THE START OF SOMETHING UNHOLY

"Well, well, if it isn't Miss Potter," Thomas said, his voice clearly laced with laughter.

He sat knee-deep in a large copper bathtub, the picture of utter contentment. Suds floated around his legs, and shaving cream covered his chin. The barber had apparently been prepared to give him a shave while he soaked in the hot water.

"Why . . . I . . ." Emily stuttered, her face getting warm. She could feel the color rising in her cheeks as she realized that she was facing a very naked and very amused man of the cloth! She was acutely aware of his lean masculine form, glistening with soap, his muscles providing enticing little curves and valleys for droplets of water to trace. Emily swallowed hard, then tore her eyes away, aware that she was staring, but not before she saw the knowing twinkle in the wretched preacher's blue eyes.

"I can explain . . ."

"Yes, please do," Thomas said, biting on his pencil-thin cigar, obviously enjoying every minute of her discomfort, "I'd like to hear that myself."

BANTAM BOOKS BY KATIE ROSE

A HINT OF MISCHIEF
A CASE FOR ROMANCE

KATIE ROSE

A CASE FOR ROMANCE

BANTAM BOOKS

New York Toronto London Sydney Auckland

A CASE FOR ROMANCE
A Bantam Fanfare Book/February 1999

FANFARE and the portrayal of a boxed "ff" are trademarks of Bantam Books, a division of Bantam Doubleday Dell Publishing Group, Inc.

ISBN 0-553-57772-7

Published simultaneously in the United States and Canada

Bantam Books are published by Bantam Books, a division of Bantam Doubleday Dell Publishing Group, Inc. Its trademark, consisting of the words "Bantam Books" and the portrayal of a rooster, is Registered in U.S. Patent and Trademark Office and in other countries. Marca Registrada. Bantam Books, 1540 Broadway, New York, New York 10036.

PRINTED IN THE UNITED STATES OF AMERICA
OPM   10   9   8   7   6   5   4   3   2   1

*For Erin, who loves Emily and Sherlock Holmes
as much as I do.
Thank you for your patience with my bad socks,
annoying songs, and the endless hours
at the computer.
You truly are the light of my life.*

Acknowledgments

Special thanks to: Stephanie Kip, for her help and enthusiasm, Karen Solem, for her guidance and support, Linda Cajio, for her help and laughter, and Marlene, who lent me my first Sir Arthur Conan Doyle. Special thanks to the Camden County Library in Voorhees for their research help.

1

The World's Second Consulting Detective

Colorado, April 1, 1894

"Excuse my rudeness," said Sherlock Holmes. "You broke the thread of my thoughts, but perhaps it is as well. So you actually were not able to see that that man was a sergeant of marines?"

"No, indeed," Dr. Watson said.

"It was easier to know it than to explain why I know it. If you were asked to prove that two and two made four, you might find some difficulty, and yet you are quite sure of the fact. Even across the street I could see a great blue anchor tattooed on the back of the fellow's hand. That smacked of the sea. He had a military carriage, however, and regulation side whiskers. There we have the

marine. He was a man with some amount of
self-importance and a certain air of com-
mand. You must have observed the way in
which he held his head and swung his cane.
A steady, respectable, middle-aged man, too,
on the face of him—all facts which led me to
believe that he had been a sergeant."

"Wonderful!" I ejaculated.

"Commonplace," said Holmes.

Emily Potter closed the dog-eared copy of the *Strand*
amid the rumbling of the stagecoach, and sank back
into the seat with a smile of satisfaction. Along with
Holmes, she, too, had figured out the mystery long
before everyone else, but it was enjoyable just watching the story play itself out. Her reading glasses
slid down her nose, and she pushed them back into
place, ignoring the odd glances she received from
the other stagecoach passengers. Besides herself,
there were two women, a businessman, a cowboy
who smelled suspiciously of whiskey, and a preacher.
Although it couldn't possibly matter, Emily noticed
that the preacher was undeniably handsome, with
piercing blue eyes and indecently long lashes. He
seemed preoccupied with the landscape that whizzed
by the coach window. Putting the book aside, she felt
the familiar surge of disappointment that the tale
was over.

Emily sighed. She hated that her active mind no
longer had anything to occupy it. Like her great-aunt
Esther, who painted nudes and was admittedly the
family eccentric, Emily simply marched to a differ-

ent tune than most women. Give her a puzzle, a problem, the most intricate enigma or most obscure crime, and she was in her element. From her earliest memories, she had been obsessed with mysteries, devouring them like candy as she helped her mother in the millinery business. While other girls shopped, went to dances, called on each other and gossiped, Emily read every kind of mystery she could find. She knew all of Poe, memorized Doyle, despised Gaboriau, and adored Vidocq. When that wasn't enough, she alarmed her mother by voraciously following the daily papers, marking the local murders in ink and poring over the details of each case. She often gave the police information about the crimes, even though they dismissed her help with fatherly smiles. Yet Emily never doubted that she would one day convince them of her methods and win their respect.

But Emily had just turned sixteen when her mother died, and thereafter she had less free time to track the activities of the criminal element. The millinery shop was still successful, so Emily continued the business, propping her beloved books between hats and feeding her habit secondhand. The books almost sufficed, but were never really enough. She longed to be like Holmes, to awaken her counterpart in the middle of the night and whisper, "Come, Watson, come! The game is afoot!"

A rustle came from the bag on the floor of the stagecoach, disturbing her thoughts. Reaching down, Emily's glasses slid to the tip of her sharp nose as she scooped inside the bag to pull out a black-and-white cat. Dr. Watson mewed contentedly, although he was tangled up in laces and yarn, thread, and artificial cherries.

"Silly cat." Emily smiled fondly, disentangling the feline. Fascinated with the mess, the cat swiped at the dangling threads, ignoring his mistress's attempts to remove them. Much of the millinery business was easily transportable, everything fitting neatly into her bag, but trimmings didn't necessarily mix well with a cat. Yet Emily wouldn't dream of going anywhere without her precious feline.

Glancing up, she saw the preacher watching her again. He turned his face away, but not before a strange little flutter began inside of her. Emily frowned. This man of God had the strangest effect on her! Surely he was just as bored as everyone else, and only looking at her to pass the time. Satisfied with this logical explanation, she placed the now string-free kitten in her lap and forced her thoughts back to the reason for her trip.

If anyone had told her a year ago that she would be making this journey out West, orphaned and unchaperoned, she would have examined them with her magnifying lens in disbelief. But she couldn't have known then that after her mother quietly passed away, she would feel a wretched loneliness. Nor could she have guessed that several years later, the death of her long-lost father would leave her with a house in Colorado with a mystery attached. Excitement coursed through her as she fished the attorney's letter out of her bag. This was a good time to refresh herself of the facts. Shaking aside the millinery materials, she opened the missive and scanned it once more.

> *It grieves me to inform you that your father has passed away. He has bequeathed all of his property and holdings to you, his daughter, in the hope of making reparation for his neglect of you in life.*

Emily's nose wrinkled. She really hadn't known her father. He'd left when she was very young, to make his fortune in the West. Unlike her mother, a romantic who'd always clung to the hope that he'd come back for her, Emily had been quite sure they would never see him again. So while his final parting stirred some small emotion inside her, it wasn't nearly as heart wrenching as it might have been. She continued reading.

> *He left you a property, a house on the outskirts of Denver. It is a handsome place, white clapboard with majestic columns, much like the old plantation homes. It has ten rooms, five fireplaces, and a parlor. The house is also fitted with indoor plumbing, something your father installed himself.*
>
> *However, I strongly suggest that you liquidate the estate. The West is no place for a woman on her own, especially a gentlewoman like yourself. I can put the house up for sale, although you won't get one-tenth of what it's*

*worth. Shangri-La, as your father called it, is
not an attractive property due to its reputation. In addition to its original purpose, which
is unmentionable to decent folk, your father
met his unfortunate end there, along with his
female companion, Rosie. Rumors that the
place is haunted abound, and no one in town
will go near the house. With your permission,
then, I'll list the property. Perhaps I can find
an out-of-towner, who doesn't know about the
murders. . . .*

But Emily had never granted that permission. Ewert
Smith, the lawyer, was astonished when she wrote
back stating that she intended to occupy the house.
Emily refolded the letter and put it back in her
valise. She couldn't pass up this opportunity. She
would investigate the crime, find out exactly how her
father and his companion were killed, who had done
the deed, and why. Even if she hadn't known him as
a daughter should, didn't she owe him that much? A
nervous tremor went through her as she thought of
the danger involved since the murderer was still at
large, but she dismissed it quickly. Holmes never let
such considerations stop him. Looking down at her
sleeve, she touched the place where the black band
circled her arm beneath her coat, in memory of the
great sleuth. Now that Sherlock Holmes's creator
had brought about the demise of the world's first
consulting detective, she was determined to become
the second.

The stagecoach lurched, and a wooden cherry zigzagged across the floor. Dr. Watson bounded after the errant decoration, skidding out of Emily's reach, and the two women beside her squealed in shock and dismay. Emily murmured an apology and tried to capture the cat, but Watson, free at last, had no intention of returning to the carpetbag. The women withdrew as far as they could within the dim interior of the coach, but the tiny feline had already disappeared beneath the older woman's skirts.

"Excuse me, ma'am." The preacher lifted his hat to her, and then seemingly as part of the same motion used it to scoop up the cat when he ventured out of his hiding place. Emily exhaled in relief although the overweight woman drew her lips tightly together as if tasting something sour, eyeing the kitten as if he were a rodent. Dr. Watson peeked out of the Stetson indignantly, but made no further protest. As Emily lifted him out of the hat, her hands briefly touched the preacher's, and a warm tingle raced across her skin. She swallowed hard to regain her composure.

"Thank you, sir. I'm so sorry, he's usually very good."

The woman only snorted in her direction, then turned toward her young companion with a meaningful lift of her brows. The preacher, seeming to sense that trouble was brewing, intervened quickly. "I couldn't help noticing your periodical. Are you a great reader?"

Emily nodded. "Yes. It was a Sir Arthur Conan Doyle story."

"Ah. A mystery. So you're an armchair sleuth."

"Exactly." Emily waited for the disapproval such a confession usually brought, but to her surprise, he seemed genuinely interested. Encouraged, she continued. "I've read all of his stories. I thought 'The Speckled Band' the best, but 'A Scandal in Bohemia' remains a close second."

"I agree. I enjoyed 'The Man with the Twisted Lip,' but thought the action in 'The Speckled Band' much more appealing." He extended his hand, his smile genuine. "I'm Reverend Thomas Hall. Please call me Thomas."

"Miss Emily Potter." Emily took the offered hand, once again feeling the odd energy spark through her. Goodness, what was wrong with her! Forcing herself to remember her mission, she let her eyes travel over the preacher. Anyone could be a suspect in this case. She couldn't forget that, no matter how upstanding he might appear to be. She studied the man without letting go of him, even bringing her magnifying glass out of her pocket and up to her eyes with her other hand to examine him from his chestnut hair to his worn boots.

His eyes were truly magnificent. Startlingly blue, they seemed to return her gaze and look right through her, twinkling with amusement. Emily blinked—how easily she was distracted! She must get back to the work at hand. He was tanned, unlike the priests she knew in Boston, but that wasn't surprising for a traveling preacher. The stubble of a black beard was beginning to show, which didn't hide his square-cut chin or firm mouth. His hands were rough, as if used to hard work, and his body was muscular, firm, and well proportioned. He clutched a worn prayer book, but it didn't look natural in his hand. There was something . . . about his posture, a readiness that was unusual for a simple man of God. Her glass paused as he withdrew his hand from hers. There was a black stain just inside his thumb. Puzzled, Emily brought her fingers up to her nose, as if to cover a yawn, and sniffed. A faint trace of manly cologne remained, along with something else. . . .

It was just as she thought. Gunpowder. He should be holding a pistol instead of a Bible.

"Did I pass inspection?" The preacher, far from being angry, seemed to find the whole thing terribly funny. His smile was devilishly appealing as he surveyed her with obvious amusement. The other passengers, particularly the females, didn't share his sense of humor and withdrew even farther from her.

"One should approach everything with as scientific a view as possible," Emily stated, undaunted. A very unusual preacher indeed. It was worth thinking about later. "Observations must be recorded, then verified with facts," she continued. "I am simply a believer in modern methods. The study of criminology, although new, is fascinating."

"Is that so?" The preacher smiled.

"Yes. Why Dave Mather, the notorious gunman, claimed to be a descendant of a Puritan clergyman, and he certainly looked like one. So did Ben Thompson and Pat Garrett, both of whom were outlaws before turning to law enforcement. You see, Mr. Hall, one can never trust appearances." She turned her glass toward the women beside her and peered at them like a Cyclops.

"I beg your pardon, miss! What do you think you're doing?" The older woman puffed indignantly.

"I'm examining your cuffs and boots," Emily explained, as if surprised at the question. "My mother and I ran a millinery shop in Boston. There I applied Holmes's theories of deduction. By examining our customers' clothes, hands, and knees, I could tell whether they were rich or poor, if they drank or had gas laid in the house. I deduced that one of our customers was a married woman having an affair, and that a girl had an addiction to snuff."

The two women gasped, then tucked their boots self-consciously under their dresses, while the businessman glanced down at his linen cuffs.

"The nerve of you, missy!" The older woman scolded. "I've never seen anything so rude! Why, young people today . . ." She sent her companion a pointed look, while the latter stared at Emily in disbelief.

"For example," Emily said, leaning forward in excitement to be able to talk about her work, "I observe that you are in mourning, but I deduce that you are not entirely sorry to have lost your late spouse. You have had some problems finding a husband for your daughter, and think that the West might provide an answer. Your husband left you with some money, but it won't last forever, and you need to secure your means. Hence, this trip." Emily sat back in her seat, satisfied.

The younger woman gasped, and looked at Emily as if she were a witch. The older one's face turned white and she stammered, "Someone must have told you this! I demand to know—"

"It is all perfectly obvious." Emily sighed, as if explaining something to a child. "You are still wearing widow's weeds, which indicates that your loss was fairly recent, and probably a close relation. You are traveling without a husband, which suggests it is his loss that you are mourning. Yet you have been to a sunny clime lately, as indicated by the slight tint to your skin, which is not your natural complexion. I can see beneath the lace of your sleeve that you are normally very fair. This leads me to believe that you have traveled for pleasure, which one might not do if one were seriously agrieved."

"But . . . my search for a husband?" The younger woman questioned nervously.

"There is a newspaper sticking out of your bag with the personal column marked. It has become common for western miners and cowboys to advertise for mail-order brides, and some of them are using the newspapers to do so. And you are not wearing a wedding ring. I deduced, given these facts, that you are interested in attracting a westerner for the purpose of marriage."

The two women sat aghast, their mouths hanging open, as astonished as if Emily had begun to remove her clothes. Unaware of their consternation, Emily turned to the businessman, intending to subject him to her deductive reasoning. But at that moment the carriage jolted, sending her glass flying. The preacher caught it deftly—then seemed reluctant to return it, perhaps because the older woman had turned an interesting shade of purple. After a moment, he placed the glass in Emily's outstretched hand, then indicated the bumpy road outside the window. "Maybe you should put it away. It will probably get broken with the way the coach is swaying."

"I suppose," Emily responded. The motion did make it difficult to continue her observations. Reluctantly, she put the magnifying glass back inside her pocket for the time being.

The ladies breathed a collective sigh of relief, and even the businessman appeared happier. The cowboy alone seemed unperturbed, continuing to sleep with his back against the seat. The tension in the coach remained palpable, however. The businessman spoke up conversationally, now that he wasn't about to be dissected like an insect.

"So, miss, are you planning to stay in Denver?"

Emily nodded. "My father left me a property on the outskirts of town. It's a nice house from what the attorney's letter says. Shangri-La, it's called."

"What?" The cowboy glanced up from under his Stetson, suddenly awake. "Did you say Shangri-La?"

"Yes," Emily answered, surprised at his interest. "It is described as a white-columned mansion, much like the old plantation houses. It even has indoor plumbing." She gave them a superior smile. "That's all the thing in Boston, you know."

The women looked puzzled, while the men glanced at each other, appalled. It must have been the mention of plumbing, Emily realized belatedly. Some people were sensitive to that kind of talk. The cowboy smirked and looked at Emily with new attention. The businessman cleared his throat. "That house is . . . not a place for a lady," he finished lamely. "Surely someone has told you of the killings? And"—he lowered his voice—"the ghost?"

Emily nodded eagerly. "Yes, of course. That was my primary interest. My father and his female companion were killed there. I want to investigate the murders and learn everything I can about them. And of course, there is no such thing as ghosts." She retrieved her notebook from her bag, pushing Dr. Watson's curious head back down again. "Now, you can probably help me. I was going to wait until I got to town to start interrogations, but as they say, there's no time like the present."

The preacher choked down a laugh, while the other passengers appeared shocked. As the stagecoach rumbled into Denver, everyone was silent, and Emily quickly recorded her observations. She was satisfied with the women, the businessman afforded little data, and the cowboy was simply a cowboy. It soon became apparent that her most interesting suspect was Thomas Hall. He had gunpowder stains on his hands, smelled nothing like Father Murphy from Boston (who always seemed to carry the odors of incense and wine), and was physically more compelling than any man she'd ever met. She was almost tempted to hold up the glass again. He was very handsome and likable, but she couldn't let that inter-

fere with her investigation of him, or admit that her
interest was in anything other than the case at hand.
For as every great detective knew, emotion was
deadly to logic. Thomas Hall was simply an element
that warranted further scrutiny.

The stagecoach finally stopped in the center of
town. Thomas waited as the passengers moved reverently aside to allow him to pass first. Outside, a
cowboy, obviously more than a little the worse for
drink, tipped his hat politely, his eye marking the
white collar of Thomas's black shirt and the Bible he
held. An elderly businessman dressed in a good wool
suit nodded cordially, while a young woman passing
by blushed and hid her face behind a lace kerchief.

Thomas accepted their deference with a forced
smile. He helped the others disembark from the
coach, wishing to God that he could go into the saloon and have a shot of whiskey to warm his bones.
But now he was supposed to be the preacher, Thomas Hall, and he couldn't afford any missteps. Especially in front of Emily Potter.

She appeared at the stagecoach door almost as
soon as he formed the thought, one hand clutching
the bag with the cat in it, in her other hand a book.
He smiled to himself as he recalled her antics with
the magnifying glass. The women on the coach had
been close to starting a mutiny, but Emily had
seemed oblivious to everything but her own objectives. He had to admire the way she'd handled those
women, and her obvious intelligence, but there was
an undeniable naïveté about her. God only knew what

she would have said to the businessman if given the chance. He reminded himself to be careful around her, for Emily was no fool. In spite of his own good sense, Thomas found himself admiring her.

The object of his thoughts was looking around as if to get her bearings. This time he surreptitiously subjected Emily to as thorough an appraisal as she'd given him. Prim and proper, dressed in a simple dove gray dress with purple plush at the sleeves, a pretty veiled bonnet trimmed with feathers, and suede gloves, she was the epitome of a spinster, a woman determined to be alone. In spite of himself, he tried to do what she had done by examining her sleeves and boots, but they revealed nothing to him. Instead, as she bent over to pick up her case, his eyes wandered over her figure, which hinted at being magnificent. She straightened, and he noticed that her face held a promise of beauty, her chestnut hair was splendid, and her mouth was downright kissable. There was a vulnerability about her, a sensitivity to life that he'd already sensed from their brief exchange.

Thomas's thoughts drifted back to the innocent brush of their fingers when he handed her the cat, and her firm handclasp when he formally introduced himself. A hot rush of sensation had swept through him at the simple contact, a sensuality so compelling that it momentarily caught him off guard. He couldn't remember ever touching a woman who evoked that kind of emotion so quickly. Her reaction told him he wasn't imagining it, that she had felt the same thing and was just as confused.

He continued to smile, but the warmth had gone out of him. Emily Potter might enjoy mysteries, but she had no idea about the one she was about to walk into. Nor that he, the Reverend Thomas Hall, would play a major role in the plot.

2

The Investigation Begins

Emily rummaged in her pocket for her glasses, excitement coursing through her at the thought of seeing her new home for the first time. But when she put on her spectacles, she gasped in astonishment at the sight of Denver.

It was a bawdy place, she could tell that immediately. The saloon was twice the size of the church, and the boardinghouse had the prosperous look of a booming business. The street thronged with life, cowboys and farmers, shopkeepers and miners. There was a dressmaker's shop, a shoemaker, a stable and a blacksmith. Emily sighed in relief as she observed that there was no milliner's shop, at least not on the main road. She was used to competition, but the less of it, the better. Even this consideration didn't distract her much. She was overwhelmed by the sights, smells, and noises of a real western town, and didn't want to miss a minute of it.

It was everything she'd expected. Whereas Boston was settled and dignified, Denver was alive, bustling and frenetic, filled, like herself, with exuberance. Joyfully, she snatched up her carpetbag, unaware of the snubs of the women with her or the calculating survey of the cowboy who was just leaving the coach.

"Miss Emily, I'd like to go with you to see the house, just to make sure you get there safely," the preacher volunteered. "Do you mind?"

"I ain't sure that's proper," the cowboy interrupted. He spat on the ground, the wet tobacco hitting the dirt with a tar-colored splat. He gave Emily a charming smile. "After all, the place has a reputation, and as a preacher, you need to keep that in mind. Ma'am, I'm Jake and I'd be more than happy to provide an escort to your new home."

Emily was about to respond, when the preacher cut in. "But the mission is close by, and I have to go right past the house." He grinned at her winningly. "I must insist."

Emily smiled uncertainly. The cowboy seemed nice, but his spitting bothered her. Logically, she realized that tobacco had to be expelled, but her feminine sensibility was still offended. Besides, there was something about this preacher that alerted her sleuthish instincts. "Well," she said to Thomas, "if you insist."

Thomas looked at the cowboy with a sharp glance. The cowboy shrugged and headed off in the direction of the saloon. Emily was careful to hide her suspicions as the preacher took her bag, then indicated the wooden boardwalk ahead.

"It's on the outskirts of town, if I understand right." He gave her a reassuring nod. "Let's try this way."

Emily followed obediently, glad now that he was there to help. As Thomas walked in front of her, she noticed once again how different he was from any other preacher she'd ever known. There was a cat-like grace to his walk, a sureness to his step. More than that, there was a presence about him that she wouldn't have expected. He tipped his hat in response to the nods that came his way, but she had a feeling that he would have gotten the same respect even without the collar.

The boardwalk ended, replaced by a well-worn path that led them behind the saloon. Emily's eyes grew wider as they approached what looked like a southern mansion: A beautiful white house rose up like a castle in a dream, complete with graciously curved windows, green shutters, and gardens on both sides. As they approached the door with its bold brass knocker, Emily turned to the preacher in astonishment.

"This is it?"

"Try the door," he suggested.

Emily experienced a brief pang when she found it was locked—until she remembered the key that had come with Ewert Smith's letter. Gingerly, she fished it out and slid it into the lock, more astonished than ever as the tumblers clicked and the door swung open. This really was the place. Thomas lit the gas, then turned up the flame, throwing the room into plain view. Emily polished her glasses, then put them back on, certain what she was seeing could not be real.

The house had been ransacked. Yet even in this dismal state, she could sense the opulence of the room, the scarlet and gilt decadence. Emily gasped as she took in the bar, the crimson chairs, the player piano, and the portrait of a woman dressed in silk and feathers overlooking everything. On the ceiling were more paintings, pictures like she had never seen before, scenes of men and women doing things she couldn't even imagine. . . .

"My God!" she whispered, turning to the preacher in horror. "What—what was this place?"

"A house of sin," Thomas said, stifling his chuckles with obvious effort. Emily studied him more closely. She was not mistaken. There was a glimmer in his eye, and a grin playing around his mouth. Odd for a preacher, she thought, making another mental note. He indicated the portrait above the fireplace. "That must be Rosie."

Nodding her agreement, Emily stared at the picture of her father's "female companion." The woman wasn't one she would call stunning, but she was attractive. Dark eyes stared out of the frame, almost twinkling with life. A naughty dimple had been cleverly captured by the artist, along with the full curve of a seductive mouth. An uncomfortable feeling swelled inside Emily as she thought of her father cavorting with this woman while he was still married to her mother. She turned back to the preacher.

"I can't believe this—" she began.

Thomas nodded, as if understanding her thoughts. "I don't know your father, but he probably never thought you'd come out here. Most women would have sold the property rather than face the dangers of the West. I guess he underestimated you."

"How incredible." The initial shock had passed and left curiosity in its wake. Like most young women, Emily knew little about the dark side of men, the things whispered about between women, always in disapproving tones. She stared at the ceiling in fascination. The paintings were unbelievable. Was it really possible for men and women to? . . . Suddenly she remembered her companion. A fleeting thought went through her mind, one that caused her terrible embarrassment. Would Thomas Hall be like that with a woman? Tearing her gaze away from the paintings in shame, she composed herself and looked purposefully at the ruined furniture once more.

"Why would someone do this?" She wondered aloud. "Do you think it was vandals?"

"Possibly." Thomas shrugged. "Or someone who was looking for something. Something of value." He gave Emily a dark, piercing look.

"Like what?" Emily glanced up at him in confusion.

"I don't know. Didn't your father tell you anything about this place, or how he got his money? Maybe he left some indication in his will, or some other documentation?"

There was something about the way he was questioning her that made her uneasy. Emily sank down onto one of the least damaged chairs. She focused on the portrait hanging on the wall. "I know my father had secrets. He was very evasive in his letters home about what he did for a living and who his friends were. My mother couldn't tolerate the idea of living on the frontier, so he went west to provide for us in the best way he could. She never said much about him, but never indicated that anything was wrong. I don't think she ever imagined this!" Emily's gaze was once more glued to the bordello paintings.

"Then it seems you didn't know much about John Potter."

The preacher sounded disappointed, as if he were expecting some other answer. Emily shrugged. "It appears that there is more than one mystery here. But it is a capital mistake to theorize without data. If you'll excuse me, I'll have to get started investigating." She rummaged through her carpetbag and withdrew the magnifying glass, then dropped to her knees on the floor.

Thomas stared in amazement as Emily, oblivious to his presence, began to examine every inch of the room. She crawled over the rug, grunting when she saw something that held meaning for her, frowning when she realized the trampled condition of the room might have destroyed a clue. Scooping up some ash near the fireplace, she put it carefully away in an envelope that had been in her bag, then scraped some threads from the carpet. At one point she withdrew a tape from her bag and measured some marks on the floor. Calculating several figures, she jotted notes in her book. By the time she stood up, her hat askew, her nose smudged with dust, she looked as wretched as the room.

"Miss Potter, what are you doing?" The preacher asked finally, astonished at her behavior.

"Collecting data," Emily replied, as if he were a fool. Then she sighed in disappointment. "Unfortunately, many people have been here since the murder. If only I had gotten here when the trail was fresh! I would have had him!"

The preacher's expression changed from amused to thunderous. "Miss Emily, stay out of this. Whoever killed your father and Rosie has never been caught. The murderer is still out there. And still dangerous."

"I know." Emily smiled at him, but saw no response in his eyes. "Don't worry. I'll be careful. I've read a hundred of these stories, and they all work the same way. Now I'll have to meet with the sheriff and the coroner, read the papers, interview suspects, and find out everything I can about my father and the girl—"

"Emily!" This time he shook her, cutting off her words. The magnifying glass bounced to the floor and Emily's jaw dropped in stunned surprise. "This isn't a story we're talking about! This is real life! Whoever vandalized this place was looking for something, and they won't let a woman stop them! The very best thing you can do is get back on that stagecoach and go home."

Emily squirmed, uncomfortably aware that she was pressed right up against him, his trouser-clad leg between her own and his black cloth jacket rubbing against her blouse. Odd sensations started somewhere within her and she frowned, wondering what was wrong with her. She saw his gaze lower and settle on her mouth, seemingly fascinated by something there. For the silliest moment, she thought he was going to kiss her, but he released her as quickly as if she were a scorpion that had climbed into his hand. Emily smoothed her dress, trying to make sense of everything. What in heaven's name was wrong with her? He was a preacher! Clearing her throat, she managed to speak coherently—at least, she thought she did.

"I'm sorry, but like my great-aunt Esther, I have to follow my destiny. I have to discover who killed my father. In the meantime, I plan to stay here and make this a good home again. As a preacher, you should applaud that. I'm going to fix up this house, meet other people, and have company. I'm going to church on Sundays, and maybe attend a dance. And I'm going to investigate. And no one is going to stop me."

Thomas walked toward the boardinghouse, fighting the urge to fling his prayer book at the closest possible target.

How the hell did this happen? He had intended to question her, get her to admit she knew something— and then she looked at him with those clear gray eyes, and he seemed to forget all logic.

What was wrong with her, anyway? What decent woman would want to live in a bordello, let alone investigate a murder there? And didn't she understand the kind of danger she was in? The house had been ransacked, and she had to know why. How much did Emily know? And what were her real intentions?

He stopped for a moment on the path, watching her shadow pass in the window of the notorious house. Nothing about the woman seemed to add up. He had to admit that her careful investigation of the room, while astonishing, made sense. No one—not even the sheriff—had done such an examination, he'd bet his life on that. And if they had, could they have found clues to the killer's identity? Could Emily?

So she was bright—yes—and naive—incredibly. The incident with the cowboy had proven that. If he hadn't intervened, the man would have taken Emily home and probably to bed. But she obviously hadn't understood his intentions, nor what conclusions he'd jumped to upon hearing that she owned Shangri-La. No, Emily was odd, but she didn't seem to be sexually sophisticated, unless she was an excellent actress. . . .

Thomas frowned as he recalled the way she'd felt when he'd shaken her in exasperation. Up close, he'd noticed that her eyes were remarkable, a strange, haunted silver that seemed to look right through him. And her mouth was so pink and moist, so very kissable. For a brief moment, something had passed between them, something that could cause enormous complications, something he wouldn't even allow himself to think about.

Emily Potter was a factor, nothing more. Thomas

turned around and started back toward town, the thought a stern refrain in his mind.

It had taken an additional hour of investigating before she felt satisfied that she had learned everything the parlor would yield. Now Emily slumped onto a gilt chair, feeling completely drained, and more than a little disconcerted.

The floor had revealed very little. She felt as frustrated as Holmes would have been to realize that dozens of people had trod over the rug since the murders, obliterating any trace of the killer. Still, she was able to fathom a few facts, and what she could deduce only confused her further.

There were foot prints she assumed had been made by her father, since she'd found a pair of round-toed boots in his closet. The evidence showed he had stood facing the fireplace, smoking a good Cuban cigar. He had turned, and was extending a glass of whiskey to someone when the shots came. Emily could see where he'd fallen, the splashes of liquor and the broken glass, the bloodstains that someone had tried to wipe up, and the nub of the cigar where it had rolled to a stop beside the grate. She shuddered when she thought of the blood, but forced the horror from her mind. This was a case, and Holmes would never let such feminine considerations stop him. Besides, she barely remembered the man. Her father.

So, she surmised, he'd been standing by the fireplace, enjoying a smoke, when someone walked in and shot him. It must have been someone familiar, for there were no indications that either her father or Rosie had struggled, and no signs of a break-in. Yet the trampled flower beds and scuffed floor hid anything else she could have seen with her glass. If only she had been here earlier! Emily sighed in frustration.

Rosie's part was a little more difficult to envision since her trail was not so obvious. She'd fallen near the steps; Emily remembered the newspaper accounts she had read, and the positions of the bodies. Yet there were signs of a smaller pair of boots, much more feminine and pointed, which had left a trail in the cigar ash, and threads from a blue dress. Had Rosie come down earlier, then returned? Emily's brow furrowed. The marks could have come from anyone, even one of the bordello girls. If so, perhaps there was a material witness to the crime. From Rosie's position, it was probably safe to deduce that when she'd come down the stairs, she'd surprised the gunman. Having no choice, the man had shot her, too, then fled. But why? What had her father done to deserve such an end?

Her eyes gazed once more at the ceiling, and she found herself blushing again. What kind of man had her father been? Emily's logical mind couldn't deny the fact that he must have been virile, and an opportunist. Did her mother suspect him at all? Was this how he'd gotten his wealth, the cash he had sent to them that was so welcomely received, the money to build this house? Did it come from—

She couldn't think about that. Emily squeezed her eyes shut, yet the paintings overhead seemed to laugh at her. Heat stung her cheeks and she was very glad no one else was present. It was foolishness, she knew that. Highly embarrassing. And, although she'd never admit it to anyone else, the place was strangely erotic. She'd even felt a tingle when the preacher, Thomas Hall, had put his hands on her—to shake some sense into her, it was true—but the sensation had been there.

It was this house. Emily nodded, satisfied with that explanation. Dr. Watson climbed out of the bag and surveyed the new residence, mewing his confusion. Emily smiled and picked up the cat, softly stroking his fur. At least the little black-and-white animal was familiar and comforting.

Fatigue overcame her suddenly and she decided she'd done enough for one day. Emily started upstairs, taking the cat and a taper with her. To her dismay, she discovered that the bedrooms had been ransacked as well. Finding the most livable, she started to enter the room, but to her surprise, Dr. Watson hissed and spat. He sprang out of her arms, then hunched his feline back and bared his teeth, refusing to cross the threshold.

"You silly cat," Emily scolded the little animal, but Watson remained unconvinced. "Fine, stay there then." Her voice sounding much braver than she felt, Emily put the candle on the dressing table and waded through the piles of clothing that had been scattered across the floor. Finding an oil lamp on the table, she lit the wick and carefully replaced the globe.

The bedroom sprang to life. Rosie's room. Emily

felt it with a certainty that passed through her like a cold chill. Picking up a silver-backed hairbrush in wonder, she gazed at the huge gilt mirror that seemed to dominate the room. Her own reflection stared back at her, as if questioning her presence. Her gaze fell to the dressing table. Row after row of perfume bottles, powders, and brushes marched across the marred surface. It was strange touching another woman's toiletries, Emily mused, especially one who had been murdered. It was almost like seeing a ghost. . . . She chuckled at the notion.

Finding fresh linens in the drawer, Emily made the bed, trying hard not to think of the activity that had taken place there. Strangely enough, the unusual preacher once more haunted her thoughts, especially when she slipped between the cool, fresh sheets. For an incredible moment, she could feel the hard length of his body pressed against her as if he shared the bed with her, his hands moving down from her shoulders, touching her, like the men and women in those paintings. . . .

Stop it! Forcing the forbidden thoughts from her mind, she squeezed her eyes shut and tried to sleep. But even then she could sense the hot, languid breath of her phantom lover against her cheek, feel the soft, feathered kisses he placed on her neck and throat. Emily squirmed, trying desperately to clear her mind, but it was useless, the images were too strong. She had never thought about such things before. Restless urgings warmed her blood, and a dreamlike passion swept over her. She wanted him, needed him to ease the nameless ache inside of her, to warm those hands stained with gunpowder against her heated flesh. . . .

That thought made her gasp. Sitting upright, Emily shook her head and mentally gave herself a scolding. Good God, what was she doing! Mortification stung her and she pressed her cool hands to her inflamed cheeks. Fantasizing about a man of the cloth! She couldn't continue to let this house or the preacher influence her, for her judgment would surely be clouded. Holmes would never have allowed passion to obtrude on a case, and Emily would have to be more vigilant. Obviously. Especially with a man as attractive and virile as the good reverend.

Lying back on the pillows, she mentally recited nursery rhymes over and over. She would force Thomas Hall from her mind if it was the last thing she did.

"Evening, Mrs. Haines. Might I inquire about a room?" Thomas put on what he hoped was his most trustworthy look as the door creaked open. An elderly woman with a shawl tucked neatly around her eyed him suspiciously.

"Not a cowboy, are you? Don't want any hooligans roughing up my parlor."

"No, ma'am. I'm the new preacher," Thomas said smoothly.

The woman's gaze fell to his collar, then her watery blue eyes squinted. "Come in and close that door behind you."

Thomas entered the house, exhaling in relief as he obediently shut the door. If there was one thing his collar was good for, it was entry just about everywhere. Even the local townsmen, after seeing that he was a man of the cloth, showed none of the suspicion normally granted a stranger, and told him everything he needed, from where to get a room to which barber had the best lime water. His smug certainty was short-lived, however, for the woman scarcely turned up the lamp before barraging him with questions.

Her face wrinkled up like an old apple as she digested his answers. She must have accepted his story, for her face cleared and she was suddenly all business. "All right, then. I don't suppose you'll be wanting the room for long, though. You'll be setting up your own mission and sleeping there like the good Reverend Flatter did. Slept under the stars until he built his church, that's how dedicated he was."

"Well, I suppose I prefer a bed," Thomas said, attempting to charm her.

But the woman harrumped disapprovingly. Nevertheless, she turned toward an oak hutch swathed in doilies and reached for a key. "I keep a clean house, and don't tolerate tobacco of any kind, nor whiskey. I also don't allow women, although that shouldn't bother you much, being a preacher and all. Room and board is ten dollars a week, paid in advance, cash only."

Thomas dug into his pocket and pulled out a wad of bills. The woman watched him carefully, then snatched the greenback out of his hand. He had already turned toward the stairs when she cleared her throat meaningfully.

"Ma'am?"

"Aren't you forgetting something, Parson?"

He stared at her, then glanced around the room. Nothing came to him. What in God's name was she expecting? Suddenly he recalled that he still wore his hat. He removed it, and grinned sheepishly.

"Sorry, ma'am." Once more he started for the stairs, but before he could place a boot on the first step, she cleared her throat again. He looked back over his shoulder in bewilderment.

"The blessing. Surely you don't enter a new dwelling without a blessing. Reverend Flatter wouldn't have dreamed of such a thing." She scowled in disapproval.

"No, of course not," he said quickly. Thomas closed his eyes and awkwardly made the sign of the cross. "Bless this house and all who dwell within. Amen." He opened his eyes and nodded, satisfied with the effort.

"Is that it?" The woman asked.

Thomas nodded. "Uh—in my congregation, an economy of words is appreciated. Good night, ma'am."

Before she could say another word, he took the steps two at a time.

Closing the door with relief, he turned up the lamp. The room was surprisingly spacious and comfortable. Thankfully, the bed had been made, and a pitcher full of water already awaited him. After tossing his garb over a chair, he splashed the grime from his face, grimacing at his reflection in the mirror. Without the black coat and white collar, he looked like himself again, and almost felt that way. An unwelcome thought entered his mind, one that lodged there like a splinter. Had Emily seen past his collar to the man beneath? Or like Mrs. Haines, did she believe him to be a simple man of God?

The question irritated the hell out of him. And the last thing he needed was to dwell on the attractive Miss Potter. If there was one thing he had made up his mind about, it was that she couldn't be as innocent as she appeared. What part Emily played in all this was a mystery, one he intended to get to the bottom of, regardless of how delectable a figure she had.

Fortified with that thought, Thomas fell into bed, barely taking the time to blow out the candle. He was exhausted, but sleep was a long time in coming. All he could picture was Emily Potter's silver eyes, her soft, sweet body pressed up against his, and her kissable mouth. Even when he did doze, he dreamed of a beautiful detective, staring at him through her magnifying glass.

3

A Ghostly Intrusion

Emily woke slowly, looking around in confusion. Gradually she recognized the furnishings and everything came back to her. She'd been dreaming again, one of those crazy visions she'd been having all night: The women in the parlor had been laughing and singing around the piano while others sipped drinks and flirted at the bar. She could still see their gorgeous dresses, their sparkling plumes, their paste jewels and rouged faces as they took a man upstairs. She could almost smell their perfume, the heady intoxication of brandy and mint, talcum powder and sweat, and hear their naughty giggles, whispered murmurings, sighs of pleasure.

Emily shuddered, forcing the visions away. No real lady ever thought such things, let alone dreamed them! Sinking back onto the pillows, she frowned, unable to banish the last dream, the one that woke her. The earlier dreams were fragmented, like pieces of a puzzle, yet the last one was as startlingly clear as if it were something she'd just witnessed in real life.

The woman was laughing, a bright, sweet laugh that sounded like the creek outside. She extended an arm that was draped in a supple blue silk and dangling with bracelets. Her fingers sparkled with rings, lighting up incredibly beautiful hands and adding drama to even a simple motion as she indicated her glass.

"Johnny, it's empty. Pour me some whiskey. The good stuff."

A man lifted a crystal decanter and poured a small quantity of amber-colored liquid into a glass. He turned toward the woman. John Potter appeared much older than the photograph on her mother's dressing table, but it was undoubtedly Emily's father. He extended the drink to the woman, still smiling, when gunshots rang out. The tumbler shattered, whiskey spilling everywhere, splashing the walls and puddling on the floor. Then everything was silent. . . .

Emily's heart was pounding. It was just a dream, she scolded herself. Only a dream. But the cold chill wouldn't leave her. Had she really seen her father? And the woman, was that Rosie?

It was the influence of this house again—and an overactive imagination, Emily rationalized. It wouldn't be the first time she'd frightened herself by envisioning the worst. After reading Doyle's, "The Speckled Band," she'd dreamed about snakes for a week. She smiled, reassured by the logical explanation, and gazed at her surroundings, fully appreciating them now in the daylight.

The room was just beautiful. Sunlight poured in through the drapes, making the shimmers of cranberry light dance across the rug. The rich furnishings and delicate curtains were even lovelier than she remembered, and the sumptuous bedclothes made her feel like a princess. In the hall, Dr. Watson chased the light beams as if they were prey, making Emily laugh at his antics.

"I suppose you haven't forgotten your fear of this room," she said.

Dr. Watson had no comment, but continued to scamper across the rug while Emily slid out of bed. "We'll have to find you some milk and something for breakfast before we renew our investigation. I brought a few apples and some rolls from the train, but that won't hold us long. I think the kitchen is the next room to explore."

Emily reached for her robe, puzzled when she couldn't find the plain cotton wrapper. Instead, one of the robes from the closet lay as if it had been tossed upon the bed. *I must have forgotten to put it away,* she mused. Feeling fanciful, she slipped into the gorgeous blue silk and caught sight of herself in the mirror. Emily started in surprise. Clad in the ice blue robe, she looked almost pretty, exotic and desirable, her hair tumbling about her shoulders in disarray as if she'd just left her lover's bed.

Blushing, Emily turned away from the mirror quickly. Clearly the erotic intoxication of this house continued to affect her. She thought of the unwelcome fantasy she had had last night about Thomas Hall, and was newly ashamed. Yes, she'd have to take hold of herself, especially since the reverend was a suspect himself. Making her way down the stairs, she tried to ignore the luxurious swish of fabric around her legs.

The parlor was exactly as she'd left it. Emily expelled her breath in relief. She hadn't realized she was holding it. She really was getting ridiculous, she mused. Scooping the cat into her arms, she walked toward the rear of the house.

The kitchen, though dimly lit, looked practical and lived in. There was a cookstove, a gaslight overhead, a walnut table with high-backed chairs, and a cupboard. A larder stood nearby, with drawers for potatoes and onions, and tins for tea and biscuits. There was even a stack of wood as if someone had been waiting for company.

"See, it's not so bad," Emily said. "With a little lemon wax for the table, some blacklead for the stove, and the lamps trimmed and filled, it will be quite comfortable."

Dr. Watson seemed far more interested in the mouseholes than her conversation, but Emily was greatly encouraged. The servants had apparently taken good care of the kitchen, for all of the utensils were stacked neatly in place, and in good working order. Whoever had vandalized the house had only rifled through the flour sifters and mixing bowls, so there was much less work to be done here than in the other rooms.

Upon surveying the larder, Emily felt no surprise to see that little food remained. The house had been vacant for some time, and the vandals had surely taken anything of value. She was pleased to see that some tea remained, and she lit the stove, intending to fortify herself with a cup. Turning up the lamp, she rummaged around in the cupboard, looking for the teapot. The light suddenly extinguished.

That's odd, she thought, glancing upward. The fixture appeared to be in good condition. There was even a black soot stain on the ceiling, testifying that the light had been used frequently. After adjusting the gas, she lit it again, making sure this time that the blue-white flame was well established before turning around. Having spotted the copper tea kettle at the rear of the cupboard, she was reaching for the vessel when the light blew out once more.

Dr. Watson hissed, his back arched, and every one of his hairs stood on end. Emily fought the feeling of dread that swept over her. "Nonsense," she said out loud. "I won't let you make me afraid. It's only a weak gas jet."

The cat snarled, his green eyes wide. Frightened, Emily glanced toward the door, almost expecting to see an intruder. The doorway was empty, but someone could be in the other room. Emily forced herself to walk across the floor. A strange, eerie sensation raced through her, and she felt a raw dampness as she approached the door. It was like walking into a cellar, yet what could have caused the feeling? . . .

A mouse scampered by and Dr. Watson pounced.

Emily nearly swooned with relief. She leaned against the doorway, smiling at her own foolishness.

"See? It was just a rodent. Watson, you frightened me to death!"

The tea kettle whistled. Emily turned back to the stove and poured out a cup, grateful for the familiar smell and hot comfort of the tea. She had to stop fantasizing about every little noise, or living alone here would become intolerable.

"I'll get someone in to look at that light," she said out loud, more to herself than the cat. "And I'll go see the sheriff today, to continue the investigation. I also want to look into Reverend Thomas's whereabouts. I'll have to keep a close eye on him, as a possible suspect. On the way back, I'll stop by the store. Once I get some food and clean the house, it won't seem so lonely."

Watson played contentedly with his prey, ignoring her. For all her brave words, Emily didn't attempt to light the gas lamp again.

About an hour later, her valise—complete with her casebook, her glass, and her extensive notes—in hand, Emily marched into town. She'd left Watson at home hunting mice, having no desire to witness his inevitable success. The sheriff's office, she recalled from her walk the previous evening, was sandwiched between the post office and the saloon. She didn't feel the curious stares of the town's ladies as she walked briskly toward her goal, her hair pulled back in a dour knot, her glasses perched precariously on the bridge of her nose. Concern for her personal

appearance was never a hallmark of hers, for Emily
was always far more interested in what was going on
around her than in herself.

Today was no different, and she approached the
sheriff's office confident in her quarry. This was
surely the best place to start her investigation. Jed
Hawkins, the local lawman she recalled from the papers, should be able to shed some additional light on
what was so dark. She hoped he'd made a detailed
examination of the site, and maybe even had his own
opinion of the perpetrator.

Knocking briskly on the sheriff's door, Emily let
herself in without waiting for a reply.

"Excuse me, I'm looking for . . . Jed Hawkins."
Emily's voice trailed off as the youthful deputy
looked up from his coffee and morning paper, annoyed at the disturbance. But it wasn't his appearance that caused Emily to lose her train of thought.
As she looked past him into the sheriff's office, she
saw that the lawman was already occupied . . . with
the good Reverend Hall.

"Miss Potter." Thomas rose and came to stand before her. "A pleasure to see you again so soon."

Emily gaped at him in surprise, refusing the hand
he extended toward her. For an embarrassed moment, the memory of her fantasy swept over her. She
had a hard time looking at him until she firmly reminded herself that she had imagined everything.
Only then could she raise her chin and confront him,
even though she was desperately trying to ignore the
heat that stung her face.

"Reverend. This is an unusual place to find a holy man, isn't it?"

Her voice rang with suspicion, but Thomas only laughed. The sheriff rose and stood in the doorway, bristling at her intrusion.

"I'm sorry, miss, but I am occupied." He turned away from her to glare at the deputy. "Fred, what the hell are you doing, letting every Tom, Dick, and Harry come in here? Can't you do anything besides drink that coffee?"

The deputy scrambled to his feet, reddening at the public scolding. "Excuse me, Miss Potter, but you'll have to wait outside. The sheriff is busy."

Emily ignored him and spoke directly to the sheriff. "But it's important. It's about my father's death."

Jed Hawkins paused for a moment and looked curiously at Emily, but his attitude didn't change. "I don't need any one else nosing around here about John Potter. I've been putting up with this for months, people traipsing in here, wanting to know all about the sensational murders. If you want to know what happened, read the papers. That's all I have to say."

Stunned, Emily was grateful that her anger made her forget all about the sexy preacher. "Other people were asking about my father? Who? Why?"

"Miss Potter, I asked you to leave. Now, if you insist on interrupting me—"

"But I have a right to know what your investigation showed!" she stated firmly. "I've come all the way from Boston, and I'm determined to find out what really happened. I've done my own preliminary work, but it is incomplete. The house is a shambles, and yielded little data. I would like to know what you saw when you came there that night of the killings, whether you examined the room thoroughly, what clues you found, and what your opinion of the case is."

Emily watched the lawman puff up like a tree frog, his face turning bright red, his eyes bulging with indignation.

"Miss Potter, I would suggest you get out of here right now before I lose my patience. I understand that you may be upset about your father, but that is not my problem. Maybe it is common back East for 'ladies' to barge uninvited into a man's office, but it doesn't happen here. Fred, show Miss Potter out!" And he slammed the door of his office behind him.

"But—"

The deputy rose and reluctantly took Emily's arm. "I'm sorry, but you'll have to leave."

"This is ridiculous!" Emily protested, staring at the slammed door in astonishment. "How can he refuse to see me? I am a citizen, just like the good reverend there!"

"You heard what he said." The deputy smiled shamefacedly, and held open the outer door. "Please, Miss Potter. You seem like a nice lady and all. You sort of remind me of . . . my mother."

Emily glared at the man through her spectacles, trying to ignore the indignation his words generated. The man was a few years her junior, she surmised, but hardly young enough to be called her son, or to think of her in such a way! She glanced down at her dowdy dress and her carpetbag, suddenly aware of how she must appear to Reverend Hall, as well.

"Please tell the sheriff I'll wait," she insisted. The deputy opened his mouth to argue, but Emily smiled sweetly and sat down on the bench outside the office. "I'm not going anywhere. One way or another, that man will talk to me."

The deputy watched helplessly while Emily brought out her notebook and began to write: "Thomas Hall visiting the sheriff at the first possible opportunity." Yes, she thought, coincidences were beginning to pile up.

The sheriff peered through the window. "Damn that woman! She's still there."

"From what I've seen of Miss Potter, she isn't liable to disappear," Thomas said smoothly, although he had to hide a chuckle. Emily had managed, in all of fifteen minutes, to thoroughly antagonize the only law in town. As it happened, her outburst had only benefited him. Whereas the man hadn't been very willing to speak to him before her interruption, Sheriff Hawkins seemed more friendly now, particularly when his presence was the only thing preventing Emily from barging in again.

Just then a head popped up near the window, and the sheriff gaped at her audacity. "She's trying to see what's going on in here!"

"Miss Potter, from what I've seen, is relentless," Thomas said dryly. He rose. "Perhaps we should continue our discussion at a later date."

"No, sit there. That danged spinster isn't making anyone leave. I don't care how long she stays." Sighing, the sheriff poured himself a cup of coffee, then sank down behind his desk in resignation. "So what do you want to know, and why is everyone so goddamned interested in Potter all of a sudden?"

"As part of my mission, I'd like to help Miss Potter come to peace with her father's passing," Thomas said, amazed at how sincere he sounded. "I have a particular interest in her, especially after meeting her on the stagecoach. The woman is, if I might say, a menace."

"She is that," the lawman agreed. He glanced up at Thomas, his gaze shrewd. "You aren't a Pinkerton, by any chance, are you? The place was crawling with them after the killings."

"No." Thomas laughed. "My interest is purely personal."

The sheriff seemed to be considering that when he caught sight of Emily's face at the window on the opposite side of the room, her forehead pressed to the glass. He flushed angrily, then continued speaking as if she weren't there. "Well, it was rumored that Potter had money. Two million dollars was stolen from a payroll, and everyone thought Potter did it."

Thomas shrugged, "I heard the rumors. From what I understand, nothing was ever found. Do you believe he had it?"

"I don't know," Hawkins said. "Someone tore the house and grounds apart looking for that gold. They never found so much as an ingot. The federal agents came nosing around here, too, and even the Pinkertons, but no one could prove a thing. That money's stayed hidden."

Thomas nodded. "I escorted Miss Potter home last night and saw the inside of the house. Nearly every article in the place has been wrecked."

"Everyone, from the lowliest vandal to the passing cowhands, has tried to find that money." Hawkins shrugged, absently caressing his white mustache. "But it ain't a coincidence that Potter and the girl were killed. Someone else knew about that gold. Someone desperate enough to murder."

"Tell me about that night," Thomas asked casually. "I am so concerned for poor Miss Potter. I don't think she's taking the danger seriously enough. Perhaps if I could explain to her . . . "

The sheriff nodded. Turning his back to the door and to Emily Potter waiting outside, he settled more comfortably into his chair. "I suppose, with you being a preacher and all, the details will remain confidential. You're right about the girl. She is in more trouble than she knows. John Potter wasn't exactly loved around here, but he wasn't hated, either. He slipped into town about a year ago, calling himself Mullen. He had that house built behind the saloon in no time flat, and seldom left it. It was a whorehouse, right from the beginning, but it wasn't exactly a typical fancy place. He brought in several girls, real lookers, too, especially Rosie. She was his favorite. He set her up nice, and made it so that she didn't have to see many other men. He put in the fixtures, had the ceiling painted, and brought in furnishings from the East. Potter had been to Europe, or so he said, and he wanted his house to be what the French had, a real gentleman's retreat."

"I saw it," Thomas acknowledged.

"Well, then you know he accomplished that all right, and soon had lots of out-of-towners coming here for a poker game and a night at Shangri-La. The locals weren't too keen on this, as you can imagine, though some of them benefited business-wise. Those visiting cowhands had money to spend. But they raised hell, drank too much, and carried on. Tension started building and the folks around here complained.

"Just when it was all about to boil over, Potter started acting loco. He bolted up the house, was real careful about who came to visit, and took to carrying his revolver with him. Something or someone was hot on his trail, I could tell that much. Yet he never applied for protection."

Thomas nodded thoughtfully. "So you think Potter had an accomplice in the robbery?"

"Potter couldn't have pulled off that job by himself, least not in my book. He was clever, but he didn't have the mind of a criminal. Also, someone had helped him escape when the Pinkertons were first after him, someone who at one time must have been on his side."

"That makes sense," Thomas said. "So you think this accomplice may have been involved in the murder?"

"The way I figure, his partner was supposed to get a fifty percent cut. But Potter double-crossed him. When his accomplice found out, he got his revenge the hard way."

"Murder," Thomas said thoughtfully. "It seems strange that his accomplice wouldn't fear for his own life in coming back here. Potter must have been dangerous, too, if crossed."

"My guess is he had two million reasons for coming back," the sheriff said dryly. "The way I see it, his accomplice, whoever it is, killed Potter and Rosie. And he still hasn't been caught."

"Why the girl? She didn't have anything to do with this, did she?"

"I think she just happened to be with him when the accomplice confronted Potter." The sheriff shrugged. "And she was a witness. Rosie probably knew the whole story, may even have known where Potter put the money, he trusted her that much. But she's dead."

"And Potter's daughter is alive." Thomas looked at the window. Was that a shadow still lurking outside? Emily was undoubtedly poised with her ear to the door.

The sheriff nodded. "Now do you see why it's important to get her out of here? Whether she knows where the gold is or not, I don't want to go back to that house and clean up another mess like I had to that night. The girl is in danger. Someone has to make her see that."

"I've tried," Thomas said in exasperation. "She

won't budge. The woman is as stubborn as a mule.
Until I can make her see reason, I'm going to find a
servant to stay there. Maybe a stable boy who could
keep an eye out."

"You could try Russ Whittaker's boy. He used to
take care of the stables for Rosie. He might not mind
coming back. All the girls fled after that night, and
even the servants disappeared. We had a tough time
trying to find witnesses."

"Were there any?"

"We did talk to the housekeeper, Bertie Evans,
who's still somewhere about. She wouldn't tell us
much. Then there was a China woman, used to do
the laundry. Her name is Sung He, and she lives at
the edge of town, near the mining camp. The men
all called her China Blue. We haven't been able to
find her, though. She disappeared right after the
murders."

"Anyone else? Odd that none of the girls saw or
heard anything."

The sheriff rummaged in his desk and pulled out a
black book of bound notes. "Here is my report. Most
of those girls scattered like fleas after the killings. We
did hear of one of them. She came back to the house
one night, apparently to get some of her things. She
ran out in a hurry, and I lost track of her. Lizzie was
her name. Lizzie Wakefield. Prettiest of all the girls."

"Lizzie," Thomas repeated. "Why was she in such
a hurry to leave? Did she know something?"

"No, I don't think it had anything to do with that.
It seems she got scared out of her wits. Folks around
here all say that, anyway."

"And what do you think?"

"Apparently, the place is haunted. Lizzie said she wouldn't go within ten feet of it again, even if her life depended on it—"

The sheriff's next words were drowned out when a crash sounded outside the office. Instinctively the sheriff grabbed his gun and got to his feet. Flinging open the door, he stared in astonishment at his office bench, toppled over on the floor, along with a bookcase and a vase of flowers his mother had brought by. Fred, the young deputy, sat behind the desk, his head in his hands. Emily was sprawled on the floor. A glimpse of snow white petticoats frothed beneath the hem of her dress, and Thomas could see just enough of her shapely ankles and stockinged calves to give him an idea of her unbridled charms. Blood pounded in the back of his head, but it was the sheriff who exploded.

"What in blazes is going on here?"

4

The Good Reverend Lends a Hand

"I can explain—" Emily began, but the sheriff only glared at her.

"I'll take care of this," Thomas said quickly, stepping over the mess and taking Emily by the arm. He yanked her to her feet, then set the bench back upright while the sheriff fingered his gun. "Thank you for your time, Sheriff. It's been most informative. Miss Potter, I think you should be getting home now, before the kind sheriff changes his mind and arrests you."

"But—" Emily started to protest, but the lawman's glance toward the cell indicated that Thomas's guess wasn't too far from the mark. "But I still need information!"

"Miss Potter will pay for any damages, won't you? I look forward to seeing you again real soon, Sheriff."

Thomas propelled Emily out the door, even as she

continued to stutter objections. He had barely closed the door behind them when the sound of the sheriff's shouting rattled the windows. Thomas flinched for the poor deputy, who'd obviously been out of his league with Emily. Quickening his pace, he half-dragged her down the street, determined to put as much distance between the irate lawman and Miss Potter as possible.

When they were several blocks from the jail, Emily was forced to stop, breathless from the exertion. She yanked her hand out of Thomas's grip, glaring at him indignantly.

"What do you think you're doing? I need to have an interview with the sheriff. There is so much information missing—"

"Miss Emily," Thomas said, cutting her off, "I don't know what your experience was back East, but lawmen here don't take kindly to females barging in and demanding to investigate. You were very close to spending the night in jail, if you haven't figured that out."

"Reverend," Emily replied haughtily, as if his words were the grossest exaggeration, "I really don't think he would have done any such thing."

Thomas gritted his teeth in exasperation. This woman could be so damned obstinate! "Miss Potter, trust me. Not even the good Lord himself could have helped you. The man was ready to kill you. There isn't a doubt in my mind that had you stayed there, you'd be conducting your interview behind bars."

Emily finally saw the truth in his words. The fire went out of her eyes and she appeared so dejected that he actually felt a pang of sympathy for her. She lifted her hands hopelessly. "Then I am defeated before I start. Even Lestrade, the intellectually inferior policeman in London, helped Sherlock Holmes. How can I investigate a case when the sheriff won't even give me the time of day?"

Thomas sighed. He should just let her realize how futile investigating the case would be, then maybe she would give up and return home to safety. Or she would confess what she knew and stop this ridiculousness. But something in her eyes made him relent. Coupled with the thoughts of those pretty ankles, the petticoat, the warmth of her hand when he'd clasped hers, he found it very hard to stand his ground. Somehow he heard himself saying something he never intended. "All right, Miss Potter, I will share with you some of what he told me. Will that satisfy you?"

"You were discussing my case with him! Why?"

Thomas forced a smile, cursing himself for being taken in by a pair of silver eyes. "Yes, we were talking about it. I decided to ask about the case after seeing the house last night and your methods of investigation. You aroused . . . my curiosity."

That wasn't all she aroused, but Thomas would be damned if he'd venture there. In truth, the simple physical contact they'd made had affected him far more than he would ever admit. This strange slip of a girl had a disconcerting influence on him, and it wasn't something he wanted to dwell on.

Emily blanched, then her eyes narrowed suspiciously. "I must say that I think it very odd for a preacher to be so interested in a murder. Where are you staying? I haven't heard of any new mission here."

"I've decided to start one, if there is enough interest," Thomas explained readily. "I think the good people of Denver will appreciate a new preacher. This seems a most unholy town. In the interim, I'm staying at the boardinghouse." When she continued to watch him with disbelief, he shrugged. "Miss Potter, since you seem so determined to remain suspicious of me, I'll be on my way. I have a lot to do myself, being new in town."

"I suppose secondhand information is better than none." She sighed in resignation. "What did he tell you?"

Thomas glanced down the street and saw the sheriff rounding the corner. The man didn't look any happier now than he had earlier. Muttering under his breath, Thomas indicated the restaurant across the street.

"I suggest we get something to eat. Your new friend is coming this way, and I don't think he's in the mood for polite conversation," Thomas said bluntly. "I also don't think you want to discuss your father's murder in public."

"Very well," Emily agreed reluctantly.

Was she really so displeased at the prospect of socializing with him? Thomas wondered how he had gotten himself into this, and for a woman who apparently wasn't in the least grateful. He led her across the street, into the immaculate restaurant that was part of the hotel. When the waitress saw his collar, they were immediately ushered to one of the better tables and given menus. They ordered soup and sandwiches.

As they waited for the food, Emily retrieved her notebook, then looked at him expectantly. "I have a list of questions here that I hope you can answer. Let's start at the beginning. Did the sheriff inspect the room? Was he able to obtain any physical data? Does he have an idea who perpetrated the crime?"

"No, no, and no," Thomas answered solemnly.

Emily's face fell, and her eyes darkened with dismay. "Then you mean he's made no progress in the case?"

Thomas tried to explain as the waitress placed their meals on the table. "Miss Potter, did you know anything at all about your father's life here? Or the rumors surrounding his death?"

Emily flushed and seemed to struggle with her answer. "No. I told you last night. My father wrote to my mother and myself, and sometimes sent money, but that was the extent of our contact with him. My mother didn't speak much about him, other than to say that things were for the best. She felt she couldn't live out here, where everything is so rugged and wild. She had family in Boston, and her customers and her church. Evidently that was enough for her."

The waitress gave Thomas a fluttery glance before moving away, which made Emily scowl all the more. Thomas ignored his curiosity about her reaction as he took a bite of his sandwich and continued his interrogation.

"That's all he told you? I suppose you never heard about the money, then.

"What money?" Emily asked.

Thomas watched her expression closely. "A stage-coach from Wells Fargo was transporting a two-million-dollar gold payroll out West when the money disappeared. Two men were in charge of the ship-ment, and everyone thought they were responsible. One of them was John Potter."

The spoon fell from Emily's hand and she stared at Thomas in shock. "What? Two million dollars in gold? And you think—"

"Your father vanished, only to turn up months later running a bordello in Denver. The other man was also accused and was fired by Wells Fargo, but no one could prove anything. The money, you see, has never turned up."

"My God," Emily whispered. "So that's why Shangri-La was vandalized!"

"Someone was looking for the gold," Thomas agreed. "No bank has registered a deposit of that amount, no individual has confessed, and your father was certainly not living the life of a millionaire. Yet all the facts point to him."

"That doesn't make sense." Emily, recovered from the surprise, picked up her pencil and began to scribble furiously. "I can't believe he did such a thing! I mean, I didn't know him well, I admit that, but to steal two million dollars . . . Even if he used some of it to build the house, where is the rest? Why didn't he use it? And how does that tie into the killings?"

Thomas sighed. Emily's surprised reaction was totally believable. Was she simply a good liar? "The sheriff thinks someone else was involved in the robbery. If your father reneged on his agreement with his accomplice and absconded with all of the money, that person would certainly have had a motive to kill."

Emily tapped her cheek thoughtfully with her pencil. "That theory certainly fits the facts, if one believes the initial supposition is correct. However, I find it difficult to accept that as truth. Therefore, the conclusion is faulty, and leading us in entirely the wrong direction."

"Miss Potter," Thomas said, trying to keep a tight rein on his emotions, "I only agreed to give you this information in the hope that you would see how dangerous this situation is for you. Whoever killed your father most likely did it for the money, and they aren't going to stop until they get it. Don't you understand? Every moment you are living in that house you are in jeopardy!"

The waitress brought their bill, which Thomas insisted on paying. As soon as the woman left, Emily rose, picked up her bag, and gave him a rare smile. It was a beautiful smile, Thomas noticed, even as her words caused his blood to boil.

"Thank you for the meal, Reverend, and the insight. I think I can manage from here. As Holmes would say, 'Ce n'est que le premier pas qui coute.' It is only the first step that costs."

"Miss Potter," Thomas said through gritted teeth, "does nothing I've said make any difference to you?"

In response, Emily laid her hand on his arm, as if patting a lapdog. "Please don't concern yourself, Reverend. I must follow my path, and do what I was created to do, just as you must." Her eyes fell meaningfully on his collar.

The simple contact of her hand made him want to pull her into his arms and teach her what he was created to do. Yet as she strode briskly away, her carpetbag in one hand, her notebook under her arm, he fought the impulse with everything he had. And he realized something else about himself, something not very flattering: For all he had intended to find out about Emily Potter, she'd obviously learned a thing or two about him.

Upon returning from the grocery store, Emily fed Watson, then finished her examination of the house. But the erotic feelings she'd experienced with Thomas just wouldn't leave her. Even when he'd grasped her hand to haul her to her feet in the sheriff's office, she had felt all tingly. She'd discovered that she liked the rough feeling of his skin against hers, which was amazingly like her fantasy, and frantically wondered if he had felt her pulse pounding beneath his fingers. The good Reverend Hall made her feel unholy indeed, but (as she had to firmly remind herself again) he was a prime suspect in the case.

Emily absently petted Watson as she studied her notes. It was inconceivable that he would visit the sheriff's office at the first opportunity, the same as herself, unless he was just as interested as she was in the murders. His presence there this morning only supported her suspicion that he was no ordinary preacher. What man of God concerned himself with stolen gold and revenge killings?

So if he wasn't a preacher, who and what was he? Emily was puzzled. Perhaps a lawman, someone working with the sheriff? He could even be a federal agent, assigned to investigate the case. Or one of the hated Pinkertons—detectives known for disguise who would ingratiate themselves with suspects, then wring confessions out of them. Thomas certainly seemed to have the nerve for such exploits, but something told her the reasons for his involvement were deeper than that. Was it possible they were also more sinister?

A chill raced up her spine. What if *he* were the accomplice to the robbery? If the sheriff's theory was right, someone out there would stop at nothing to get that gold.

Putting aside her casebook, Emily tried to clear her mind. One could not theorize with so little information, she reminded herself, for invariably one started trying to fit the facts to the theory instead of the other way around. Also, although Emily couldn't explain it, even to herself, she didn't want Thomas to be the killer. Aside from the way he made her feel, there was something likable about him, something that made her want to trust him. Still, the thought was more than a little disconcerting, and one she couldn't entirely dismiss—especially not for the sake of a tingling sensation and some broad, masculine shoulders. . . .

Emily decided to do some cleaning, to give herself

something to do other than wonder about Reverend
Hall, and to start making Shangri-La into a proper
home. Physical activity was the best cure for an overactive mind, her mother had taught her. Climbing
the stairs, she started with her bedroom—Rosie's
room. Emptying the contents of the wardrobe onto
the bed, she gasped at the collection of clothes Rosie
had accumulated. There were richly printed dressing
gowns from India, and intricate lace chemises that
enticed the eye. There were brilliant jewel-tone ball
gowns, and day dresses of sprigged muslin. There
were nightclothes such as Emily never knew existed,
gowns and short shifts, shimmering rails and exotic
lingerie. She touched the luxurious material in
wonder. For a fleeting second, Thomas Hall again
popped into her mind, but she refused to entertain
the thought. Blushing furiously, she forced herself to
inspect the rest of the wardrobe. There were cloaks
and shoes to match everything, clever boots, slippers,
and beguiling wraps. Emily shook her head in amazement. The cost of one of these beautiful gowns could
feed a family for weeks! Yet she had already made up
her mind to get rid of the clothes.

When she finished packing as many of the gowns
as she could manage, she began rounding up the
jewels and perfumes. Something feminine within her
made this difficult, but she reminded herself of the
poor, scrawny miners she'd encountered on her trip,
of the half-starved children she'd seen playing in
their camps. Any proceeds from this stuff would
surely help them, so she deliberately packed most of

it, leaving only a few items remaining in the dresser. When she came to the last flagon of perfume, attar of roses, she hesitated, examining the beautiful bottle.

Rosie wore this. The thought came unbidden, and she put the bottle down quickly, as if it had burned her. There was something about knowing how the woman smelled while still alive that chilled her. It made Rosie seem so real, as if she were here. . . .

As she turned back to the bundles of clothes, Emily smelled a soft fragrance. Roses. It filled the air—the sweet smell of a garden in July. Breathing in the heady scent, she looked over her shoulder at the table. She must have left the stopper off, or knocked the bottle over . . . but her brow knotted when she saw the flagon.

It was full, and tightly stoppered.

Yet the air was thick with the perfume. Amazed, Emily breathed it deeply. Then a cold breeze blew over her, as if she'd stepped outside in the dead of winter, that same raw, damp chill she'd felt earlier. She stood frozen in disbelief as a sudden certainty came over her.

She was not alone.

The cold chill passed right through her. The scent continued to fill the air, sweet and rich, almost as if the woman herself was standing right beside her.

"Rosie?" Emily whispered squeakily. Her own voice sounded strange to her. Only silence answered her, but she was more convinced than ever that there was another presence in the room.

A ghost? Emily sank down onto the chair, her knees shaking. The hair rose on the back of her neck.

She'd read about such doings, but never thought to experience them herself! Eagerly, she reexamined her surroundings, but there was no visible evidence. It was more of a feeling, the way one knew when a cat had entered the room long before actually seeing it.

The candle flame went out, just as the gaslight had earlier. Her hands shaking, Emily tried to relight the wick, but the match blew out as quickly as she struck the flint.

"Rosie, now stop that! If you really are here, why don't you just appear and stop playing these games! Some ghost you are!"

She felt better voicing her fears and taking control of the situation. She found another flint and successfully lit the candle. As she glanced up, Emily smelled the perfume again, and felt the same, eerie presence she'd experienced before. Her eyes rose to the mirror that faced her. Slowly, one by one, the matches slipped from her fingers. She saw her own reflection, and right beside it, the bawdy image of a saloon girl.

"Rosie!" she cried breathlessly, taking in the scarlet dress, the black plumes, the dancing earrings. Her eyes, like the eyes in the portrait, were magnificent. She grinned, as if still enjoying life, and Emily could hear her naughty laughter. "My God, it's really you!"

"Well, it ain't Queen Victoria. How are you, sweetie?"

5

Suspicion

Emily stared in amazement, her mouth hanging open like an overstuffed drawer.

"Don't look so horrified, honey, it ain't that bad. I won't hurt you. I couldn't even if I wanted to." The saloon girl giggled. "Sorry about the gaslight downstairs. Seems I can cause that kind of thing, even if I can't get out of here."

Emily forced her mouth closed and swallowed hard. "Then I'm not imagining this? You're really here?"

"In the flesh, I would say, but that isn't quite correct, is it?"

"Rosie." Emily lowered herself into the chair at the dressing table, trying to force her mind to accept what she was seeing. "But you're—"

"Dead." Rosie said the word with glee. "It's still a little hard for me to accept, but that seems to be the case. I was shot, sweetie, not far from where you sit. Hurt like hell, I must say. When I woke up, I was a ghost, and stuck inside the mirror. It's like being yourself but without a body."

That was too incredible a concept for Emily to imagine. She touched the mirror, half expecting her hand to go right through to feel the satin of Rosie's dress. Instead, her fingers rested on cold, hard glass. Ignoring the spirit's laughter, she looked behind the gilt frame, even going so far as to lift the heavy glass from its nail, but the back of it was smooth and firm, the hook a simple scrap of tin.

"There has to be something," Emily said to herself. "I've seen those new experiments with moving pictures. There must be a projector."

Replacing the mirror on the wall, Emily ignored the vision's smirk of amusement as she fetched her magnifying glass. She searched every inch of the wall for a hole, a crevice, or a mechanical device that could cause what she was seeing, but she found nothing. The wall was simply a wall, the bed, a bed, the ceiling plastered and firm. And yet . . . how could this be? She knelt and peered under the bed. Nothing but a plethora of dust balls.

"Satisfied?" The phantom seemed to be holding back laughter. "It's been kind of boring, these past few weeks, with nothing to see or do here. I couldn't even get downstairs, or I'd have scared the hell out of those cowpokes who wrecked the place. I did a pretty good job as is, though. Anyhow, I'm real glad you've come. You're right pretty, honey, and you look a little like your pa."

The familiar mention of her father made her flinch. Emily brought her magnifying glass up to the mirror, examining the image in minute detail, but even the trusty lens didn't shed any light on this mystery. The reflected image seemed as real as if the woman were standing behind her. "Then you were my father's . . . consort?"

Rosie paused, translating this into her language. "Oh, you mean mistress. That's certainly a nice way of putting it. Sweetie, my relationship with your pa had nothing to do with you or your mother. They were separated for so long. But he never forgot you. He spoke of you constantly."

Emily bristled, although Rosie's explanation was meant to be reassuring. "I've heard such things are common on the Continent, but it isn't quite so readily accepted here," she said coolly. Was she really arguing ethics with a ghost?

"Why, I know, and I can understand how you feel," Rosie agreed blithely. "But if it makes you feel any better, I was the only girl he visited. He built this house for us . . . and for you. It is lovely, isn't it? I wasn't too crazy about the downstairs, those paintings and all. Your pa assured me they were art, but I think they were just to please the fellas, you know? And I don't have anything against that. Why, if it makes a cowboy come quicker, then my girls are happy, too. Know what I mean, honey?"

Emily didn't have the slightest notion what she meant. She frowned, her nose wrinkling. This was all too bizarre to sort out, even with a wonderfully logical mind like her own. "Is my father with you?" she asked finally.

Rosie shook her head. "No, I think he moved on. I didn't see him after everything happened, but he got himself shot before I did. Same killer, I would say."

Goose bumps popped up on Emily's arms. In spite of her disbelief that this was really happening, a clue was a clue. "Do you remember anything about—?"

"No, I can't," Rosie said quickly, her plumes dipping like an exotic peacock's. "I've tried and tried, but can't recall who it was that walked into our house that night. I think all that gets erased when you come to this side, so you can't cause trouble for the living."

"Why haven't you moved on?" Emily found her fear lessening, being replaced by fascination. Even if this were just a weird dream, it was incredible. "Shouldn't you be wherever my father is?"

"Sure," Rosie agreed. "But I got trapped in this mirror. Caught between two planes, so to speak, and here I am."

A knock on the door interrupted Emily's reply. She watched Rosie's reflection fade away to nothingness. "Wait!" Emily cried, but the mirror was just glass once more, and the only image she could see was her own.

"Drat!" she muttered, picking up the candle. Maybe it was all just a dream. Emily's logical mind could conceive of no other explanation. She was alone too much. Perhaps it made one fanciful. Or it was this house! Surely it was that, and not that she was losing her mind. . . . Outside the door, Dr. Watson mewed, staring at the blank mirror with his back arched and his fur standing straight out. Had he seen the same thing she had? Downstairs, the rapping became more persistent, and Emily had no more time to think as she rushed to get the door.

Thomas stood on the front step. "Good evening, Miss Emily. I hope I'm not intruding?"

"Reverend." Emily stared at the man, her eyes narrowing. She wanted to talk to the ghost, to learn everything she could about the murders, and about her father. But once again, Thomas had gotten in her way. Her previous suspicions came back to her as she scrutinized him more thoroughly. Could he be a coldblooded killer?

"Mind if I come in?" Thomas walked into the hallway without waiting for her answer. It was only then that Emily realized he wasn't alone. A small boy doffed his cap, his hair sticking straight up like a cocklebur, and followed Thomas into the house. He appeared undersized and thin, his shoulders seeming to sag beneath the weight of his suspenders. He looked down at the floor shyly.

"Miss Emily, I'd like you to meet Darrel," Thomas said formally. "He's looking for work as a stable boy, but he can do just about anything: toting wood, cleaning, you name it. He worked here once before, when your father owned the place. I thought you could make use of him, being out here alone."

"Hello, Darrel." Emily was distracted from her thoughts about Thomas and she smiled stiffly at the small boy. About thirteen or fourteen, the lad appeared capable and bright. He seemed not at all self-conscious about being in the house, in spite of the lurid paintings and furnishings. He peered curiously over Emily's shoulder.

"Why don't you help yourself to some milk and biscuits in the kitchen?" Emily said, blocking the boy's view. "I want to talk to the Reverend Hall a moment, then I'll be back for you."

At the mention of food, the boy's face lit up. "Thank you, ma'am." He looked to the preacher for approval.

As soon as Thomas nodded, the boy scampered through the door. Emily turned to the preacher, her mouth pursed. "I appreciate your good intentions, but I have no horses and no need for a stable boy."

"I know." Thomas shrugged, as if he had been expecting her protests. "I spoke to the boy's father. He is quite willing to let you compensate the lad when your business starts paying. You did say you intend to reestablish the millinery shop, didn't you?"

"Yes, but—"

"I won't take no for an answer." He began lecturing her in a solemn church tone. "Miss Potter, it isn't safe for you to be alone out here. You saw the condition of the house. I've told you about the gold. You need someone living on the property, someone who could at least send for help if it should become necessary." He hold up his hand when she started to protest once more. "Don't thank me, I consider it the good Lord's work."

Emily felt as if she'd been run over by a train. This man was arrogance defined! If he hadn't obviously been intent on helping her, she would have given him a piece of her mind for meddling in her life. Still, she supposed she could use the boy for toting parcels and helping with the repainting. She forced down her annoyance.

"I'm sure I can find work for the boy. If it's all right with his father, I'll feed him until I can afford to pay him. Now if you don't mind—"

"Not at all. In fact, I was just thinking how good a hot cup of tea would be with a fine Christian woman like yourself. You drink tea, don't you?" The preacher smiled, and Emily noticed again how good-looking he was, and how his eyes crinkled at the corners, making them seem even more intense. That odd little thrill raced inside her again, reminding her what it was like when he touched her.

But just as quickly Emily dismissed the notion. She couldn't forget her suspicions about Thomas's role in this case, no matter how he made her stomach flutter. Still, until she knew who he was, she couldn't be rude. Reluctantly she led him to the kitchen, where Darrel was happily eating a biscuit. Crumbs on the table indicated it was not his first. Thomas gazed around the kitchen approvingly as Emily filled the teapot.

"Looks like you've done a lot with the place already," he commented.

"I've managed to clean up most of the broken furnishings, but I've got a long way to go," she said. "Once I sell a few hats, I can paint and wallpaper, and maybe replace a few pieces of furniture."

"I'm surprised your father didn't leave you some

money," Thomas commented. "Aside from the gold, he should have had something. The income from the house should have at least provided a good living."

Emily's nose wrinkled as she realized the meaning behind the preacher's words. Had her father been living off Rosie and the girls? But if he'd had the gold, why didn't he just use that? It all seemed to grow more confusing by the moment.

The tea kettle whistled, and Emily began pouring the hot water into the teapot as Thomas took a chair. She tried to ignore the fact that his physical presence nearly overwhelmed her. Unwillingly her mind went back to that moment in his arms when her body had tingled upon the simple contact. She shook her head. First she was seeing ghosts, and now she was having thoughts about seducing this charlatan minister!

She was so deep in her reverie that she splashed her hand with the hot water. Waving it in front of her, she tried to stop the burning pain, but the cool air just seemed to make her skin sting more.

"Did you hurt yourself? Let me see." Thomas's voice lost some of its remoteness as he held her hand under the gaslight and examined the red patch. "Looks like a scald. Let's put some cold water on that. Darrel, hand me that pitcher."

"No, I'm fine," Emily protested, but it did little good. Thomas ignored her, gently pouring cold water over her fingers. The pain was soothed instantly, and Emily sighed in relief as the ache became a bearable throb. "Thank you," she breathed gratefully.

"It looks like a bad burn. Blisters could develop,

which means a chance for infection. You really should let me put something on that. I have some salve in my room at the boardinghouse. I can bring it over."

Emily looked up at him. Suddenly she realized that he was rubbing her wrist. His hands, lightly callused like fine sandpaper, felt wonderful against her bare flesh. A strange awareness raced along her skin, and Emily swallowed hard at the unfamiliar sensations. The starch of her prim collar seemed to scratch her flesh, and her corset felt as if it were laced far too tightly.

Fidgeting with her collar, she spoke quickly. "Why don't I accompany you instead? That will be quicker."

She had to resume her logical thinking, which had deserted her in his presence. But in the dim recesses where her brain still functioned, she realized it wasn't a good idea to stay here with him. In addition to not knowing who he was, he posed another kind of threat, one that at the moment seemed even more eminent.

"Are you certain?" he asked, an understanding twinkle in his eye. "I'm not sure that's proper, seeing as I'm a single man of the cloth. And Mrs. Haines isn't too fond of female callers."

"I'll wait outside," Emily replied. It hadn't escaped her, even in her current state, that she could at least verify where he was staying. Besides, if he were innocent, who could be a better escort than a preacher? No one in their right mind could find fault with that, especially if she stayed demurely on the porch. The burn on her hand twinged. Thomas

Hall, Emily decided, was becoming a distraction she couldn't afford.

Thomas accompanied Emily into town, certain what she was up to. She was as suspicious of him as he was of her, and had figured out a way to confirm his cover story. He had to admire her methods.

She walked stiffly beside him, careful not to brush against him. A smile curved his lips when he thought of the charming blush he'd seen on her cheeks when he'd massaged her hand and felt her racing pulse. Miss Potter wasn't all cold logic. Yet knowing she had reacted to him physically didn't help much, for there was nothing he could do about it. Nothing at all.

His amusement changed quickly to frustration. Having this woman so close to his bedroom didn't help his control over the odd attraction that was sparking between them. All he could picture was Emily sprawled out on Mrs. Haines's patchwork quilt, that chestnut hair tousled about her naked shoulders, her eyes smoky with passion. She would be so soft, so sweet, begging him to touch her, kiss her, make love to her. . . .

He quickened his pace, heedless of the fact that she was a good three steps behind him. The last thing he needed was to have erotic thoughts about Emily Potter! Yet the vision wouldn't leave him and his blood was beginning to pound in his veins. When he reached the house, he saw her puffing to catch up to him. Opening the door, he gestured to the porch. "Wait here."

Emily nodded, obediently standing beside the door.

She was so pretty, her face flushed from exertion, her hair loosening from its knot to allow a few curls to frame her face. Perspiration gleamed on her forehead, and she looked like a woman who'd just had a good tumble. He couldn't help his short-tempered growl as he headed into the house. Insanity must have propelled him to do this. Why should he care if her hand got infected? The woman thought the worst of him, and didn't appreciate anything he did for her. Moreover, he still wasn't convinced she was innocent in the matter of the gold. Why then did Emily continue to concern him?

"Reverend Hall! There you are!"

Thomas gritted his teeth and turned slowly in the foyer. He wanted nothing more than to fetch the salve, get rid of Emily, and relax with a hot bath and a cold beer. Although drinking wasn't considered one of the deadly sins by everyone, it wasn't in good form for him to appear in the saloon so soon after his arrival in town. Yet he needed a drink. Emily Potter was beginning to get under his skin.

Mrs. Haines accosted him, oblivious to his tired yawn, then thrust a shawl-covered mound toward him. It was then he noticed another woman, her face partially hidden by her bonnet. As he took the proffered bundle, the other woman smiled shyly.

"This is Mrs. Olson, and that is her new baby boy!" Mrs. Haines declared. "Isn't he beautiful!"

Thomas gazed down into the reddened face of the newborn. A thatch of black hair stood up from his head, and his tiny fingers poked aimlessly at his blanket. The baby stared at him cross-eyed, then began to gnaw at his fist. When that didn't appease him, he rooted at Thomas's chest, apparently looking for his next meal. Like most newborns, he resembled nothing more than a wizened old man, and Thomas forced an awkward smile.

"Beautiful. Yes, absolutely."

When he looked up, he saw Emily standing on tiptoe outside, doing her damnedest to see what was going on. He frowned at her sharply, then turned back to the women with a preacherlike smile.

The baby, hearing an unfamiliar male voice and having no success in finding his dinner, screwed up his face and inhaled. A moment later, he let out a yell that pierced eardrums and made teacups rattle on the shelves. Appalled, Thomas tried to bounce the infant, but his only reward was another scream.

"Why, that's odd. All babies loved Reverend Flatter. Never held a one that he couldn't quiet. You remember Reverend Flatter, don't you Mrs. Olson?" Mrs. Haines asked, her eyes narrowing as the baby continued to fuss.

"Oh . . . yes." The woman watched Thomas manhandle her baby, her eyes wide with apprehension.

Thomas felt incredibly foolish as the baby wrenched himself into a knot, in preparation for another bawl.

"Yes, and a wonderful man he was." Mrs. Haines was beginning to wax poetic. "Like I said, he loved babies, and they just loved him."

"Well, it seems I don't have Reverend Flatter's talent in that area," Thomas said miserably as the baby squirmed. "Here." He thrust the offending creature at his mother. "I have a friend outside who needs medical care. I was bringing her a jar of salve."

"Oh, bring her in!" Mrs. Haines reached for the door.

"That's all right, she can wait outside," Thomas tried.

"Nonsense!" Mrs. Haines waved a hand in dismissal. "This will take a few moments. She can't stand out there in the heat like that. Come in, Miss? . . ."

"Potter. Emily Potter."

Emily walked triumphantly through the door to stand next to the women, obviously relishing every moment of his discomfort. Thomas glared at Emily, then shifted his gaze back to Mrs. Haines. "What will take a few moments?"

Mrs. Olson looked at him in confusion, pressing the child back into this arms. "Reverend, I was hoping that you . . . I mean, he is newborn, and we want to save him from the fires of hell and all. . . ."

"Hell?" Thomas stared at her while the baby let out another squall, more robust than the first ones.

"He needs to be christened, of course," Mrs. Haines said briskly. "You do perform them, don't you?"

Thomas wrestled with the baby, trying desperately to keep from dropping his charge. An odd grin of satisfaction curved Emily's lips.

"Of course, Reverend," Emily agreed politely. "You must christen this child at once! God forbid anything should happen to him."

Thomas shot her a murderous look. Forcing a

smile once more, he looked at the other two women pleadingly. "But don't you think it would be better to wait until my mission is established? I mean, for his sake." He gestured to the screaming baby with his chin, since his hands were full holding on to the little creature.

"Not at all." Mrs. Haines looked as offended as if he'd suggested the baby didn't deserve a christening. "One can never be certain in these times what will happen. I told Mrs. Olson you'd perform it without delay."

"I see." It seemed he had little choice. The three women eyed Thomas steadily, one with suspicion, the other two in expectation. He felt as if he were being tested, and God help him if he didn't pass. "All right, but it will have to be the short version. Then you can bring him back later and we'll do it again. Is that all right?"

Mrs. Olson nodded, relieved, Thomas supposed, that he wasn't dooming her son to eternal damnation. Fumbling in his coat, he grimaced as he realized his prayer book was upstairs. To fetch it would only prolong his agony.

"Our Father, who art in heaven. Hallowed be thy name," he mumbled quickly.

Emily's brow lifted and she silently mouthed "Our Father?"

Thomas ignored her, and lowered his voice, muttering a prayer. The cadence had a pleasing effect, and the older women appeared satisfied by the time he ran out of phrases.

The baby, however, screamed indignantly, drowning out his words, and Thomas felt something wet penetrate his shirtsleeve. It trickled down his arm and off his little finger. Swallowing hard, he finished quickly. "I christen thee . . ."

"Francis Olson." The baby's mother beamed.

"Francis Olson, in the name of the Father, and the Son, and the Holy Spirit, Amen."

"Amen," the two women repeated. To his amazement, Mrs. Olson was smiling at him.

"I'll take him now. He must be hungry. Thank you so much, Reverend."

Thomas handed the baby back to its mother, silently groaning at the wetness of his coat. Emily squelched a giggle, but when he glanced up at her, she was straight-faced. Mrs. Haines noticed the dark stain spreading across his jacket, and her usually harsh face softened. She gave him a blissful smile.

"Isn't that sweet! He christened you! You know, they say it's good luck."

The two women tittered while Emily gave him a knowing glance. Thomas held his dripping arm away from his body. Luck. He had a feeling that his was running out.

6

A Clue

"Excuse me," Emily said to the man bent over the filing cabinets. "Could I speak to you for a moment?"

Old Doc Johnson, who also functioned as county coroner, was next on her list of people to see. Emily could only pray that the man was more help than the sheriff had been. He would at least be able to verify the cause of her father's and Rosie's deaths. And a well-written coroner's report, she knew, was often a detective's best ally.

Emily tried unsuccessfully to hide a yawn as the man turned toward her. She had spent a sleepless night tossing and turning, glancing continually at the mirror and waiting for the ghost to swirl into life in the gilt frame. But the phantom had put in no further appearances, and she had almost convinced herself that the earlier vision was due to exhaustion and the strange atmosphere of the bawdy house.

That also explained the strain of being around the overly zealous and attractive Thomas Hall. A delicious smile curved her lips as she thought of him attempting to christen Mrs. Olson's baby. For a preacher, he'd seemed very inept at this basic task, and obviously had not been at all happy to have her witness the incident. His struggle only made her more certain that he was no minister, although she wasn't any closer to discovering who he really was.

"Well?" The doctor brought her out of her reverie. A wiry little man with a sheaf of hair carefully combed over his bald pate, he had bright, beady eyes that traveled curiously over her simple dress and bag.

"I'm Miss Emily Potter, and I'd like to see your report concerning my father's death." Emily smiled brightly at the man, avoiding the sight of the dissecting table in the center of the room. Swallowing her repugnance, she tried hard not to think about what went on here. But the smell of chemicals and death seemed to fill the air, and Emily heard her stomach rumble in protest. She let her gaze drift over the papers scattered around the office. "I assume you are Dr. Willard Johnson. It occurred on—"

"I know when it occurred," the man said, his face wrinkling unpleasantly. "And I know who you are! You're that Miss Potter that everyone is talking about! The one sticking her nose into all kinds of business! Well, I won't give it to you."

He returned to his files as if the matter were done.

Emily stared at him in disbelief. Holmes never

had these problems. Forcing a smile, she tried to remain polite.

"I'm sorry that it's an inconvenience, but I really do need to see those forms. If you're busy, I can look myself—"

"Don't you touch my files!" The doctor was as upset as if she'd proposed setting the building on fire. He took a step closer to her. "I've organized these files since 1885, when I took over for my father, God rest his soul. No one touches these files now but me."

He gave a firm nod, as if he had laid down the law, and went back to his work.

Emily watched him in exasperation. "I see. Dr. Johnson, I am sorry about your loss. I am also sorry that you are trapped in a job that you obviously dislike, that you are in love with someone and your feelings are unrequited, and that your secret ambition is to write poetry, not pronounce a body dead. But I'm afraid I can't help you much in these endeavors."

The man shut the file so quickly he caught his hand in the drawer. Letting out a howl, he sucked on his finger, then stared at Emily as if she were a witch.

"How did you know all that? Who's been telling you about me?"

"No one," Emily responded simply. "But when I see a man filing endless papers, with a half-scribbled poem tucked beneath his forms, it isn't too hard to guess that he is ill suited for this work. Furthermore, though I can't read the entire verse, I can see enough to know that it is dedicated to a woman who doesn't return the poet's love. It is simplicity in itself."

"It *is* wonderful." The man's bravado, which was really only the thinnest veneer, dissolved completely. "Surely you would have been burned had you lived in Salem two hundred years ago."

Emily bowed at the compliment, then gave the man a gentle smile. "I am investigating my father's death. Since you lost your own father, I'm certain you are familiar with my feelings. May I see the file?"

"No." The doctor shrugged as Emily gaped at him. "I believe you are telling me the truth, and think you would make a fine detective, but I don't have the file. I lent it out this morning."

"Lent it out?" Emily repeated incredulously. "To whom?"

"Reverend Hall. He said the sheriff wanted to take another look at it."

"Thomas Hall." Emily suddenly wanted to strangle the preacher. "Do you know when he'll return the file?"

"He should be back any minute," the coroner answered confidently. "Why, here he is now."

Thomas entered the room, looking even more handsome than she remembered. His hair may have been a little too long, but it was neatly slicked back, and his black shirt outlined his muscular arms to perfection. He was missing his coat, and he looked in need of a shave, but the rough shadow around his chin only added to his sensual appeal. It was almost sinful that a man look so good. Emily gave him a frosty stare, which he acknowledged with a nod before launching into an exuberant greeting.

"Miss Potter! What a pleasant surprise, though not entirely unexpected." He stopped next to the grisly table, holding the file under one arm.

Emily didn't know what was more annoying, his slow grin or cocksure attitude. Obviously he'd beaten her to the punch. Again. "Reverend Hall. Why on earth aren't you out christening babies?"

"You mean being christened by them," Thomas corrected, laughter dancing in his eyes. The doctor coughed, and Thomas glanced in the poor man's direction before looking back at Emily. "What are you doing this morning? Making more friends?"

His veiled reference to the debacle with the sheriff didn't intimidate her in the least. "Dr. Johnson is quite willing to assist me in my case. Unlike some of the other gentlemen in town," she stressed the word "gentlemen." "But I find it quite a coincidence, running into you again in such an unusual place."

"It is a coincidence," Thomas agreed, though his gaze twinkled. "One might think we were on the same trail."

Having him make light of her suspicions didn't help Emily's mood at all. One thing was for certain, she had to find out what he was about, and the sooner, the better. "May I please have my file?" she asked coldly.

"Of course." Thomas handed her the folder, then watched as she opened it. "Although I think you'll find it a disappointment."

Emily glanced at him sharply, then examined the documents inside. The Reverend Hall was correct.

The paperwork was obviously completed by someone who paid little attention to detail, and had dashed off the reports as quickly as possible.

"This is ridiculous!" Emily said, dismayed by the shoddy files. "Death by gunshot wounds! A child could have figured that out."

"It wasn't one of my more literary days," the medical man explained weakly. "The truth of the matter is, I don't like filling out those reports. Writing about death makes me squeamish."

Emily glanced at the man incredulously, then looked at the minister. Thomas appeared to be trying hard not to laugh. He cleared his throat several times, and even had to walk toward the door, as if suddenly interested in something outside. Emily returned her attention to the folders, but there was nothing else to be gleaned from them.

"I'm sorry they weren't much help," the doctor said when she handed the files back to him.

"If you remember anything of use, maybe something that should have gone on record, please contact me." She handed him a card with her new address scribbled on the front.

"I will." The little man went back to his files, stuffing the scrap of poem deeply into his shirtsleeve.

Thomas followed Emily outside, then down the boardwalk. She had gotten about ten paces when she turned to him, her eyes sparkling with outrage.

"How could he write a report like that? In Boston he would have been fired a long time ago!"

"I know." Thomas shrugged. "But this isn't the

East. There probably aren't a whole lot of folks out here signing up to be coroners."

"And I want to know what you were doing there," Emily continued, facing him down. He had a lot of explaining to do and she was determined not to lose her head, no matter how handsome he looked. "What possible interest could you have in my father's death?"

Thomas shrugged, as if his purpose were obvious. "The sheriff mentioned the coroner's report when we met yesterday. He thought it might contain something useful. As you can see, it didn't."

"You didn't answer my question," Emily persisted. "Why would it concern you?"

"I have a special interest in this case," he said, his eyes locking with hers. "Since a certain young lady seems set on getting herself in trouble over it. I consider it my Christian duty to watch over her, and to assist her in any way I can."

"So your interest is in . . . me?" Emily asked incredulously.

"Yes," Thomas affirmed simply. "Why else would I care?"

That indeed was the question, Emily thought. She stared at him as if he were the corpse and she were a coroner, dissecting him on one of those tables. "I find that very difficult to believe."

"As Holmes would say, once you remove all the possibilities that couldn't have happened, whatever remains, no matter how improbable, must be the truth."

Emily scowled, not at all happy to have her mentor's words thrown back at her. "I plan to move forward with my investigation, no matter what the obstacles."

Thomas's expression changed from amusement to stern disapproval. "Miss Potter, that report, feeble as it was, said death by gunshot wounds. This is not a story we're talking about. Someone murdered your father. Someone premeditated his death, shot him, and left him to die in his own blood on the floor. And they wouldn't stop at killing you!"

He grabbed her, intending to stop her progress down the boardwalk, but he missed her shoulder and caught her arm instead. She wound up very close to him—too close. Emily could see the crinkles around his eyes that deepened when he got angry, and the lustrous blue that was suddenly even more intense. A strange fluttery feeling welled up inside her, very much like the last time this man had touched her. Her nerves must be getting very bad indeed to react this way.

An elderly woman passed them, and Thomas instantly released Emily. The woman's gaze went from the handsome preacher to Emily. The old woman smiled at him in approval, then gave her a look that clearly marked her as a baggage.

"Good morning, Reverend. I heard from Mrs. Haines that we had a new preacher in town. You must come to tea. I have a new pig I'd like blessed, and Mrs. Haines said you're just the man for me."

Thomas shifted from one foot to the other. "Well, I . . . you see, I am engaged. . . ."

Emily picked up her bag and beamed at him.

"Good day to you, Reverend. I wouldn't dream of detaining you."

Turning smartly, she left him in the old woman's clutches.

As she marched away, Emily giggled. The sound would have been astonishing to anyone who heard it, coming from the dour young woman. Thomas Hall was badly in need of a comeuppance, she thought. Perhaps blessing a pig would do just that.

When Emily got home, she went straight to the kitchen, intending to review the case thoroughly. Clutching the coroner's useless report in her hand, she snatched up her casebook and ignored Watson's plaintive meow as she marched past him, her mind in a whirl.

Before she could reach the kitchen door, it swung open. Emily gasped, thinking of the incident with the gaslight. She put her hand over her heart in relief as Darrel came toward her, a pile of wood in his hands. The young boy looked abashed when he realized he'd upset her, and he stared at the floor.

"Sorry, ma'am. I didn't mean to scare you."

"That's all right, Darrel." Emily managed a weak smile. "I simply forgot you would be here. Did you find everything all right?"

Darrel nodded. "The reverend helped me make my bed in the barn."

"Ah, the good reverend." Emily tried to keep the sarcasm from her voice. "How did you meet Thomas Hall, if you don't mind my asking?"

"Ah . . . the sheriff told him about me." Darrel shifted awkwardly, still balancing the logs in his arms. "He asked me if I would come work here."

"How nice." Suspicion burned brightly in Emily's mind. Could the preacher have sent this boy here as his spy? It wasn't beneath Holmes to use children for such ignoble purposes. Could Thomas Hall be equally ruthless?

Emily bent down until she was at eye level with the boy. "Darrel, what exactly did Thomas ask you to do?"

"Ah . . . he just asked me to help you. You know, carry wood, sweep. Like I used to for the other ladies." But he refused to meet her gaze and began edging toward the door. "If you don't mind, ma'am, I'm setting to sweep the porch. Is that all right?"

Before she could answer, he sped out the door. Emily rose and watched him run, tapping a finger against her lip. So the sheriff had introduced Thomas to the boy. Why? And why was Thomas at the sheriff's office, then at the coroner's, reading the file on her father?

Emily recalled his explanation, and her pulse quickened at the thought that it was really due to his interest in her. Could Thomas be feeling the same confusing emotions for her that she felt for him? Glancing into the mirror, she saw her dowdy dress, lack of jewelry, and her maidenly knot. Try as she might, she could see no feminine beauty or frippery that would entice a man. Her heart sank. She must be utterly foolish to believe Thomas could be interested in her.

And yet, there was something about the way he looked at her . . . something sweetly compelling in those deadly blue eyes. She shook her head, forcing the notion from her thoughts. Romance had no bearing on logic, she firmly reminded herself. Thomas was a suspect at the moment, her most important suspect. As attractive as he might be, she'd have to proceed with her plans. It was high time she followed him and found out who he really was and what he was really doing here. She was a detective first, a woman second.

7

Hot on the Trail

A twig stabbed into Emily's cheek, nearly putting out her eye. Grateful for her glasses, which were the only reason she hadn't just been transformed into a Cyclops, Emily swatted the offending rhododendron branch away from her face. Shifting her bottom on the uncomfortable bed of dead leaves and flowers, she peered through the thicket outside Mrs. Haines's boardinghouse once more.

Where was he? He should have come out sometime before noon, Emily reckoned, since he had always managed to be under her feet by midafternoon. Opening her casebook, she glanced at the scribbled notes from the coroner's report and her conversation with Thomas regarding the sheriff. The two-million-dollar notation glared at her, and her nose wrinkled as she underlined the figure.

Could her father really have stolen that much

money? A shudder went through her as she realized how little she knew about her next of kin. And what facts she did have weren't promising. He'd left her and her mother to go west and make his fortune. Perhaps he had fallen into the wrong company, and chosen a road that lead irrevocably to disaster. The house and Rosie's presence certainly indicated that. Yet something just didn't add up. If he had stolen the gold, where was all the money?

Then there was Rosie. Even though she hadn't appeared again, Emily couldn't stop thinking about her. Was it really possible for a murdered woman to come back from the dead? She couldn't credit such a thing. She had to have imagined it. But why would she conjure the spirit of her father's paramour?

There were just too many threads here. She would have to find someone who knew her father and Rosie, someone who would talk. Emily hummed a little ditty designed to clear her mind. After all, she couldn't figure out everything in one sitting. This afternoon her focus was the handsome Reverend Hall.

It was as if he heard her thoughts, for a moment later, the preacher walked purposefully out of the boardinghouse and toward town. Emily kept as still as possible, not allowing so much as the rustle of a rhododendron leaf to give her away. Thomas paused for a moment beside the path, and Emily held her breath. Did he see her? He searched in his pockets for something, then finally proceeded on his way.

She exhaled slowly. That was close. Evidently he had paused to light a cigar, for she saw the faint glow of tobacco in his hand as he walked. She waited until he was at least fifty feet ahead, then climbed out of the bush, oblivious to the twigs and leaves stuck to her. Then she began following him.

It was more difficult than she'd anticipated, for she had to keep a good distance between them and yet not let him out of her sight. Thomas appeared to be window gazing, pausing at one store, then another, nodding politely to the townspeople. If she didn't know better, she would think he knew he was being followed. Emily was forced to dodge between buildings, hiding behind a fat matron with a parasol in order not to be seen. She ignored the startled glances of the town's ladies, focusing only on her quarry. Her eyes rolled in disgust as two young women curtsied outside the dry goods store, giggling, while their mothers tried to detain him. He was quick on his feet, she'd give him that, for he managed to keep moving without insulting anyone.

Abruptly, he stopped, then glanced back as if searching for someone. Emily ducked quickly into a cobbler's shop, positioning herself at the window so she could continue to watch him. The proprietor gawked at her, taking in her leaf-bedecked dress and the twig protruding from behind one ear.

"Excuse me, ma'am. Can I assist you?"

"No." Emily peeked out the door once more. Thomas was gone. In that one second that she'd turned her head to answer the man, he'd disappeared. Exasperated, she dashed outside, brushing past the surprised groups of bankers standing on the granite steps of their institution. Frantically she looked up and down both sides of the street, then sighed in relief as she spotted Thomas entering the barbershop.

Determined not to lose him again, Emily stood directly outside the establishment and peered covertly into the shop. There were three chairs inside, and a counter laden with shaving soap, lime oil, colognes, and towels. Emily thought she could hear Thomas talking with the barber, but both men seemed to have disappeared into a back room.

Now what? Emily's mind worked frantically. Thomas could be innocently getting service from the barber, but if so, why wasn't he in the chair? What if he were secretly meeting someone? The barbershop would be the perfect place. Concealed from public scrutiny, he could conduct any kind of activity, with the watchful eye of the barber on the door.

As the minutes ticked by, Emily grew more suspicious. Surely if he were simply getting a haircut, he'd be in the chair by now. She couldn't just stand here and let an opportunity slip by, and yet she couldn't enter the strictly male domain without giving herself away. Fuming with impatience, she surveyed the property. Perhaps she could slip in the back door and try to hear what was going on.

An alleyway between the shop and the bank provided the perfect route. Emily quickly disappeared into the shadows, then rounded the back of the building. A thrill raced through her as she saw a screen door slightly ajar, and she slipped into the storeroom unnoticed.

Thomas's voice came from the next room. Emily pressed her ear to the wall, but the thick wood muffled the words. Noticing a door with a keyhole just a few feet away, she crept closer and crouched down, listening intently.

"Could use a new preacher. Got a priest, but the more good influence here, the better."

"So I've seen. Denver seems like a nice town, but a little rowdy. And the unmarried women here are pretty persistent."

Emily heard a chuckle. "I can well imagine that. Good-looking preacher like you. You're every mama's dream. The poor Reverend Flatter left town last fall just for that reason. I don't think the ladies would ever accept his . . . preference."

"Well, that's not exactly my problem," Thomas said dryly, and Emily rolled her eyes.

The barber chuckled, then Emily heard the quiet clink of glass. "Looks like I forgot the lotion. Must have left it on the counter in the shop. I'll fetch it and be right back."

Emily could hear his footsteps receding. Was he gone yet? Was someone else there? What were they doing? She leaned against the door, pressing her ear firmly against the keyhole. Unfortunately, the hinge gave under the pressure, and Emily toppled into the room.

"Well, well, if it isn't my dear Miss Potter," Thomas said, his voice laced with laughter. Suds floated around his legs, and shaving soap covered his chin. The barber had apparently been prepared to give him a shave while he soaked in a hot tub.

"Why—I—" Emily stuttered, her face getting warm. She was facing a very naked and very amused man of the cloth. Acutely aware of his lean masculine form glistening with soap, his muscles providing enticing little curves and valleys for droplets of water to trace, Emily swallowed hard, then tore her eyes away. But not before she saw the knowing twinkle in the wretched preacher's blue eyes.

"I can explain. . . ."

"Yes, please do," Thomas said, biting on his pencil-thin cigar. "I'd like to hear that myself."

"I—" Emily tried to speak, but couldn't form a coherent sentence. Good God, how could a man look so sinfully sexy? She was transfixed. Her mouth actually watered. His legs, bent at the knees, were firm and solid, covered with dark hair, while his arms, relaxed against the metal tub, showed a strength that was clearly not of an ecclesiastical nature. Only a teasing handful of bubbles hid the rest of him from her, and she could only guess it was just as wickedly magnificent.

"If you were that eager for my company, Miss Potter, all you had to do was say so," Thomas said dryly. "I'd have been happy to oblige."

"I—I didn't come here for that! I mean—your company! I mean—" Emily's words tripped over each other, her eyes drawn unwillingly back to his magnificent form. If she crossed the few feet between them, she could touch that warm, bare skin. . . .

"I see. You were thinking, perhaps, of ordering a bath? A little unusual, maybe, but then this is you we're discussing. Please feel free to join me in mine." He gestured invitingly to the water with his cigar.

"Oh!" His meaning struck Emily fully as she pictured what he implied. If her cheeks had been hot a moment ago, they were feverish now, and her mouth went suddenly dry. Instinctively, she took a step backward. Thomas opened his mouth as if to warn her, but she had already crashed into the clothes tree. It fell to the floor with a terrible noise, and Thomas's hat flew into the tub. Water splashed his face and extinguished his cigar.

"Oh, Thomas, I'm *sorry*!" Mortified, Emily dove for the hat before it was ruined, too. Her fingers plunged into the suds next to the hat when she felt her wrist captured tightly in Thomas's fist, preventing her from going any further.

"Looking for something?" His voice was teasing, yet his eyes burned like blue-black coals. He retrieved the hat himself with his free hand, then tossed it on top of his clothes. "When a lady goes fishing around in my bathwater like that," he drawled, "it can only mean one thing."

"Why—I—let go of me!" Emily twisted, trying to break free, but Thomas's grip was like steel.

"I don't think so." He drew her closer, so close she was forced down on one knee. She had to brace herself on the tub to keep from falling in. Emily's mouth dropped open as she saw the wide expanse of his chest through the rainbow prisms of the bubbles. Desire, hot and intoxicating, shot through her, heightened when he lightly trailed a suds-covered finger from her cheek down to her neck.

"Emily." His voice sounded hoarse and oh so seductive. "It isn't a good idea to invade a man's bath like this, do you realize that? It makes him think that maybe you want this, that maybe . . ."

A strangled little cry came from Emily's throat, and she closed her eyes, savoring his touch. It was like wet fire, heating her flesh more than the burn on her hand, making her think of indecent things, things no lady ever dreamed of. A drop of water fell from his arm and splashed her dress. The wet cloth made the tip of her breast even more sensitive, and she felt the delicious ache spread through her skin. Swallowing hard, she opened her eyes, and saw her own smoldering passion burning brightly in his. His face drew closer, and she knew he was going to kiss her.

"Here it is," the barber's voice chirped happily. "I had used up the last bottle so I had to get a new one."

Emily watched in horror, her heart pounding, as the barber strolled back into the room with a towel thrown over one shoulder and a bottle of shaving lotion and a razor strop under his arm. His triumphant smile disappeared when he saw Emily practically draped across Thomas's lap. Emily shot to her feet as Thomas quickly released her wrist.

"I—I—" she stammered in renewed mortification.

The barber's face grew thunderous. "What in the hell is going on here?"

"It's not what you think—" Emily squeaked, her voice several notes higher than normal.

"What she means is, she fell in here by mistake." Thomas attempted, but the barber wagged a finger at both of them.

"I don't go for any fooling around in my shop. If you're one of those new saloon girls, tell Nancy to keep her business under her own roof. And you a preacher! You ought to be ashamed—"

"No! Please, let me explain—" Emily blushed furiously. "I . . . was passing by, and saw Thomas, er, the Reverend, disappear in here. I thought it rather odd that he wasn't in the chair, and suspected that something foul was going on. I didn't think to cause any trouble. I just . . . wanted to make sure he was all right."

Emily wasn't sure why she felt compelled to help Thomas maintain his preacher facade, but she did. Gratitude flashed in his eyes, then was gone so quickly she thought she'd imagined it, replaced by the outraged innocence of a holy man.

"That's exactly what happened! How dare you accuse me, a man of God." He shook his head dismally, as if unable to bear all the wickedness in the world.

The barber glanced at Thomas, who appeared righteously indignant. Drawing his brows together, he addressed Emily sternly, now that he had the guilty party.

"Young lady, most women do not intrude on men's baths," the barber said in a preacherlike tone of his own. "I understand that the reverend here has garnered quite a bit of attention from the unmarried ladies in town, but none of them have gone to this extreme!"

Emily looked at Thomas. He still maintained that scowl of indignation, but Emily saw the twinkle in his eye. Crossing his arms behind his head, he reached for the cigar, but not before she saw the seductive wink he sent her. This preacher radiated an animal magnetism that had almost been her undoing earlier, while the barber was behaving much more like a man of God!

"Who is your father?" The barber persisted.

"Huh?" Emily tore her attention away from the smirking Thomas once again. His implication was quite clear.

Emily flushed in horror, then stammered, "I . . . my father was killed."

"Then you live alone?"

At her nod, the barber began once more to deliver a sermon. "Then I suggest you hightail it out of here before your reputation suffers further damage. And if you want the minister's attention in the future, I think you should go about it the way a decent woman would, such as inviting him to dinner. You young girls these days should be ashamed of yourselves, throwing yourself at a man of God like that."

The barber shook his head and clucked, as if equally shocked at her brazenness. Emily opened her mouth to object, but clamped it shut. She realized that the barber's explanation for her presence, while not flattering, was much more believable then anything she could concoct. Emily turned and with as much dignity as she could muster stalked out of the room.

Thomas Hall may have won this round, but the game was far from over.

As soon as she left, the barber bolted the door, still shaking his head over Emily's boldness. "That young miss needs to be taken in hand! My pa would have taken a razor strop to any of his girls that behaved like that."

"She could use it," Thomas agreed, allowing his amusement to flow freely now. He chuckled out loud. Emily's expression had been priceless. He'd been expecting that, as a Sherlock Holmes devotee, her next move would be to follow him. Yet not even Emily could have predicted this turn of events.

That thought made him pause. Once again the prudish Miss Potter wasn't nearly as prudish as he would have thought. While he would never guess it from her manner, her reaction to him was telling. Initially when he'd captured her hand to keep her from finding anything other than his hat, he'd thought to embarrass her, even teach her a lesson, but when he'd looked into her eyes, the passion he saw made him forget everything except having her. His laughter died as he realized just how close he had come to acting on that desire.

"I'm glad you can laugh about it. I do apologize, Reverend. Please don't think all of our young ladies are like that. The nerve of that woman, barging in here like some hussy!"

"Oh, I don't think of Miss Potter that way." Thomas felt oddly compelled to defend her. "I just think she didn't expect to get caught. You know how young girls are. Curious and all that. And Miss Potter has twice the curiosity of most girls."

"Then you know her?"

The razor blade felt cold against Thomas's throat. "Sort of. We came in on the same stage together. Her father was John Potter. The one that owned Shangri-La."

"Oh, that Miss Potter." The barber nodded as if it all made sense now. Wiping the blade on his cloth, he pinched Thomas's nostrils to get a closer shave. "I hear she's been causing a ruckus all over town. I guess the apple doesn't fall far from the tree. With her taking that house over and all, I'm surprised she hasn't opened shop yet."

Thomas struggled to sit up as righteous anger swept through him. "Miss Potter is nothing like her father," he said sternly, surprised by the indignation he felt. After Emily's outrageous behavior, he *should* let the man think whatever he wanted. Yet the barber's assumptions infuriated him. "And she certainly isn't a . . . bordello girl. She's just different, that's all."

"No offense, Preacher." The barber shrugged indifferently, then plopped a steaming towel down on his face. "I didn't know you were so—involved with her."

Thomas could image the man's smug expression even with his eyes closed. "I'm not involved with her," he said dryly, lifting the towel to speak. "Miss Potter happens to be an acquaintance. I'd hate to think this town is so ungodly that anyone would take pleasure in spreading rumors about her."

"Well, you're right about that," the barber said quickly, abashed. He removed the towel, then carefully splashed cologne on Thomas's face. The sting nearly brought Thomas out of the tub, but the barber only nodded thoughtfully. "Miss Potter may just be different, but if I were you, I'd keep an eye on her. She looks like trouble."

Thomas sank back into the tub and let the warm water envelope him. Silently, he couldn't agree more.

Emily slipped a black fishnet stocking over her toes, frowning as she inched the difficult material up over her ankle, then her calf, pulling the stocking up to her thigh where a black lace garter waited. Tucking the material beneath the tight garter, she reached for the second stocking and repeated the process. Satisfied, she stood before the mirror, astonished at her reflection.

A black satin corset pushed her breasts upward indecently, making them threaten to spill over the flimsy garment at any moment, and a matching lace petticoat rustled around her thighs. It was amazing the difference that a few carefully chosen clothes made. Thank God she hadn't thrown everything of Rosie's out, because this saloon-girl outfit was perfect. She looked experienced, a seductress among men, not a little milliner from Boston who stammered helplessly at the sight of a naked man in a bathtub. Giggling, Emily slipped on the yellow dress trimmed in black lace and felt very naughty indeed.

Seating herself before the mirror, she drew her hair up into a thousand little curls, allowing a few tendrils to frame her face. There was no lack of hairpins in Rosie's drawer, so even with a few mistakes, Emily was able to pin her curls into a charming upswept hairdo that brought out her eyes. Borrowing Rosie's rouge, she deepened the pink of her mouth and her already flushed cheeks. Yes, even Thomas Hall, the would-be preacher, would have to take a second look to know it was her.

Unwillingly, Emily's mind went back to the incident with Thomas at the barbershop. In spite of her inexperience, Emily was certain Thomas had been as aroused by her presence as she had been by his. His bold invitation made her legs weak just thinking about it. A delightful fantasy flashed through her mind, of doffing these seductive clothes, and splashing into the tub with him. She would be sitting in his lap, her arms draped over his shoulders, her face right up against that rough beard. She could almost see Thomas's stunned surprise, then feel his hands against her skin, tracing a bubble as it slid tantalizingly down her throat, all the way down to her breast. . . .

Good Lord, where were these wicked thoughts coming from? Emily fanned her face, hoping to cool the hot color. It must be the clothes. That had to be why Rosie and the other saloon girls dressed this way. It made one feel positively indecent.

Still, as the yellow satin dressed shimmied over her slender hips, she enjoyed the confidence the odd garb gave her. Emily slipped little jet earrings on her tiny earlobes, gems that glittered with each toss of her head, and made her eyes sparkle. A touch of kohl, and a few of Rosie's plumes finished the look, and she stepped back and smiled in pleasure.

Emily Potter was gone, and in her place was a

seductive barroom wench, one who knew the ways of
the world and feared nothing. Forget Thomas, she
told herself, and move on with the case. And the saloon was the most logical place to go next. The
saloon girls knew everyone, and given the fact that
her father's home had been a bordello, it seemed
certain that the two places would have customers in
common.

Confident in her objectives, Emily took the back
way into town. Discretion was the better part of
valor, she reminded herself, and successfully avoided
observation until she found herself outside the bar.

The Silverdust Saloon was a typical western gin
mill, complete with swinging doors, a rustic facade,
and a cowboy hitting the boardwalk just as Emily
tentatively approached. Tension coiled inside her as
she stepped aside, giving the cowboy a sympathetic
glance. Ignoring her, he thrust his hat down hard on
his head and stormed away, muttering that he would
return and blow all their fool heads off.

Summoning all her courage, she stepped through
the swinging doors. Inside was just as raucous as the
outside appearance had promised. Smoke hung
thickly about the room, and a mahogany bar with a
huge mirror behind it took up one entire wall. The
town's men were either absorbed in games of faro
or standing at the bar guzzling whiskey. The saloon
girls struggled to keep the men's glasses full, dodging
the drunken miners and the rowdy cowhands, all the
while expertly avoiding the groping hands, and slipping extra tips from the tables unobserved into their
pockets.

Her tension eased and fascination began to creep over her. This was it! She really was living her dream, and detecting just as her hero Holmes would have done! She, as the world's only other consulting detective, would become part of this scene and discover what clues she could. The idea was heady.

"Hey, girlie, fetch me a beer." One of the men thrust his glass at her and Emily started, then realized that she obviously blended in perfectly. Taking his mug, Emily gave the cowboy a smile, then headed for the bar.

"You new around here?" The barkeep took the glass and filled it quickly, scraping off the excess foam. "Nancy hires 'em, and doesn't tell me a thing."

Emily nodded, her feathers dancing. "I'm here to see Nancy. I'm looking for a job."

"I'm Nancy." A hefty woman deftly positioned herself between Emily and the bar. Emily saw that the woman was pretty, but had so much rouge and rice powder on her face that her own complexion was completely hidden. Drenched in perfume and paste jewels, her hair a conspicuous shade of red, she looked every inch a soiled dove, used to dealing with drunks and cowboys.

"Emily." Emily extended a hand in a ladylike manner. Nancy raised a brow, then accepted the gesture. Her critical eye ran over Emily, taking in her dress, the rouge, and the too-tight slippers she wore. Her brows knotted together in suspicion.

"Hey, girlie, where's my beer?"

"Keep your shirt on, Charlie," Nancy yelled back without even turning her head. She smiled at Emily, though her eyes were still questioning. "Don't you pay them no mind. These cowboys all get lickered up after riding the trail. They're just letting off steam. So what's a lady like you doing here? And don't try telling me you're just a saloon girl, 'cause I know better. The way you hold your head, your walk . . . you ain't no ordinary dove. Now, you either tell me what's goin' on, or I call the sheriff."

Emily sighed. Just like Watson, she knew when the jig was up, and to try to fool Nancy was impossible. Truth was her only hope, and she shrugged her bare shoulders. "I'm John Potter's daughter. I just came into town and I need a job."

"Potter!" Nancy's penciled brows thrust upward like the wings of a blackbird, and she whistled in surprise. Instantly her suspicious manner changed. "Why didn't you say so? Hell of a man, was old Johnny, though I didn't know that was his name until recently. We all called him Mullen."

"You mean he was here under an assumed name?" Emily asked, excited. "The coroner's report listed him as Potter!"

"Yes, the sheriff identified him soon enough, although using another name is not exactly uncommon out in the West. Most of my girls don't use their own names. Anyway, Rosie and I were good friends, and she had nothing but nice things to say about your pa. We had an understanding, a business agreement, if you will, about the girls. Rosie stayed away from the Silverdust, and I sent her johns. It worked just fine."

Emily nodded, though the full implication of all that escaped her, and she quickly dismissed the

shudder that passed through her at the mention of
the ghost's name. "I was wondering if any of the girls
knew something about what happened that night."

Nancy nodded. "So that's why you're here! I
reckon' if my pa died like that, I'd want to know,
too." She tapped her foot for a moment, then her
face brightened. "There was a girl. Lizzie Wakefield,
she called herself. I hear tell she's living in Boulder."

"Hey, Nancy! Can't you have teatime later? I want
my beer!"

Nancy sighed, then glanced back to Emily. "I suppose we can talk later. Are you really in need of
work?" When Emily nodded eagerly, the woman
grinned. "All right, table three is all yours."

Emily took the mugs the bartender offered and
walked stiffly onto the floor, careful not to spill an
ounce of their precious contents. She could barely
contain her excitement, and couldn't wait to flaunt
her success in the reverend's face. She'd only been in
the bar a few minutes, and she already had one clue.
Lizzie Wakefield in Boulder. She placed the drinks
before the cowhands and was about to return to the
bar when a voice stopped her in her tracks.

"Hey! I know you—you're that woman that owns
the whorehouse! Boys, this lady is from Shangri-La!"

The cowboys let out a whoop, and Emily felt her
face flame. Glancing up, she saw the cowboy from the
stagecoach when she'd first arrived in town. Unbelievably, he'd recognized her in spite of her changed
appearance. The cowboy stood up and pulled her into
his arms. The tray dropped to the floor with a clatter,
and the barkeep threw up his hands in disgust.

"Well, if you ain't a pretty thing," the cowboy said, touching her feathers appreciatively. "You sure look much better like this than you did on that stage. If I'da seen you in this dress, I'd never have let you git away."

"Let go of me!" Emily tried to pull away, which only made the cowboys laugh harder.

"Hey, I like that! Is that what you plan to do at the house? Play the lady, then turn into a whore? That's a right good idea, honey, if I don't say so myself! Why, I want to be the first customer!"

He tried to plant a kiss on Emily's cheek, but she turned her face away and the cowboy got a mouthful of plumes instead. The other cowboys roared, while Emily renewed her struggle to break free. Frantically she looked around for Nancy, but the woman was nowhere to be seen. The breath was knocked out of her as the cowboy bent to put his shoulder in her belly and lift her clear off the ground.

"Let's not wait for the grand reopening, sweetie. I'll be your first customer now."

More laughter and shouts of encouragement broke out as the cowboy started toward the door with Emily thrown over his shoulder like a sack of flour. But he hardly got three steps when a voice stopped him cold.

"All right, Jake, put that girl down."

8

The Plot Thickens

Emily nearly swooned in relief. But the man who held her turned quickly, whirling her around in the process. She was starting to feel sick. Her stomach lurched again as Emily felt the cowboy reach for his weapon.

"Stay out of this, Preacher. I don't want to kill no man of the cloth."

"Then drop that damned gun," Thomas swore.

Emily heard the collective gasp, and even she couldn't help glancing up at the Reverend Hall. Dressed simply in minister's garb, he looked anything but helpless or holy. The sharp blue quality of his eyes seemed deadly cold as he squinted at the cowboy, almost as if he were a gunman himself.

"Look, Preacher, this doesn't concern you—"

"Doesn't it?" Thomas's words cut the man off.

"I'm not telling you again, cowboy. Drop that gun and let that girl go."

Emily had thought that of the two men, Jake was the more dangerous one, but now, Thomas's presence made the rough saloon patrons look like children. She glanced back once more. Thomas stood facing the cowboy, his knees slightly bent, his hand held just outside his coat as if . . . as if he were preparing to draw. The other cowboys looked at each other, apparently as surprised as she. None of them seemed happy with this development. Shooting up a bar was one thing; shooting a preacher, quite another. Especially one who looked all too familiar with gunfights. Slowly Jake let his gun drop.

"That's right. Now you step aside and let that girl go. Miss Emily, come here."

Jake let her down slowly, but before he could say another word, Thomas yanked her backward, out of his grip. When she was standing safely behind him, the preacher addressed the cowboys once more.

"I don't want to hear anything else about this incident boys, do you understand? You've made a mistake where Miss Potter is concerned. I'll let it pass under the circumstances, but I don't want any more trouble over this. Remember, the good Lord knows all."

The veiled threat in Thomas's voice was unmistakable. The men stood back as the preacher hauled Emily out of the saloon. As soon as the door swung closed behind them, the bartender turned to Jake, a cool whistle escaping from this lips.

"Did you see what I seen, boys? Or was that a Bible that preacher had under his coat?"

Outside, Emily tried to thank Thomas for his help, but he refused to speak to her. Instead he hauled her along by one arm as if she were a disgraced schoolgirl. Emily struggled to keep up as her tight velvet slippers tripped on the rocks and holes in the dirt road. Yet Thomas didn't stop or even acknowledge her protests. He escorted her home, thrust her inside, and slammed the door behind him.

Sensing trouble, Watson sprang from the window to race upstairs. Emily raised her face to Thomas, rubbing the bruise on her shoulder where he'd grabbed her. Angry as she was at his callous treatment, she had to admit the man had helped her. She tried to smile, although it died on her lips when she saw his clenched teeth and blazing blue eyes. Emily swallowed hard. Once again, he hardly looked like a man of the cloth. Instead, he looked even more dangerous than he had at the bar. And suddenly . . . sexy.

"Reverend Hall," Emily said weakly, before she could lose her nerve. "Thank you for your help. I didn't realize things could get so out of hand. For a minute, I thought you were going to pull a gun yourself!"

Thomas ignored her words, taking hold of her as if he meant to shake her.

"Dammit, Emily! What in the hell were you doing in that place, dressed like this?"

Emily gasped. Not only was the preacher still

swearing but he was furious. And determined to take it out on her. For once, her famous courage flagged. She was in the grip of a madman. Thomas may have rescued her from the saloon, but who would rescue her from him?

"You little fool!" he continued, his voice harsh. "What were you thinking? Or do you think? Was this another one of your adventures, like when you barged in on my bath, or is there some other explanation?"

Thomas had never been so angry with anyone in his life. He stared down at the girl he held so tightly, and saw that her shoulders were beginning to redden beneath his fingers. Swearing under his breath, he eased his grip. He didn't want to hurt her, but he didn't want her to escape his wrath either.

She'd nearly blown his disguise. Thomas had been certain he would have to pull his gun, and then it would have been all over. As a child he'd spent years practicing with his rifle, until he'd become famous for the accuracy of his shot. It wasn't a talent he was proud of, but it had saved his hide more than once. If a gunfight had broken out, Reverend Hall would have had to disappear, leaving more than one grave to his credit.

And all because of her. Thomas's fingers still held her shoulders, those impossibly pretty, creamy white shoulders that led down to a frothy neckline baring a full, enticing bosom. Thomas hadn't been able to believe his eyes when he first saw her, for it was the most incredible transformation he'd ever seen. A fairy godmother's wand couldn't have created anything more dramatic—Emily, in her spinster dress and schoolmarm demeanor, changed into this glittering, golden butterfly.

His eyes swept over her again, as if trying to convince himself once more that it was truly her. He had to admit that her hair, pulled up with a only few curls dangling around her face, was beautiful, a peculiar shade of red brown like polished mahogany. Jet black earrings danced from her tiny ears, while her plumes, a little bedraggled, still dipped and swayed enticingly. And the dress—the dress looked as if it had been made for her. It fitted her tiny waist impossibly well, displaying a generous portion of her round breasts above a spray of black lace. Her figure, as he'd guessed, was spectacular, from that neckline all the way down to where the dress hitched up to show scandalously fishnet-stockinged legs. It didn't take much for his mind to imagine the little black garters that held those stockings up, and his anger doubled with the pounding swell of his arousal.

Emily's silver eyes grew even wider and she backed up until the door hit her bustle. With feminine instinct, she seemed to know that something had changed, and she was in a different kind of trouble now. At least he had the satisfaction of seeing that he finally had her attention, although she was far less terrified than he would have liked.

"I . . . I was investigating! This is a case, and I need clues to solve it," Emily was saying, as if that explained everything. When his fingers tightened on her again, she squirmed in his grasp, rubbing the abused flesh. "You're hurting me!"

"Investigating! Emily, those were real men with real guns. How many times do I have to tell you that this isn't some story you're reading! If one of the other girls hadn't come to the boardinghouse for help—"

"But don't you see? I realized that the saloon girls might know something, and they did! I got my first real clue!"

"Damn you!" Good God, what was wrong with this woman? Thomas was about to launch into another tirade when he stopped himself. "What clue?"

Emily's lips, red where she had nervously bitten them, relaxed into a triumphant smile. "I found out about Lizzie Wakefield."

Lizzie Wakefield? Hadn't the sheriff told him . . . "What did you find out?"

Emily grinned, as delighted as if she'd found a pot of gold, rather than a piece of information. "Lizzie was a bordello girl who lived at Shangri-La when my father and Rosie were there. Nancy told me she might remember something."

"She didn't happen to tell you where she was?" Thomas asked casually.

Emily nodded. "Nancy said she might still be in Boulder. Isn't that wonderful?" She reached up and gently touched his collar, sending a shudder of awareness through him. "I must say, you were most impressive when you showed up and faced down those men. You even had me frightened. And I really don't think those cowboys meant any harm. Like Nancy says, it's just their way of letting off steam. It seems to me that everything worked out for the best, after all."

Thomas shook his head. Although he was secretly impressed at what she'd managed to find out, her rationalization frightened him. She truly seemed to have no idea what had been in store for her. And he could tell that further lectures would get him nowhere. She was so bright, yet so incredibly naive at the same time. His gaze fell once more on her rouged face, her heavily lined eyes, and her moist, red mouth. There was more than one way to make a point, Thomas thought, and it was time to take action.

"Since you have no objection to cowboys letting off steam, perhaps you won't object to this, either."

And before Emily could protest, he yanked her into his arms and covered her mouth with his own.

"Thomas!" Emily cried out in shock, yet the sound was instantly diminished as his mouth took fierce, erotic possession of her own. It felt better than anything she had ever imagined, or could even begin to imagine. His mouth teased her, enticed her with a sweet temptation and an aching tenderness, while his hand curved up to cradle her hair and slide into that silken splendor. One by one her plumes dropped, and Emily heard her hairpins clatter to the floor. His other hand tightened about her waist, pulling her impossibly closer until she could feel his heartbeat keeping wild rhythm with her own.

She didn't entirely understand what was happening, but, lost in a world of pure sensation, Emily surrendered completely. She slid her hands from his chest, where she'd attempted to push him away, to wind them around his neck. Something hard pressed against her, and a soft, kittenish whimper came from the back of her throat. Dimly, she noted that the fiery stirrings racing through her blood ended—shockingly—where her lace garters met. Desire, new and freshly awakened, made her skin incredibly sensitive. The lace trim at her neckline seemed to torture her aching breasts, and the nipples, encased in pure satin, throbbed and puckered beneath the smooth fabric.

Then Emily heard Thomas groan and whisper her name. "Good God, Emily . . ." Was he feeling something similar? His hand slid from her hair to her throat, leaving a trace of fire where he touched, then lower to rest just above her breast. The warmth penetrated her skin and she whimpered again, this time from wanting. She craved his touch, certain it was the only thing that would ease the ache he'd created in her burning flesh, and take her wherever this incredible experience was leading. A fleeting memory of her fantasy crossed her mind, and she realized that she wanted it to happen! Although she'd been taught that this was wrong, that men would take terrible liberties if encouraged, and could ruin a girl, no one had told her how wonderful it would feel. Nor had anyone prepared her for the sweet, aching tenderness of a man's kiss, or the hot black ardor of her own passion. Why? Here was yet another mystery.

When his hand covered her breast, she thought she was still imagining it, for the sweet, gentle touch and scorching heat were almost more than she could bear. Moaning softly, she pressed herself more fully into his hand, her eyes opening wide at the odd tingling that pulsed through her.

"My goodness!" She gasped as his mouth finally eased from hers and he pressed fiery hot kisses along the expanse of skin bared before him. When his fingers touched the roughly textured nub of her nipple, she nearly swooned in his arms. "Are you certain that this is . . . right?"

"Yes, it's very right, Emily, my sweet Emily." Amazingly, the rough texture of his hands felt wonderful against her soft skin, and Emily closed her eyes once more, drinking in the sensations. When he pushed down the lace and bared her breast completely, she was astonished, and even more so when his hot, wet tongue laved the nipple with sweet caresses. She clung to him, panting helplessly as wave after wave of emotion assailed her. Good Lord, what was wrong with her? Could it really just be the dress, or the house? Perhaps it was her artistic aunt's blood in her. Something had to make her act in such a brazen manner, especially with Thomas Hall!

Thomas recovered from this madness first, for as he lifted his head and saw her, the pure innocence of her awakening desire, the soft fluttering of her black-edged lashes against her milky skin, and the round O of her mouth, reality finally penetrated. He realized he was very close to doing the same mischief the cowboy had intended, and he was shocked at himself. He'd meant to teach her a lesson, yet instead he'd learned that he'd never wanted a woman as badly as he wanted the one in his arms. It took every ounce of gentlemanly training to realize he had to release her before he disgraced her and himself. With an oath, he pulled the scandalous dress up to cover the beautifully formed breast with its wet pink nipple, then he withdrew from her embrace.

"Thomas?" Her beautiful silver eyes widened and she leaned against the door once more to regain her balance. Her expression was one he would never forget: flushed with pleasure and sexual awakening, she looked like a rose, gently unfolding before his eyes.

Thomas groaned. Dear God, how had he gotten himself into this mess?

"Emily, I'm sorry. I'm sure you agree this shouldn't have happened. I didn't mean to take advantage of you. You just have a way of . . . pushing me beyond rational thinking."

"I do?" She seemed to sort through this, and Thomas didn't like the logical path her mind was sure to take. The last thing he needed was for her to think he had a weakness where she was concerned. Good God, the woman ran him ragged enough already with her propensity for trouble.

"I just meant to show you what can happen when you . . . tempt a man too far. To parade around in a dress like that indicates that such attentions might not be unwelcome."

That came out badly and he knew it. Most women would have slapped his face at that point and called him a liar. But not Emily. Her brows knotted together, as if working out a puzzle, and her gray eyes were unfathomable silver pools.

"I see. Then you think simply my choice of dress indicates a propensity for sexual attention? That's rather curious, isn't it? Do you suspect it's the satin, or the lace? Perhaps the feathers . . ." Emily glanced into the mirror, and seemed shocked at what she saw. Her hair had fallen around her shoulders in a charming tumble, and her rouge was smudged. Yet after a moment her eyes narrowed as if she had returned to trying to make sense of what he was saying.

"Emily!" Thomas said in frustration. "I meant that you seemed unaware of what could have happened. I was just trying to help you understand. . . ."

"The lesson was well received," Emily said, as if discussing the latest scientific theorem. Her finger tapped against her cheek in a meditative way. She turned back to him, her head cocked to one side like a particularly bright student eager to engage the teacher. "I especially enjoyed the kissing part, and have no objection if you wish to continue the lesson. I thought it most informative."

"That's it." Thomas turned on his heel and pushed past her to the door. Emily Potter was a curse, he decided, a curse sent especially to visit him.

Emily sank down into a chair, still breathless from her encounter with Thomas. Good Lord, the man nearly made her faint, and it wasn't from her tight laces! She fanned herself, wondering what Holmes would have done in such interesting circumstances, but she reminded herself that as a man, Sherlock probably didn't run into these problems. At least, not in quite that way. . . .

"Whew, honey! That looked like a hot little session you two had going!"

A ghostly whistle caught Emily off guard. It was her! Jumping out of the chair, Emily raced upstairs to the mirror. There, once again, was the vision she'd tried so hard to convince herself wasn't real. Sprawled in a sitting position with a nail file, Rosie's ghost rolled her eyes appreciatively and gave Emily a broad smile.

"Looks like my dress still has what it takes. You had that man positively eating out of your hand, honey. Lord, you'd have made a fortune working for me."

"Why do I keep imagining you?" Emily touched the glass again. It was as solid as any mirror she had ever encountered. Logic seemed to mean nothing, for once; she was seeing a ghost, one that had apparently witnessed her intimacy with Thomas. Her cheeks got even redder under the already scandalously dark rouge.

As if sensing her thoughts, Rosie chuckled. "Don't worry, honey, I closed my eyes after he started kissing you. But the sparks in that room were enough to set a house afire. He wants you all right, and he doesn't like it one bit."

Emily frowned, her nose crinkling. In spite of her disbelief, she couldn't help being drawn into the conversation. "Why wouldn't he like it? Isn't it . . . pleasurable for men as well?"

Rosie hooted so loudly that Emily was sure the

whole town could hear her. When she could finally speak, she wiped her eyes and gazed at Emily as if she were nothing more than a precocious child. "Of course men like it, sweetie, why do you think they pay for it? It's just that they like to think they're in control of the whole situation. When a man tries to kiss a woman into submission and finds himself seduced instead, he doesn't know quite how to handle it. That's what happened with your preacher man."

Emily pondered this. The very feminine, very secret part of her was pleased at Rosie's words, especially given the way Thomas had stalked out. Still, her smile quickly changed to a frown as her mind shifted thoughts. "I still don't understand how you can be here at all, Rosie. I saw the official report of your death!"

"Oh, did you visit Willard Johnson?" Rosie asked with some amusement. "Nice little man, isn't he? Always paid well, too. He was sweet on Lilly Belle, one of my prettiest girls. Saw her every Friday."

"Lilly Belle?" Emily repeated stupidly. "You mean old Doc Johnson was one of your—"

"How did you put it?" Rosie cut in brightly. "Consorts? Why, yes, he was a regular."

Sinking onto the bed, Emily stared at the reflection before her, for once at a loss for words.

"So what *is* your relationship with the handsome preacher man?" Rosie asked, not seeming to notice that anything was amiss with Emily. "It seems the two of you are in the thick of something here."

"Not in the least," Emily answered defensively, finding her voice. She wasn't quite willing to accept

Rosie's existence, much less use her father's dead mistress as a romantic confidante! "Mr. Hall is under investigation. I am trying to learn everything I can about him. He is a suspect in my case. That's all."

"I see." Rosie's eyes twinkled. "That's an approach I don't think we ever used. Did you learn anything by throwing yourself into his arms?"

"He had a gun," Emily said, ignoring the ghost's mocking tone. "I felt it when he . . . kissed me."

"My, you are a cool hand. I don't think his gun is what I'd have been feeling in that man's arms," Rosie said in admiration. "Are you sure that's what it was?"

Emily's cheeks burned with embarrassment as Rosie's meaning became clear. "I don't care to continue this conversation," she said firmly. "You are, after all, simply a figment of my overanxious nerves. I shall just ignore you and—"

Every chandelier in the house shook. Emily's mouth dropped as the player piano downstairs belted out a bawdy tune, the windows open and shut by themselves, and the curtains flapped like flags in the wind. Nothing she was seeing could be explained by any logic, and certainly not by an attack of nerves, unless Emily was willing to concede that she had gone mad. Slowly the noises stopped, the curtains settled back into place, and Rosie faded from view.

"I'm real, sweetie, and the sooner you accept that, the better."

"Rosie!" Emily cried, but the mirror was just a mirror again. Her own reflection, looking frightened and wan, stared back at her. Reaching out, she touched the glass, ready to pull her hand back quickly. But Rosie was gone.

Shivering, Emily leaped into bed and pulled the covers over her, her mind in a whirl. The house was haunted! There was no question remaining in her mind, for as Thomas had so smugly reminded her, when you eliminate everything that cannot be fact, whatever remains, no matter how improbable, must be true. She gazed at the mirror, but it remained a silvery flatness.

Suddenly lonely, Emily's mind went unwillingly to that heated kiss with Thomas. In spite of her uncertainty about him, she'd felt safe in his arms. A need welled inside of her, one that before she'd met him, she hadn't known existed. It was as if she'd unlocked a door, and now that it was open, things would never be the same again.

As she tried to sleep, she left the light on and hugged a pillow, determined to quell the emptiness inside her. It was a hell of a thing, sharing the house with the ghost. And it looked as though she'd better get used to it.

9

What Lizzie Wakefield Has to Say

The next morning, Emily boarded the stagecoach for Boulder. The few men traveling with her scarcely paid her any attention, dressed as she was in her usual subdued clothing with her hair pulled back into a prim knot. Her spectacles slid down her nose as she read and reread the old news clippings regarding the crime, hoping there was something she'd missed in the drab reports.

But there was nothing. In disgust, she flung them carelessly into her case, earning a hiss from Watson. Forcing her thoughts from the frustrating lack of evidence, she tried to focus on the scenery. Visions of Thomas crept into her mind unbidden. Once they were there she had no choice but to entertain them, of course. A delicious warmth bubbled inside her as she thought of their kiss, and she had to fight to keep from squirming in her seat at the strange restlessness that came over her. Rosie's words came back to her and she couldn't help the little tingle of pleasure she felt at the thought of arousing Thomas's passions beyond his control.

Emily shuddered as she recalled the ghost's appearance the previous night. She could no longer excuse what she'd seen as being a case of nerves. Rosie the ghost was real, no matter how much reason argued against it.

The coach finally pulled up beside a narrow boardwalk where a sign flapping overhead announced that they had entered the town of Boulder. It was a mining town, filled with tents boasting the sale of pickaxes, pans, shovels, and whiskey. Emily disembarked slowly, taking all of this in, and then stopped to stare in amazement at the mountains overshadowing everything. They seemed like giants shouldering their way out of the earth. Yet, as beautiful as it was, Boulder seemed like a lonely place compared to Denver, and Emily wondered why Lizzie would want to live here.

Lizzie Wakefield of Boulder. That was really all she had to go on, and, from what she could see, Boulder was a sizable town. There was a church, a saloon that was twice its size, a restaurant, a bank, a hotel, a dry goods store, and a barbershop. She started for the store, but when a woman came out of the restaurant to polish the front of its glass window, Emily approached her instead.

"Hello, I'm looking for someone in town. Could you help me?"

The woman glanced up from her task and frowned,

taking in Emily's plain dress and odd manner. "Who are you looking for?"

"Lizzie Wakefield. I hear she lives in town."

"She sure does. If you go down Main Street, make a left by the church, head on down the dirt road until you come to the first street, make a right, then a hard left, you'll find her."

Emily sighed. She'd have to confess the truth, no matter how embarrassing. "I'm sorry, but I have a problem with directions. I just know I'll get lost."

The woman started to chuckle, then straightened, placing her hands on her hips. "It's like that, is it? I know what you mean. I get lost anywhere outside a three-block square. A boy picks up her laundry Monday mornings. If you'll wait a few minutes, you can follow him right back to her house. Why don't you have a cup of coffee? I made some apple pie as well. You look like you could use a little food, if you don't mind my saying so. By the way, I'm Sally."

"Emily." Emily returned her smile. The woman's tone was warm, and her invitation so enticing that Emily couldn't resist. Taking up her case, she went into the restaurant with the woman and ordered the pie and coffee, painfully aware that her coins were dwindling at a rapid rate. She'd have to start her millinery shop soon, Emily thought, accepting the cup the woman handed her. The pie was as wonderful as promised, tart and still warm, and the coffee was aromatic. Sally continued cleaning, even though the place was spotless, and talked constantly.

"Lizzie a friend of yours?" She barely waited

for Emily to nod yes before she continued. "Pretty woman. She's been here awhile. Since that ruckus at Shangri-La, anyway. She lives quietly, comes into town once in a while. She must be more popular than I thought, though."

"Why do you say that?" Emily asked, discreetly pouring some of her milk into a saucer for Watson.

"There was a man here earlier inquiring about her. Good-looking, too, with dark blue eyes . . . Preacher man, he was."

"A preacher?" Emily tried to hide her astonishment. "He was here? Asking about Lizzie?"

"Yes. In fact, you might run into him. You won't forget him if you do see him, that's for sure. Downright handsome, if I *do* say so myself. Why, there's the laundry boy now."

Emily leaped up, placing a few of her precious coins beside the plate. "Thank you, the pie was wonderful."

"You're welcome. Good luck, and tell Lizzie not to be a stranger."

Emily followed the boy down the dusty road, her mind spinning. Thomas had been here before her. Why? Suspicion, cold and unnerving, wound its way through her thoughts. Could Thomas have been pumping her for information last night? Was his seduction simply part of a scheme to learn what she knew?

A cold ache spread through the pit of her belly when she realized she had been used. Fortunately her logical mind came to her rescue, reminding her that she had been suspicious of him from the beginning. Yet she couldn't completely dispel the pinprick of disappointment that shot through her, or the hurt that came after.

The laundry boy entered a tiny white cottage nestled in a grove of cottonwoods. Emily saw a housekeeper answer the door, snatch up the bundle, then slam it closed. The boy walked away grumbling, but without another word to Emily, tossing a penny into the air. Emily waited a few minutes, then when all was silent, she knocked on the door.

The housekeeper answered almost immediately. "What do you want now?" Her eyes popped open wider when she saw Emily, then narrowed into tiny slits. "Who are you?"

"I've come to see Lizzie."

"Lizzie don't see no one," The woman said, and began to slam the door once more.

Deftly Emily put the case between the jamb and the heavy door. "Tell her I was sent by a friend. Tell her Nancy sent me."

"I don't care who sent you, she doesn't see anyone." The woman tried once more to close the door, and then Emily heard a sweet, musical voice from somewhere inside.

"That's all right, Aggie, you can let her in."

Emily gave the housekeeper a smug look, then marched past her into the parlor. The woman muttered something unintelligible, glancing up and down the road as if expecting to see other intruders, then—at last—slammed the door again.

"Would you like some tea? I was just going to have some myself."

Emily stared at one of the most beautiful women she'd ever seen. Lizzie Wakefield was blond and blue-eyed, her hair swept up in charming disarray with a few springy curls framing a face that could only be described as angelic. Her eyes were huge and doelike, fringed with black lashes, and her skin was luminous. Even without rouge, she was lovely, and the black lace wrapper she pulled more tightly around herself revealed a perfect figure.

A momentary flash of jealousy went through Emily as she pictured Thomas speaking with this woman. Reminding herself that Thomas was a suspect, and not of any possible interest to her, she smiled and extended a hand, inhaling the essence of rose water that Lizzie wore.

"My name is Emily Potter. I just need a little of your time, if you don't mind."

The woman waved a hand toward a chair, then waited until Aggie had left the room before speaking. Her eyes ran over Emily's face and she nodded, as if confirming something for herself.

"I heard John's daughter had returned to Shangri-La. I must say I was surprised that you took over the house." She seemed a bit nervous, as if agitated by the thought. "Have you . . . seen anything strange since you've been there?"

"The house is haunted, if that's what you're asking."

The cup dropped from Lizzie's hand and crashed to the floor. Lizzie gave Emily a tremulous smile, then scrubbed at her gown with a linen napkin.

"I'm sorry, you did give me quite a start! You say Shangri-La is . . . haunted?"

Emily nodded. "I know you may find it hard to believe, but it's the truth. Rosie appeared to me. I know she and my father were murdered. I have to find out who did it, and see that justice is done."

"I see." Lizzie took a new cup from the tray, and poured herself more tea. She managed to stop shaking long enough to fill the cup, then she drank deeply of the brew. When she looked back at Emily, her blue eyes were wider, but calm.

"I believe you. You see, I went to the house one night after the killings to get my things and I, too, heard Rosie."

"You did!" Emily leaned forward, her voice filled with excitement. It was such a relief to hear that someone else knew she wasn't crazy.

Lizzie nodded. "No one believed me, but I know Rosie's voice, and I know it was her. What exactly did she tell you?"

There was an odd inflection in the woman's tone and Emily shrugged, reminding herself to be cautious. "Not much. She doesn't remember who did it."

Lizzie frowned, her beautiful brows drawing closer together. "But why can't she remember?"

"She thinks it all got erased when she passed to the other side," Emily explained.

"She didn't say anything about the money?" When Emily's eyebrows flew up, Lizzie continued. "It's legend in these parts. Mullen, I mean Potter, was supposed to be hiding out. A few months before the murders, a man came to the door to ask for him, a man with a wooden leg. Potter nearly climbed out the window he was so scared. Shortly after that, he started locking the doors and windows, and wouldn't go anywhere without his gun."

"Because of some money?" Emily asked carefully.

Lizzie shrugged. "Everyone thought your father had stolen a payroll. Two million dollars' worth, from what I hear. Vandals tore the place apart after he died, but no one ever found a cent. You haven't found anything?"

Lizzie searched Emily's face, but the former bordello girl's eyes were fearful.

Emily shook her head. "No, and I'm not really convinced there is any money. I'm more interested in solving the murders. Is there anything else you remember that might help? Where were you on that night?"

Lizzie's hands began to shake once more and she placed the cup on the tray before her. "I told the sheriff everything I knew. I was at the house earlier, but I went out that night. By the time I returned, it was over. I'll never forget it, seeing them lying there. Rosie almost looked like she was asleep, except for the blood. I just couldn't believe they'd been killed."

"Did you enter the parlor, then?" Emily asked eagerly.

Lizzie shook her head. "No, I ran right back out. When I returned, the place had been cleaned up and the bodies were gone, thank God. It was so horrible!"

A tear formed in her eye and she wiped quickly at it with the back of her hand. Emily felt compassion for the beautiful, agitated woman as she tried to compose herself. After a moment, Lizzie valiantly continued. "In any case, I couldn't stay there. I left town determined to start over. I still can't get that vision out of my head, nor the sound of Rosie's voice."

Emily scribbled a few notes, then looked up again. "Is there anyone else who might remember something?"

Lizzie nodded slowly. "Well, there was a woman, Bertie Evans, who took care of the place. You shouldn't have much trouble finding her—someone in town should know where she is. She was the housekeeper, and knew just about everything that went on."

Emily took a deep breath before asking her final question. "I heard there was a preacher man here this morning. What did he want?"

"Please!" Lizzie cried, distraught. "I'd never seen the man before! Just let me be!"

"Miss Wakefield." Emily rose and faced the woman sternly. "You must know something that makes you so afraid."

"Miss Potter, please listen to me." Lizzie leaned forward urgently. Her face grew deathly pale, and the light in her eyes made her look as if she'd gone mad. She grabbed Emily's arm and held so tightly Emily couldn't pull away. "You must listen. For your father's sake, stay out of this. Sell the house, leave this place. Or you, too, will die."

Outside, all was still. Unnerved by the woman's words, Emily looked around, making certain no one was following her. The stretch of road before her was lonely, and as she walked she disturbed a grouse from the brush. It made her feel a little better to think that no one else had passed that way for a time, but when she reached a crossroads, the uneasiness inside her grew again.

She didn't know how to get back. She hadn't paid enough attention when she'd followed the boy to the house. Determinedly she picked the left fork, but had only walked a few hundred feet when she realized nothing looked familiar. She had retraced her steps and started down another path when the sound of a horse's hooves made her heart skip. Turning quickly, she felt a strange mixture of apprehension and relief when she recognized the horseman.

"Thomas!" she breathed. Then fear crept up her spine as she remembered what Lizzie had told her. Was her warning about Thomas? Emily didn't really believe he was dangerous, but the evidence was mounting. Was it simply that she didn't want to think he was a killer, after the intimacy they'd shared?

He sat astride a black quarterhorse, his preacher's collar completely at odds with his demeanor, once again. He looked anything but pleased to see her, and his eyes seemed to pierce right through her.

"I guess I don't have to ask you what the hell you're doing here. This isn't a good part of town to be wandering around. Give me your bag."

Emily handed him the case and before she could protest, he had thrust it over the saddle horn and hauled her unceremoniously onto the horse in front of him. Emily's corset cut into her and she gasped for breath, struggling to stay upright.

"Who do you think you are!"

"Just a humble preacher, helping his fellow man, or woman, stay out of trouble," Thomas responded, apparently unperturbed by her outburst. Emily scrambled for balance, gripping the saddle horn, trying desperately to maintain some kind of dignity. Thomas solved part of her problem and exacerbated the other by pulling her into his lap. In spite of the awkward position, at least her skirts settled into place. Furious, she turned to give him the set-down she felt he deserved.

"You have some nerve! I gave you no leave to follow me here, nor to interfere! Just who are you really, and why are you involved in all this?"

She was almost sorry she spoke. His face turned hard and his arm stiffened around her, just below her breasts. "Emily, I warned you to stay out of this. Someone has to look after you, and unfortunately, it looks like I've been elected. You just don't seem to understand that this is dangerous. Nothing you discover can possibly help. The sheriff has already been to see Miss Wakefield, and has her sworn statement. I'm not telling you again to leave it alone."

It occurred to Emily that he was angrier than she was. He spoke in that gritted-teeth tone that she was beginning to recognize as genuine fury. Still, she was too angry herself to be cowed by it. She lifted her head defiantly.

"I will not leave it alone. I have a right to investigate. He was, after all, my father. The sheriff may be willing to talk to you, but he's been of no use to me at all. And at this moment what I want to know is, why are you involved in this? Why aren't you preaching or something, and staying out of my life?"

"Emily." She thought his teeth would break from the force with which he was clenching them. The arm holding her tightened again, and she was pulled against him so intimately that she blushed. Fortunately her face was turned away from him, for she was now seated directly between his legs and the contact was oddly exciting. The hard muscles of his thighs cradled her bottom, and she couldn't help but recall his naked form in the tub, or how it felt to be held more tenderly in his arms.

When he scolded her this time, it was considerably more strained. "This isn't a game. I came here this morning because I knew you'd show up and question Lizzie. What you don't know is that Miss Wakefield is the lover of an outlaw, and outlaws don't take too kindly to strangers. You were liable to get your fool head blown off."

"Lizzie is involved with an outlaw!" Emily whistled through her teeth, forgetting her suspicion of Thomas in her excitement. "No wonder she's living in seclusion! Do you know who it is? Maybe he's somehow connected—"

"Emily! For chrissake, don't you listen—"

The words had no sooner left his mouth than gunfire spat out from the surrounding woods. Emily ducked as Thomas pushed her head down toward the withers of the horse, then kicked the gelding into a gallop. The scream died on Emily's lips as the gunfire blasted around them, the sound deafening as well as terrifying. The bark was torn off a cottonwood as a bullet made contact just inches from her face, and she cried out again, wrapping her arms around the gelding's neck. Watson popped out of the open bag, curious about the sounds and sudden motion. Emily reached blindly for him.

"Forget the damned cat! Stay down!" Thomas yelled as another volley of gunfire burst from the trees in front of them. Forcing Watson back into the case, she closed her eyes, unable to bear looking at the ground as it sped past her. Emily choked as clouds of dust from the horse's hooves rose up around them. Dust which was probably all that saved their skins, she realized when she could breathe again.

The noise finally died, and the ground beneath them appeared to grow harder. Sounds of normal everyday life replaced the fusillade of bullets behind them, and she surmised that they must be near town. It was only then that Thomas slowed the horse's frantic pace. Emily peeked between the horse's ears and saw that they were back on the main street. There was the bank, the stagecoach stop, the hotel and restaurant, and the townspeople, all going about their day as if nothing unusual had happened.

Her heart felt as if it might pound its way out of her body. Glancing over her shoulder and seeing Thomas's nod, Emily straightened. Her spine had practically been bent in half. Her corset cut deeply into her sides. But her discomfort was the least of her concerns as she frantically opened her case. Her breathing slowed to something much closer to normal when Watson poked his head out indignantly and mewed. She sighed and slumped backward against Thomas.

"Good Lord, what was that all about?" Emily asked tremulously.

"What do you think I've been talking about all this time?" Thomas said, although he too seemed shaken. "You aren't meeting with the ladies' sewing circle, Emily. These are dangerous people and dangerous times. Maybe now you understand what I've been trying to say. You've got to trust me."

She wanted to. God, how she wanted to. With his arms around her, even though her heart was thumping frantically, she felt oddly safe and secure. Yet there was no logical reason for that. Thomas Hall could be a coldblooded killer, who would murder her just as someone had murdered her father. Until she knew for sure, she couldn't continue to let her guard down like this, not for one moment.

That thought made her withdraw from his embrace. When she spoke, her voice was carefully controlled. "You are right, Thomas, I see that now. I should be more cautious, and will act accordingly in the future. Now, if you'll just help me down, I can wait for the stagecoach here."

She felt him stiffen as if he'd been slapped. Emily gulped, wondering if he suspected her thoughts. His reaction indicated that he was upset, but why should he be? She was only taking his advice.

"Forget it," Thomas said bluntly. When Emily turned to look at him in surprise, she met a cold stare. "I know you, Miss Potter. Once the excitement wears off, you'll go back to investigating and get yourself killed. I'm taking you straight home."

"But that will take at least six hours!" Emily protested.

"You may as well get used to my company, then."

Emily tried to dismount, but Thomas managed to hold her still—at the expense of losing the reins. The horse bolted, and by the time Thomas had the animal under control again, they were well out of the bustling town. Fuming, Thomas dismounted and yanked Emily down to the ground next to him.

"Dammit, woman, you're going to get us both killed!" He turned her to face him, determined that once and for all, he would show her who was master. But her eyes were wide with fear, two luminous pools of silver, and her lips were parted, red and inviting. His skin still ached deliciously from where she'd been pressed against him, and his trousers strained tightly against his erection. Every inch of his body cried out for her.

"Emily, sweet Jesus, Emily," he swore, and covered her mouth with his own.

10

The Conflict Becomes Even Thornier

Emily whimpered a confused protest. Thomas eased the pressure of his mouth, molding her soft lips gently to his. Urging her closer, he caressed her waist, letting his hands slide over her curves, deliberately stoking her passion and calming her fears. A moment later, he got his reward when he felt her melting against him like wax, pressing her soft, sweet body to his.

Thomas groaned, feeling pleasure rush through his veins. Cupping her head in his hand, he slipped his fingers into the silky strands of her hair, enjoying the wonderful texture. At the soft moan in the back of her throat, he parted her lips with his tongue, then plunged boldly inside. She tasted sweet and ripe, like a luscious wine, and his hands slid down her back, wanting nothing more than to pull the dour dress from her and make love to her.

"Emily . . ." Why did it have to be her? She was an eccentric, would-be detective who never knew when to let well enough alone. Yet her mere proximity drove him mad, and he could think of nothing but possessing her. He wanted to love her, to tease her and tempt her until she was begging for release. He had to have her; it was as simple as that.

The thought made his blood pound. He lifted his face, wanting to see her expression, and was enthralled when he did. She looked like a ravished angel. Her eyes fluttered, their depths like precious molten metal, and her mouth was flushed with their kiss.

"Emily, I want you so badly. I want to make love to you. Please say yes."

She met his heated gaze uncertainly. "Thomas, I feel so strange. It's like every pore of my body has awakened, and my blood seems to sing through my veins. Is it always like this? No one ever told me so!"

He chuckled, his desire even more aroused by her innocence. "Yes, it's supposed to be like this, when it's right between two people. I want you, Emily. I can't promise more than that, but I want you."

She wound her fingers around his neck and leaned against him. She was giving him what he had been coveting, dreaming about, yearning for since he first laid eyes on her . . . and then he winced when she came into contact with his gun. Thomas saw her expression change. Her head lifted, and she looked directly into his eyes with an honesty that was as compelling as it was heartbreaking.

"Thomas, I want to know the truth. What is going on here? I need to know before I can . . . commit to anything else."

"I don't know what you mean," he whispered, because it was the only response he could give, letting his fingers fan through her hair.

"You aren't a minister. You've been following me everywhere, you handle a gun like an outlaw, you swear, and you kiss like . . . like I don't know, but I'm sure it's not holy. I need to know, Thomas."

She waited and he shook his head. Why did she have to be so intelligent? "Emily, I'm just a traveling preacher. You have nothing to fear from me. That's all you need to know."

She looked at him sadly. "Then I can't make love to you, Thomas. I know what you're telling me isn't right. It's the Science of Deduction, you know. Now could you please take me home?"

His mouth opened to object to her "Science," but the hint of a tear in the corner of her eye proved his undoing. He couldn't stand to see her cry. And God knew what would happen then. Instead of arguing with her, he helped her back up onto the horse, then climbed on himself, feeling a sickness in the pit of his stomach. To hear Emily confess that she couldn't trust him cut him to the quick in a way he would never have suspected. Forcing aside the emotion, he reminded himself that he had no other choice. Yet there was one feeling he couldn't quite get past, and that was regret.

As soon as Emily left, Lizzie sprang into action. "Aggie, help me pack. I'm getting out of here."

The housekeeper nodded in agreement. "That's the best idea I heard all day. But how's Jake going to feel about this?"

Lizzie paused, looking up from the suitcase she was packing to meet Aggie's eyes. "I don't know. Sometimes I think he'd be relieved. All he wants is that damned money, not me."

"You should never have taken up with him to begin with," Aggie said. "You know what I always say. When you sleep with a rattler, you're going to get bit."

As if to punctuate her glum pronouncement, shots rang out and the two women stared at each other in fright. "Oh, my God," Lizzie murmured, placing her hand over her heart. The gunfire continued, the sounds a short distance away, and the former bordello girl broke out of her frozen stance.

"Hurry! We've got to get out of here!" Aggie cried.

Lizzie nodded, but the color had drained completely from her face. Pulling the shades, she dragged out another box and began filling it with dishes. Aggie worked silently beside her, folding towels between pictures, tying boxes with twine. They had barely finished the downstairs when the door flung open and a man strode inside.

"Jake!" Lizzie gulped. "I didn't know—I wasn't expecting you. . . ."

"I can see that." The cowboy stood in the center of the bare room, his rifle slung over his shoulder. His eyes immediately fell on the boxes and trunks, and the housekeeper standing protectively by Lizzie. His face hardened perceptibly. "What the hell is going on here?"

"I thought I'd take a little vacation," Lizzie answered softly. "This town is awfully quiet these days, and my feet are itching for some fun. I thought a spell in the mountains might do me good, or maybe a few weeks in town. That's all."

Jake snorted and pulled Lizzie from the housekeeper's grip. "This wouldn't have anything to do with that schoolmarm who was just here, would it? I heard she was in town, asking questions and poking her nose where it didn't belong. What was she doing here?"

Lizzie shrugged. "She's John Potter's daughter, Jake. She was only asking about her pa. She wondered what happened to him. Someone must have given her my name. That's all, Jake, I swear."

"What did you tell her?"

"I told her I didn't know anything," Lizzie said quickly. "Why would I tell her anything else?"

He seemed to weigh that answer, but his black eyes glittered menacingly. "What else did she say? Does she know where the money is?"

Lizzie shook her head. "No. I asked her point-blank, but she doesn't have a clue. You weren't shooting at her, Jake, were you? You didn't kill her—"

"What if I had?" The outlaw grinned. "Ain't no more than she deserves. But I just fired a few warning shots to scare her off. The last thing I need is some spinster woman raising all kinds of questions." His smile died as his gaze fell on the boxes once more, taking in the dishes and linens, her photographs in their delicate frames. When he looked up, his expression was dangerous.

"You know, most women wouldn't pack up everything for a vacation. Another man might think you were running out on him. That isn't what you'd planned is it?"

"No, Jake, it isn't like that at all," Lizzie pleaded. "Why would I run out on you?"

"I don't know, but it don't matter because you ain't. You're coming with me." Ignoring the protests of the housekeeper, Jake kicked opened the door and pulled Lizzie toward his horse.

"No, please, just let me go," Lizzie sobbed.

But the outlaw was heartless. "Git on that horse. You ain't leaving me, honey, not by a long shot. No woman ever leaves me."

Emily pulled off her hat that night and flopped down onto the bed. Watson meowed and she absently pulled him out of the bag to set him on the floor, but the cat sprang from the room, still frightened of the mirror. Emily stared into her reflection thoughtfully.

Thomas's proposition today, while shocking, nevertheless made her pause. She'd been so overcome with passion that she'd actually considered agreeing, especially when she recalled the magic he was able to make her feel in his arms. He was a dangerous man in more ways than one, Emily realized, pressing her hands to her heated face. He always seemed to know exactly what she was thinking, where she would turn next, and how to arouse her—expertly.

"I must be losing my mind," she declared out loud. The last thing she needed was a physical involvement with a suspect in her father's murder. Yet the man had only to touch her and she melted in his arms. Worse, when she confronted him, he made it clear that he had no explanation for his actions. Was his seduction simply part of a plan, or was he really attracted to her?

It was yet another mystery. As Emily put her purse on the dressing table, its meager weight forcibly reminded her that her money was running out. She was no closer to finding the gold than she had been the first day she set foot in Shangri-La, and she certainly couldn't afford to keep investigating without finding a source of income. As much as she wanted to continue the case, she had to eat.

"What's the matter, sweetie? You look so glum!"

Emily nearly leaped out of her skin as the ghost swam into view. Staring at the bordello girl's spirit, Emily shook her head in wonder.

"I just can't get used to this. Are you always there?"

Rosie giggled, fanning herself with her plumes. "Sorry about the noise the other day, but you needed a little convincing. Yes, I'm always here, but I only show myself when necessary. It uses up too much energy to appear for nothing. So why are you sad? Did that handsome preacher man do you wrong?"

Emily sighed. "Not exactly. I just wish I knew who he really was. Until things are clearer, I have to keep my guard up."

"Ah. Then you kissed him again?" When Emily's mouth fell open, Rosie chuckled. "You forget, honey. While detecting may be your forté, mine is men. So what happened between you and our little minister?"

"He . . . propositioned me," Emily said slowly. She was reluctant to confide in the bawdy ghost, but she desperately needed to talk to someone. "He asked me to make love to him."

"Did he, now?" Rosie's painted eyebrows flew up. "And did you?"

"Of course not!" Emily huffed, though she was afraid Rosie knew exactly how close she'd come. "Why on earth would I do that?"

Rosie looked at her as if she were mad. "Why? Well, for all the normal reasons, sweetie. To be courted by a man like that . . . he'll bring you perfumes and flowers, make you feel pretty . . . and when a man like that makes love to you, you'll never ask 'why' again."

Emily flushed hotly. "Thomas Hall is a factor in this case, nothing else." She couldn't tell Rosie how she felt about the man. Then the ghost would really laugh.

"I see." Rosie's eyes twinkled, as if seeing a lot more. "Then is that why you're sad?"

"No. I suddenly realized that I have to start making some income. I'm going to have to set up my milliner's shop. The materials I ordered should be arriving any day. The only problem is, I don't think I have enough money to pay for a space in town."

"Mmm." Rosie was thoughtful a moment, then her face lit up. "I know! You could use my parlor! It could be a sitting room where ladies could try on hats!"

"I don't know if women would come here." Emily remembered her own reaction when she'd first entered the house. She pictured her mother walking into the parlor. It would never work the way things were now . . . but still, it was a possible solution. "Maybe I could redo it. You know, paint the ceiling, subdue the furnishings a little. . . ."

"Sure! I think having the shop here will draw lots of customers." Rosie perked up, her face alight. "Most women are curious about what goes on in houses like ours. Maybe it would draw customers out of curiosity, if nothing else!"

Emily tried to envision that. "Maybe, if someone in town made it fashionable. We could make a kind of ladies' club, almost like a gentleman's gambling club. They could come here, try on hats, discuss books, maybe play cards. Who knows? We might even learn something about the murders."

"What fun!" Rosie agreed eagerly. She clapped her hands like a child. "I don't see what could go wrong!"

"All right, I'll give it a try." Emily straightened, putting her notebook aside and starting for the stairs. She had to admit, she was touched by Rosie's enthusiasm and obvious desire to see her succeed. This was a side to the bordello girl that she had never thought to witness, and it made it difficult to continue disliking her. Strange as it was to have a ghost on her side, it made her feel as if she weren't entirely alone.

Emily proceeded into the parlor to assess the room. She had a lot of work ahead of her to make it even slightly presentable. Detecting would have to wait a spell, she decided with regret. Her only consolation was that even Holmes occasionally ran into monetary difficulties.

And he didn't have a ghost to bail him out.

11

Miss Lizzie Is Gone

The following day, Thomas headed back toward town, grateful to have his horse and his thoughts to himself once more.

What was it about Emily that completely shattered his control? He'd certainly been with more beautiful women, women with a lot fewer complications, but he'd never had a woman turn him inside out from wanting as she did.

Maybe it was simply because she was trouble, and someone he should stay a million miles away from. Thomas knew that the best thing for everyone would be to put as much distance between himself and Emily as possible, but that never appeared to work. She was always under foot, always in danger, and he seemed to be her unappreciated rescuer. And someone was getting nervous about Emily's prying. If whoever it was felt threatened enough to shoot, they were threatened enough to kill. It was time he had a real heart-to-heart talk with Lizzie Wakefield, and without Miss Sherlock's help.

Thomas stopped at the post office, nodding his head to the clerk who acknowledged his collar respectfully. There was one letter for him. Taking the missive outside, he tore open the envelope. It was from Wells Fargo. Skimming past the niceties, Thomas stopped when he came to the paragraph he'd been searching for:

". . . In answer to your inquiry, Miss Potter is exactly what she appears to be. Her former neighbors describe her as quiet but eccentric, and the Boston police speak in admiring terms of her detective abilities, and wish her well. It appears highly unlikely that she knew about the gold, or her father's nefarious activities. . . ."

Thomas quickly read the rest, then stuffed the envelope in his pocket. All his suspicions of her had proved unfounded. Emily had never been involved in the payroll theft, hadn't come here to pick up the missing gold. Emily was completely innocent of any deception. If only he could say the same for himself.

Mounting his horse, he retraced the path he had taken the day before. Knowing that Emily Potter really was an amateur detective made his reasons for avoiding her invalid. He was no longer concerned about her role in the crime. And now more than ever she needed protecting. The seductive memory of the kiss they shared came back to haunt him, and Thomas knew one thing for certain: It would be harder than ever to resist Emily Potter now.

Pleasantly immersed in memories of hot skin and quicksilver eyes, it took him several hours to return to Lizzie's house, and seconds to sense that something was wrong.

The shades were drawn, and the house looked deserted. Tying his horse behind a tree, Thomas drew his gun and crept closer. He half expected one of yesterday's gunmen to come charging out, but everything was quiet. Too quiet . . .

Thomas stepped carefully through the open door, and his breath caught in his throat as he saw the body. It was the housekeeper. She had been shot. Twice, by the looks of it. Frantically he scanned the room for other signs of bloodshed, but there was nothing else. His fingers clutched his weapon as he searched the back room and the kitchen.

No one was there.

Back in the parlor, he saw the boxes filled with linens and china. What had happened? Did the housekeeper's murderer kill Lizzie also, or take her captive? Or had she somehow managed to escape?

Thomas stood in the center of the room, and surprisingly, Emily came to mind. He recalled the way she'd investigated the crime scene upon arrival at Shangri-La, an inspection that he had to admit (although he would only do so privately) made sense. Borrowing a page from her book, he searched the carpet, looking for additional bloodstains, but found none. There were no signs of a struggle. Stepping outside, he saw two furrows from a pair of small, delicate boots, where they had been dragged through the mud. Hoofprints told the final story.

Lizzie had been getting ready to bolt. Someone had stopped her, taken her captive, then killed the housekeeper. Why? What did Lizzie know that had everyone so damned scared? And what was Lizzie running from?

They were questions without answers. Thomas mounted his horse, then headed back to Denver to report the housekeeper's death to the authorities. No one in Boulder would talk now.

Miss Lizzie was gone.

"Okay, honey. No, it wasn't quite like that . . . yes, that's better. And that one picture should go over the bar."

Emily stepped back in satisfaction, surveying the parlor. With Rosie's coaching and Darrel's help, she'd managed to whip the room into shape. The piano gleamed from the corner, polished down to the bare wood, and the gaslights glowed softly overhead. A needle and thread repaired the sofa cushions, which had been carelessly slashed when the vandals had searched for the gold. It took considerable balance to stand on the upholstered chairs and rehang the pictures that had fallen from the walls. Emily tried not to look too closely at some of them, for they were amazingly detailed portraits of female nudes. Warmth still rose within her whenever she looked up at the painted ceiling, however, and she doubted she'd ever get used to that.

My God, men were different creatures, Emily mused, fanning herself from the heat of both her erotic thoughts and the exertion. The slightest thing seemed to arouse them, and the blatancy of this room must have strongly appealed to their baser instincts. Try as she might, she couldn't look at those pictures without thinking of Thomas, and how easily she could have been drawn into the same sultry act. She had to admit she was curious, and more than a little aroused. Goodness, if this place had this effect on her, what would it do to the women in town?

An unbidden image sprang to her mind, of Shangri-La in its prime. She could see the girls fanning themselves with their black plumes while men surveyed them, fantasizing, plunking down their wages for a night of ecstasy. They would follow their chosen girl up the staircase, into one of the bedrooms above. . . .

"I can't leave the pictures up," Emily decided firmly, squeezing her eyes shut. Somehow, she couldn't see the good women of Denver looking at one of those portraits and not falling into a dead faint. She didn't want to hurt Rosie's feelings, though. "I think the rest is all right, but the pictures have to go." She resolutely began to remove one of the portraits.

"Why? I think they're lovely, especially that blond," Rosie cooed in protest. "Looks a little like me, don't you think?"

Emily's embarrassment deepened as she realized the implication of that. Thank goodness, Darrel had gone to the barn. She could just see Rosie, sprawled on the couch, wearing nothing but a carefully draped shawl and a smile. Closing her eyes firmly, she hefted the portrait down and placed it discreetly behind the sofa. The others followed suit until the walls were bare.

"I just don't think the women of Denver are ready for all this," Emily said, brushing her hands on her skirts.

"Well, if you're certain, there are some landscapes in one of the bedrooms that you can hang." Rosie said happily.

"The bordello girl's voice surrounded her, and Emily smiled as she thought of the ghost surveying her parlor with pleasure. Although her image couldn't leave the mirror, Rosie was able to see anything in the house, and could speak anywhere. Yet Emily was the only one who could hear her. She tried to explain it all to Emily, that her spirit was not earth bound, but it made no sense to her. Once she accepted Rosie as a phantom, Emily didn't even try to apply logic to the rest.

"Now you'll need some fresh flowers, and music. The piano is a player, so all you have to do is wind it up. I really like the way you fixed my curtains, sweetie. That was horrible when those vandals tore them right off the wall! It makes the windows seem so naked, doesn't it?"

Emily had to hold back a bubble of laughter. Apparently naked windows offended Rosie's sensibilities, but naked men and women didn't faze her in the least.

She took one more look around, wishing she felt as certain of success as Rosie did. Some of Emily's hats lay neatly on a polished rosewood table, displayed to show off their best features, while books of designs were opened invitingly nearby. The shelves were also filled with books, for in spite of Rosie's protests, she'd added her collection of mysteries, her books on poisons, her encyclopedia of important persons, and her files. Other women besides herself must be interested in intellectual pursuits as well as enticing a man, she explained, and she insisted that the books be given shelf space. Rosie was forced to agree, even though she declared that no man ever wanted to read in her house.

"We should hold a reception!" Rosie said enthusiastically. "Invite the women to the grand opening. We'll have a real party in the house again!"

"Excellent idea!" Emily agreed. "Now I think we need to get started on some new designs for the hats. I'll go to the post office and see if the supplies have arrived yet."

Emily had taken only enough time to draw up some posters advertising her grand opening before setting off toward town. Walking through the dusty street, she passed a few of the town's ladies and smiled in a friendly manner. But she was mystified when they pulled their skirts aside and crossed to the other side of the road.

Puzzled, Emily stared after them. Maybe they just didn't appreciate her hat, which was the newest Paris fashion. As she ventured into the post office and tacked one of her posters to the wall, she felt several pairs of eyes on her. Attempting to act as if nothing were out of the ordinary, she walked up to the clerk.

"Hello. I'm Emily Potter. I've been expecting a shipment from Boston, some fabric and trim. Has it arrived?"

The clerk looked at her, then glanced at the women who stood in the far corner. He cleared his throat, his face reddening in embarrassment.

"Yes, I believe it has arrived. But don't you think it would be better if you came around back?"

Emily looked at him in confusion, then her face cleared. "Oh, I see. It is rather bulky, and it probably would be easier to fetch it that way. Thank you."

The man met Emily on the other side of the building. "The package is large. I have a wagon here you can borrow." He gestured to a rickety old cart. "Just bring it back when you're finished. I'm sorry I couldn't receive you around front. Nancy and the other girls all know that."

"Oh, I'm no longer at the saloon, so I can come around front next time," Emily informed him, though she didn't care for his tone. This was a complication she hadn't thought of. Apparently her reputation had suffered some damage from her stint at the saloon, if not from her possession of the notorious house.

"Ah . . . of course," the clerk said awkwardly. His tight-lipped mouth curved upward. "Why don't you bring that wagon back tonight? We could get better acquainted."

Emily instantly stiffened. Forcing a smile, she watched as the clerk tossed a thick bundle onto the cart, then left as quickly as she could, pulling the wagon while Watson followed. Her face heated as she thought of the clerk's meaning, and a sudden idea crossed her mind. Could Thomas have the same impression of her? Is that why he thought he could proposition her? It didn't seem as likely, since he knew her intention was to investigate. Still, Emily was learning just how little she knew of men.

Inside the dry goods store, four women stopped talking when she entered. Emily adjusted her glasses and saw to her dismay that one of them was the older woman on board the stagecoach when she'd arrived in town. Watson bounded toward the woman as if he, too, recognized her, and Emily scrambled to scoop him up. The woman nodded in her direction and whispered something to the others. They all stared at her.

Emily ignored them and placed her poster in the window. She walked to the counter and tried to make her voice as normal as possible.

"Could I have some lace, please? Five yards will do. And some of that white thread."

Emily requested the items from the shopkeeper, who also stared at her with open curiosity. She attempted to overlook his rudeness, but it was almost impossible. Instead, she focused on the walking stick beside him, a handsome specimen with a gold-plated tip.

"Miss Potter, I have to ask you something." The man placed her packages on the counter. "Miss Jenkins there claims that you can read a person's mind simply by looking at their cuffs. Is that true?"

Emily sighed with impatience. "Not exactly." When the man raised his brows in triumph, she went on. "I can tell a lot about a person by their cuffs and boots.

It isn't anything anyone else couldn't do. And it certainly isn't mind reading."

"I see." He handed her the change, then smiled in a superior manner. "I don't suppose your talent helped at the saloon?"

The women tittered, but Emily kept her composure and simply shrugged, collecting her purchases. But the man wasn't about to let her off that easily.

"See! I knew you were a fraud. You couldn't tell anything about me!" He turned toward the women with a smirk, as if dismissing them all as silly females.

Emily smiled, turning toward the door. "Other than the fact that you've developed a weakness for whiskey, that it has led you from a lofty position at the bank to your present occupation, that you have a small dog who continually chews your belongings, that your wife has left you, and that you are desperately trying to forget a woman named Rita, I can't tell a thing."

The gasp behind her was audible. Emily turned and gave the man a nod, noting his white complexion and gaping jaw. Normally she didn't like to employ her talents just to put someone in their place, but her pride had taken a solid beating that morning and she had had enough. The women looked equally astonished and watched the clerk in bewilderment, waiting for him to deny her charges.

Instead, he sputtered, "But how—you just came into town. How did you know? . . ."

"It was elementary. You have a walking stick inscribed from the bank. Banks only give such presentations to valued employees or important customers.

Since you are working here and don't appear to have great wealth, I deduced the former. Since you were once held in such high esteem, and now are employed in a dry goods store, I have to assume that some evil influence created your downfall. When I see that your stick is chipped in several places, and observe the scent of whiskey on your breath, it wasn't hard to figure out."

"But my dog?"

Emily gestured to his boots impatiently. "There are at least three bite marks on your boots. They are only an inch apart, hence a small dog."

"And my wife? And Rita?"

Emily waved her hand in the air while the women stood looking at each other, speechless. "You no longer wear a ring, but there is a clear white mark where it once resided. Also, I saw that the back of your watch was once inscribed 'Rita,' but you scratched over the name. I observed it when you laid it on the counter. Good day."

She left the store, with the women and the clerk still in stunned silence. She never saw Thomas move away from the window where he'd witnessed the entire scene, nor did she see the long, thoughtful glance the preacher gave her.

After Emily departed, Thomas walked casually into the store. The shopkeeper had just removed Emily's poster, and was busy rolling it up while the women whispered and tittered. Without saying a word, Thomas took the poster from the man's hands and put it back into the window.

"Excuse me, sir, I mean, Reverend, what are you doing?" the shopkeeper huffed indignantly.

"Being neighborly," Thomas answered dryly. "As a man of God, I consider it my duty to make sure all of his children treat each other kindly. What is that saying? Do unto others . . ."

"Do unto others as you would have them do unto you," one of the woman corrected him with a superior look.

Thomas shot her an unappreciative glare. "Thank you. Miss Potter is a good Christian woman, and I aim to see that she gets a warm welcome here in town. I don't want to hear of anyone causing her any trouble. Are you in agreement?"

Thomas stared down the shopkeeper, his eyes like steel. The man swallowed hard and indicated the poster. "But I can't have that hanging in my store! I'll lose business. Miss Potter has a reputation—"

It was as far as he got. Thomas stepped closer and grabbed the man by the collar. Tension radiated from the preacher, and the glitter in his eyes got even icier. At the moment he appeared more like the wrath of God than a man of God. The women shrank back.

"Miss Potter is a lady, and should be known as such," Thomas said, his jaw tight with anger. "Now, if I hear any different, I'll have to come calling on you. For I have an observation in addition to Miss Potter's. You are a coward. Do you understand me?"

The shopkeeper nodded, his eyes wide with fear. Thomas let him go, then brushed his hands as if to remove filth. "Good." Thomas forced a smile, remembering his calling. "As a man of the cloth, I'd hate to have to prescribe a public penance. Good day, shopkeeper. Ladies."

Thomas walked out, and the women exchanged a wondering glance with the shaken clerk.

Anger still burned in his gut as Thomas walked toward Shangri-La. The thought of that weasly shopkeeper passing judgment on Emily made his stomach wrench, even though he himself had once done the same thing. These parochial townspeople didn't know her, didn't understand her, and never would, Thomas fumed. It would be best for all concerned if Emily just quit this place and went back East, especially after all that he had witnessed yesterday.

The picture of Lizzie's housekeeper lying in her own blood wouldn't leave him. If he hadn't gotten to Boulder when he did and taken Emily away . . . he couldn't even think of the rest. He had the horrible feeling that she was tangled in a web where death and disaster were the certain outcome.

After leaving Boulder, he'd ridden into the Chinese settlement outside of town to look up China Blue, the laundry woman who'd worked at Shangri-La. It had occurred to him that she might be in as much trouble as Lizzie and Emily, especially if she had been there the night of the murders.

But he had had little success finding the woman. No one in the encampment would even talk to him. He could only hope that someone had understood why he was looking for China Blue and would warn her about the danger she might be in.

Now he could only vent his aggravation on the shopkeeper. Lizzie was gone, her housekeeper brutally murdered, and China Blue either dead or in hiding. There was only one other person that the sheriff had named as a possible witness: a housekeeper who had worked in the bordello. Tomorrow, Thomas would probe that lead a little further. He had to admit he didn't like the way things were going. And yesterday's murder proved just how far the killer would go.

He stopped outside Emily's house, watching her charming silhouette in the window as she lit the lamp. Thomas smiled, thinking of her deductions concerning the shopkeeper and the women's astonished reaction. He had to admit, she was good, but even her brilliance wouldn't keep her out of trouble this time. He felt a strange hollowness as he realized that if she took his advice, he'd never see her again, but he couldn't let that stop him. Reaffirming his resolve, Thomas climbed the porch steps. He was going to talk some sense into her.

The door flew open at his second knock. Emily and Darrel's eyes widened at the sight of him. "Reverend Hall!" Emily spoke first. "I wasn't expecting company. . . ."

"That's all right. Can I come in, Miss Emily? I have something to tell you. Darrel, would you mind waiting outside?"

The boy stopped his work and dashed out the back door before Emily could say another word. She bit her lip uncertainly, as if not at all sure she wanted to hear anything he had to say. Thomas felt the same strange stirrings that she always engendered in him and thought back to their encounter outside Boulder. Damn! Pushing the memory aside, he entered the house—then stared at the parlor in astonishment.

It looked just like a real bordello. Thomas's jaw fell open as he took in the mended curtains, the lace undersheers peeking beneath like petticoats, and the newly fixed sofa. Perfume emanated from somewhere—the gaslights, it seemed—and the rose-colored shades threw a seductive pink light over everything. Books were everywhere, some of them open, and hats were displayed on every available table and shelf. The player piano tapped out a tune that he dimly recalled had suggestive lyrics, while strategically placed mirrors caught every movement. And above it all was the ceiling, the couples entwined in frankly sexual positions, laughing at him.

Thomas's throat went dry. "Emily . . . my God, what are you doing?"

"Do you like it?" Emily beamed. "I am going to establish my shop here."

"Emily, you've lost your mind." Thomas's hat dropped to the floor and he turned to her in disbelief. "You can't mean—"

"Why not?" Emily said defensively. "Just think, Thomas, what this could mean! Women would have the same privileges as men: a retreat for their own needs. They could come here, try on hats, look through the pattern books, and socialize. What's wrong with that?"

"You have lost your mind." Thomas put a hand on her forehead. Her temperature felt normal, but he

was again forcibly reminded of the soft feel of
her skin, like rose petals. His fingers remained on
her flesh longer than necessary as he marveled at the
silky texture. Visions of the couples cavorting overhead burned into his brain, and he realized what
he was thinking. He pulled his hand from her as
quickly as if he'd been burned. As he glanced around
the room once again, consternation creased his
brow. How far would Emily take this? Surely, she
wouldn't—

His voice was hoarse as he took her by the shoulders and spoke. "You can't plan to . . . have men here
to . . . pleasure these women?"

"Of course not!" Emily seemed insulted by the
suggestion. She pulled out of his grip. "I hadn't even
thought of such a thing! I envision Shangri-La as a
place for women to go, a place to enjoy some of the
things men take for granted. What's wrong with
that?"

"And where do you plan to find these women?"
Thomas asked, incredulous.

"I've hung posters in town, and I'm going to hold
a reception!" Emily said triumphantly. "I think I will
attract women with intelligence and talent. What
better way to gain customers, build relationships,
and sell hats in the bargain?"

Thomas suddenly understood the shopkeeper's
resistance to hanging Emily's poster. "Emily, listen to
me. This idea is insane. Not only will decent women
refuse to come to a whorehouse to buy hats, you'll
never have another chance to establish yourself here.
The townspeople already think you are some kind of

saloon girl. If you pursue this, your reputation will be in shreds!"

He was pacing the floor in extreme agitation. Lord, how could a woman become full grown and know so little about the world? She seemed genuinely puzzled by his disapproval, and she gazed at the fruits of her labor as if trying to see them with his eyes.

"Do you really think . . . I was so sure they would be curious. . . ."

"Emily," Thomas sighed, trying once more to rein in his impatience. "You're right, they would be curious. But most women aren't like you. They wouldn't brave the loss of their good name over anything, let alone an opportunity to glimpse a whorehouse. And when word got out about what this place looks like, their husbands wouldn't get a moment's rest. Don't you see? Every marriage in town would be threatened, and everyone would say you were the reason. You'd be tarred and feathered, and driven out of Colorado!"

She paled, and to Thomas's great relief, seemed to consider his words seriously. "Maybe I should paint the ceiling. I did take the pictures down."

He came closer to her and lifted her chin. "Emily, I really think you should just leave. This isn't the place for you. You are so intelligent and so . . . different. You need the stimulation of the East, places where you can safely practice your detecting. I came here to tell you that Lizzie is gone."

"Gone?" Emily's eyes widened. "Where?"

"I don't know. She was planning to bolt—I saw

her trunks near the door. But something happened. Now she's gone and her housekeeper is dead. She was shot."

Emily sank down on the sofa, folding her hands together. "My God, Thomas, Lizzie gone! And the poor housekeeper . . ." Her voice cracked and Thomas sat beside her, putting a comforting hand on her shoulder.

"That's right. And I don't want to see anything like that happen to you. I can't keep you safe. No one can."

When she looked up at him, his heart plummeted. Her silver eyes were thoughtful, like deep pools of water, and her chin lifted.

"I'm sorry, Thomas, but I've already told you I can't leave. Don't you see what this means? We're getting closer! Whoever killed my father is worried that we are on his trail! I can't quit now, or ever!"

It was useless. He had hoped the shock of the housekeeper's death would frighten her, but not Emily. She was more determined than ever, and he knew he could talk himself blue in the face, but it wouldn't matter.

"Then I'm sorry, too, Emily. You leave me no choice. If you don't have sense enough to take care of yourself, I will do it for you."

"Thomas, you don't have to do that!" Emily gasped. "If you think just because we shared a kiss—"

"I'm afraid I do. Emily, I almost made love to you. You know it and so do I. Maybe that means nothing to you, but when you allow a man certain liberties, you allow him other privileges as well. I have decided a few things. I want you as I've never wanted any other woman, and I'm going to have you."

Before Emily could do more than utter a flabbergasted squeak, he continued in the same rough tone.

"Furthermore, even though you don't trust me now, you are going to learn to. You might as well get used to me, sweetheart, because I'm about to become your Watson."

12

My Dear Watson

Emily struggled to find her voice as Thomas's words penetrated. "You mean—"

"Yes," Thomas said firmly. "I am officially your partner. That means there isn't a clue you uncover, a witness that you question, that I won't know about. Don't even bother to look over your shoulder, because I'll be there."

He meant it. He planned to stay on her, day in and day out, sticking his nose into her investigation, following her like a shadow. And at the first sign she'd slipped up, he would take preventative action.

Every ounce of independent will within her rose up in protest. Even her mother had capitulated when she'd realized Emily would not be deterred from detecting. And now this "preacher" with the faulty disguise thought he could stop her?

But she *had* been in danger. The housekeeper's

death reminded her that whoever she was chasing was getting desperate—desperate enough to kill again. Thomas was certainly capable of defending himself. The saloon incident had shown her that. In truth, he had already rescued her more than once.

So she did need help. And he was offering it—forcibly, but offering it all the same. She squinted at him as she took his measure. He could be her brawn, while she was the brains. And she would be able to keep an eye on him and whatever he was up to that much easier.

But what about his other words? She swallowed hard. He wanted her and meant to have her. Dimly she realized she had only herself to blame for this situation, for she certainly hadn't tried very hard to discourage him. In fact, she had welcomed his kisses and caresses, and let him know it.

And now he thought he could order her into bed with him. Emily opened her mouth to put him in his place, when a voice sounded clearly in her ear.

"You get more flies with sugar than with vinegar, honey! If you want your way with a man, sweet-talk him!"

"What!" Emily sputtered, shocked to hear Rosie's gleeful suggestion. Thomas looked sharply at her, and Emily realized she had spoken out loud. Thank heavens, he seemed not to have heard Rosie. But maybe the ghost had a point. Emily decided it couldn't hurt to try.

"You're right, Thomas." She managed to keep her tone low and soft. "I should have realized it before. This investigation is dangerous. I'm not leaving, though. I want to stay here and make a living. Perhaps I'll just leave the detecting to the sheriff."

Her glance flickered upward to hide the lie she was sure showed in her eyes and to her amazement, she saw Thomas sigh with relief. "I'm glad you've finally seen reason. I apologize for threatening you, but I feel that strongly about this."

"I understand. Thomas, I want you to know that I really do appreciate your concern. . . ." Emily broke off, listening to the whisper again.

"Nice touch. Now ask him to supper."

"Supper!" Emily spat, then quickly regrouped as Thomas faced her in surprise. "I mean . . . I was going to prepare supper for myself. Would you care to join me?"

"I'd be obliged. I spent all day riding, and frankly, I could use a good meal. Thank you, Emily."

"That's it, sweetie, you got him now!" Rosie hooted in her ear and Emily got up quickly, afraid Thomas would see the grin plastered on her face.

"I'll go get it started." Schooling her features once more, she gave him a smile that he returned. A brief shudder went though her as she realized that even dusty and unshaven, he was, in Rosie's words, a hell of a man.

But now she was stuck with him. Marching into the kitchen, she whispered to her invisible matchmaker while putting the potatoes on to boil.

"What did you make me do that for? We were getting along just fine. He could have gone home."

"You were doing a real good job of bringing him

around, but you needed more," Rosie explained. "If you're going to work with him, you really have to make him think of you as a friend, not the competition. No man likes a woman who beats him."

"That's too bad," Emily said indignantly, bringing out a roast. "At least he said he was Watson! He's no Holmes, that's for sure."

The feline namesake of the man in question rubbed against her leg. Rosie chuckled while Emily set out two plates and put some beans on to cook, but she couldn't keep quiet when Emily started placing the dinnerware on the well-scrubbed table.

"You don't mean to eat in here?" Rosie demanded.

Emily nodded. "Yes, I do. Your parlor seems to set him on edge, and I don't want to tempt fate. I think these humble quarters will be much better." Emily didn't want to add that the erotic feeling of the parlor only enhanced her attraction to Thomas, making her own resolve weaken.

"At least fetch a bottle of wine," Rosie protested. "There should be some in the cellar, if that houseboy didn't take it all."

Grumbling, Emily plodded to the basement and picked the dustiest bottle out of the wine rack.

Back in the kitchen, Rosie insisted on candles. When Emily said a firm no, a pair of candlesticks floated in from the parlor. They settled down on the table with a soft hush.

"Rosie!" Emily cried.

"Did you say something?" Thomas asked from the parlor.

"Just that the roast is almost ready," Emily improvised, closing the door so he wouldn't see the ghost's hijinks.

"Don't be such a worrywart," Rosie said indignantly. "Now we just need to tend to you. I think my silver wrapper would look wonderful with your hair and eyes. Don't you think so, honey? And do your hair up again. Thomas loved it last time you wore it that way!"

Emily didn't know where to direct her frustrated glare. "I'm not setting out to seduce him!" she growled at the empty room.

"It's always easier to deal with a man from your strengths," Rosie said, enunciating each word slowly, as if speaking to a child. "If you are going to be partners with this man, you have to gain the upper hand. It never hurts to look your best. Trust me, I know."

Emily couldn't argue with that. Rosie had been a legend among men. Her name was always spoken respectfully in male company, with a little awe thrown in. Resentfully, Emily raced up the back stairs and tossed aside her simple dress. The bordello ghost nodded from the mirror, giving out instructions as Emily changed.

"That's right. Oooh, that's gorgeous. And I have earrings to match. Look in the top drawer, there's a pair of crystals. Now some perfume . . ."

Feeling utterly foolish, Emily obeyed the ghost. Dabbing the perfume behind her ears, she boldly added another drop between her breasts. Who knows? Emily mused. Maybe she *was* going about this all wrong. Maybe by treating Thomas as an equal, she'd given up the most effective weapons she possessed. She'd soon find out.

Giving her hair a final pat, she raced back down the steps to find the potatoes nearly boiling over. She dished out the meal, pausing to catch her breath before she called to Thomas.

"Dinner's ready!"

He appeared instantly. When he walked into the kitchen, Emily experienced a moment of sheer, feminine pleasure. His gaze swung quickly from the enticing meal to her and stayed there. Thomas's jaw dropped, and when he spoke, his voice was hoarse.

"Emily. You didn't have to . . . I mean, you look wonderful."

She dipped her head, hiding a blush, but couldn't deny the thrill that went up her spine. "I just thought I'd change into something more comfortable. We are going to be friends now, Thomas, aren't we?"

He nodded, taking the seat she pulled out for him. His gaze was fastened on the low neckline of her wrapper. "Yes. Friends. That's what we'll be."

"Good. I'm so glad that you came by tonight, Thomas. We got off on the wrong foot, and you showed me the error of my ways. I am obliged to you."

A glimmer of suspicion sparkled in his eyes then, and she heard Rosie whisper, "Don't lay it on too thick. The man's not stupid. Give him the wine."

Realizing her blunder, Emily quickly filled Thomas's glass. He took it from her, their fingers touching, the sparks positively jumping between them.

"This is delicious," he said between forkfuls of food. Drinking deeply of the wine, he savored it as a gentleman would.

"You seem to know good wine," Emily remarked. If only she could be sure what he was up to! Her gaze swept over him, and she noted to her keen frustration that there was very little she could deduce about him. His cuffs told her nothing; his boots, only that he'd ridden hard. His eyes, that peculiar shade of blue, gleamed with intelligence. His chin was firm and unshaven, his hands dexterous and capable. Her eyes traveled back to his collar. Perhaps if his guard were down he would mention something about his past, or who he really was.

"Yes, it was a regular part of our menu where I grew up."

"Virginia?" Emily hazarded a guess. He nodded, and she continued to pick at her food. "I suppose you lived in one of those beautiful manor houses in town. Richmond?"

"Why, Miss Potter, are you investigating me?" His voice sounded teasing, but Emily recognized the warning note.

She looked directly at him. "Do I need to, Thomas?"

Silence hung between them for several seconds before Thomas resumed his meal. "No. You have nothing to fear from me. I've told you that before. I know you don't trust me now, and maybe for good reason. But you will."

Emily felt some relief at his words, but a nagging feeling of doubt lingered. Thomas held his glass up to the light, turning his attention back to the wine in an effort to change the subject. "Was this left in the house?"

"Yes. Apparently the vandals weren't too interested in the wine cellar when they tore the place apart."

"No, they wanted the money." Thomas's gaze met hers. "Have you found any trace of it yet?"

"No," Emily told him, shaking her head. "That's why I need to start the shop. I do think I'll take your advice and tone down the parlor. It is a little much."

"I'll say," Thomas agreed, his voice thickening with some emotion—or was it the wine? Emily's thoughts went back to the seductive room, and she knew he was having the same trouble getting those images out of his head. Everything about this house was sexual—the graceful lines of the rooms, the erotic paintings, even the swish of her wrapper, the feel of silk on flushed skin. . . .

"Could I have another glass?" Thomas pushed his goblet toward her. Emily refilled the glass, hiding her satisfaction. It pleased her to know that Thomas wasn't as fully in control as he liked to pretend. She placed the glass before him, smiling as he downed it in one gulp, like whiskey.

"That was wonderful. Really, the best meal I've had in ages. I should be going, though. Tomorrow is the Sabbath."

"Are you holding services, then?" Emily was genuinely curious. To her knowledge, the Reverend Hall had done very little ministering since his arrival.

His eyes twinkled as if he knew exactly what she

was thinking. "Not yet. I'm meeting with some of the local ministry, to see if my help is needed," he explained. "Denver is an unholy city, from what I've observed."

He was out of the chair and headed for the door when Rosie's voice entered her head once more.

"Invite him for brandy in the parlor!" the ghost shouted in her ear. Emily tried to ignore her, but to her consternation, two crystal glasses floated across the room, followed by a bottle. Taking Thomas by the shoulders, she turned him quickly toward the fireplace until the brandy had landed safely on one of the polished wood tables.

"Emily?" Thomas asked in surprise.

"You can't go yet!" she said, frustrated by Rosie's tricks. "I just thought . . . we'd have a brandy and light the fire."

She let her hands slide down his shoulders, then self-consciously dropped them to her sides. Thomas looked into her eyes as if he thought he could understand what she was doing by gazing into their depths. No such luck.

Pure innocence radiated from her, and he nodded once in reluctant agreement.

"One drink. I'm really tired, and have to be getting back—"

Emily poured the brandy and put it beside him, not trusting herself to touch his hand again. The chemistry between them threatened to ignite at the slightest provocation, and she turned deliberately away from him to light the fire.

Darrel had stacked the wood earlier, making it

fairly easy to get the tinder going. Yet when she bent forward, she could have sworn she heard a groan. She turned quickly to see what she could only describe as a look of pain on Thomas's face.

"Are you all right?"

"Fine," he croaked, tugging at his collar. Emily nodded in confusion, getting up to place a roll in the player piano. The music tinkled, the fire crackled, and the brandy was wonderful. Emily took a seat beside him again, and gave him a warm smile.

"That's it, honey. A little closer. Good girl!" Rosie whispered encouragingly.

"Emily." Thomas seemed to be struggling with something, then totally gave up. He reached over and took the glass from her hand, setting it aside. Then he pulled her into his arms and kissed her senseless.

Emily sighed with the pleasure of it. The feel of Thomas's shirt beneath her fingers, the rough scratchiness of his beard against her skin, the erotic promise of his touch that simply begged to be fulfilled. Everything worked against her resolve not to succumb to his physical charms. The silk wrapper caressed her, inflaming her already heated skin, the brandy and wine intoxicated her, and Thomas's kiss made her blood throb. She pulled him even closer, wanting more. Slowly he relaxed against her, and his mouth eased from hers. He embraced her tightly, tenderly, for a few long minutes. Emily never would have believed it was so pleasurable just to be held. She felt so warm, so safe, and so wanted. Then she heard something.

He was snoring.

"He's asleep!" Emily cried out, in her dismay forgetting to be circumspect about talking to Rosie.

"Are you certain he's out?" Rosie whispered.

Emily stood, her heart dropping in disappointment as Thomas's head rolled to one side. He snuggled more deeply into the couch, then resumed snoring.

"Yes," Emily pronounced. Her body ached with unfulfilled sexual promise, her blood still rang in her ears, and she was mortified that Rosie had witnessed her humiliation.

"Well! I never had a man do that in my house before!" Rosie sounded personally offended.

"Maybe this will work to our benefit," Emily said practically.

"What do you mean?" Rosie asked, perplexed. "You don't mean to . . . pick his pockets? We didn't even do that! At least, not much."

Emily was already unbuttoning Thomas's coat. "I'm not going to steal anything, I'm just looking for information. I have to find out who he is. *Especially* now."

Rosie gasped, but Emily ignored her. Thomas's snores grew louder, and Emily was sure it would take Sherman's army to wake him at this point. A true detective would never let such an opportunity go by. She slipped her fingers deftly into his pocket and pulled out a letter.

"Read it, sweetie," Rosie encouraged, all her objections forgotten.

"It's dated June fourteenth, and it's from the Wells Fargo Company." Emily's brow wrinkled in puzzlement. The same firm from whom that two-million-dollar payroll had been stolen. She opened the missive and scanned it quickly.

"Dear Thomas," it read.

> We received your last communication, and are glad to hear that you are making progress. There has been no fresh evidence to report from our side, nor any indication yet of the whereabouts of the gold.
>
> In answer to your inquiry, Miss Potter is exactly what she appears to be. Her former neighbors describe her as quiet but eccentric, and the Boston police speak in admiring terms of her detective abilities, and wish her well. It appears highly unlikely that she knows about the gold, or her father's nefarious activities.
>
> If there is anything else I can tell you, let me know. We are eagerly awaiting your results.
>   Will Jenkins.

Emily frowned, rereading the letter, particularly the part about herself. From somewhere high above, she heard Rosie's laugh.

"Looks like your gentleman friend was as suspicious of you as you are of him," the bordello girl hooted. Emily only nodded slowly, lost in thought. What did Thomas have to do with Wells Fargo?

Thomas awoke with a start a few hours later. At first, he couldn't believe what he was seeing: couples in various sexual positions cavorting in erotic splendor. Leaping to his feet, he gradually recognized his surroundings.

He was at the bordello. Emily's bordello. Emily herself was gone, probably to bed. The fire had long since died, and the gaslights had been turned down to a rosy gleam. Two empty glasses stood on the table beside the sofa, and he reluctantly remembered the brandy and the kiss that followed.

Surely he didn't . . . couldn't have . . . The wine and brandy had gone to his head, he knew that, especially after yesterday's exertion and the shock of seeing Lizzie's housekeeper dead. His fury returned as he recalled Emily's stubborn refusal to listen to him, her insistence on using the bordello as a millinery shop, then her odd reversal. She'd invited him to dinner, seemed to want his friendship. . . .

Friendship. His body still burned and he knew it hadn't happened. He hadn't made love to her. Maybe it was for the best, for this situation got more complicated by the moment. He had practically declared himself her bodyguard, and now she wanted to be friends? It simply didn't add up.

But then, Emily wasn't like other women. He strode to the bookcase and fingered one of her hats, amazed at the elegant stitching, the beautiful feathers that crowned it, and the artistic arrangement of flowers and veiling. It was so different from her usual logical approach to everything, and so . . . romantic.

His fingers left the hat and wandered to the books. There were volumes on poisons, weapons, and crimes. There were legends of outlaws, train robbers, and common lawbreakers. There were detailed accounts of Jesse James, Sam Bass, Butch Cassidy, and Billy the Kid. Every two-bit ruffian whose name had ever graced a wanted poster, and even some who hadn't, had a place on her bookshelf.

Thomas sighed, putting on his hat and locking the door softly behind him. Despite all the danger this case had thrown at him, it was Emily who posed the greatest threat. She was artistic, self-supporting, unrealistic, nosy, terribly clever, and completely and utterly beautiful. And he had just made her a promise that would force him to be around her every single day. He didn't think he could stand the torture.

Thomas climbed the stairs of the boardinghouse. Emily Potter had just become his responsibility. And now he was going to have to live with it.

13

The Man with the Wooden Leg

"I'm sorry, miss, but you cannot have access to my newspapers. Run along, dear, I'm busy."

Emily stared at the newspaper editor, unable to believe what she was hearing. This couldn't be happening again! Yet the man squinted once more into the light and leaned over his copy as if she weren't there. With a cup of coffee in one hand and a pencil in the other, he read over the morning paper, grunting in satisfaction.

Emily sighed. It was going to be another uphill battle. She'd left the house bright and early that morning, hoping to avoid Thomas's interference. Even though she had pretended she would no longer investigate, she didn't trust him to believe her. Yet it was oddly comforting to know the handsome preacher-turned-Watson was there to protect her, if she needed him.

Still, the last thing she needed was another obstinate male getting in her way. Forcing a smile, she stepped between the copies of the *Rocky Mountain News*, moving closer. A huge Hoe press took up half the room, and she practically had to climb around it to reach the tables covered with papers, gas lamps, files, and a telegraph where the newspaperman worked.

He looked up impatiently. "Look, I told you, Miss—"

"Potter," Emily finished for him, extending a hand to introduce herself.

His keen eyes swept over her and she counted three different expressions that crossed his face. Emily knew he was reviewing the rumors about her, and correlating them with his own judgments. She didn't fault him for it, for as a newsman, it was a necessary part of his job. Just as seeing those papers was part of hers. He ignored her outstretched hand, and Emily let it drop, leaning forward to meet his eyes.

"I only want to look through your papers," she said evenly. "I won't damage anything. I'm doing some research, and I need access to old copies of the paper."

"What kind of research?" The man cocked his head at her like a sparrow.

Emily brightened. Maybe, once he understood her need, he would be more willing to help. "I am investigating my father's death. I have copies of the Boston *Atlas*, but I thought a local paper would have a more thorough account."

"I'm sorry, but I won't allow that," he said in a

paternal tone. "While I understand your curiosity, this is a matter for the sheriff. Leave it where it belongs. I have two daughters just about your age, and they, too, love to read the sensational stuff. Murders and mayhem! If you don't mind, I've got a paper to put to bed. You can leave the same way you came in."

Emily sputtered helplessly, "But I don't understand! What objection could you possibly have to me looking at the files?"

The newsman plunked down his coffee cup and glared at her. "Miss Potter, I gave you my answer. If you continue in this manner, you will leave me no choice but to summon the sheriff myself. Now be a good girl and run along."

His voice had changed. Now he was actually pleading. Emily glanced toward the files, her logical mind racing. Could she break in here later, and get what she needed? Her eyes went toward the window, and she began to form a plan. The editor had gotten up and was starting to walk toward her. Before he could physically throw her out, the door opened and a tall man in preacher's garb strode inside.

"Thomas!" Emily and the newsman declared at the same time.

"Morning, Miss Potter. Mr. Tebbel. Is there a problem here? I could hear your voices in the street."

The newspaperman's demeanor changed immediately, while Emily stood by in stunned silence.

"No, there's no problem, Reverend. Miss Potter wanted access to my files. I told her no. I advised her to leave investigation to the sheriff."

"Sound advice," Thomas agreed somberly. Emily

wanted to kill him. But a moment later, he surprised her again. "Still, I don't think it would do any harm to let her look at a few articles. Miss Potter came all the way from Boston to claim an inheritance that was most unusual, to say the least. Her curiosity about her father and his death are natural. I think you could provide her some comfort by accommodating her request."

The newsman didn't look convinced. Thomas stood beside him and laid a hand on his shoulder. "I'll stay with her and make sure she puts everything back in order."

It was one thing to push Emily around. It was quite another to bully a preacher who had made it known he would do what it took to get what he wanted—in spite of his collar. The editor swallowed hard, feeling the pressure of Thomas's hand on his shoulder. Nodding, he gestured to a wide table with more empty space than the others.

"You can look at them here. But don't take anything home, and don't mark them up."

"Thank you." Emily smiled gratefully, a smile she extended to Thomas as well. Although it bothered her to accept his help, she had to admit that he'd gotten much further with the newsman than she had. Maybe this partnership really would work. He returned her smile, and the twinkle in his eye reminded her uncomfortably of the previous night. Holding her head as high as she could, Emily reached for her case, then turned to the filing cabinets.

Mr. Tebbel was meticulous, if nothing else. Emily

could see that the files were arranged chronologically. Fingering through them until she found the date of her father's and Rosie's death, Emily took out the paper and laid it on the table. Oblivious to everyone around her, she scanned the articles, taking copious notes, squeaking with satisfaction when she found an item of importance, grunting when something didn't match her theories. She didn't stop with that issue, however, for in subsequent ones she found more details, and in previous ones, a few additional references to her father. One obscure item that seemed unrelated caught her attention, and she copied it down word for word.

Thomas watched her in amusement. He accepted a cup of coffee from the editor, and tried hard not to respond when the man made a twirling motion beside his ear, indicating that Emily wasn't playing with a full deck. He sank down into a chair and picked up one of the papers, wondering what in God's name she thought she was going to find. He chuckled at the sudden memory of her expression when he'd walked in. Emily had looked as if she'd seen a ghost.

Thank God Darrel had come to fetch him when he did. Thomas knew Emily was determined. He also knew that in spite of her agreement give up detecting, it would take a bit of doing to make that happen. But she was like a bloodhound on a scent. Intrigued in spite of himself, Thomas watched her dig through the papers. Research was fine, but nothing beat action. Yet as his thoughts wandered back over the last few days, he had to admit that he hadn't made much progress on his own. China Blue was gone or in hiding, Lizzie had disappeared, and the whereabouts of Bertie Evans, the housekeeper from Shangri-La, were still unknown.

Yet the murderer was closing in, he was sure of it. Although it went against his grain to encourage her, Thomas felt that at least her research was less dangerous than her roaming the countryside investigating. And he meant what he'd said to her last night.

He'd keep her safe, no matter what.

The noon hour arrived and the editor stopped the huge press. Piles of fresh newspapers lay in a neat bundle at his feet, and the scent of paper and ink filled the air. A pack of newspaper boys gathered outside, and as the clock struck twelve, the editor opened the door and stood to one side.

"All right, no running. Get these papers delivered. And remember, if I find a single paper in the trash or by the railroad tracks, you're all fired. Understand?"

The urchins raced in, snatched up papers, and raced back out. Emily never looked up. When the room cleared, the editor indicated the boardwalk.

"I'm going to get lunch. Like to join me?"

"No, thanks. I'll stay and help Miss Potter. I feel it's my Christian duty."

The editor appeared perplexed, but nodded and left the office. When he was gone, Thomas picked up Emily's notes and began to read through them. As soon as she noticed what he was doing, she tried to snatch them back, but Thomas refused to release them. Looking up, he faced her outrage with a frown.

"Emily, what has this got to do with the case? Your

notes are all about some outlaw named Emmet Colter."

"You're right, Thomas, it has absolutely nothing to do with it. Now could you please give them back?"

He held them closer to his chest. "Emily, I thought we had agreed to be partners. How can I help you if I don't know what you're doing?"

Emily sighed in resignation. He obviously planned to make good his threat, and there was nothing to be gained from fighting him. "Read this!" She thrust the paper under his nose.

Thomas scanned the newsprint, but he had no idea what had caught Emily's attention. There was an article about the elections, one about a robbery, then one about the drought. The rest appeared to be editorials and items of local interest. He didn't see anything that had any bearing on her father or the killings.

"What am I supposed to be looking at?" Thomas asked, mystified.

"Right there. The robbery. Don't you see?"

Thomas reread the article. It was about Emmet Colter, an outlaw who had plagued mining towns and the railroad alike in the last few years. There was a price on his head; Thomas had seen the wanted poster in the post office himself. Apparently there had been gunfire following the robbery of the Union Pacific. Colter had made off with a few thousand dollars, but he'd been shot in the leg as a result.

"So?" He handed it back to her.

Emily stared at him as if he were an imbecile.

"Don't you see? Our first real break!" When Thomas shook his head, Emily sighed. "Thomas, this article is dated four months before the murders. Lizzie said my father was afraid of a man with a wooden leg. Colter was shot in the leg, and he couldn't have gone to a real doctor, for any doctor would have reported him. He probably treated it himself, and gangrene set in."

Thomas couldn't keep the admiration from his voice, although he tried. "Much as I hate to admit it, you may have something there. I still don't think you should be endangering yourself this way, but I have to give you your due. That's a damned good job of detection."

She blushed, and Thomas realized she was more pleased with his comment than she would have been had he praised her beauty. Her eyes shone, and she folded her hands together like a child.

"You really think so?"

"Yes. It's not conclusive, but it makes sense. I'll give this information to the sheriff and maybe he can find Emmet. But if I catch you chasing after an outlaw yourself, there's going to be hell to pay. Emmet isn't a man to toy with. Just like the housekeeper, a man like that wouldn't think twice . . ."

Thomas's voice trailed off as he realized what he'd just said.

Emily clapped her hands in glee. "I'm right, aren't I? You think Emmet was involved in her death! Thomas, the trail is getting warmer! Don't worry, I have no intention of becoming one of the Colter gang's victims. I'll be careful."

The editor returned before Thomas could argue further. It was all he could do to get Emily out of the office before the newsman murdered her.

"Goodness, he certainly wasn't very friendly."

"Emily, this is his life's work. I know you may find it hard to believe, but most men resent a woman who pokes around in their business."

"Yes, but—"

Emily was interrupted when a woman ran out of her house and accosted Thomas. Tears streamed from her eyes as she stopped in front of the preacher, clasping her hands together in supplication.

"Preacher! Please, you've got to come! My old pa is passing on, and we need someone to read him the last rites, proper-like."

Emily glanced at Thomas. His jaw had tightened and he held the woman's hand nervously, shaking his head.

"I've got other obligations—"

"But you must come! If you don't say the prayers over him, he's doomed to damnation! My poor pa . . ."

The woman's wails grew louder. She was well dressed, obviously affluent, and used to being obeyed. Other people stopped, watching and whispering. The woman fell to her knees, hugging herself, her sobs growing more wretched by the moment. Emily reached down and helped her up, comforting her with soft words.

"It's all right. Reverend Hall will come. There is nothing else pressing right now, is there, Thomas?"

He looked like he wanted to strangle her. The

expression disappeared as quickly as it came and resignation followed. "I'll go get my prayer book."

"The Reverend Flatter never needed his book," the woman declared, wiping the tears from her face. "He had them all here." She tapped a finger against her temple.

"I like to be accurate," Thomas said pointedly. "Especially when dealing with eternal damnation."

"But there isn't time!" the woman declared. She grabbed Thomas's coat and began dragging him toward the house. "He's liable to go at any moment!"

Emily could have sworn she heard Thomas curse as the woman pulled him along. More people had gathered to watch. The woman yanked Thomas through her front door and up to her father's bedside.

Emily stood a little behind him, watching Thomas lean over an elderly man who was obviously dying. His breath came in wheezes, and his eyes were closed. They opened slightly when Thomas entered the room, but they seemed unable to focus on anyone except his daughter.

"Adelia? Is that you?"

"I'm here, Pa, and I've brought the minister with me. Don't worry, you won't go to your grave without a proper blessing."

The man's eyes closed again, and his lined face relaxed. Thomas's presence seemed to have brought him some peace already.

The preacher stared down at the dying man. The woman stood on the other side, then looked questioningly at Thomas.

"Well?"

Thomas cleared his throat, then gestured awkwardly at the bed. "Do you have some holy oils or something? I believe that's part of the process."

"Oils?" The woman's nose wrinkled. "Where would I get oils?"

"Perhaps some nice bath oil would do," Emily proposed. "Or cooking oil. Thomas wasn't able to fetch his supplies, after all."

The woman nodded, and Thomas threw Emily a look of such gratitude that she had to hide a smile. The daughter returned seconds later with a bottle of pungent bath oil that reeked even before he unstoppered it. Thomas ceremoniously opened the flask and doused his hand with the stuff. As Emily watched him fumbling with the bath oil, the last trace of uncertainty about Thomas Hall's status as a preacher left her mind.

He didn't have the first idea what he was doing.

Everyone waited as Thomas stared at the man, mumbling a chant that no one could hear. Emily held back her comments as the lavender-scented bath oil dripped down his hand and onto the man's head. The elderly man sighed, sniffing the air as Thomas made a crude attempt to anoint his forehead. He dabbed at the man's face with his sleeve, trying to blot some of the spilled oil. Tiny droplets of sweat beaded on his skin, and he bit his lip. The woman frowned and was about to comment when Thomas raised his hands.

"Good Lord above, have mercy on the soul of this

man. He led a good life, practiced your word, tread the holy path. . . ."

The woman tugged at his sleeve. Thomas glanced over at her and she shook her head. "My pa made his fortune gambling. I don't know if that's the good Lord's work—"

"I'm sure He understands," Thomas answered quickly. Emily choked, and he gave her a quelling glance before starting the unusual prayer again.

"May he rest in peace through eternity. *Et cum spirit Tu. Tu. O.* Amen."

"Amen." The woman nodded, then beamed at Thomas. "That was a very good last rites, though I've never seen it done quite that way."

"Neither has he," Emily couldn't resist adding.

Thomas shot her a look, then glanced back at the woman. "I'm sorry. I could have been more eloquent if I'd had my prayer book."

"No, I thought it was wonderful. Didn't you, Pa?"

The man didn't respond. It took Emily a long moment to realize that he was no longer with them. Astonished, she glanced at Thomas, and saw the understanding come to him as well. A peaceful silence fell over the room as the man's spirit departed. The woman fell to her knees and resumed her sobbing. Emily laid a comforting hand on her shoulder, then looked back at Thomas. He indicated the door, and they quietly withdrew, leaving the woman alone with her grief.

Outside, Thomas absently smoothed back his hair, then paused as the scent of lavender hit him. He sniffed his hand and groaned, and Emily burst into laughter.

"You're the prettiest-smelling preacher I've ever met."

"Very funny." He gave up any attempt to remove the oil, aware now that his efforts only rubbed it deeper into his skin.

They had reached her door and Thomas stood undecidedly on the porch. Emily's face lifted to his and her smile reached her eyes.

"I'm not going to ask how you knew where I was, but thank you for your help. That newsman had no intention of assisting me. Without your . . . interference, I wouldn't have gotten anywhere."

"You're welcome. But I meant what I said. Stay away from Emmet. I'll give the sheriff the lead." After another moment he turned and started to walk away, then stopped in his path. "You are done for the day?"

"Sleuthing, yes." Emily grinned. "But I do need to work on some hats. My reception is Tuesday, and I have lots to do."

"I see." He looked at her regretfully. "Miss Potter, do you think it inappropriate to have supper with me in town one night this week? Maybe Wednesday? I'd like to repay you for your kindness last night."

He was referring to the meal, of course. Emily had to fight to keep from blushing as she remembered their kiss—and the fact that she'd rifled through his pockets when he fell asleep.

"I think that would be nice," she agreed, a bit surprised at how nice it really did sound.

"Good. I'll come for you around seven. Is that all right?"

Emily's eyes searched his, then she smiled. "Seven would be just fine."

"Now I know he's lying."

Rosie materialized in the mirror, yawning as if Emily had awakened her. She rubbed at her eyes, then glanced around the room in bewilderment. Her gaze fell on Emily and her beautiful brows lifted in surprise.

"What did you say, honey?"

"I said I know he isn't a preacher." Emily tossed aside her bag and sat meditatively on the bed. "There isn't the slightest doubt in my mind."

"How do you know?" In spite of her fatigue, Rosie appeared intrigued.

"He was asked to perform the last rites in town today. You should have seen him—he looked like a bachelor handling an infant. He didn't have the faintest idea what to do."

Rosie clapped her hands together. "What fun! What happened?"

"He muddled through it, but he knew I was onto him. So he's in disguise, but why was he investigating me? And what does he have to do with Wells Fargo? Thomas Hall is certainly a tangle in this web."

Emily flopped onto her stomach, her mind racing with possibilities. Rosie frowned, her painted beauty mark dimpling. Then Emily sat up suddenly, her eyes sparkling.

"I know! I'll search his room!"

"What?" Rosie looked at her as if she were mad.

"It's the only way," Emily said logically. "I can't continue to work with him until I know if he's friend or foe. Otherwise he'll know everything I do and could use it against me. Somewhere in his room, there has to be something telling who and what he is."

Rosie chuckled. "I see. That shouldn't be too hard. Most men are more than eager to show you to their bedroom. But how are you going to pull it off, honey?"

"He asked me to supper on Wednesday," Emily said. "Maybe that would be a good time to . . . accompany him back to his place." Emily blushed at the thought.

"Sure!" Rosie agreed. "Tell him you need to change in privacy, or something like that. Men will agree to just about anything if they think it's seduction."

Emily wasn't entirely sure what she meant, but a possible scenario began to emerge in her head. "Now that he's sworn to be my bodyguard . . ."

"What?" It was Rosie's turn to look surprised.

Emily nodded. "He means it, too. He followed me to the newspaper office this morning. I don't know how he knew where I was, especially at that hour. I swear he must have eyes in the back of his head."

"Hmmm." Rosie considered this development, and her smile broadened. "Why, honey, I think this man's sweeter on you than we gave him credit for. Why else would he put his own neck at risk to protect you? Whether he wants to admit it or not, you've gotten under his skin."

"Do you really think so?" Emily couldn't hide her pleasure at the thought.

"Sure, I think so, and why not? You're pretty, you have a wonderful figure, you're bright and fun and . . . well, I could just go on and on."

Emily looked into the mirror beside Rosie. For the first time in her life, she didn't see her crooked spectacles, the cat hair that clung to her dress, her unfashionable outfit or straight nose. She saw herself as Rosie did, someone pretty, fascinating, and . . . desirable.

"Maybe . . . perhaps there is some hope. . . ." Emily hardly dared to voice her thoughts.

"Why, of course there is. He'd be crazy not to fall for you. You just keep coming to me for advice, and we'll make Wednesday a night he'll never forget." Rosie brushed her hands together as if it were as easy as pie.

Emily smiled, though her practical mind was already planning.

14

The Reception

"How does it look?"

Emily stood back to survey her work. The parlor was aglow from her scrubbing, and candles lent their soft gleam to the hardwood floors. Crepe paper twirled between the chandelier and the fireplace, making the room look festive and inviting, and doilies added a lacy touch beneath the serving dishes.

Darrel stood by the table, his cocklebur hair plastered into place with Rowland's macassar oil. He was dressed in a white shirt and his Sunday-best dark trousers, and at a distance, could pass muster for a very short waiter. He appeared proud of his position, and practiced hoisting a silver tray on one arm, balancing the brimming Champagne glasses. Emily held her breath as they tottered precariously, but so far none of them had been broken.

The large parlor table had been transformed into

a buffet, and Emily looked over the result with satisfaction. She'd been able to scrape up enough money for a ham, thinly sliced, cold potato salad, snap beans, fruit, cheese, and peach ice cream. She even found some tongue as an appetizer, and a meringue pie, which provided a touch of elegance to the rustic spread. Lastly, she'd managed to entice the wine merchant into parting with a bottle of Champagne for a pittance. The golden liquid bubbled merrily in the glasses, announcing to everyone that a party was about to happen.

It would work. Emily smiled, pleased with herself. She glanced down at her dress, a simple gown of beige trimmed with fur. Although Rosie thought it boring, Emily had to explain that it was considered elegant, and most proper. The house was bawdy enough, and Emily felt strongly that she must appear as sophisticated as possible to make the women feel at home. Smoothing a wrinkle from the gown, she heard Rosie's laughter.

"You look grand, honey, stop worrying! And I really do like that dress, although one of mine would have been just as nice. Everything looks right pretty."

"You think so?" Emily asked and saw Darrel glance up in confusion. Frowning, she remembered that he couldn't hear Rosie. "I just said I think everything looks all right," she told him.

"Oh." Darrel nodded, though he plainly thought Emily a little daft.

"Yes, it looks wonderful. Those ladies will be piling in at any moment! You'll be a spectacular success!"

Emily stood beside the fireplace. Deciding that she looked too eager there, she moved to the bookcase and pretended to be looking through her volumes. Thinking that might look too scholarly, she perched on the edge of Rosie's settee with a glass of Champagne. Watson mewed and sat under the table, eyeing the food, while Darrel stood at attention.

No one came.

The clock struck half past eight, and Emily began to pace the floor. The Champagne fizzed less exuberantly, the ham began to get shiny and the tapers dripped onto the tablecloth. The player piano tinkled out a song, while Darrel removed all but one glass from the tray, his arms obviously aching.

Still no one came.

By nine o'clock, the potato salad had begun to congeal, the ice cream was now a bowl of milk and peaches, and the Champagne had lost all of its pretense to fizz. The piano continued to play, but the music came out in tired strains. Dismissing Darrel, Emily collapsed into a chair and was forced to face the truth.

No one was coming.

Tears, hot and stinging, came to her eyes, and to her intense shame, she began to sob out loud. Never could she remember having been so blatantly rejected before. The room swam in firelight and colors as she looked through her tears at the bawdy ceiling, the crimson chairs, the hats and the books. She was a failure. She'd extended a hand toward the women of town, and that hand had been firmly slapped.

"Oh, don't cry honey, I'm sure something went

wrong. Maybe no one saw your posters." Rosie's voice came from nowhere and the scent of roses filled the room.

"I'm not crying," Emily sobbed. "It's no use, Rosie. They don't understand me. And they certainly don't like me."

"It's not that bad," Rosie assured her, though she too seemed completely at a loss. "Maybe they need to get to know you. You know, at church functions or something."

"My money won't hold out much longer." Emily cried like a disconsolate little girl. "I don't have time to go to church and court the women! I have to get the business off the ground, but if they won't come . . ."

The rest was too difficult to finish. If they didn't come, Emily would be forced to pack up, go home, and quit the case. There would be no investigation, no excitement, no chasing after clues and untangling the mystery. She would never know who'd murdered her father, and there would be no Thomas, either. Emily was amazed at the jolt of pain that followed that thought. She would have to return to Boston, to her quiet existence, where years of spinsterhood and books lay before her, doomed forever to imagine "what if."

Watson sprang up into her lap and Emily hugged the cat, grateful for his warmth. The disappointment she suffered was keen. Nothing would fill the emptiness inside of her, nothing except . . .

A knock at the door. Watson leaped from her arms, and Emily brushed frantically at the dampness staining her cheeks. Rising to her feet, she smoothed her dress, while Rosie whispered encouragement.

"That's them! They've decided to come! Now pinch your cheeks, honey, you look right peaked."

Emily obeyed, then walked smoothly to the door as if nothing could possibly be wrong. She opened the portal and forced a smile, her heart in her throat. She would be the most charming hostess ever, even if only one person showed up. In the darkness, she saw a lone figure standing on the porch and for a moment she thought everything would work out after all.

And then she realized it was Thomas.

"Hello, Emily, I just thought I'd stop by and see how the reception's going. . . ." His voice trailed off as he looked behind her and saw the table laden with food, and no one to eat it.

Emily straightened, trying to appear as dignified as possible. She looked him in the eye and tried desperately to keep the pathetic quiver from her voice. "Thomas, you were right. They didn't come."

The preacher looked at her for a long moment, put his hat aside, then took her in his arms. Emily melted into the comforting warmth, the acceptance, the understanding in his embrace. The sobs came fast and furious now, and he held her more tightly, smoothing her hair, quietly caressing her.

"Shh. Go ahead and cry if it makes you feel better. Emily, I'm so sorry. You can't honestly think I'd be happy about this, can you?"

She looked up at him and shook her head. "No. I don't suppose that would be Christian. But you were right, Thomas. They don't like me and won't accept me. I've failed."

"Stop that." Thomas practically carried her to the sofa, holding her as if she were made of precious china. "They don't know you, Emily. All they know is what they've heard. Think about it. You come into town, masquerade as a saloon girl, scare the bejesus out of the townspeople with your science of deduction, and then invite them to a whorehouse for tea and cakes. Don't you think it appears a little odd?"

She pulled away from him and nodded, suddenly unable to argue with the logic of his words. "But I just thought—"

"I know what you thought, and it wasn't a bad idea. The women just have to get to know you, then they'll understand."

"It's no use." Emily looked up at him, her eyes swollen from crying. Self-consciously, she tried to smooth back her hair, but she knew she looked a fright no matter what she did. "I need the money, Thomas. That's why I had the reception—to get my business off the ground. Now I'll have to go home. I know that's what you've been encouraging me to do, but I can't stand the thought! Oh, God, Thomas, I don't know how I can do it!"

Her sobs welled up anew and she struggled valiantly not to cry again. Thomas stared into her face for a long moment. Then he sighed as if coming to a difficult conclusion.

"All right. This goes against everything I believe in, for I do think you're safer in Boston. But I can't stand to see you like this. There's a shop in town that would be perfect for your millinery business. I spoke to the owner this morning, and he said you could have it for five dollars a week. It's located just outside the dry goods store and the bank, so you'll have plenty of traffic. All you need to do is hang out your shingle."

"You don't understand," Emily said forlornly. Her hands folded in her lap, and when she looked up, he could see how hard the next words were for her. "I don't have five dollars. It might as well be five million."

"I see." Thomas frowned, then his gaze fell on the discarded paintings stacked in the corner.

"I've got it, Emily. Why don't you sell off the paintings?"

Emily heard Rosie's gasp, and her head came up quickly. She glanced at the empty spaces where the portraits had hung, and the blush deepened on her cheeks. "You mean, the nudes?"

"Yes." Thomas chuckled at her expression. "I know some of the men in town would pay a fortune for one of those. And the Silverdust would certainly be interested. What do you think?"

Emily nodded, her heart lightening. "I think that's a grand idea. Do you think it will work?"

Thomas nodded. "I'll take care of the details. I don't think you hawking paintings of nude women will add much to your reputation. And as a preacher, I'll have to get an intermediary to help sell them. But I can make the arrangements tomorrow, then we'll go see the shopkeeper. Is that a deal?"

Giggling, Emily threw herself into his arms. "It's a

deal. Thank you, Thomas. You have no idea what this means to me."

Gently he disengaged himself from her embrace. Emily looked up, puzzled, but Thomas looked decidedly uncomfortable. She couldn't hide her disappointment, especially since those delicious sensations she always felt in his arms had started to stir up inside her, hot and thick. He got stiffly to his feet, and distracted her by pointing to the table.

"I haven't had supper, so a plate of that ham would be welcome," he said hoarsely. "Do you mind?"

"No, of course not." She practically skipped to her feet to fetch him the meal. She made him a heaping platter, gathering a smaller portion for herself at the same time. Even Watson got his share, for he had been sitting beneath the table patiently all evening.

They drank flat Champagne, ate their fill, and talked. For the first time since she'd met him, Emily felt they really were beginning to be friends. Her heart warmed at the thought, and hope now burned again inside her. He had come to her rescue—again—like the knights of old, pulling her from the depths of despair. Surely now he would tell her the truth about who he really was, and why he was involved in her case.

They had scarcely finished eating when a sharp knock sounded at the door. Emily and Thomas looked at each other in surprise, then Emily got to her feet. She opened the door expecting Darrel, but an elderly woman stood on the porch steps.

"Hello. Are you Miss Potter?"

"Yes."

"Are you having a party tonight?" The old woman's voice came in staccato notes.

"Why, yes!" Emily said, delighted.

"Well, then. Can I come in, or are you going to make me stand on the porch all night?"

Stunned, Emily stepped back and held open the door. The woman extended her hand briskly. "I'm Eleanor Hamill. I saw your poster today, and I've heard a lot about you. I meant to come much earlier, but I plumb forgot and fell asleep by the fireplace. Am I too late?"

Thomas rose and came to the door, his hat in hand. "I'll be going, Miss Emily. Wonderful party. I really enjoyed myself."

The preacher nodded to the woman, then stepped away into the darkness. Emily felt a peculiar lurch in her heart as he left, then turned toward the woman, who looked approvingly after him.

"That's that new preacher, isn't it? I told those old biddies in the sewing circle that you were all right, they just weren't giving you a chance. Wait until I tell them that even the preacher thought enough to stop by. Here, take my cane."

Emily took the woman's cane and bonnet from her outstretched hands, trying not to laugh at her peremptory manner. Eleanor fixed herself a plate, not saying a word about the abundance of food and lack of guests. Instead she seated herself beside the fire and ate her meal with obvious relish.

"Interesting surroundings," the woman remarked

between mouthfuls of food. Her gaze drifted around the room, taking in the crimson-and-gilt chairs, the portrait of Rosie hanging over the fireplace, the bar and the piano. Finally she looked upward at the ceiling with a squint. "Always wanted to see the inside of this place. My eyes aren't what they used to be, but that looks just like the Sistine Chapel. Ever been to Europe?"

"No," Emily said, choking back her laughter. She studied the woman before her with interest. Eleanor was obviously well-to-do, and had dowager written all over her. She also had a no-nonsense attitude that Emily liked right away. Her gown was of the best quality, tailored almost like a man's suit, and her gloves were of the finest calfskin. When she removed the gloves Emily could see that her index finger was covered with a rubber hood, and her cuff was smeared with ink. Her small glasses were perched on the edge of her nose so she could look over them, and her sharp blue gaze seemed to see everything at once. Smiling, Emily gestured to her books.

"Since I observe you are a great reader, please feel free to enjoy any of my works."

The woman chuckled, then put aside her plate. "I am not surprised at your observation, since I've heard of your powers. I am a reader of the *Strand,* and love the Sherlock Holmes stories. As soon as I heard what you were able to do, I knew exactly who your mentor was. I, too, mourn his loss."

"You are a fan?" Emily was astonished anew by this woman.

Eleanor Hamill chuckled. "But of course. My

dear, we have much to discuss." She raised an arm and Emily gasped at the black armband she wore, just like her own—the official method of mourning Mr. Sherlock Holmes.

Thomas walked past the boardinghouse toward the saloon. Although it wasn't seemly for a preacher to visit such a place—especially not twice—he didn't care. He needed a drink. He needed a dozen drinks to figure out what the hell he'd just done.

He'd made it easier for Emily to stay. Why?

Cursing under his breath, he pushed through the swinging doors and strode into the smoke-filled room. Faro dealers took up one side of the saloon, while cowboys danced with brightly gowned girls. The barkeep looked his way and Thomas gestured to the bottles behind him.

"Whiskey."

An amber glass was pushed in front of him and Thomas downed it in one shot. The liquor burned all the way to his gut, but didn't bring him much relief. Thoughts of Emily wouldn't leave his head, and he cursed himself ten times for being a fool.

She was more trouble than she was worth. Yet when he'd seen her forlorn face and witnessed the humiliation she'd suffered, he knew he had to do something. But he also knew he'd been avoiding an important issue for too long. For when he succeeded in *his* mission, Emily would suffer much greater pain than she did today. He felt as if he were riding at a flat-out gallop to a place called disaster.

15

Emmet Colter Makes a Move

"Well, honey, you're a success!"

Rosie beamed as Emily entered the bedroom. It was well past midnight, and Mrs. Hamill had just left. Tired as she was, Emily couldn't stop the smile of pleasure at Rosie's words.

"Yes, it was a success, in its own way. Eleanor Hamill is a real Sherlock Holmes devotee. Why, the minutiae she remembers is just marvelous! And she has the most fantastic brain. I could talk with her for hours."

"I think that's just wonderful." Rosie yawned, stretching her arms over her head in such a way that Emily couldn't help but observe that Rosie was dressed for bed in a black negligee so sheer it made her blush. But Rosie didn't notice, for she continued chatting away.

"She seemed like she was real interested in you, and would take you under her wing."

"I think so." Emily nodded in agreement. "She's already asked me to tea, and to meet with the Ladies' Sewing Circle. I sure hope it works. Thomas is going to help me set up shop in town, so it looks like we just might be on our way." Emily looked fondly at the reflection in the mirror. "You know, Rosie, I never thanked you for your support. You are . . . I mean were . . . are . . . a good friend."

"Why, thank you, honey." Rosie looked genuinely touched. Her beautiful eyes seemed almost misty, and she glanced away, embarrassed at the show of emotion. Brushing at her cheeks, she looked back at Emily, and her expression was filled with both appreciation and regret. "That's real sweet of you to say. Actually, you're my first real friend, too, outside the working girls. I'm learning all kinds of things from you. I only wish I were still alive to make use of them."

The silence that followed was almost palpable. Emily had to acknowledge to herself that Rosie might someday simply vanish from her life. As painful as that thought was, Emily refused to give it credence. No one really knew when their time would come. She would simply enjoy Rosie's company all the more, knowing it for the gift it was.

"Now that we have that out of the way," Emily said briskly, returning to her logical thoughts, "it's time to take the next step in the investigation. Tomorrow I'm going to find Bertie Evans."

"Hmm." Rosie frowned, her beautiful brows

drawing closer together. "I don't think your preacher man's going to like this one bit."

"He doesn't have to know," Emily said practically, but her own brow wrinkled in thought. Keeping Thomas at arm's length was no longer as appealing as it once was.

The next day, Emily awoke early and worked feverishly on the hats. She wanted at least a dozen models to display in the shop, for it would show the women what she was capable of doing.

By late afternoon, she had to take a break. She rose and brushed her hands together, removing tiny snips of thread and pieces of feathers. Smiling in satisfaction, she surveyed the hats lined up on the table.

They were gorgeous. There was a white Parisian bonnet, with a plume of dove feathers and pink ruching. There was a dark blue sun hat piled high with fashionable netting, a stuffed bird, and fruit. There was a beautiful dark green day bonnet with a pale silk lining, cock feathers, and elegant fawn-colored ribbons. Beside it was a pert short velvet cap with a cocky arrangement of dried baby's breath and a neat black satin bow in the back, meant to be worn at a rakish tilt. Emily had even included a velvet snood for winter, decorated with ostrich feathers, and a yachting-style hat that was perfect for the new bicycling fad. While it wasn't a complete collection, it was a good overview of her skills.

She was pleased with her efforts. Although some of her creations had been transported from Boston, her updating had helped them tremendously, and her own good taste was apparent. There were no monstrosities in her collection, such as bonnets with stuffed mice, beetles, or lizards, nor any of question-able wearability. All were obviously well constructed, and simply beautiful.

Straightening, she put on her glasses and took up her case. On second thought, she put on one of her hats, adjusting it in the mirror until it looked perfect. A walking advertisement never hurt, she thought, ty-ing the ribbons beneath her chin. Watson, sensing that she was about to renew her sleuthing activities, leaped up to join her. Emily smiled and let him into the bag. As she was preparing to leave, Darrel ven-tured in through the back door.

"Are you going out, miss?"

Emily was about to reply, when a thought made her hesitate. Somehow Thomas had discovered her whereabouts surprisingly quickly when she'd gone to the newspaper office. The last thing she needed was for him to find out she was trying to trace Bertie Evans. Although she couldn't be sure that Darrel had informed on her, it didn't escape her attention that the boy had been hired by Thomas. She shrugged absently.

"No, I thought I'd just take a little walk. I've been working so hard on those hats, and I need some fresh air. Can you do something for me? I'd like those boxes brought down from the attic to transport the hats. If you could please take care of that now, I would appreciate it."

Darrel glanced up the stairs, then back at her.

Emily could almost hear his thoughts. Unable to come up with a graceful way out of the task, he turned and ventured toward the upper floors of the house. Emily waited until she heard the attic door slam, then snatched up her case and started toward town.

Her plan was successful. Emily strode onto the boardwalk, unhindered by Thomas. Congratulating herself on her own cleverness, Emily crossed the road and headed toward the post office. But she never saw the cowboy step out of the saloon, nor did she see him watch her enter the post office door, following her movements with dark, shifty eyes.

Inside, Emily grimaced as the clerk recognized her. Thank goodness, no one else was there, and instead of his outright rudeness she only had to endure his leering stare as she approached.

"Miss Potter. I was wondering when I'd see you again. I was hoping you'd take me up on my offer to meet me later."

Emily glared at him coldly, with all the interest a scientist shows a particularly gruesome insect he's about to dissect. Refusing to give in to his insinuation, she gestured toward his post box.

"I am trying to locate a Miss Bertie Evans," Emily explained, using the story she'd concocted last night. "She used to work at my house, and I have some letters that need to be forwarded to her."

The clerk's face fell, but he turned toward his books, grumbling. "You're the second person asking after her this week. What's so interesting about a housekeeper?"

"I have no connections with anyone else making

inquiries," Emily answered primly. "You wouldn't happen to remember who else asked for her?"

The clerk shrugged as he flipped through the huge book, but his manner softened. "That preacher man, the one that's new in town. He said she used to be in his congregation, and he wanted to invite her to his service on Sunday. Though why she'd want to come all the way from Greeley to hear him speak is beyond me. Here it is. Evans. Bertie. She's at number four Ninth Avenue, in Greeley. I'll take her mail." The clerk thrust out his hand.

"Oh, I forgot to bring it with me. Aren't I silly? I'll have to go back home and fetch it!" Emily shrugged, playing a dimwit with considerable success. There were times when it paid to be female, she thought.

The clerk seemed more annoyed than suspicious. "I'm closing in a few minutes. Bring them tomorrow."

Emily walked outside lost in thought. So intense was her analysis that she didn't notice the cowboy loitering by the post office door, scowling as he watched her go. All she could think about was Thomas, and why he was asking about Bertie Evans.

The dreaded suspicion welled up inside her again, and she knew she'd have no peace until she had some answers. Whose side was Thomas Hall on anyway?

She stood outside the shop that he'd told her about and surveyed the tiny store with its neat little window and bright green door. He was right. It was perfect. Which only added to her suspicions.

Turning abruptly, she started home. She couldn't

continue to play this cat-and-mouse game. As outrageous as it was, she would follow through with her plan. Tonight she would see Thomas, get inside his room, and look through his belongings. She would do her best to unmask him once and for all. And whatever she discovered, she would have to live with. But knowledge was far better than this uncertainty.

Emily was sure of it.

Someone entered the post office, banging the door shut behind him. The little clerk snorted in annoyance, then spoke without turning around.

"I'm closed! Whatever it is will have to wait till tomorrow!"

"I don't wait on no man," a voice said coldly.

The clerk turned slowly, his throat dry. He saw the outlaw standing at the counter. His eyes shifted from the likeness on the poster hanging right behind him, back to the man himself. Emmet Colter looked uglier and meaner than even the wanted poster indicated. His fingers were hitched in his trousers, just enough to show the handle of his gun, and his stance was menacing—or what the clerk could see of him above the counter. But it was his eyes the clerk would never forget. Cold, black, and heartless, they were the eyes of a killer.

The clerk swallowed hard. "What can I do for you?"

"Who is that woman that was just here, and what does she want?"

"Miss Potter?" the clerk stammered. "She was

asking for the address of the housekeeper who lived at Shangri-La. That's all."

Emmet's lip curled with disdain, then he spat on the floor. "I don't like that Miss Potter asking so many questions, and I especially don't like people helping her. Now, what did you tell her?"

The clerk felt as if he were going to faint. Sweat broke out on his brow. Slowly, he weighed the risks—and then the small amount of backbone he still possessed caused him to lay his finger on the books, then shrug.

"Silverton. I said she's in Silverton."

Emmet's smile broadened, and he fingered the pearl-handled pistol in his belt. "All right then. Now, if I hear you ran to the sheriff, I may have to pay you another visit, and I don't think you want that."

"No." The clerk shook his head nervously.

"Then we understand each other." Emmet tossed a coin on the counter, and the clerk closed his eyes in relief as the outlaw sauntered out the door.

Opening his eyes when he heard the door shut, the clerk exhaled the breath he'd been holding. He steadied his nerves, then drew himself up to his full five feet five inches, and brushed the coin to the floor.

He was no man's doormat. He was a representative of the U.S. Mail.

"You look wonderful."

"I feel like a plucked chicken," Emily said, trying to breathe, though the tight dress made that a challenge. Under Rosie's ministrations, she'd bathed and powdered herself, then corseted and laced her undergarments with considerable difficulty. She'd forced her feet into tiny velvet slippers, and jet earrings pinched her lobes. Yet the result was worth it. Rosie gave her an approving smile as Emily surveyed the results of her toilette with pleasure.

Rosie had been right. The red dress was perfect—the neckline daringly low and fringed with scalloped black lace, framing her face and making her skin appear like cream. The waist was tiny, but Emily had managed to squeeze into it, and the gown fell to her feet in an elegant swish of crimson satin. The bustle in the back was small, in the current fashion, and required only padding instead of the horrid steel contraptions that used to be built into dresses. Still, it felt quite strange to Emily as she turned herself to look at her silhouette, and saw that she actually had a decent figure.

"Now some lip rouge. Just lean over the mirror and I'll show you how to put it on. You made a mess of it when you went to the saloon. Purse your lips like this."

Emily giggled, then followed Rosie's suggestions. It was like nothing she could ever have imagined, seeing her face right next to that of a specter in the gilt-framed glass, especially receiving a lesson in applying lip rouge. Yet she was grateful for the assistance.

There was a knock downstairs and Emily straightened abruptly. "He's here. Are you sure I look all right?"

"You look beautiful. Now let that boy answer the

door. You don't want to appear too eager. And spray
on some of my cologne. That's right."

Emily applied a discreet dab of perfume to the
cleft between her breasts. Rosie cocked her head as
she examined her protégé. "Now remember what I
told you. Let him invite you back to his room. Act
real innocent, like you haven't any idea what he has
in mind. Then when things get hot and heavy, tell
him you need a few minutes alone, that you're overcome by passion. Men love talk like that."

Emily looked up doubtfully. "You really think that
will work?"

"Of course, honey. Now hold your shoulders high.
That's right. It makes your bosom look bigger."

Emily made her way down the steps, trying not to
fall. It was more difficult than she would have
thought, for the shoes were just too small and she
could barely take a full breath in the dress. She
couldn't imagine how women like Rosie put up with
this all the time. Yet when she entered the parlor,
Thomas's expression was worth every moment of discomfort.

"Emily?" Thomas got to his feet, his mouth falling
open in surprise. Emily came to him, her hands outstretched as Rosie had instructed, and gave him the
full benefit of her smile.

"Hello, Thomas." Her voice sounded sultry, even
to her own ears. That, she had also learned from
Rosie.

"You look . . . wonderful." There was a burning in
his eyes as he took in the sight of her. "It amazes me
to see the two sides of you. It's almost as if there's the

Emily I know every day, and then this exotic woman that you keep in hiding."

Emily smiled at his compliment. She noticed that he had changed from his minister's garb to a suit, which looked unbelievably good on his lean frame. His coat was black with satin-covered buttons, and his trousers were a gray stripe, subdued and very stylish. He wore an immaculate white shirt and a gray tie, which had been knotted in the newest fashion. Yet he appeared very much the country gentleman, elegant and extremely masculine.

Emily felt her heart flutter. "You look very nice, too. Decided to put away your preaching garments?"

Thomas smiled, and she noticed again how the crinkles around his blue eyes deepened. "Just for the night. I didn't think the good Lord would find too much fault if I took a lady out to dinner in proper dress." He let his finger trace a line from her earring to the neckline of her gown.

"No, I don't think so." Emily swallowed, trying to ignore her body's reaction to his touch. Lord, but his hand felt like a flame! She shivered in spite of herself, and was sure she saw his smile widen.

"Oh—this is from the sale of the paintings. I wanted to give it to you before we went out."

Thomas extended a wad of bills to her and Emily gasped at the thickness of it. "Why, Thomas, this is incredible!"

He nodded. "I told you they would go over well. My intermediary was very successful. Apparently you just had to get to the right men. You know, ones with wives or sweethearts who don't understand them."

Emily looked up, her eyes alight as she caught his insinuation. "Thomas, you didn't! Why, that's almost blackmail!"

"I beg your pardon, but a man of the cloth would never engage in anything so despicable. Now, Miss Potter, are you ready?"

Emily put on her hat, the smart black one that looked perfect with her dress, then picked up Rosie's lacy shawl. Thomas extended his arm, and with pleasure Emily slid hers through the crook of his elbow.

Just before they left the house, Emily heard Rosie's voice again and was barely able to choke back a reaction. "Remember what I told you, honey. Wait until things get hot, then get him out of that room. Your answer lies there."

"Are you all right?" Thomas asked, turning to look at her in concern.

"Fine." She waved at the air. "Just fine."

16

The Preacher Is Unmasked

It was impossible for a woman to be so beautiful.

Thomas sat across from Emily in the dining room of the Hotel de Paris, sipping a wine that could only be called excellent, and savoring the beef burgundy, scalloped potatoes, almond beans, and French pastries. In spite of the good meal, he found he couldn't take his eyes off Emily, nor could he remember enjoying an evening more.

The duality of her personality still astounded him. By day she looked like a schoolmarm, all dowdy clothes and spinsterish spectacles, but at night the temptress emerged, dazzling in a burgundy gown that dipped daringly low in the front, and a hat that could only be an Emily Potter original. He didn't know much about women's millinery, but he knew enough to recognize quality and genuine artistic ability. The hat she wore tonight was obviously for

evening, and it complimented her dress, drawing
one's eye to her face, setting off her upswept hair-
style to perfection. She was so talented, as sure of
herself with satin and feathers as she was with her
magnifying glass and logical discourse.

His gaze lowered. A froth of black lace had been
discreetly added to the neckline of her gown, but it
hid little of the smooth expanse of creamy skin that
gleamed like rose petals. The lights caught her hair,
giving it a reddish cast like polished wood, and those
silver eyes seemed to twinkle merrily. And her conversation was as interesting as she was lovely, for
Emily could talk of many things. Even if most of
them included poisons, famous murders in the last
decade, and outlaw legends, he was fascinated. This
was Emily Potter.

His eyes fell to her enticing cleavage again and he
frowned, aware that she'd caught the attention of
other men in the room. Emily saw his look and her
brows drew together questioningly. With his wineglass, he indicated her dress.

"I was just admiring your gown. I don't think I've
ever seen that one before. Isn't it a little . . . bare for
Boston?"

"Oh, this isn't mine," Emily said with that forth-
rightness he so admired. "This belonged to Rosie."

"Rosie?" When she nodded, he stared at her
incredulously. "Emily, isn't that a little strange, to
borrow a dead woman's clothes?"

Emily appeared to have a sudden coughing fit and
had to swallow hard, catching her breath. When she
could speak, she giggled like a young girl.

"I suppose. But to me, Rosie is as alive as ever."

"I see," Thomas replied, though he didn't see a damn thing. Aware that a man across from them was trying desperately to look down her dress, he scowled. "Maybe next time you could borrow something a little more discreet."

"Oh, Thomas, don't be a bother," Emily waved her hand dismissively. "This dress is in the latest style, and is no more low-cut than any other woman's here."

"Not that there *are* many others," Thomas remarked dryly. Still, when his gaze ran over Emily, he felt the familiar sexual tension between them begging to be alleviated. The first time he'd kissed her had never left his mind. If anything, the memory was burned like a brand into his brain, making every innocent brush of her skin a lesson in torture.

He didn't know how much longer he could hold out. Thomas truly wanted to do the right thing, but he had to have this woman, had to know the depths to which he could take her. He had to see her eyes half-closed again, in that innocent enjoyment of seduction, as her body trembled with a passion that still left him stunned.

As if she knew what he was thinking, she looked at him through lowered lashes and spoke softly. "I want to thank you again for the other night, and your help selling the paintings. You really have become a true friend to me, Thomas."

That word again. Thomas shifted uncomfortably, wondering if she knew what she was doing to him, wondering if she was enjoying it. He drank deeply of his wine, hoping to kill the hunger inside of him, but moment by moment, it just grew stronger. It was time to lay his cards on the table, Thomas thought. He had to know where he stood.

"You're welcome. Emily, I am proud to be called your friend, but I was hoping for a deeper relationship with you. Especially after what we've shared."

He waited for her response, and when it came, he wasn't disappointed. She lifted her face and looked directly at him with an expression he'd never forget.

"You mean that night, when we kissed at the bordello, and . . . you did other things." When he nodded, she continued softly. "I've been thinking about that, too, Thomas. I know I told you I couldn't make love to you unless you told me the truth, but I'm starting to see things differently."

"You are?" It was his turn to have a sudden coughing fit.

Emily absently twirled her wineglass. "Yes. I've come to realize that you are following your own line of inquiry for your own reasons, just like I am. I can only hope the day will come when you trust me enough to confide in me. Until then, I have only two choices. I can continue to pretend that I only want friendship with you, or . . ."

"Or?" Thomas's mouth was suddenly parched, and the word was little more than a rasp.

Emily lifted those gorgeous silver eyes and looked directly into his heart. "Or I can spend the night with you."

For a second, he couldn't breathe. Thomas stared

at this beautiful woman, the anticipation nearly killing him. To his astonishment, she rose and gave him that Mona Lisa smile that nearly made his blood boil. Laying her slender hand on his shoulder, she said, "I choose the latter."

"Are you sure?" He asked hoarsely, unable to believe his luck, but wanting to make certain she knew what she was doing.

Emily nodded truthfully. Even with all of Rosie's coaching, it was a conclusion she'd come to by herself. She wanted to experience everything this man had to give her, to know the full pleasure she could find in his arms. If there was one thing her life as a spinster in Boston had taught her, it was that being proper and approved of meant wretched loneliness. And Emily had had a lifetime of that.

Now she wanted to live.

"Yes, I'm sure."

Thomas picked up her wrap and signaled for the waiter. Just as he was placing the lacy shawl around Emily's shoulders, the man who'd been devouring her with his gaze all evening approached.

"Excuse me, but I felt I had to make an introduction. Ewert Smith, attorney at law. You aren't perchance Miss Potter?"

"Yes, I am," Emily said, surprised.

"Thomas Hall." He extended his hand. "Nice to meet you. Now if you don't mind, we're on our way out. . . ." But the attorney barred the doorway. His eyes wandered over Emily's bosom, and his ruddy face deepened in color.

"Well, well. I'm very surprised you're still here! Haven't changed your mind about selling the house, have you?"

"No," Emily said firmly. "I believe I told you that in my letter."

"I know. But I figured, you being a flighty female and all, you'd have second thoughts when you saw the place. You don't look the worse for wear, though. That is truly a magnificent hat. And I could swear I've seen that dress before, as beautiful as you are in it."

"Excuse us, Mr. Smith, but we've got an engagement," Thomas interrupted.

Ewert turned to Thomas and grinned, patting him on the shoulder. "Now I know why you've taken such an active interest in the lady. It's no secret—everyone in town knows that the good Reverend Hall has taken Miss Potter under his wing."

Emily glanced up, aware of an odd tension in the air. Forcing a smile, Thomas spoke in that tight, barely controlled tone she'd heard several times before.

"Your interest is very kind, Mr. Smith. Now, as I mentioned, the lady and I have plans."

"I can imagine. Good day, Reverend Hall. Miss Potter. Oh, and Miss Potter, I'd like to call on you soon, see how the house is coming along. You wouldn't mind that, would you?"

"No," Emily answered before she could think.

"Good. I'm looking forward to it." The man put on his derby, then sauntered out of the room as if he'd already made a conquest. Thomas's face darkened and he silently took Emily by the hand. Outside, he walked toward the boardinghouse, his expression menacing as Emily tottered to keep up with him. Finally she stopped in the middle of the street, her toes aching in the tiny shoes.

"Thomas! I can't run that fast."

He stopped, managing a rueful smile as he noticed how breathless she was. "I'm sorry, Emily. That man just got the better of me. The way he leered at you. . . . I was ready to belt him."

"Thomas! Why, you're jealous!"

Her words appeared to hit him like a brisk slap in the face. Thomas gazed at her in astonishment, then, unable to argue with her logic, he began to chuckle.

"You're right. I guess I am jealous. I'm jealous of any man who looks at you like that, who wants you . . . because I want you."

A thrill of feminine pleasure coursed through Emily, and when Thomas reached for her in the dim light and pulled her into his arms, she simply sighed in satisfaction. No man had ever wanted her like this before. No man had ever been jealous of her, especially not a man like Thomas. It was a heady experience, and she felt as if she were dreaming, and if she pinched herself, it would all be over. She leaned against him, focused on his mouth traveling to her throat, pressing feverish kisses there.

"Emily, my God, I can't wait to have you. Let's go upstairs to my room. Unless you'd prefer Shangri-La?"

"No!" Emily answered immediately. Dimly she remembered why she was doing this. She had to find out once and for all who he was. Besides, she could just imagine Rosie's comments the next morning if she saw Thomas in her bed.

Arm in arm, they approached the boardinghouse, which fortunately appeared deserted. Thomas took Emily up the stairs and into his back bedroom. The room was cozy, decorated with flowered wallpaper and amber-shaded gaslights. A large poster bed dominated the center of the room, covered with a cream-colored quilt. He started to remove his coat, hesitating when he saw the look on her face.

Emily stared back at him like a frightened deer. Her eyes wandered to the bed and she stared at it as if transfixed.

"What's wrong? Emily?"

He lifted her chin and gazed into her eyes, then smiled warmly. "Emily, don't be afraid. I'd never do anything to hurt you. You know that, don't you?"

She nodded, her eyes wide and luminous. "Thomas . . . do you mind if I have a few minutes to myself? I need to . . ." God, what did Rosie tell her to say? "Prepare."

He looked puzzled, but he nodded. "The Silver-dust is across the street. How about if I get a bottle of brandy for a nightcap? It might calm your fears."

"That would be perfect. Thomas, you are so thoughtful."

He leaned closer and kissed her soundly on the mouth. Some of the tension left her and she could feel her body respond, warming to his touch. For a moment, she totally forgot what she planned to do. She really cared about this man, and the promise of what lay ahead intoxicated her.

Easing from her embrace, he smiled. "I'll be right back." Then he closed the door and was gone.

As soon as she was alone, Emily nearly collapsed on the bed. Part of what she'd told Thomas was the truth. The enormity of her decision was just beginning to hit her. Good God, what had she done? This wasn't all part of a plan . . . oh, the plan! She eyed the meager furnishings: a bureau, a washstand, a carpetbag, and a night table. Instantly her detective instincts focused on the bag. *If I were concealing something*, she thought logically, *I'd hide it there, where it was portable.*

Her conscience nagged at her, but she reminded herself that once she knew the truth, all would be well between her and Thomas. There would be no wall of mistrust, no wondering, no fear that this man was neither friend nor foe. Emily knew deep in her heart that she was really starting to care for him. She couldn't afford to let her feelings go unless she knew for sure what side he was on.

Opening the bag, she sifted through the papers. There was a letter that appeared to be from a female relative. Tempted as she was, Emily couldn't bring herself to invade his privacy that much, and she put it back. Next was a note from the sheriff, verifying that Emmet Colter had a wooden leg, and that he had been seen recently near town. That looked promising, but there was no other indication that the lawman knew who Thomas really was.

Frustrated, Emily dug deeper. She knew no more than when she'd entered the room, and he could return at any moment. She scanned the other

documents until she found what she instinctively
knew she was looking for.

Another letter from Will Jenkins of Wells Fargo.
Her fingers were shaking as she opened the missive.
"Dear Thomas," it ran.

> *I am pleased to hear that things are pro-
> gressing. As I mentioned, the company cannot
> take responsibility for your presence, but I as-
> sure you that you have my support. In my
> heart, I've always known you weren't responsi-
> ble for the loss of the payroll, and if you can re-
> cover any portion of it, I will do my best to get
> you reinstated. I hope your disguise as Rever-
> end Hall isn't hampering you unduly, and that
> you achieve your goals to keep Miss Potter out
> of danger.*
>
> *Please keep me posted as to what you un-
> cover. We eagerly await the results of your in-
> vestigation. Ewert Smith, whom we've hired as
> assistant attorney, can help you with any legal
> difficulties and perhaps furnish local informa-
> tion. Any assistance I can provide is at your
> disposal. . . .*

Emily gazed at the letter, rereading it. Thomas was
the second man accused of stealing the gold! He
worked for Wells Fargo! Relief sped through her as
she realized he was innocent of any criminal activity,
and that like her, he was doing his own detective
work. Thomas Hall was neither thief nor murderer—
nor preacher, either.

Back at the Silverdust, Thomas ordered the bottle of brandy and a small glass for himself. A wry smile came to his lips as he pictured Emily, suddenly shy, her eyes wide with apprehension.

Her natural jitters didn't upset him; if anything, her reticence only made her seem more womanly, innocent, and virginal. He tipped his glass back, letting the brandy warm him, though he was already feeling quite flushed with the heat of desire.

One of the saloon girls, a bold brunette with huge dark eyes, tried to get his attention, but Thomas had absolutely no interest in the bawd. Instead, his mind returned over and over again to Emily. The way she'd looked at dinner, the way she'd propositioned him, the way she was waiting for him back in his room— she was a potent combination of innocence and intelligence, curiosity and uncertainty. The passion she'd displayed on previous occasions assured him that what he'd find in her arms would be unique, just like Emily herself. In spite of the fact that he'd had other women, Thomas felt himself looking forward to this night in a way he never had before. Moreover, he realized he was beginning to care about her. He wanted her to reach fulfillment, and find ecstasy in his embrace, as he knew he would in hers.

The barkeep shoved the bottle of brandy at him and demanded payment. Thomas reached for his money, then realized that he'd left his wallet with his money in it at the boardinghouse.

"I'll be right back," he told the man, then picked up his hat and headed back to his room.

Emily Potter would not be disappointed this night, he swore to himself. He'd see to it. But as he stepped into the room, he froze at the sight before him.

"Well, well, my dear Emily."

Emily felt her breath catch hard in her throat. Looking up in horror, she saw Thomas standing just inside the door. His face was grim as he surveyed her, sitting on the floor, his letters scattered around her like confetti. He reached down, picked up his wallet, and held it before her.

"I forgot my money."

Their eyes locked for a long moment. Then Emily rose, her face beet red, her hand still clutching the letter. Thomas held her gaze, then let the wallet drop to the bureau meaningfully. Kicking the door closed behind him, he faced her like a judge in the final hour.

Emily was caught.

17

Emily Confesses

Emily's first thought was to run for it but when Thomas kicked the door shut, he had effectively cut off the only means of escape. She glanced toward the window, but it was too far away from where she stood. Trembling, she forced a smile, then took a few casual steps toward the door.

"I think I'll be going now. Thank you for a wonderful evening—"

Thomas's hand shot out and grabbed her wrist. Emily's breath caught as his fingers closed on her like a vise. Blood seemed to stop flowing to her hand, and the letter fluttered to the floor unheeded, like a giant snowflake.

"Let me go!" she demanded.

"Not on your life." Thomas's voice was deadly cold. He pulled her, still struggling, against him, and held her there.

This was even worse. Emily could feel every hard, muscled inch of him, the rough pressure of his legs against her thighs, the scratchiness of his shirt rubbing her bare neckline. She suddenly wished she'd worn something a little less revealing, for she could tell he was as affected by their nearness as she was. Logically, of course, she knew she wouldn't be in this situation if she'd worn something a little less revealing. A predatory energy emanated from him and she struggled more fiercely, causing him to tighten his embrace.

"Emily, I want to know what the hell you were doing going through my things. Or do I even need to ask? Is this all part of your sleuthing campaign? Pretend to have a personal interest in me in order to get into my room? I don't think even your precious Holmes would have stooped so low."

Thomas's voice was a snarl, and Emily swallowed hard. "Well, actually, there was that servant he pretended to be engaged to, in order to get information about her mistress. . . ."

"Goddamn it, Emily!"

Her breath seemed to vanish as he crushed her even harder against him. Maybe he really didn't want to discuss Sherlock Holmes, Emily thought dimly. Gazing up at him, she saw the fury in his eyes, coupled with something else, something that in another man, she would have thought was hurt or disappointment.

But after all, she reasoned, Thomas was playing the same game she was. He had investigated her, as well as everyone else who had anything to do with the murders. He should understand.

"I'm waiting, Emily," he said through gritted teeth, "for an explanation."

There was no way out. Emily felt the sexual tension between them, the threat he posed in more ways than one. Only now was she truly beginning to understand her vulnerability—when it was far, far too late. There was nothing left but to tell him the truth, and to let the chips fall where they may.

"I . . . Thomas, I had to know who you really were. We both know you aren't a preacher—that last rites ritual!—but I came to you repeatedly and asked you to tell me, and you wouldn't. So I did what I had to do."

"You agreed to make love to me, only to come here and root through my letters to satisfy your curiosity?"

The outrage in his voice made her quake. Emily tried another tack. "It wasn't like that! You're twisting my words! Thomas, as any detective worth his salt knows, you have to understand the players. I don't know what side you're on! How could I trust you, when you could have been the murderer yourself!"

He looked as though she'd slapped him. Emily's panic increased as Thomas simply stared at her, his eyes blazing. When he suddenly released her, she felt a moment's relief, but it disappeared as she watched him lock the door and toss the key under the bed. Her throat went dry as he slowly began to unbutton his shirt.

"What . . . what are you doing?" she asked tremulously.

He looked at her as if it were a ridiculous question. "Emily, I should think that's obvious. You agreed to make love to me tonight, and that's what we're going to do. Like you, I want to do a little detective work of my own. I want to discover just how far you'll go for the sake of the Science of Deduction. I suggest you remove your clothes."

Emily felt her pulse pound as the meaning of his words penetrated her brain. He couldn't really mean to . . .

His shirt hit the floor, then he sat on the edge of the bed and began removing his boots. A little squeak came from somewhere inside of her, and her gaze fluttered once more around the room, like a caged bird. Edging closer to the window, she managed to get within three feet of it before Thomas rose and took hold of her arm.

"It's not that simple, Emily. We have a bargain, remember? You got what you wanted. Now it's time to pay up." He gestured roughly to her gown. "Start with the dress."

The look in his eyes was hard, implacable. He still gripped her arm tightly, and she realized, for all her cleverness, she hadn't prepared for a predicament like this.

"Do you need help?" he asked softly. She shook her head, and he raised his brows sharply. "Then what are you waiting for? Come, Miss Emily, I am anxious for my part of the deal."

Emily's gaze rose to meet his, shame and fear beginning to overwhelm her. Tears welled up from somewhere inside her, and she fought them unsuccessfully, quickly looking down at the floor. All of her logic, all of her studies, all of her wisdom, meant nothing at this moment. Her eyes were filled with the sight of him, lean and powerful and bare to the waist, standing so close to her. His chest, hard and well muscled, seemed like iron, and the small amount of black hair there tapered down to where his trousers began. Confronted with brute male force and the sudden realization of her vulnerability as a woman, she threw herself on his mercy.

"Thomas . . . I can't. Not like this."

He looked at her for a long moment, then lifted her face to his. To her horror, the suppressed tears spilled out, and she wiped them quickly away, seeing a smear of rouge come with them. It didn't matter now—none of it mattered. With a dismal sense of loss, Emily realized that she had somehow ruined everything. The only thing left was to tell him the whole truth.

"I'm sorry. I really felt you left me no other choice! I had to know, especially since . . ." She opened her eyes and looked through the moisture at him. "Especially since you were beginning to mean something to me."

That cost her, and she saw, to her tremendous relief, that he understood. Some of the anger seemed to leave him as he gazed at her, weighing what she said, looking for any sign of falsehood.

"Do you mean that?" he asked, his voice rough.

Emily nodded. "I admit that I had decided to look through your things tonight. When I first thought of it, I felt apprehensive, but I couldn't come up with an alternative. I thought that it was better to do that, and know I could trust you, than to start to . . . fall in love with you without knowing the truth. Thomas, you investigated me. I don't blame you for that. How can you blame me?"

"What did you say?"

"I said that I know you investigated me—"

"No, before that."

Emily stared at him and felt more exposed than if she had been wearing one of Rosie's negligees. "I said I was afraid I was falling in love with you. That's why I had to know."

A weight seemed to come off his shoulders. Emily watched him digest this, then his hand fell from where he'd been holding her arm.

"I don't think there is anything else you could have said to me tonight that would have mattered except that." He slid his fingers up the side of her throat, softly touching a stray curl that had escaped her hat, then back down, to the bare neckline of her gown. Emily's breath hitched as the warm, wonderful sensations ignited within her. The rough feel of his hand, the closeness of his half-naked body, the scent of him, clean and masculine, filled her senses. She was overwhelmed with desire, and powerless to stop him when he took her into his arms.

"Don't be afraid, Emily. I won't hurt you, I just want to pleasure you. It is inevitable, this thing between us, isn't it? My God, Emily, let me . . ."

His mouth covered hers, and Emily sighed with intense pleasure. The fear was gone, replaced by wonder as his tongue flirted with hers, teasing her, making her want more. The erotic images from the bordello flitted through her mind and she pressed eagerly against him as he plunged his fingers into her coiffure and removed her hat. Emily was aware that he placed it aside carefully, but none of that mattered at this moment. Her body was aflame, his bare chest pressed against her sensitive skin, and her blood felt like honey flowing thick and sweet through her veins. His kisses went teasingly lower, then he freed her breasts from the bodice of her dress and closed his lips over one of them.

"Oh, Thomas!" Emily luxuriated in the pulsing madness that seemed to possess her. His tongue was like a flame as it tortured her nipple into a hard little point, then went on to treat the other to the same delicious torment. Arching up against him, Emily let her dress fall to her waist, allowing him to taste even more of her aching breasts, wanting everything that his lean body promised.

"Tell me," he said roughly, his eyes burning with a strange light. His tone, and the way he fumbled with the buttons of her gown were even more exciting to Emily. "Tell me how much you want this."

Cold air hit newly bared skin and she gasped at the myriad of sensations. Shivering, she stepped out of the gown, dimly understanding now why Rosie's dresses were always so easy to unfasten. She nearly melted into the heat of his embrace, marveling at the throbbing ache of desire that culminated between her legs.

She lifted her face to his, and in a breathless voice, she managed, "Yes, I want this. I know I can trust you. Oh God, Thomas, don't stop—"

His smile seduced her and she trembled as his lips lowered, inching down her chemise with each fiery kiss, until she wore only the black silk stockings Rosie had given her. She saw his brief look of surprise, and attributed it to the belief that colored stockings were considered very fast. Yet that, too, only added to the sizzling eroticism of the moment. Emily had one more fleeting thought about Rosie—she certainly knew her stuff—then Thomas lowered his head even more and she was swept away, incoherent.

"Oh my . . . Thomas, you can't! You must stop, please stop—oh my God, don't ever stop!"

Emily was aware of the sounds coming from her, but for once she was unable to form a conscious thought. The feelings he generated in her were simply too powerful. His mouth dazzled her, his tongue seemed to know exactly how to tease her, torment her, until she was writhing before him, her back against the wall, his hands holding her up by her silk-encased thighs. She would have fallen if he hadn't held her, and when the tremors wracked her, she did fall, and he caught her in his arms.

"Thomas," she murmured, letting the unfamiliar emotions wash over her. Never in her life had she felt like this. Never had she thought that such a delicious reward lay at the end of such a sinful deed.

"I know, sweet." He carried her to the bed, smoothing back her hair, holding her as if she were precious, fragile. His eyes swept over her as he removed his trousers and the rest of his clothes, and his voice was dark with passion. "So beautiful. So sensual. My dear Emily."

He gathered her into his arms, wedging himself gently between her legs. Emily felt the first hard thrust of him and she gasped, but he held her close, caressing her, easing her fears. "Easy, Emily. It may hurt just a bit at first. My God, you are so hot, so tight. I don't know if I can hold back. . . ."

"Don't hold back," Emily breathed. The feel of him, hot and full against the most sensitive part of her, was exquisite. When he slid into her, she felt a stinging pain, then gradually, it subsided. She sighed as her body expanded to accommodate his male hardness, taking all of him inside her.

"That's it. Now put you legs around me. Yes, like that. Oh, God . . ."

Emily wrapped her stockinged legs around his back and felt him thrust even deeper. Excitement sparked within her and she arched her back against him, moving with him. Thomas whispered encouragement, then with a throaty cry, met his fulfillment. Tenderly he held her against him, and Emily could feel the pulsations of his body drain away in rhythm with her own.

A few moments passed, and he pressed a kiss on her neck. Emily felt a kind of satisfaction that she'd never known—emotional as well as physical. There was the closeness of the man beside her, the completeness of sexual fulfillment, and the knowledge that he would keep her safe, warming her. She smiled at him and Thomas's mouth quirked softly.

"I take it you didn't think it so bad."

"I thought it was wonderful," Emily sighed. "Thomas, I . . . I am so sorry for what I've done. You do realize why I had to look at your letters?"

"I'm not happy about it, Emily, but I do understand. And now I guess I'll have to tell you the rest."

She nodded and waited patiently.

"I haven't told you who I really am because it would be dangerous for you to know—not because I didn't trust you. And you're not going to like what I'm about to tell you." He paused, drawing in a long breath. "About a year ago I worked for Wells Fargo. My real name is Thomas Brant. You correctly guessed, from my accent, I suppose, that I come from Virginia. My father died in the war, and my family was left penniless. I tried my hand at a few things, but other than my accuracy with a gun, I didn't have many advantages.

"In any case, the job at Wells Fargo promised a lot. My ability with the rifle was a benefit to them, and I was sent to guard a shipment of gold. It was a payroll sent from one of the banks in the East."

Emily sat up, suddenly sure that she did not want to hear what he was going to say, but unable to stop him.

"Your father was my partner," he continued. "I didn't know him well, but he acted as a mentor to me, teaching me the ropes, pretending to be my friend. I had to admit, I bought it. I admired him. It was a long trip, and he talked of nothing but you, and of the way he would secure your future."

"Thomas, I don't know . . ."

He held up his hand. "Emily, in one respect you

are right. If we are to have this kind of relationship, there can't be secrets between us. Let me finish. About halfway through the trip, your father shot me and left me for dead. He disappeared with the gold. No one knew where he'd gone. I was suspected in the theft as well, and lost my job, my income, and my name. My family suffered as well as myself. The only way for me to clear my name is to find that gold."

"I don't believe this," Emily said, stunned.

"It's all true," Thomas told her gently. He showed her the scar on his shoulder. "This is where I was shot, Emily. After I was fired, I contacted my old supervisor, Will Jenkins, and told him I was going to find that gold. Will, thank God, never believed I was guilty. He agreed to help me, and he put me in contact with Ewert Smith, who suggested the role of traveling preacher as a cover. From Ewert, I learned of your father's fate, and your arrival. At first I was certain that you knew about the money, and that you'd come back to claim it as your inheritance. I'd set out to stop you, but after I got to know you, I realized you were innocent."

. Emily stood up and began to dress. Thomas watched her from the bed, his eyes never leaving her.

"It's the truth, Emily. You wanted that."

"It's not! You're wrong, Thomas. My father never stole that gold! Why do you think we haven't found it? It doesn't exist!"

"Emily, I know how hard this is for you to hear. But I think your father may have had an accomplice, someone who was supposed to get half the money. I think he double-crossed this man, and that man killed him and Rosie. Are you listening to me, Emily? This is the danger I've been warning you about!"

Thomas got out of the bed and stood beside her, but Emily refused to look at him. Quickly fastening the last of her buttons, she found a knot of tears in her throat. This couldn't be true, it just couldn't be. Her father wasn't exactly citizen of the year, Emily knew that. He'd left her and her mother, taken up with a soiled dove, and lived in a bordello, but that was very different from ruining a man's life, especially Thomas's! Surely her mother couldn't have loved a man that low. The facts added up, but for the first time, logic failed her.

"Emily, don't do this. Listen to me—"

"I'm leaving. Thomas, I'm sorry about what happened. I think we both realize this was a mistake. Please let me go."

"Emily, damn it." Thomas touched her cheek, trying to coax her to talk to him. But she stood next to the door with her head down, refusing to meet his eyes. Helpless, aware that nothing he said at this moment would make a difference, Thomas slowly put on his clothes. Retrieving the key from under the bed, he unlocked the door. Before she could bolt, he took her arm.

"I'm walking you home, Emily. Don't argue with me about this. Especially after what I told you tonight, you have to be more careful."

She considered that for a moment, then reluctantly nodded. They walked in silence from the boardinghouse to the former bordello. The moon rose high in the sky, illuminating the path, but the lack of conversation between them was painfully awkward and Emily almost wished for complete darkness to hide in. When they reached her porch, he finally spoke.

"Emily I just want you to know one thing. I remember what you said to me before all this happened, and it meant the world to me. I know you need time to sort through all this, but when you're ready to talk, I'll be here."

Emily squeezed her eyes shut. She had to get out of here, had to get as far away from him as possible. As soon as he opened the door, she turned and ran inside.

18

—❦—

A U.S. Male

"Well, well, looky here. What have we got, boys?"

Jake grinned as Emmet Colter hobbled into the abandoned miner's shack. Lizzie looked up, her eyes wide with terror. She was seated in a chair, her hands tied behind her, her mouth gagged. She watched Emmet approach as a deer would a hunter, leaning as far back in the chair as her bonds would allow.

"I brought Miss Lizzie to visit," Jake said, and the two outlaws broke into drunken laughter. "Seems she was fixin' to fly the coop. I brought her back here where I could keep an eye on her."

"I ain't seen you in a long time, sweetheart," Emmet said, but his eyes were narrowed dangerously. "Not since that detective on the train filled my leg with lead. Sad that I ain't much use to a woman now, though. I know you missed me."

"We've got something else to worry about." Jake stood up and began to pace in front of the door. "That spinster woman, Emily Potter, has been stirring up trouble all over town. She's been asking questions, poking her nose everywhere. She had even been to see Miss Lizzie. Lizzie claims she told her nothing, but somehow I don't rightly believe that."

"I was in town yesterday and heard the very same woman asking the postman about Bertie Evans. There are too many loose ends here, and too many people getting wise. That preacher man's still sticking to her like flies on horse dung. I don't like the looks of it. We should have finished the housekeeper long before this."

"I thought you didn't want no more killings," Jake said, but his grin belied the regretful tone of his words.

Emmet scowled. "The boss doesn't, but it seems we left a few messes behind. The housekeeper shouldn't be hard to silence, and she's in Silverton— far enough away that it won't be traced back to us. The postman almost peed his pants when he told me where she was."

Jake chuckled at the picture of that. "I'll take a little ride to Silverton, then. Housekeepers are getting to be my specialty."

Emmet smiled, then waved a hand toward the hills outside. "You know, I ain't nearly as concerned about Bertie Evans as I am that China woman. She turned up yet?"

"Naw." Jake shook his head. "We looked everywhere, but those Chinese wouldn't tell you a thing. Clam up quicker than a virgin's legs as soon as you ask them a question."

Emmet smiled, but his voice was deadly when he spoke. "We've got to find her. Of all of them, she could cause some real trouble. The boss wants this thing done clean. I want that China girl found, and I want her dead. And if Miss Potter gets in the way, the same goes for her, too."

"So, honey, how did it go? I can't wait to hear the details!"

Emily stood before the mirror, slowly removing her gown. Confusion overwhelmed her, and her face screwed up into a knot as she tried to puzzle it all out. To further complicate matters, she felt very strange physically as well; her body still glowed from Thomas's lovemaking, and a stinging ache between her legs reminded her that after tonight, nothing would be the same.

Rosie sat up, her excited smile changing quickly to concern. "What's wrong, Emily? He didn't propose anything outlandish, did he? My God, those holy men are always the worst. I remember one minister, who wanted to play Indians, and tied me up—"

"No, nothing like that," Emily hastened to reassure her. But when she spoke again, her voice was blandly logical, as if she were speaking about the weather. "That part was very nice, and more enjoyable than I would have thought. But he caught me looking through his papers."

"He did?" Rosie froze in horror. "Oh, my. What did you do?"

Emily sighed in self-disgust. "I did the worst thing I could have done. I told him the truth. I told him that I was afraid I was falling in love with him and I had to know who he really was."

"Thank the Lord." Rosie let out the breath she appeared to have been holding. Her smile returned and she eyed Emily with admiration. "That was real clever of you! You've learned more from me than I thought! Normally I wouldn't advise saying that to a man until you were certain of his feelings for you, but in this case, the timing couldn't have been better. What did he do?"

Emily looked at the floor. "He seemed relieved. I guess he thought that I was only pretending to want him, just to spy on him. What I told him was true, though. I am beginning to care for him."

"I know," Rosie said softly. "I think he feels a lot for you, too. He just may not be ready to tell you about it. But honey, this sounds like good news. Why do you look so glum?"

Emily lifted her chin and looked directly at the phantom. "Rosie, I have to ask you something, and I really need to have the whole answer."

Rosie nodded, sitting at attention. "I'll try. What do you want to know?"

"Thomas told me a lot of things tonight. He worked for Wells Fargo, and his real name is Thomas Brant. He was transporting a gold shipment, a payroll, with my father. Thomas claims my father stole the money and tried to lay the blame on him. He also thinks there was an accomplice who killed you both when my father double-crossed him, and that, whoever it is, is still determined to get the money."

"Good heavens!" Rosie's expression became sympathetic. "Now I can see why you're so upset. That is terrible! I can't imagine such a thing. . . ."

"I need to know," Emily whispered, pain filling her voice. "I really need to know about my father."

The ghost gazed at Emily with fondness. Her voice, when she finally spoke, was soft and understanding.

"Your pa wanted so much to help you. You're all he ever talked about, honey, and that's the truth. He was so proud of you! He kept anything that reminded him of you, and the few letters he received from you, he treated like they were gold. I don't know if he was capable of doing such a terrible thing, but if he did, he did it for you."

Emily shook her head in disbelief. "But why? I never asked for money. I never wrote to him of any desire for wealth, or tried to make him feel less of a man because we didn't have it. Frankly, I didn't think much about him at all. He left me when I was so young, I never even knew what kind of man he was."

Rosie nodded, a tear spilling down her face. "I know, honey. You know how men are sometimes? They start out thinking that they want success, and that usually means money. It's only when they get older that they start to think about other things, and what success really is. I think that's what happened to your pa."

"It's all so confusing." Emily sighed, and Rosie nodded.

"I know, and it only gets more so. But that's life, isn't it?"

Emily looked at the ghost, thinking of what an odd thing it was for her to say. Yet perhaps, being on that side, it was easier to see.

"I still can't accept this," Emily said softly. "If I did, I would have to admit that my father was a thief and worse. And Thomas . . ." Thomas would have every reason on earth to despise her. How could he hold her, make love to her, if he really believed her father caused his ruin?

As if reading her mind, Rosie spoke softly. "Why don't you just wait and see what turns up? Your preacher man doesn't seem to be holding your father's actions against you. I think he genuinely cares for you, and he's sure put himself out to help you. And if you solve this mystery, you may very well get your answers then."

Emily smiled, watching the ghost fade from sight.

The next morning, Emily summoned Darrel to fetch the hats. Then, she made her way into town to borrow the post office clerk's cart once more.

Rain poured, making her journey a misery, but Emily pressed on. Last night, while falling asleep, she had figured a few things out. The shop had to be opened immediately, and she needed to attend the functions that Eleanor Hamill had suggested to her. Further, she had decided to paint the ceiling of the house and tone down any other vivid reminders of what went on there. Emily realized she couldn't count on all the women having Eleanor's astigmatism, and she finally understood that Thomas was right—at least about this. She needed to win the approval of the town's women, come hell or high water.

Thoughts of Thomas were twice as unsettling this morning. Unfortunately in this case, Rosie's advice didn't work, for the hot bath she'd suggested had only reminded her of the delicious lovemaking they'd shared the previous night. It troubled her greatly that he hadn't returned her words of affection, and she still couldn't believe what he'd said about her father. The fact that Thomas did bothered her intensely.

Maybe that's why he hadn't professed any strong feelings for her. Perhaps, when he looked at her, all he saw was her father. Several people had remarked on their likeness, and Emily swiftly recalled Thomas's efforts to question her when they first met. Could he still be using her for his own gains? He was determined to find that gold, and she might be the only lead he had. To her dismay, Emily had realized a startling truth. Since finding out his identity, her doubts about Thomas had only gotten darker.

Frustrated, she ran swiftly through the rainfall and into the post office. Closing her umbrella, she saw gratefully that no one else was in the place— due, she supposed, to the weather. She managed a smile as she approached the desk, but when the clerk looked up and recognized her, his face drained of color.

Emily sighed. This again. "Sir, I was wondering if I could beg a favor," she asked prettily.

"Miss, would you mind coming around the back?" The clerk's manner was nervous and jerky. He circled around the counter to where she stood, then to Emily's amazement, began to draw the shades.

"Look, I told you I don't work at the saloon anymore—"

"Miss Emily." The man turned toward her and Emily's words seemed to dry up. He looked terrified, and he indicated the office in the back. "I meant there. Can you step in for a moment? There is something I need to discuss with you."

Nodding, she followed him into the office, noting anxiously that he bolted the door behind them. She saw, too, his furtive glance out the back door, then he bolted that firmly as well. When all was secure, he turned to her, and even then, he lowered his voice to a whisper.

"Do you remember the last time you were here, asking about that housekeeper?"

"Bertie Evans. Yes, I remember." Emily frowned. Something was terribly wrong here. This went far beyond being embarrassed by having a tart on the premises. She waited patiently for him to gather his nerve.

"After you left, Emmet Colter came in here, asking the same things. He wanted to know who you were, what you wanted, and what I had told you. When I mentioned the housekeeper, he got angry and asked me where Bertie was."

"Good God." Emily sank down into a chair, staring at the piles of mail before her without really seeing them. "Emmet Colter! Here? Why?"

"I don't know," the clerk said, still literally shaking in his boots. "But I thought I should warn you. My life is in your hands, for if Emmet finds out I said a word to you, he'll kill me. I can't go to the sheriff, much as I'd like to 'cause word would get around too quick. Then Emmet would come looking for me."

The significance of the clerk's words was sinking in. "Then I was right! He *is* involved in this. But if Emmet knows where Bertie is, I've got to warn her—"

"That's not necessary." For the first time, the clerk looked genuinely pleased with himself. "I told him her address was Silverton."

"How wonderful of you, and how brave!" Emily said with sincere admiration. The clerk flushed, but his gaze remained steadily on her.

"Emmet knows where you are. Keep an eye out, Miss Emily. Keep an eye out."

19

A Vanishing Ghost

When the rain finally stopped, Emily was able to transport the hats safely from the house to the millinery shop. She put them neatly on the counter, displaying them in their full glory in an effort to entice any passing traffic into the shop. Again, she had to admit Thomas was right about the place. Its location couldn't be better, and without even having to advertise, she would attract exactly the crowd she needed. Now, if only the townswomen would give her a chance, she knew she could be successful.

While waiting for customers, Emily propped her notes between the hats and began her work, just as she had during her days in Boston. Retrieving a tablet of paper and a pencil, she began scribbling the facts of the case. Her encounter that morning with the postal clerk had left her wary—and more frustrated than ever.

Rosie and John Potter: Murdered.

Known enemies: None. John Potter reportedly stole a gold shipment, and may have cheated an accomplice.

Coroner's report: Death by gunshot wounds.

Sheriff's report: Unobtainable. Feels deaths were caused by accomplice because of dispute over gold.

Fact: John Potter was afraid of a man with a wooden leg.

Fact: Emmet Colter has a wooden leg and is a known outlaw.

Fact: Lizzie Wakefield confessed that the housekeeper, Bertie Evans, may remember something.

Fact: Lizzie is missing, and her housekeeper was killed. Lizzie is the consort of an outlaw—possibly associated with Colter.

Fact: Emmet Colter asked about Bertie Evans. Possibly afraid of a witness?

Chewing her pencil, Emily nodded to herself. The web around Colter was tightening. But she knew time was running out. Even now, Emmet was probably riding to Silverton to look up the missing Bertie Evans. When he realized she wasn't there, he wouldn't drop his pursuit; most likely, he'd redouble his efforts. The postal clerk had bought them a few days, but that was all.

Rising, Emily folded the slip of paper and put it into her pocket. She knew what she had to do: find

Bertie and warn her of the danger, then find out what she knew before Emmet could silence her forever. And the only way she could do that was with Thomas's help.

Closing the shop, she started resolutely down the street, grateful that the rain had stopped. As she rounded the corner, she saw the hotel where they'd had dinner. A blush heated her cheeks as she recalled the night they'd spent together, and the scene that followed. Thomas's accusations about her father troubled her in so many ways, but one thing nagged at her more than anything else. What if he was right?

A crowd had gathered at the edge of town, and Emily paused, curious, to see what was going on. She heard what sounded like preaching, and saw the women listening with rapt attention. She was within a few feet of the knot of people when she recognized the voice.

Thomas. Of course.

"My friends and good townspeople, I appreciate your time given this evening to listen to my humble prayer. We have spoken of Christian forgiveness, of understanding, and of human charity between each other. No other town has impressed me with the goodness of its people the way Denver has. No other city can boast of the kind hand of friendship that has been extended to me, a poor traveling preacher.

"I now ask that you extend that same courtesy to one of our brethren, our less fortunate sister, Miss Emily Potter. Miss Potter, who by circumstances and unfortunate family connections, is considered a bit eccentric, but is nevertheless an innocent herself.

She is deserving of your charity, your forgiveness, your Christian friendship."

A murmur went through the assembled women. Emily's cheeks grew red. Pushing her way through the crowd, she tried to signal to him to stop, but he ignored her.

"You may well recognize her name. Her father, John Potter, was killed in that house down the road, a beautiful place known as Shangri-La. We all know that that name means paradise. John Potter may have called the house by that name for his own reasons, but I can assure you that it has truly become a paradise. Miss Potter is a wonderful woman, bright, intelligent, and gifted, and a magnificent milliner. Last week, she extended an invitation to the women of this town, an invitation that was rudely snubbed, by almost all of you."

Tears of humiliation came to Emily's eyes. Good God, why was he doing this? He wasn't truly a preacher—he'd admitted that much at least. Why wouldn't he stop? Yet as she peered at him through the crowd, she noticed that the women, especially ones with young, unmarried daughters, appeared to be affected by what he was saying.

"So I, as a member of this holy profession, am asking you to reach out to this woman, who only sought to brighten your lives. You will find Miss Potter to be a good woman, a woman who will enrich your lives the way . . . she has enriched mine."

Emily lifted her head and her breath caught at his words. Thomas's eyes met hers and Emily knew he spoke to her. Something in her heart swelled until she felt it would burst, and she bit her lower lip.

"I think if you visit her shop, you will be delighted by her millinery talent, and will enjoy her company. Miss Eleanor Hamill, as well as myself, will attest to Miss Potter's character. I will consider it not only a personal favor, but a gift to the Lord. Thank you, good people."

To Emily's amazement, the crowd began applauding, and the women touched handkerchiefs to their eyes. Dodging behind a water barrel, Emily heard the ladies whisper among themselves that they planned to call on Miss Potter immediately. Embarrassment mixed with pleasure as the women recalled tales of Emily's deductive brilliance, and the reports of Mrs. Hamill were duly retold. Waiting until they dispersed, Emily approached Thomas with a rueful smile.

"That was an interesting speech, Reverend," Emily said softly, putting emphasis on the last word.

Thomas grinned. "Think so? Wait until Sunday. I plan to lay it on twice as thick if you don't have customers by then."

"Thank you, Thomas."

The words came out simply, but sincerely. Emily's eyes met his. He nodded, picking up his prayer book from the cracker barrel that had been his makeshift podium, then offered her his arm.

After a moment's hesitation, Emily took it. Neither one spoke as they started down the path to her home. The silence hung heavily between them until Thomas broke it.

"Emily, I should have thought of a better way to tell you everything, but I couldn't think of one at the time. I'm sorry if I hurt you. I just thought you should know the truth as I see it."

Emily nodded. "I understand, but it's so hard to accept that my father was a lying thief as well as everything else—" Her voice broke off, then she looked back at him and held up her hand to indicate a truce. "I think it's better if we don't discuss this. But I do want you to know that you were right about one thing. Emmet Colter is onto me."

"What?" It was Thomas's turn to look astonished, and Emily quickly relayed what the postal clerk had told her. When she finished, Thomas took her by the shoulders.

"That's it. Game's over, Emily. Emmet Colter is a coldblooded killer. He'd think no more of plugging you than he would a rabbit. You're going home. I don't care if I have to put you on that train myself."

Pain welled up inside Emily, surprising her with its intensity. He didn't want her. She didn't know why she was taken aback by his reaction, for it was no different than what he'd said all along. But now, after last night, she wanted something different.

Looking directly at him, Emily took a deep breath and held her ground. "I'm sorry, Thomas, but I've told you before. That's out of the question." Before he could argue, she rushed on. "Think about it. If Emmet Colter really thinks I have two million dollars, I hardly expect that there is any place I'd be safe. And to run would suggest that I have something to hide, namely that I've found the money. My life wouldn't be worth a pittance."

"But you would be safer—"

"No safer than here. I'm sorry if I've become inconvenient for you, Thomas, but this is now my home and I intend to stay. Rosie did warn me that men sometimes wanted their mistresses out of the way, but I didn't listen, and that's my fault."

"Rosie?" Thomas asked in confusion, then his voice turned hard. "Surely you can't think—"

"It is my privilege to think whatever I want," she said primly. "But all of this is beside the point. I'm not leaving. I'm going to Greeley to warn Bertie Evans. I thought we could go tomorrow—"

"We?" Thomas's fingers tightened on her arms. "Emily, *we* are not going anywhere. You are going to run your shop, like a good little milliner, and I will see to Bertie." When Emily opened her mouth to protest, he placed a finger against it. "No buts. Emily, I refuse to discuss this. It's my way or no way."

"But I have to interview her! She'll tell me more than she'll tell you!"

"Emily, I am investigating this case the same as you. Besides, after my little speech today, you will probably be deluged with customers tomorrow, out of curiosity, if nothing else."

Her frustration was apparent. She looked like a bottle of shaken sarsaparilla beer, ready to explode. Thomas chuckled in spite of himself, and softly touched her cheek. "I promise to give you a full report when I get back. Remember, even Holmes trusted Watson to interview suspects occasionally."

"I know." Emily had to give him that one. "But Rosie thinks—"

"Emily, why do you keep insisting that you can speak to this dead bordello girl? This is incredibly surprising, especially from you."

Emily stood on the porch, her eyes taking his measure. Then she made a decision. Taking Thomas's hand, she pulled him toward the house. "I think it's time you two met."

"You don't have to do this—"

Thomas protested in vain as Emily dragged him up the stairs. It was all he could do not to gawk at the lurid parlor as they passed through, especially with the fantasies that refused to leave his mind. Watson meowed, leaping out of their way. Heedless, Emily hauled him into her bedroom, then lit the candle on the dressing table.

"Now watch. Rosie! Thomas is here. He wants to say hello."

The gilt mirror hung before them, a magnificent creation of ornate gold frame and silver glass. Thomas and Emily looked expectantly at their reflections.

"Rosie?" Emily called again.

Nothing.

Stamping her foot in frustration, Emily turned to Thomas. "But she is here! She's in the glass! I can feel her even now!"

"Emily." Thomas took her in his arms in an attempt to soothe her, but Emily pulled away.

"You don't believe me."

"Let's just say I'm skeptical. You've been working very hard, and in a strange house like this—"

"Thomas! I've seen her, talked to her. She's been helping me with the case!"

"Emily, it doesn't matter if I believe you or not. You believe it. That's all that counts."

His hand went to her chin, softly caressing the rounded curve. Emily shivered, the delicious feelings rising up in her quickly even at the simple touch. They both suddenly became aware of the bed yawning in the center of the room, looking entirely too available and entirely too enticing. The previous night's lovemaking was fresh in both their minds, and the room suddenly felt far too small.

"I should go." Thomas's hand reluctantly left her face. He waited for a moment, to see if she would object. When she didn't, he appeared disappointed, then turned quickly, walking toward the door as if afraid he'd change his mind. He stopped only long enough to speak over his shoulder. "I'll go see Bertie Evans tomorrow, I promise. If it makes you feel any better, put together a list of questions you want answered. I'll try to get as much out of her as I can."

Emily nodded, still shivering from desire. She watched him walk out of the room, wanting with all her heart to call him back. Now that she knew the sweet reward that lay in his arms, she only wanted more. Yet the mystery of her father's death hung over her head like a guillotine, and until she knew what had really happened, she just couldn't risk making herself any more vulnerable.

Besides, Thomas probably thought she was crazy. Even as the thought formed in her mind, Rosie appeared, her eyes sparkling impishly.

"Rosie! Why didn't you come when Thomas was here?"

"What and ruin everything?" The phantom giggled. "I thought you two were doing just fine without me, honey."

"Well, that's nice. He probably thinks I've lost my mind. In fact, I'm sure of it."

Rosie hastened to reassure her. "I don't believe he thinks any such thing. So you two have kissed and made up?" The ghost sounded hopeful.

"Not exactly. He tried to make me go back to Boston." Emily fought to keep the stinging pain from her voice, but Rosie picked up on it instantly.

"Boston! Why?"

"Emmet Colter knows about me, and isn't too pleased that I've been asking questions. When I told Thomas, he insisted I leave."

"I see." Rosie tapped a manicured finger against her cheek, then her smile broadened. "Honey, don't take that as a sign that he's not interested in you. Sounds to me like he's really worried about you."

"Yes, but after last night, don't you think . . ." She let her voice trail off, unable to finish the sentence. She felt like a fool, an unsophisticated child who still expected a glass slipper.

Rosie nodded. "I understand. Don't feel bad, honey, men just look at these things differently than we do. Thomas wants to keep you safe, and he thinks the best way to do that is to send you back East."

"Well, I refused," Emily said flatly. "Worse, I wanted him to take me to see Bertie Evans, but now that he knows about Emmet, he won't let me come."

Rosie sighed thoughtfully. "I know you won't agree with me, but I think that makes sense. You would lead Emmet straight to the woman. You might even cost her her life."

"I hadn't thought of that." Emily's eyes grew wide.

"Let the preacher man do the dangerous work. You're the brains here, after all."

Emily nodded, brightening at that thought. "Tomorrow I open the shop. It's so frustrating that I can't be in two places at once! I'd really like to do more research and see what else I can find out about Emmet. But after Thomas's little sermon today, I may actually have customers."

"What sermon?" Emily was so used to the ghost's presence, she'd forgotten again that Rosie couldn't "see" what happened outside Shangri-La. She quickly explained the incident in town, and the ghost giggled uproariously.

"Well, if that ain't the funniest thing! Our preacher man, who ain't even a preacher, preaching to the choir!"

"Tomorrow is also the meeting of the Ladies' Sewing Circle. Eleanor promised to introduce me around."

"Maybe once your business is doing well, you could hire someone to help," Rosie suggested. "Then you could do two things at once."

"That's a thought," Emily agreed, slipping under the bedclothes. "In fact, that's a brilliant idea."

20

Eleanor Hamill Saves the Day

It was late morning when Thomas rode into Greeley, Emily's words weighing heavily on his mind. Emmet Colter in Denver! He swore aloud, picturing the outlaw with his cruel eyes, peg leg, and menacing smirk. Although he'd never met the man in person, he'd seen enough posters and newspaper drawings to remember his features clearly. That such a man could be after Emily was enough to make his blood run cold.

Perhaps he could persuade her to move into the hotel, at least until things cooled down. Shangri-La, for all its graceful beauty, was dangerous in its isolation. Although the reason for the house's location was obvious, it still troubled him to have Emily out there alone, except for an imaginary ghost. He had already spoken to the sheriff about protecting her, but the man simply didn't have enough help. He could only promise to keep an eye on things. Still, it was better than nothing.

Thomas's thoughts went back to Emily's claim that Rosie was haunting the house. The sheriff had made the same comment. Although Thomas had chalked the man's story up to fancy, Emily was the most logical person he'd ever met.

He shook his head. Frankly he didn't know what to make of it, except that perhaps her nervous strain was beginning to show itself. And he couldn't blame her if it did. Emily Potter wasn't safe anywhere now, and until that gold was safely locked away in a bank vault, she never would be.

His horse slowed to a walk as he approached Greeley's center, and he realized that something meaningful within him had changed. Whereas the most important thing to him had been the recovery of the gold, Emily's safety now held as much weight, if not more.

Climbing off his horse, Thomas tied the animal to a hitching post and walked into the dry goods store. A lone Indian looked askance at him from a dark corner of the shop, while the shopkeeper himself beamed at the prospect of a customer.

"Need help, sir?"

"Just directions. I'm looking for Bertie Evans."

The shopkeeper frowned, shaking his head thoughtfully. "I don't recall anyone by that name. Do you have an address?"

Thomas handed the man a slip of paper and his

face cleared. "Oh, that would be Miss Higgins. She's only been in town a few months. Lives alone. You can't miss the place, it's just past the canals."

"Thanks." Thomas walked out of the store, his frown deepening. Bertie Evans had changed her name. Why? From one viewpoint, it was a prudent thing to do, especially after her association with the bordello, but it could also mean something else: Bertie knew something, and had correctly guessed that someone would eventually be asking for her.

Remounting his horse, Thomas followed the man's directions, past the remarkable canals that irrigated the area. Named for Horace Greeley, the town was really an oasis in the midst of a prairie. Green undulating fields stretched before him, a stark contrast to the vast emptiness of the plains. It was an experiment that was obviously a success.

As Thomas approached the modest house, he saw a woman hanging clothes outside. From her appearance, he guessed her to be Bertie, and he approached her cautiously.

"Miss Higgins?"

The woman glanced up, clothespins in her mouth. She nodded, her eyes narrowing as he came closer. Bertie was a short, plump woman, like a little sparrow, with wonderfully alert eyes and a brisk manner. Thomas removed his hat and saw her tension wane as she noticed his collar. She removed the pins from her mouth.

"Morning, Preacher. What can I do for you?"

"I came to talk to you about Shangri-La. It's important."

Her eyes widened and she glanced back at the cottage, as if preparing to make a run for it. Thomas gave her his most ingratiating smile.

"Don't be afraid. I'm not the law, nor any kind of trouble. In fact, I'm trying to prevent that. You are Bertie Evans, am I correct? Do you know a man called Colter?"

The woman's eyes grew impossibly larger. She nodded in answer to both his questions, her face draining of color.

"I have learned that Emmet was involved in the murders of John Potter and Rosie. You do know that Potter's daughter, Emily, has taken over the house? And that Lizzie Wakefield is missing?"

The woman trembled. Sinking down onto a bench, she began to shake from head to toe. "I don't know nothing! I came up here to get away from that place! I only want to live in peace, to forget that night."

"I understand," Thomas said gently. He laid a hand on hers, trying to comfort her. Her skin felt like ice. "I came here to help you. Emmet's looking for you, and it won't be long until he tracks you down."

"My God!" The woman rose quickly. "I have to pack! Emmet Colter! Lord have mercy . . ."

"Please, Miss Evans," Thomas tried again. "I'm trying to help Miss Potter, and trying to prevent any more killings. Part of my reason for coming here today was to warn you. The other part is that I need your help. Whatever you can tell me about the murders would assist us tremendously."

To his surprise, the woman nodded, and he had to

admit—if only to himself—that Emily's coaching had been valuable. Bertie Evans indicated the house, and she walked inside a few feet ahead of him, her plump body quivering like a plate of jelly. He felt sorry for her, but was grateful that he'd found her before Emmet did. He kept picturing Lizzie's housekeeper, lying dead on the floor.

"I'm sorry, Reverend. Your news has me so scared I didn't think to offer you tea. Would you like a cup?"

Thomas nodded, and the woman bustled about the kitchen, obviously more comfortable with something to do. She brewed the tea, setting out cups, her every motion a measure of efficiency.

"I don't know what all I can tell you except that I'll never forget that night. I was in the kitchen, in the rear of the house, cleaning up after dinner. Rosie and Mr. Potter had just finished up, and were making plans for the evening. It seems to me they expected a guest, for they asked me to remove the supper dishes earlier than usual."

"That's interesting." Thomas made a few notes. "Do you know who they expected?"

The housekeeper shook her head. "No. I could hear them talking, then Rosie must have gone upstairs, for it got real quiet. The China girl, Sung He, had been helping me in the kitchen, then she went up to see Rosie. Right around the same time, there was a knock on the door. I heard Mr. Potter answer it himself."

"Was that unusual?"

"Yes. Normally, one of the servants would open

the door and bring the calling card into the parlor, but Rosie had given the butler the night off. I thought it was odd, but with what went on in the house, mysterious callers sometimes came. I didn't think much more about it."

Thomas noticed the woman's face get hot as she glanced at his collar once more. He struggled to hide his smile as the woman continued reluctantly.

"I thought I heard Mr. Potter talking softly, friendly-like. He sounded like it was someone he knew well. I couldn't hear his company, but I was all the way in the back of the kitchen, scraping plates. I was thinking of going in there, to see if they wanted anything, when it happened."

The housekeeper's eyes glazed over, as if she were picturing something terrible. Thomas nodded encouragingly. "Please. Go on."

The woman shuddered. "Next thing I know, I heard gunshots. The plate fell out of my hand and crashed into the sink. Somehow I knew he was dead. I think Rosie must have come down the stairs, for I heard her cry out as well. I didn't think twice. I just ran toward the woods out back and hid in the shrubbery. I saw someone run out the back door after me, then heard the sound of horse's hooves coming around the house. It looked like the rider was searching for someone. I didn't move. I just lay there, sick to my stomach, praying I wouldn't die."

Thomas leaned closer and patted the woman consolingly as she began to sob. "That's all right. Did you see who was in the yard with you?"

She lifted her face, tears streaming down her round cheeks. "When I finally got the nerve to look around, I realized that it was Sung He who had run out of the house, and that she was hiding near the woodshed. The horse finally rode off, then I saw her slip into the hills and she was gone."

"I see." Thomas scribbled furiously, the excitement building within him. Sung He, from the woman's account, was a possible eyewitness! No wonder no one would tell him where she was!

But the killer must have seen her as well, for why else would he circle the house instead of riding off? He surmised that Bertie's guess was right—the killer had seen the Chinese girl run, and had searched the grounds for her.

"What happened then?" Thomas asked gently as the woman fought to compose herself.

"I never went back. I came here, to save up enough money to go out to California, or somewhere safe. When things seemed to die down, I stopped worrying. I got a job here working in the Trapper house, and thought to live out my life quietly. Looks like that ain't going to happen, now."

Her face was so miserable that Thomas felt truly sorry for her. He smiled in an attempt to comfort her. "Do you have any relatives you could visit for a few weeks?"

The woman nodded, then blew her nose. "I can telegraph my sister back East. We don't get along as a whole, but she might be able to take me in for a spell." She looked up hopefully. "Are you sure you're not mistaken about Emmet?"

"I wish I was." Thomas rose. "Go to your sister's. I'll make certain you're notified once Emmet is behind bars."

"Thank you, sir," the woman said, as she looked forlornly around the meager house she would soon be leaving.

Emily walked into the town hall, her basket under her arm and her heart in her throat. Somehow facing outlaws seemed easier than attending the monthly meeting of the Ladies' Sewing Circle. Swallowing her trepidation, she forced herself to hold her head high as she entered the room.

The women milled around a table covered with sweets, glasses of lemonade, and cups of tea. They chattered animatedly among themselves, until one woman spotted Emily and lightly nudged her neighbor. She glanced Emily's way, notified her nearest acquaintance, until one by one the hall fell silent.

Emily wanted to run. Thomas had warned her how hard this would be, but the reality was worse than she'd ever dreamed. Faced with the possible rejection of all of the town's ladies en masse, she became even more aware of how desperate she was to make a good impression. Yet the censorious expressions she saw gave her little hope. She wondered how long it would take them to throw her out.

"Ah, there you are, Miss Potter. I despaired of your arrival."

Emily's shoulders slumped in relief as Eleanor Hamill approached, rapping her cane sharply on the floor. The imperious old lady indicated a chair along the wall.

"You are to sit beside me. I wouldn't dare miss one word of your captivating conversation this evening. I must say, we are all delighted to have you. Aren't we, Edith? Joyce?"

The ladies glanced at each other helplessly, forced to nod in Emily's direction. "But of course! We are very glad to have you. Pray take some refreshment and join us."

The knot in Emily's throat seemed to dissolve and she put her case next to Eleanor's seat. As she filled a plate, she felt someone staring at her. Across the table, to Emily's dismay, was the woman who had been on the stagecoach with her when she'd come into town— the same woman who'd witnessed her "Science of Deduction" at the dry goods store. Emily smiled weakly, but her adversary practically harumphed her displeasure aloud. Taking up three cakes, she gave Emily a wide berth.

"Don't let Amelia bother you," Eleanor whispered, taking Emily's arm. "I daresay you made an impression on her that she won't forget. Some people just don't understand Holmes's brilliance."

"I see." Emily more than saw, especially when the woman began tittering to her companion. Still, she had Eleanor's support, and that was a start.

Following the older woman to their seats, Emily tried not to notice that some of the others had reached for their stitchery and some simply stared at her. Although a few of the braver souls, emboldened by Thomas's speech, had made their way to her shop that morning, most of the faces were unfamiliar and far from friendly. Emily forced down a dry cake, and followed it up with a swallow of bitter tea.

"Miss Potter, I'm so glad you decided to join us this evening. I must say, we've heard so much about you."

The woman Eleanor had introduced as Edith spoke softly, but her kind words were followed by more than one choking sound. Emily could hear the hisses of disapproval. She smiled as graciously as she could at the woman.

"Thank you. I do appreciate that. I know I've been remiss in not introducing myself earlier, but I've had so much to do. I finally set up shop in town, and am in the process of fixing up my house. I'm sorry I didn't meet many of you at my reception."

In the silence that followed this remark, Emily realized she'd made another misstep. Eleanor leaned toward Emily. "*They* should be sorry, my dear, for I had a wonderful time that evening. The house itself is magnificent, and you've already done wonders with it. And the books!" Turning back to the sewing circle Eleanor said to the room at large, "Are any of you familiar with the works of Sir Arthur Conan Doyle?"

The ladies looked perplexed, and Eleanor nodded as if confirming her own suspicions. "That is exactly what I thought. It is little wonder Miss Potter has been so misunderstood by you all, for she is attempting to emulate Doyle's fictional hero, a Mr. Sherlock Holmes. Holmes, you must understand, is the world's only consulting detective."

"A detective!" one of the younger woman exclaimed. She turned to Emily in amazement. "You don't mean to say you are a Pinkerton? I've never heard of them employing women."

"Nor I," Emily answered truthfully. "But I have never let my sex be considered a hindrance. I think a woman's mind is as fine as any man's, in spite of those recent theories suggesting that because our skulls measure smaller, we aren't as capable. By studying Holmes's methods, and learning the Science of Deduction, I've been able to shed light on cases that were very dark to the local authorities. I daresay even here in Denver, I've been able to practice successfully."

"I heard about the incident at the dry goods store," another woman said softly, putting her sewing aside. "Is it true you were able to tell everything about the man simply from examining his cuffs?"

The women leaned closer, and to her amazement, Emily realized they were genuinely interested. She glanced at her mentor, but Eleanor simply winked and sat back in her chair. Encouraged, Emily continued.

"Well, I also had some help from his watch and the plaque he displayed there. By reading these clues, one would have to be very dim indeed not to deduce the man's story. I wasn't proud of that event, for I was motivated more by my own pride than science. Still, it is helpful to sharpen one's skills continually."

"I find that fascinating," the younger woman who had been on the stagecoach remarked. "And I think your notion of a woman being equal to a man in intelligence is gratifying. I have always thought much the same thing, and I am delighted that one of us has the courage to say it. I've been thinking of calling on you, to ask a favor, so it must be fate that brings you here today."

"I'd be glad to help," Emily said, delighted.

"I met a man," the young woman whispered shyly. "And I thought, given your talent, perhaps you could meet him and advise me of his true character. I'll never forget your scientific deductions on the stage-coach."

Amelia, who'd been glaring at Emily all the while, snorted loudly. "I suppose your little stunt at the Sil-verdust was a result of your 'Science,' too. Miss Pot-ter, I am going to be blunt, and I'm sure I speak for most of us here. I find you a disreputable person, and I must admit I am dismayed that our little club had admitted you at all."

Stunned, Emily watched as the good humor that was just beginning to preside evaporated. More than one woman suddenly seemed to remember the ru-mors about Emily. The frowns of disapproval were beginning to return when Eleanor put her tea aside, then stood up next to Emily like a professor defend-ing her protégé.

"Mrs. Merryway, I can quite understand your interpretation of Miss Potter's actions, but I assure you that Holmes would have understood completely. Assuming the dress and character of a completely different personage enabled Holmes to obtain infor-mation he could never have known otherwise. That is precisely what Miss Potter has done. I must say, she is a very convincing actress, for no one initially suspected anything out of the ordinary. The stage lost a great performer when you decided to turn to detecting, Miss Emily."

Silence ensued once more. Emily felt as if she were on trial. Yet it seemed as if the verdict might be favorable. First came one shy smile, then another, until the woman beside her extended her hand in welcome.

"I am Victoria Sands. Perhaps you could come to tea on Tuesday. I am fascinated by your work, and would love to hear more about it. I also adore your bonnet. Do you have many more like it?"

"I, too, would truly like to know you," another woman added. "I admired your hats today through the window, but I couldn't summon the courage to come in. And I would love to see the inside of your home. I've often thought how beautiful that house would be, if used for other purposes."

The woman's implications became clear, then laughter broke out among them all at once.

"Why, Mary, you couldn't know of any such thing! I am scandalized!"

"Miss Potter, is it truly lurid? And are the rumors of a haunting true?"

"Is it true that Rosie's portrait hangs there?"

Emily nodded, on surer ground now. "Yes, it is true. The house is beautiful, and it *is* haunted, by a very benevolent ghost."

"A ghost! How wonderful! You know, I belong to the Spiritualist Society. We've attempted seances, but never heard from the other side. My group would be fascinated, as well as appreciative, if we could visit. And we've a lot of hat buyers among us."

"And I'd like to make an appointment for your counsel," the young woman from the stagecoach said boldly. "Is Tuesday convenient?"

Amelia Merryway scowled in disapproval, but it was entirely too late now. With Thomas's help and Eleanor's support, the women of Denver had decided to embrace her.

It was a wondrous feat indeed.

21

※

A Late-Night Visit

"You did it? You won over the dragon ladies of Denver! That's terrific, sweetie!"

"Yes, I really think I did." Emily grinned as the ghost slowly materialized in the mirror. "Thank God for Eleanor Hamill. She really helped me when it seemed, for a moment there, that they would attack."

Rosie shuddered. "I can't remember much of my time on earth anymore, but I remember them. Bunch of old biddies, that's what they are. Why, they used to cross to the other side of the street when I approached, and wouldn't give me or my girls the time of day."

Emily's smile was sad. "Did they really treat you that way? I can't imagine anyone knowing you and thinking you any less than the most noble and kind of women."

Emily's voice was sincere and Rosie blushed, then wiped at her cheek. "Why, thank you, honey. That's real sweet of you to say. It means a lot to me, and I know it would have to your pa, too. He cared quite a bit for you, sweetie."

"I suppose." Emily frowned thoughtfully. "You know, if he really did have that gold, wouldn't he have wanted me to find it? There has to be a clue, something I've overlooked. . . ."

"Have you really searched this whole house? Your pa designed it himself from the ground up, and it's a puzzle all right. There are so many rooms, secret doorways—"

"What?" Emily was completely at attention now.

Rosie nodded. "Yes. There's one in the hall, so we could hide out if the lawman decided to make arrests. Although he was more often one of our customers—"

Emily let that remark pass, too intrigued by this new possibility to think about it. "Maybe that's it! If my father knew of my interest in detecting, maybe he thought I could figure it out! And if the gold is nowhere to be found . . ."

"That would make things a lot easier between you and Thomas, wouldn't it?" Rosie speculated. "Speaking of the handsome preacher man, he was here earlier."

Rosie let this bomb drop with all the subtlety of a naval tactician. Emily sat up.

"Thomas? Here?"

"Why, yes! He knocked on the door a good long spell, and when you didn't answer, he must have tried the knob. I don't know if you or Darrel left it open, but I heard him swearing downstairs that you've got to be more careful. He seemed right upset. Even said something about taking it out on your hide."

Emily blushed, but instantly got to her feet. "He must have learned something from Bertie that he wants to tell me. I've got to go to him!"

"Honey, how are you going to do that?" Rosie leaned forward, obviously amused. "He's living at the boardinghouse, isn't he? You can't just go traipsing in there. We didn't even do that."

Emily laced up her boots, but her fingers slowed as she tied the knots. "I see what you mean. The night I went there with Thomas, the place was dark, but there's liable to be people about now. Still, I can't wait until morning." She sat back on the bed, her keen mind working. Suddenly, a huge smile came to her face. "I have an idea."

Outside, it was dark and starless, a perfect covering for her covert operation. Emily felt a grin come to her face as she thought of Thomas's reaction. Would he be pleased, or would he resent her intrusion? And what if someone were with him, perhaps another woman?

That thought stung, but Emily forced it aside. If Thomas was romantically involved with someone else, she thought logically, it was far better to know now than to get in deeper with him. Still, the vision of the townswomen, all trying to get his attention at his "service," haunted her.

The fire escape looked a bit rickety as she approached, but Emily tested the first step carefully, and finding that it would support her weight, ascended to the second. One by one she climbed, until thankfully she reached Thomas's window. She peered inside.

He was in the room, and quite alone. Emily would have exhaled in relief if she hadn't realized in the next instant that he was in a bath, just like the time she'd barged in on him at the barber. Her fantasy of joining him in the tub flashed before her eyes, and she sinfully allowed herself to entertain the thought of doing so. He was so strong, so muscular, so . . . sexy. His back was to her, but she devoured the sight of his half-naked body surrounded by bubbles, and she could see that his feet stuck out of the small tin tub. A cigar smoked from beneath his teeth, and a glass of whiskey lay on a table at his elbow. He appeared absolutely content with the world, and completely unaware that he was about to have a guest.

Suppressing a giggle, she made her way around the back and slipped into the hallway, making a mental thank-you note to the Lord that the door on this floor had been left ajar. As she approached Thomas's room, a maid came up the stairs carrying a bucket of hot water.

"Is that for this room?" Emily whispered.

The girl nodded, looking tired.

"I'll take it," Emily replied. When the girl's brow flew upward, Emily hastened to explain. "I'm the reverend's sister. It's quite all right."

The maid was so harried she left the bucket and departed without another word. *Rosie must be rubbing off on me,* Emily realized, for six months ago, she wouldn't have dreamed of such scandalous—surely—and immoral—no doubt—behavior. She couldn't wait to see the look on Thomas's face.

Tiptoeing into the room with the water, she softly closed the door behind her. Thomas lay in the tub, his eyes closed. Without looking up, he gestured to the tub.

"Just pour it in. The water's getting cold."

"Certainly," Emily replied, then dumped the water over his knees.

Thomas's eyes flew open as he recognized her voice, then howled as the hot water poured over his cooled skin. Emily stepped back, a laugh escaping from her as he half rose from the tub, gasping from the heat. A moment later, when it became bearable, he sank down into the suds again, a wry smile coming to his face.

"Very funny. Miss Potter, I believe you have a tub fascination. You are continually invading my bath. How did you get in here?"

"The fire escape," Emily said blithely, rewarded with the look of incredulity on his face. "I heard you were at Shangri-La earlier, so I came right away. What happened?"

"The fire escape? You mean you climbed . . ." He turned toward the window in disbelief, then glanced back at her. "You heard I was at the house? How—"

Emily started to respond when he cut her off.

"No, I don't want to hear about your ghost again.

But yes, however you found out, I did come by tonight to tell you what happened."

"Then you found her?"

Thomas reached for his drink, took a long swig, then nodded, extinguishing his cigar. "Yes, Bertie Evans was in Greeley under an assumed name."

"Thomas, that's wonderful! And so clever of you!" Emily said, truly impressed. She pulled up a chair, heedless of Thomas's nudity, then leaned forward with her hands on her knees. "Now I want to hear everything. Did you question her the way I instructed? Does she remember anything helpful? Does she know Emmet Colter is after her, and does she know why?"

Thomas grinned, his white teeth a roguish flash against his grizzled chin. "Patience, my dear. I'll tell you everything. You do realize, Miss Potter, that it is extremely immoral of you to break into my room like this, and converse with me in my tub? The women of the town would be scandalized."

"No one has to know," Emily said practically. "Besides, this was too important. I just couldn't wait."

"Well, next time you'll have to." Thomas assumed his preacher tone again. "Emily, we're both working to build up your name in this town. One indiscreet act like this could ruin it all."

"Oh, Thomas, I can't be concerned about that now! Stop teasing and tell me."

Thomas's eyes rolled in mock disgust, but he related the story of his meeting with Bertie Evans, giving Emily every possible detail he could remember. Her gaze shone with interest as he told her about

Sung He, and she nodded slowly, as if mentally committing the facts to some secret vault.

"Then someone did see the murders! I knew it! Now if we can just find Sung He. . . ."

"That, unfortunately, is easier said than done. I've already tried."

"What?" Emily's jaw dropped. "When?" Thomas told her about his previous visit to the encampment at the edge of town, and the secretiveness of its Chinese inhabitants.

"No one would tell me a thing. They are suspicious of strangers to begin with, but it's little wonder they hide China Blue—they must know the danger she's in."

"There has to be a way. I seem to recall Holmes partaking of opium once, to enter one of the Chinese dens in London. Perhaps . . ."

"Oh, no," Thomas said sternly. "For a woman of your brains, you sometimes have very little sense. You aren't going into any opium den, not even in the interest of science. Furthermore, you have to start locking your door and taking some precautions. I was going to talk to you about this tomorrow, but since you decided you were lonely for my company tonight, we may as well talk about it now."

Emily sighed, then looked at him doubtfully. "I detect a sermon coming on."

"You are correct. Emily, I believe you should take lodging in town, at least temporarily. I still think the safest place for you is at home in Boston, but if you are too stubborn to listen to common sense, then we'll have to go for the next best thing."

"No!" Emily looked at him as if he were an imbecile. "I can't do that! If Shangri-La is unprotected, someone else could find the gold! Also, if Emmet or one of his crowd is after me, no hotel door will stop them. You know that."

Thomas gritted his teeth in frustration. "Emily, why can't you make things easy? I'm trying to protect you!"

"I think you're trying to get rid of me!" The words came out before Emily could stop them, the pain apparent in her voice. Thomas looked as stunned as if she had slapped him. The hurt that Emily had been suppressing came to the surface, and she blurted out everything.

"Ever since our night together, you keep suggesting that I leave town. Well, if you think just because you had the milk, you no longer need the cow, you are very much mistaken. I appreciate your help, Thomas, but I can manage on my own, if need be, and I'm not going anywhere."

Thomas looked at her strangely.

"Is that what you really think? That I don't want you anymore?"

"What else am I to think?" Emily shrugged as if it didn't matter, though her eyes stung suspiciously. "You certainly have reason to dislike me. Especially with what you believe about my father."

Thomas shook his head, then looked down at the bathwater. His voice was filled with amused frustration as he held up a wrinkled hand.

"Emily, we need to talk about this, but I need to get out of this water before I look like a prune."

"Thomas, I'm sorry! Why didn't you say something? Please, come out of there. Don't mind me," Emily said, flustered, suddenly aware that the water had stopped steaming and goose bumps had appeared on Thomas's arms.

Thomas raised a brow. "Most ladies would be a little shocked if I simply strode out of the tub, with no care for their feminine sensibilities. However, if that doesn't concern you at all . . ."

He started to rise and Emily gasped, overwhelmed by the sight of him, dripping and magnificent, his muscular body emanating sensuality. She raced for the towel, ignoring his chuckle as she handed it to him, a blush heating her cheeks. Thomas wrapped the towel around his hips, then came to stand directly in front of her. Lifting her chin upward, he gazed into her eyes.

"My God, I can't believe you'd think so little of me. I guess I'll just have to show you. . . ." Heedless of his wet body, Thomas pulled her into his arms. Emily's mouth parted with a gasp, but before she could say a word, he kissed her thoroughly. Her struggles dissipated almost immediately, warmed by the hot, wet feel of him against her, the smoky, whiskey taste of his mouth, and the erotic pleasure that began to wend its way through her flesh.

When he finally eased his mouth from her, he gazed into her face, his expression soft. "Does that feel like someone who doesn't want you?"

Emily shook her head. All thoughts of desertion left her as he communicated his feelings in a way that was timeless. The pain left her, replaced by a wonder and joy that was so intense, she wanted to cry out. Instead, she reached up and wrapped her fingers around his neck, wanting every delightful sensation he offered.

Smiling, he lowered his head to her once more. This time, he deepened the kiss, his tongue thrusting through her teeth, making her moan. Emily arched against him, her body pressed tightly to his, her skin burning through the layers of clothing she wore. She gasped as Thomas lifted her and carried her to the bed. Lying there, she propped herself up on one elbow and felt his hand caressing the silky flesh of her thighs, then the opening in her drawers.

"Thomas! My word . . ."

"I know, sweet. I didn't plan on this either, but if you come sneaking into a man's room at night, you'd better expect something like this. Come, Emily. Open your legs for me. Oh, my God, Emily, you are so hot and sweet. . . ."

Emily gasped, feeling his fingers rub expertly between the folds of her flesh, then enter into the hot moistness between them. Writhing, she was helpless against the sensations that spiraled through her, her body arching, wordlessly crying out for more. Thomas withdrew the finger, slid it upward, then gently massaged the most sensitive part of her until Emily cried out, reaching a shuddering climax almost immediately.

"Please," she whispered.

"Wait, I'll undo your clothes."

"No, now!" Emily wriggled restlessly beneath him. She heard his chuckle, then he tossed the towel aside and came to her.

"Whatever pleases the lady," he murmured, then entered her swiftly.

Emily sighed, her body filled with his hardness. It was even better than before, more urgent and complete. It took her only a few strokes to reach her climax once again. The intensity of her response seemed to excite him even more, for he thrust deeply into her, his body pulsating. After a moment she felt him relax and he wrapped her in his arms as if he could not seem to bring her close enough. Then he lifted his head and smiled down at her. "Emily, promise me you won't ever become a maid. I don't think I could handle the thought of you servicing men's baths this way."

Emily giggled, but his words warmed her strangely. She cuddled closer to him, not caring that her corset cut into her, nor that she was still clothed. She felt wonderful, cared for, and protected.

"I did mean what I said earlier, though. I want you to consider the hotel. If not, then I want that door locked at all times. Do you understand me?"

"Yes, sir," Emily smiled, but Thomas didn't share her mirth.

"I'm not teasing, Emily. I'm serious. This whole thing is closing in on us—I can feel it."

"All right, Thomas, I'll think about what you said." Rising from the bed, she glanced out the window. "I guess I'd better get going. Thanks to you and Eleanor Hamill, I may actually have some customers tomorrow."

"I'll walk you home."

"Thomas, you don't—" Emily stopped herself. "All right, I'd like that."

"And I'm checking the house before I leave."

Emily smiled, watching as he pulled on his trousers. He really was, as Rosie would say, a hell of a man. For however long this lasted, she would enjoy it.

22

The Secret Chamber

"Sorry, boss, we couldn't find hide nor hair of that damned housekeeper. My men rode all through Silverton. Bertie Evans is gone."

When he finished speaking Emmet sipped the excellent whiskey at his elbow, waiting for the explosion that would surely come. He was seated in the private Pullman car of the Union Pacific, and he couldn't help but admire the thick velvet draperies, polished wood tables, opulent gold trim, and comfortable tufted chairs. As a traveling office, it offered many advantages—luxury, servants, and transportation. For the criminal element, it offered even more, for a moving target was extremely difficult to track. Unfortunately, the wealthy occupants, legitimate or otherwise, had to rely on the outside world for information, and that didn't always sit well.

Emmet expected that this time, it wouldn't sit well at all. The boss didn't like disappointments, and disliked failure even more. Emmet was smart enough to know that this job was in jeopardy, and it was too lucrative to let go without a fight. They had been promised a nice cut of the big money when it was found. What the boss didn't know was that Emmet planned to make 100 percent of the profits. This was a hell of a lot easier than robbing trains, Emmet thought. And he'd be damned if he'd let it slip away.

After getting the negative reports from Silverton, he'd gone back to confront the postal clerk, only to discover that the man had vanished. Even more disconcerting, his replacement, who at the show of Emmet's gun produced a forwarding address in Greeley, could tell him nothing else. Greeley yielded the same results as Silverton, and the inescapable conclusion: Bertie had been warned off.

After a long silence the boss spoke coldly. "I didn't hire you to produce a litany of failures. I expected better, Emmet. You were known as a man of action, a man who could get the job done."

"I will get it done," Emmet swore, his fingers tightening on the glass until they turned white. His frustration boiled over, and he voiced the thought that had been eating at him for days. "I've got a gut feeling that it's that damned schoolmarm, Emily Potter, that's behind all this. That woman's worse than any Pinkerton. She's been asking questions, digging up information, even posing as a saloon girl to learn what happened to her old man. Jake says she went out to see Lizzie, although we took care of that little problem. I think she's the one who warned Bertie off."

The boss paused and appeared to digest this information with interest. "Miss Potter? You think Potter's daughter is directly involved?"

Emmet nodded his head. "If it wasn't for your message, I'da shot her and been done with it the day I saw her at the post office, walking around like she'd got a stick in the back of her dress, them spectacles slipping down her face. She was snooping around, poking her nose into everyone's business."

"Interesting. So Miss Potter is trying to find out who caused her father's death. That could mean trouble. But you can't kill her. Not yet. She may still lead us to the gold, and I want that money. I was cheated out of it once; I don't intend to let it happen again."

"That's the only reason that spinster lady's still alive," Emmet snarled. "She's stirring up too much dust. That housekeeper's gone, and China Blue is missing. The China girl's really the one that can hurt you, though. She was there, remember."

It wasn't his neck on the line for the killings, and they both knew it. Emmet was getting a little tired of this game, and more than a little tired of taking orders. He pulled his hat down and discreetly glanced around the interior of the luxurious car, looking for the safe. Maybe it would be better to do it now, shoot the boss, and just take the money. As if reading his mind, the boss stood up and faced him.

"Don't even think about it, Emmet. Do you really

believe I'd be so stupid as to keep my money with me? You'll get paid as long as you perform. But I'm losing patience. I may have to take matters into my own hands."

Emmet gritted his teeth. He'd already run through the money from the last train robbery, and he needed income until they found Potter's two million. After that . . . well, that was another matter. He stood up quickly, balancing awkwardly with his wooden leg.

"I'll shut that housekeeper up, if I have to track her back East myself. And that China girl's as good as dead. You can bank on it."

"Good. You do your part in this, and I'll see that you're rewarded. However, I do think it's time I got more involved. I want to keep closer tabs on Miss Potter. If that gold is found, I want to know it. And I cannot tolerate any more incompetence."

"Don't worry," Emmet spat, touching the butt of his pistol. "That gold will be found."

A few days later, Emily stood in her hat shop, ringing up sales. A pile of receipts lay in a box at her side. Many of her display hats had already been sold, and she had standing orders for at least twenty more. Business was brisk, already much better than in Boston, for as Emily had originally noted, there was little competition. She also realized that the western women, tired of last year's fashions, very much appreciated her newer styles and her unerring touch when it came to decorations. If things continued at this pace, she would have more than enough income to get her through the winter, even if she never found the gold.

That thought led to other, more disturbing, ones. Thomas had been instrumental in helping her get started. A shiver of pleasure went through her as she thought of their lovemaking, and the tender things he'd said to her. He'd gone out of his way to reassure her, but he'd also held firmly to his belief that her father was, well, a crook. And if Thomas did clear his own name and prove her father had stolen the gold, it would create an impasse between them that might never be overcome.

The only solution was to discover the truth herself. She'd meant what she'd said to Thomas: She was falling in love with him. As a result, it was even more important that she find out what really happened, and put this dark cloud behind them. Now if she could just find more time to investigate!

Her nose wrinkled as she glanced down at her notes. She had so many clues, and with Thomas's new information, it was even more imperative that they find China Blue before Emmet did. The laundry woman was possibly a material witness, and as such, held the key to the entire mystery. In spite of her promise to Thomas, she fully intended to try and find the woman herself.

Then there was the missing gold. Emily was still intrigued by what Rosie had said to her. Although she'd checked out the secret door the ghost had told her about, she hadn't found anything. Yet that didn't discourage her. If the gold was somewhere in the house, she'd have to take a logical approach to finding it. Thus she planned to go over the measurements of the house, to discern whether there was unaccounted space where the gold could be hidden. Perhaps her father had built a secret room to hide the money. If so, she would find it.

In between customers, Emily tried to review the case, but it was a difficult task, especially in light of the distractions. Every time she began to make progress, she was interrupted. Finally she realized it was futile. Even Emily couldn't do two things at once, much as she hated to admit it.

"I need help!" she said to herself, but somehow the words slipped out.

A woman who'd been looking at the hats paused at her elbow, turning to her with a curious expression. "Excuse me. Did you say something?"

Emily sighed. "I'm sorry, I was thinking out loud. Business is a little better than expected, and I just realized I need to hire someone."

"Really?" The woman put down the bonnet she was holding, and a shy smile came to her face. "Isn't that funny? I am a widow in need of income, and I was just thinking what a perfect occupation this would be. If you're serious, maybe we should talk. My name is Lynette Stockbridge." She extended her hand.

Emily felt as if God had overheard her. Putting on her spectacles, she looked over the woman before her, even as she accepted the proffered hand. Lynette was about five foot three, with soft blond hair and a slender figure.

"Have you any experience?" Emily asked her.

The woman nodded, then dug through her purse.
"I worked for Mrs. Bates in Philadelphia for many
years as her seamstress. I came out here a little over a
year ago with my husband. Unfortunately, he passed
on, and I've been struggling since. I'm certain I could
learn how to stitch hats or can take care of customers."
She held out a rumpled letter of recommendation.

Just then another woman approached and tapped
her fan on the counter. "May I have some help here?"

She was an older, heavyset woman, with a beaked
nose and a tight mouth. A demanding type, Emily
could tell immediately. She glanced at Lynette.
"Why don't you assist this woman? I'll be right back
here if you need anything."

Lynette turned to the older woman. "Certainly,
Madam. I'm sorry you had to wait. What can I show
you?"

"I need a winter bonnet. Not one of those new-
fangled things that wouldn't keep a baby warm, but a
good, solid winter bonnet. In black. I am in mourning for my husband. I cannot possibly wear colors."

"I am sorry," Lynette said softly. "I know what it is
to lose a husband. But the mourning period isn't
quite so long now, and I can't help but picture how
lovely this one would look on you. However, I do
have some plainer bonnets, if you prefer."

The older woman's manner changed at the compliment, and she reluctantly allowed Lynette to tie
the ribbons beneath her chin. Looking into the mirror, her eyes opened appreciatively.

"Why, it does look nice, doesn't it?"

"Very nice," Lynette agreed. "And that blue is

definitely your color. The ladies of the sewing circle will be green with envy. Did you just need the one, or would you like to look at the pattern book? Miss Emily can custom design a lovely bonnet for Sunday, or perhaps something special for Christmas."

"I could use a pretty bonnet for the holidays," the woman said happily. "Can I sit down?"

"Certainly, right over there. And let me bring you some tea while you look."

Emily smiled, watching as Lynette efficiently bustled the woman into a seat, then waited on the next woman. She successfully sold the first woman two more hats, then convinced the other that she should place orders for new ostrich feather bonnets, since she had the deportment to carry the style off. Both women left impressed and satisfied. When she returned to the counter, Emily put a hand on her shoulder.

"You've got a job, if you want it."

"Really? Oh, that's wonderful! This is perfect! We are going to make great partners, I just know it!"

"When can you start?"

"Right away," Lynette said enthusiastically. "Today, in fact."

"Good. I'll be in the back for a while. If you need anything, just call me."

Emily went gleefully to the rear of the shop, her notes under one arm, her glasses tipping at the end of her nose. Finally she could sleuth undistracted, and make some real progress on a case that was quickly getting hot. Things were working out better than she could have hoped.

———

A few days later, Emily and Lynette were working silently and companionably together sewing hats when the door to the shop opened softly. Emily glanced up. A rush of emotion went through her as she saw Thomas watching her, his eyes warm and admiring, taking in the pretty scene of the two women bent over their needlework. Sunlight filtered through the lace curtains, making soft, dappled patterns against the floor, and bringing out the highlights in Emily's hair. Dr. Watson played contentedly with a ball of yarn, while Lynette's needle flashed silver in the gentle light.

Emily rose, putting her work aside. The sweetness of their lovemaking, when she had so boldly intruded on his bath, was still fresh in her mind and she gave him her hand, feeling a warm tingling when he touched her.

"Good morning," Thomas said, his eyes twinkling. He glanced curiously at the other woman. "How are the hats coming?"

"Wonderfully." Emily smiled. Lynette glanced at Thomas, then Emily, obviously sensing the emotion between them. "Reverend Hall, this is Mrs. Stockbridge. She's helping me with the shop. Mrs. Stockbridge, Reverend Hall. He is a local preacher."

"Reverend." Lynette bowed her head, then looked up at Thomas again. "I've heard so much about you. The ladies in town are very taken with you."

"Thank you." Thomas seemed pleased with the compliment. "I try to do the Lord's work." He turned back to Emily, his gaze inviting. "I had a few things to do in town and I thought you might like to come for a walk. It's a beautiful day."

Lynette nodded quickly, waving her hand at the couple. "Go. I can easily finish what's in the bag here. If any customers come in, I'll help them."

Emily smiled and slipped her arm through Thomas's. "It looks like I'm free. I won't be long," she promised.

Outside, Emily turned to Thomas excitedly. "Isn't she great? I can get so much accomplished now! I was so lucky to find her!"

"I didn't know you were thinking of hiring help," Thomas replied. He paused at the dry goods store, taking out his shopping list.

"I didn't plan to. She just walked into the shop one day. She has been a tremendous help already."

"She does seem like a nice lady," Thomas commented, filling his sack with a razor, shaving soap, and a few other toilet articles. "And I'm glad you have someone in the shop with you. I didn't like the idea of you alone there, and exposed."

A shiver went through her as his hand softly caressed her cheek. What was wrong with her, that the simplest touch of this man turned her into jelly? "I have everything under control," Emily assured him. "You'll see."

Emily returned home, overjoyed by her success. With Lynette's help, her productivity would increase dramatically. She would be able to fill the orders she already had in record time, and would soon have new stock to put on the shelves.

And she would have time to investigate. She hadn't told Thomas that part, for she knew what his reaction would be. Yet, as soon as she put Watson on the floor, she sent Darrel outside to cut wood. Fishing out her measuring tape, she took the remaining measurements of the house: the outside walls, then the interior rooms. Suddenly she gave an excited shriek. She'd found what she'd been looking for: four feet of unaccounted space.

This was it! A secret chamber must be hidden within the walls, just as she and Rosie had suspected. Now all she had to do was pace off the rooms to find the exact location of the discrepancy.

Emily stood with her back against the wall, then began to walk carefully between rooms. "Nineteen feet for the parlor. Twenty-one feet for the kitchen. Yet the total house measures forty-four feet. Somewhere here . . ." Emily put the pencil behind one ear and began to tap on each wall with a hammer, as intent as a bloodhound caught up in the scent. It took several hours of work, and a few slips of the hammer, but she finally discovered a section of wall behind the fireplace that didn't sound as solid as the rest. But she didn't hear the door open behind her, nor did she see Thomas's scowl as she crawled across the floor, gently rapping and listening to the hollow sound.

"Here it is!" Emily rose, unaware of neither the smudge on her nose, nor that her hair had fallen from its prim knot. Disheveled and excited, she whirled around, nearly shrieking when she saw Thomas standing on her threshold. "My Lord, you scared me!"

"Emily, didn't I tell you to lock this door at all times?" he said grouchily. "Lynette said you'd gone home for the afternoon, so I thought I'd check and make sure everything was all right. What in God's name are you doing?"

Emily shrugged, as if the answer were perfectly obvious.

"I've just discovered a secret chamber in the house. I think the gold may lie here!"

Thomas's expression changed from annoyance to interest, then admiration, as Emily explained her thought process.

"Rosie told me there were secret doorways in the house, and that got me thinking. I tried to put myself in my father's shoes and imagine what he must have thought before he died. He knew someone was after the gold, and he wanted to protect the treasure. The only logical hiding place was in this house, which is why he left it to me. He must have known that I wouldn't sell it, and he probably had confidence in my ability to figure it out."

"And how did you?" Thomas asked, intrigued in spite of himself.

"I simply measured all of the interior rooms, then the exterior of the house," Emily explained. "There are four feet unaccounted for. Our answer lies somewhere behind that wall."

Pointing to the plaster barrier, she dug out her pencil and confirmed her findings. Handing the measurements to Thomas, she saw his brows rise as he verified her calculations, and a smile crept over his face.

"I've got to hand it to you, Emily. You really are a
hell of a detective. Are you just going to stand there,
or will you let me help you break down this wall?"

A flush crept over her face at his sincere compliment. His acknowledgment of her abilities meant
the world to her, and Emily didn't care if he knew it.
Putting her papers aside, she dashed down to the
basement, returning with a miner's pickax. She
handed it to Thomas, then stood back as he slammed
it into the plaster.

The wall cracked, then the pickax slipped easily
through. Excited beyond measure, Emily used the
hammer to pound at the weak material. Bit by bit
the wall disintegrated, until there was an opening
large enough for them to see inside. Plaster dust
filled the room. Emily choked, then backed away
from the wall, coughing heartily.

"I'll get a candle," she murmured, waving at the
air. Thomas nodded, then went back to work, enlarg-
ing the hole.

A lit taper in hand, Emily rejoined Thomas. Both
of them held their breath in suspense as she thrust
the light into the secret chamber, and the blackness
dissolved. The yellow gleam illuminated a tin box.

"The treasure!" Emily breathed reverently. "Do
you see it, Thomas?"

He nodded, staring in awe at the small, stout
metal box gleaming in the darkness. Using the
pickax, he was able to pull it close enough to the hole
they had made, where Emily, with her slender arms,
could grab it.

"Here it is," she said in hushed tones as she pulled the box through the broken lath and plaster and set it on the floor of the parlor.

Neither spoke for a moment. The treasure might solve some of their problems, but it would inevitably compound the conflict between them. Fleetingly, Emily almost wished she hadn't been so clever— for once the gold was found, Thomas would have no further reason to stay in Denver. The thought was unbearable.

Worse, the presence of the gold would confirm Thomas's theory that her father was a thief.

As if he knew exactly what she was thinking, Thomas looked at her with compassion. "I'll have to break it open. Do you mind?"

Emily shook her head. The box had to be opened, they'd come too far for anything else. Even though she was afraid of the outcome, a thrill raced up her spine as Thomas took up the pickax once more and split the lock with one swift motion. The broken padlock tinkled to the floor, rusted and useless. Emily reached down in breathless anticipation and flipped open the lid.

Inside there was a stack of papers. Emily's face fell as she leafed through them and discovered her father's will, some letters, and a few other documents. One by one, she took the missives from the box, then peered at its flat, smooth bottom.

"This is it?" Part of her hadn't wanted to find the gold, because of what it would prove about her father, but the disappointment still stung. Emily stared at the gaping metal box in disbelief. She pushed against the bottom of the box, thinking to find some second layer or hidden compartment, but there was nothing.

"I'm afraid so," Thomas sighed. He seemed disappointed as well. Glancing over the documents as Emily handed them to him, he shook his head. "It looks like the original of your father's will. Why did he go to such lengths to hide it? The rest of these papers seem to be personal letters, and have no bearing on the case. I'm so sorry, Emily."

Tears stung her eyes, and she wiped them away quickly. "I shouldn't be so surprised," Emily said logically. "The chance of finding that gold was a long shot, but I really thought I was onto something here. It still doesn't make sense for my father to hide this will so well. Ewert Smith has a copy in his office downtown. It has to mean something."

"Maybe we'll never know, Emily, but that was a damned brilliant bit of detecting. I'm just sorry it yielded so little."

His kind words made her really feel like crying, and instinctively, she found herself in Thomas's arms. He held her tightly, and when she lifted her face to his, Thomas leaned closer and kissed her—a soft, soothing kiss that made her feel warm and fluttery.

It was amazing the effect this man had on her. Her sense of failure dissolved. Everything felt so right in Thomas's arms. Could they ever get past the damned gold? It seemed that the stolen money hung between them like a black cloud. Once she had proven that her father had never stolen Wells Fargo's money, perhaps Thomas would put the past behind him. But if he were right . . . she couldn't bear the thought.

"Thank you, Thomas." Emily stepped back, her own thoughts troubling her. Thomas smiled, then wiped at a suspicious drop of moisture on her cheek.

"You're welcome. Now I guess we'll have to see to fixing that wall."

"Oh, goodness, I completely forgot the time," Emily said, flustered. "Lynette is probably wondering what happened to me by now."

Thomas leaned closer and pressed a kiss on her forehead. "Emily, I really am sorry. Maybe we could have supper tonight. I'll bring the plaster and fix up the wall for you. How does that sound?"

"It sounds just wonderful," Emily said sincerely.

"Goodness, I hope I'm not intruding." Lynette's voice was soft as she stepped through the door. "I brought today's receipts. I thought you might want to review them. . . . My God, what happened here?" She stared at the plaster dust and the giant hole in the wall. Then her gaze fell to the metal box on the floor.

Emily smiled, stepping forward to take the box of receipts from her. "Just a little accident. Nothing serious, but it did delay my return."

"I was concerned," Lynette said. "But the shop was so quiet, I was able to get so much done."

"That's wonderful," Emily said.

Thomas cleared his throat. "I understand you've

been a great help to Miss Potter, who is a very special friend to me. I deeply appreciate the assistance you've given her."

"It's been my pleasure," Lynette responded graciously. She glanced at Emily. "I think the relationship will be truly beneficial for us both. Now if you'll excuse me, I'll be on my way. I want to get home before sundown."

"Thank you," Emily called after her, placing the receipts to one side. When Lynette had gone, she turned to Thomas again, but he was already reaching down and pulling her into his arms. He kissed her deeply and thoroughly, practically singeing her eyebrows with the heat of his passion. When he released her, he gazed down at her, his eyes afire.

"That should hold me until tonight."

Emily shivered, then leaned against the door, watching him walk down the path with a masculine saunter that was both appealing and dangerous at the same time. A thrill of pleasure came to her as she anticipated the coming night and she raced upstairs.

She needed help. Fast.

23

— ❦ —

A Romantic Notion

"Rosie!"

The ghost swam into sight as Emily bounded up the stairs. "Who was here, sweetie? I heard you talking to someone. The voice sounded familiar."

"Oh, you must mean Lynette. She's my new assistant."

"Lynette." Rosie let the name roll off her tongue. "That doesn't ring a bell, but there was something wrong, something I felt. Like a presence I've known before . . ." The bordello girl shook her head, as if it were too much of a struggle to remember. "Anyway, I'm so sorry about the box. I really thought you'd found the gold this time. You must be very disappointed."

Emily nodded, breathless, eager to move on to the subject she was most interested in at the moment.

"He's coming here, for supper! What if something . . . happens again?"

Rosie grinned, her dimples deepening with delight. "So he wants to take supper with you, does he? My, our man has more stamina than even I would have given him credit for. You don't need my help for that, sugar. Just a nice roast beef, some potatoes, apple pie is usually good—"

"I'm not worried about the food!" Emily flopped onto the bed feeling excruciatingly shy. Then she forced herself to speak what was on her mind. "I think I need . . . instruction."

"I see." Rosie looked more than delighted. "This is becoming a regular habit, isn't it? We'll have to start working on getting you two hitched. Even the best of methods aren't foolproof."

Emily paused at the thought of marriage. Herself, wed to a man like Thomas! At first, she couldn't imagine it, but then she remembered the kind things he had done for her, the way he held her when she was distressed, the caring in his touch and voice. She looked hard at the phantom. "Do you really think a man like that would ever want me?"

"He wants you now, doesn't he?" Rosie said joyfully. "We only have to nudge him a few more steps."

Emily shook her head. "Until the issue of the gold is cleared up, I don't think we can be happy together."

Rosie's mouth curved down in sympathy. "I see. Well, getting back to the subject at hand, you want to remain protected tonight if things . . . develop. Am I understanding you right?"

"Yes," Emily stammered, the blush deepening even further as she recalled his parting kiss.

"All right, then." She gave Emily an appraising look. "Are you certain you still require it, honey?"

"What do you mean?" Emily looked confused.

Rosie smiled, then looked pointedly at Emily's belly. "You've already been with him more than once. Are you sure it hasn't taken yet?"

Emily's eyes widened. She mentally calculated the days. A sigh of relief escaped her and she shook her head.

"No, I've had my time since then. It's all right."

Strangely, even as she said the words, a sense of sadness permeated her. Bearing Thomas's child was an incredible idea, and one that she was almost sorry to lose.

Rosie nodded. "Good. I'll help you, then. But it would be much better to wait until after you're wed. These old biddies in town will be counting the months as is."

Emily looked up at the phantom and gave her a warm smile. "Rosie, I'm so glad you came into my life. There is no one I could have asked about this. Not even my mother, if she were still alive."

"Why, thank you, honey. I enjoy your friendship, too. I don't know how much longer I'll be here. There are days when I start to feel myself fading, and it's getting harder and harder to materialize. I don't know what it all means, but at this point, every moment is precious."

An ache grew inside Emily as she imagined her life without Rosie. Tears moistened her eyes, and when she glanced up at the mirror, she found it hard to talk.

"I hope you won't leave anytime soon."

"I'm trying not to. But if it happens, just remember. I'll always be with you, whether you see me or not."

Emily nodded, then wiped quickly at her face. "I've got to get ready," she declared, afraid she'd really burst into tears if she thought about it much longer.

"I'll help," Rosie said. "We've got a man coming to dinner, honey."

"Did you find her?"

Jake sauntered into the den, a wicked grin on his face. He took a swallow of whiskey, catching the drips on his face with his sleeve.

"Yeah, I found her all right. She was heading back, just as we thought. It wasn't hard to get her train— the man at the ticket counter told me everything once I put a gun to his head."

Lizzie's head came up as the outlaws spoke, and her beautiful eyes widened in horror.

"Jake, you didn't . . . you said no more killings!"

"What happened?" Emmet asked impatiently, cutting her off. "Did you finish her nor not?"

"I did," Jake said proudly. "I tried to find out what she knew and who she told, but that Bertie Evans wouldn't say a word. She plumb fainted as soon as I hauled her off the train, and I had to slap her face to bring her around. She was so scared she couldn't talk, so I shot her then and there. Whatever she knows, she ain't telling no one now."

"Jake! That poor woman—"

"Shut up! You should have left the gag on her!" Emmet snarled, backhanding Lizzie. A red mark appeared on her cheek, swelling almost immediately. Jake turned on Emmet, the whiskey bottle in his hand, his grin vanishing.

"Say, Emmet, what did you do that for?"

"She had it coming. I'm getting tired of her carping. You and I need to talk, Jake. The boss ain't at all happy with the way things are going. Miss Lizzie here is starting to get in the way."

Lizzie's eyes rounded and her voice was pleading when she spoke. "Emmet, please don't kill me. I'll never tell anyone. I'd hang, too, if I did. You know that."

"Emmet, she ain't no trouble." Jake shrugged. "I don't think we need to shoot her yet. We could always use her for a hostage. No law in these parts will want to shoot a woman. Besides—" his unsavory grin deepened—"I ain't done with her yet."

Lizzie couldn't repress a shudder, which only made Jake laugh. Emmet watched the interaction between them, then nodded as if deciding something.

"All right. But if she gets in the way, she's done for. Once we find the gold, I don't give a damn what happens to her. In the meantime, we've got to find that China girl."

"Right," Jake agreed. "I'll go tomorrow. One of them has to know where she is, and this time,

I'll make them talk." With that, he cocked his gun meaningfully.

"That was a wonderful supper, Miss Potter."

Emily was sitting with Thomas on the porch of Shangri-La. Darrel had taken his dinner and gone home, leaving them alone. It was a beautiful night. Stars twinkled overhead, and the music of grasshoppers and crickets filled the air around them. The scent of fading summer roses mixed with the crispness of the cooler air, and the promise of fall was ripe and hopeful.

It had been a perfect evening. Thomas had come back with his tools, as promised, and fixed the plaster wall. Darrel had offered to help, and Thomas had worked very patiently with the boy, teaching him now to do the repairs, making him feel important. Emily watched in amazement as Thomas deftly patched the hole, then smoothed it over with plaster. Everything he did was done well, she noticed. The evening was strangely domestic, with Thomas performing a traditional male task while she cooked dinner. It made her feel comforted, safe, and . . . loved.

That emotion was one that caught her by surprise, and she thought back to the conversation she'd had with Rosie. The idea of marriage was something she hadn't given a lot of thought to, mainly because she'd always assumed she'd be a spinster like her great-aunt. Women like them, the eccentrics, didn't often marry. Instead, they spent their later years baking cookies for nieces or nephews, sewing lace onto handkerchiefs, and making quilts for charity while everyone gossiped about their oddities.

The thought of spending her life with a virile man, bearing his children, and keeping house like this was very appealing. But Emily knew she could never give up detecting. It was just too much a part of her. And she wasn't certain Thomas would ever settle for that. Actually, she wasn't certain of his feelings at all! Still, the picture was heady and unbearably pleasant. He put his arm around her as they sipped their coffee. Neither of them spoke for a few moments, and the silent companionship filled her heart with happiness.

"I could get used to this." It was Thomas who finally spoke, but he echoed her thoughts.

Emily looked at him shyly. "Do you think so?"

He turned to her, a smile curving his handsome mouth. "Why, Miss Potter, I'd almost think you were fishing for a declaration."

"I was not!" she said indignantly, although he was perfectly correct. "I was just logically assessing your comment—"

"Is that so?" Thomas took her cup from her hand and put it aside. Before she could protest, he swept her into his arms and gave her a heated kiss. "Now, you tell me what that has to do with logic."

Emily sighed, giving herself up to the pure pleasure of his embrace. Her fingers slid into the soft hair at the nape of his neck, and her body pressed closer to his. He felt good, warm, and hard, his arms strong as they tightened around her. Just then Emily thought she heard a twig snap, and a discreet cough came from the path.

"Excuse me. I hope I haven't come at a bad time."

They broke their embrace quickly as the figure of a man appeared in the gloaming. Emily straightened her dress, grateful that the night air would soothe her inflamed cheeks. Thomas looked anything but pleased as the visitor stepped into the porch light.

It was Ewert Smith.

"Hello, Mr. Smith," Emily said quickly, her voice sounding embarrassed to her own ears. "We were enjoying the night air. I'm glad to see you do the same."

"Why, yes," Ewert said with a smirk. "Although some of us enjoy it more than others."

Thomas glared at the man, while Emily fought to keep from laughing. She rose and indicated the coffee cups.

"Would you care for some coffee?"

"Why, that would be right neighborly." The man sat down on the steps and stretched out his legs, apparently settling in for a long visit.

Thomas sighed in disgust, and Emily went to fetch the coffee. When she returned, they were talking softly. She had to hide a smile as she overheard Thomas subtly encouraging the man to be on his way, but Ewert was either dense or without sufficient motivation to leave. He accepted the cup from Emily, and sipped the coffee, enjoying himself.

"You are as talented as you are lovely, Miss Potter," Ewert said. "Is this a distinctive brew?"

Emily heard Thomas's snort, and she giggled softly. "No, it's nothing special."

"It must be your angelic touch," Ewert declared.

"I swear I haven't enjoyed a cup of coffee like this in ages."

"Shouldn't you be getting home?" Thomas asked abruptly. "It looks like rain later."

"Oh, I think not, it's a wonderful night. Very clear. I just brought few papers for Miss Potter to keep. I thought you might like some of your father's personal belongings, and there was another copy of his will among his effects. I'm sure he wanted you to have them."

"Thank you, Mr. Smith. That is very kind of you." Emily accepted the papers and gave Thomas a superior I-told-you-so look that he obviously didn't appreciate. While she scanned the documents, Ewert's eyes never left her breasts. The low-cut dress she wore, one of Rosie's suggestions, more than amply displayed her generous figure, and Ewert devoured her by the glow of the gaslight.

Thomas walked into the house for a moment, returning with Emily's shawl. He placed the black lace garment over her shoulders, discreetly draping her bosom. Emily glanced up and smiled a thanks, while Ewert, understanding Thomas's motives, gritted his teeth in frustration.

"These look like business letters and documents concerning purchase of the house. I'll put them away, along with the rest of his papers. Thank you for bringing them."

"Why, you are quite welcome. I almost wish I had more, so I could have an excuse to come over and visit again. The house looks lovely. You've obviously done a great deal of work on it."

He might have been fishing for an invitation to come in, but Thomas interrupted quickly.

"Emily would ask you inside, but I had to fix some plaster today. The house isn't presentable."

Ewert got reluctantly to his feet, while Emily shot Thomas a questioning look.

"Well, I'd better be going. Thanks again for the coffee." Ewert handed Emily his cup and walked slowly down the path, waving once more before he disappeared from sight.

As soon as the man was out of earshot, Thomas swore aloud. "That licentious bastard! If he stared at your bosom any more, he'd have fallen inside your dress."

"Thomas!" Emily said, shocked but delighted. "He didn't do any such thing. It was kind of him to bring my father's papers."

"Yes, real kind." Thomas snorted. "Emily, how can you be so naive? Don't you see what that man wants?"

Emily's nose lifted. "No, I don't see anything except that your imagination is overheated."

"That's not all that's overheated," Thomas growled. The cup fell from Emily's grasp and rolled across the porch as he pulled her into his arms but neither of them paid any attention to it. "I can see I'll have to make an honest woman of you soon, so that love-smitten lawyers aren't howling at your door."

Emily's mouth parted in astonishment, but before she could speak, he captured her words under a hard kiss. Every tingling inch of her flesh seemed to burn against him as he swept his hand into her hair, holding her head firmly, while his mouth took erotic possession of hers.

It took Emily a minute to realize the whimpers she was hearing came from her. Desire, hot and heady, coiled within her like a snake, then spread through her blood like heated syrup. Her breasts tingled, and a now-familiar throbbing started deep inside her. When he put his hand on her breast, the sensation was almost unbearable, and she moaned in sheer pleasure.

"Emily. My God, this is always so good between us. I don't think I can wait much longer. I desperately want to make love to you."

"Yes, Thomas. Yes." From a distance, Emily heard her own response, and it was all that he needed.

He pulled her to her feet and Emily led him through the door and up the stairs. The house was very quiet, but an odd uneasiness crept through her. When they entered her bedroom, Emily couldn't help glancing at the mirror. There was no reflection, no bawdy saloon girl's giggle, but she couldn't get Rosie's presence out of her mind.

"Emily, my sweet girl." Thomas embraced her once more, and kissed her thoroughly. Emily delighted in the pure sensation of it, the feel of his hands caressing her back, the teasing way he toyed with her buttons and then began to undo them, one by one. In the mirror, she could see her reflection, then gasped as one breast popped out, fully exposed.

"Emily, come to me, sweet. Bend closer, that's it. . . ."

His hoarse encouragements, exciting as they were,

could not make her forget the picture of herself, naked and writhing, in Rosie's mirror. Could the ghost see her even when she wasn't visible? The thought was like a bucket of cold water being poured over her head. Reluctantly, she pulled away from Thomas's embrace, quickly fastening her dress.

"Emily, what's wrong? What is it?"

Shyness nearly overcame her and she shook her head. How could she explain this? He had never believed her when she'd told him about Rosie. Still, she couldn't help the way she felt.

"Thomas, I can't. . . ." Emily faltered, then made herself continue. "This is where Rosie appears! I just can't, knowing that she might be there!"

Thomas gazed at her incredulously, then looked at the mirror. Frustration was keen in his voice as he indicated the sheer glass. "But there's no one there! Look!"

"Thomas, I know you don't believe me, but it's true. And I just . . . can't."

"Are you sure there isn't another reason?" Thomas's voice sounded harsh. "Like maybe you've had a better offer?" When Emily stared at him in confusion, he continued. "I suppose a barrister might be a better prospect than someone like me, with a name to clear and a fictitious position. Has he been here before, or were you planning a little rendezvous with him later?"

Emily gasped, then drew herself up to her full height. "How dare you! Sir, I am asking you to leave. Now."

Thomas started to say something, but Emily

brushed past him and ran down the stairs. At the bottom she held the door open, his hat in her outstretched hand.

"Emily—"

"I bid you to leave, sir," Emily said firmly.

Thomas walked helplessly out on the porch, then turned and continued down the path. As soon as he had gone, she slammed the door. From the bedroom, she heard delighted laughter, and she braced her hands on her hips, finding little humor in the situation.

"I don't see what's so funny," she scolded, while Rosie giggled merrily.

"Why, I think it's precious, honey. Your preacher man is so jealous he can't see straight. That's exactly what that man needed, a little competition. A few more episodes like that, and you'll have him hooked."

"Do you really think so?" Emily ran upstairs and approached the glass. Rosie swam into view.

"Yes, I certainly do. He's been entirely too confident of your affections. Let him see that another man is interested. It's a ploy that always works, honey. Trust me."

"Why do you suppose that is, anyway?" Emily asked, trying to see the logic of it all.

"Did you ever see dogs mark their territory? Then when another dog comes around, they bark and growl and dig up the dirt? Why, they'd do anything to defend it! That's what just happened, honey. You can count on it."

24

⚘

Another Yarn

Emily walked down the stairs for breakfast the following morning, hiding a yawn behind her fist. Tying her robe tightly about her against the morning chill, she tried to force herself to wake up. The emotional events of the previous evening had left her drained, and she'd slept soundly as a result. Stumbling toward the kitchen, she wanted nothing more than a cup of hot, black coffee.

At the bottom of the steps she paused, dimly aware that something was wrong. Backtracking, she returned to the parlor. The front door was wide open. Guilt filled her as she recalled Thomas's scoldings, but then she remembered locking the door right after she'd slammed it on him.

That's odd, she thought, turning to look around the room. It was then she saw that the parlor was in disarray, and that the strongbox that she'd left in the center of the floor was missing. Fear crept up her spine. The curtains billowed at the window in the rush of clean fall air, showing clearly where the intruder had gained entrance.

From what she could tell, the only thing missing was the box. A sensation of vulnerability made her knees weak. During the hours she'd slept, someone must have opened the window, crept in, and searched the room. Finding the box, the robber or robbers had secured the treasure and brazenly walked out the front door.

They must have been after the gold. Vaguely Emily recalled the sheriff remarking that the house had been broken into several times, and she recalled the vandalization she'd witnessed when she'd arrived. She shouldn't be surprised that it had happened again, unless . . . it meant something more.

Fear dissolved as her mind went to work. The first few hours after a crime was committed were crucial, Emily reminded herself, since most of the evidence would ultimately be destroyed by footprints, weather, and time. Her instincts guided her, and she walked outside to examine the windowsill and the soil beneath it.

The flowers there were untouched. But Emily saw that the earth behind them was trampled, as if someone had deliberately avoided the phlox. The sill was swept clean of dust, indicating that someone had recently come in contact with it, almost certainly as they climbed into her house. Taking out her glass, she examined the window closely. There, where the sill met the sash, was an indentation where a knife had jimmied it open.

The mark was trim and clean. There were no scratches, and neither the breakage that would have been created by a thick tool such as a crowbar, nor the splintering that a screwdriver might have caused. Scanning the grounds carefully, she looked for a cigarette butt, a box of matches, a spot of gray ash, but her burglar had obviously been careful and the earth revealed nothing about who had passed that way. So intense was her concentration that she ran straight into Thomas as she rounded the corner of the house.

"Emily! What are you doing out here?" He snatched at her shoulders, stopping her in her tracks. Before she could answer, he went on quickly. "I'm sorry. I've done a lot of thinking, and I came to apologize for my behavior. I was presumptuous last night, and you had every right to throw me out. I'd like to talk about this."

"Not now, Thomas! I'm on a scent!"

She brushed past him and into the house, her glass noting every suspicious trace. Dropping to her knees, she had just started to examine the rug when she heard his footsteps behind her.

"Scent? What are you talking about? Good God, what happened?" Thomas stared in dismay at the vandalized room.

"Someone broke in during the night," Emily explained, glancing up from the floor impatiently. "Thomas, I must ask you to step to one side until I've gathered all the evidence. You might inadvertently disturb something."

"What the hell do you mean, someone broke in! What happened? Are you hurt?"

She stared at him through her glass, her expression clearly saying that he wasn't using the brain God gave him, then she shook her head. "No, I'm obviously not hurt. The only thing they seem to have stolen is my father's strongbox. That's rather telling, don't you think?"

"What do you mean?"

"Well, either they thought it contained valuables, which is not illogical given its appearance, or they came purposefully looking for it. My only happiness is that when they open the box, they won't find anything. I removed the papers."

Emily produced them triumphantly from inside her robe. Thomas swore as he caught a glimpse of her creamy skin, and the hint of a rosy nipple as well. Slamming the door shut behind him, he crossed over to where she knelt and hauled her to her feet.

"That's it. Emily, go pack. I'm taking you to the hotel right away. You are not staying in this house alone one more night. Christ, when I think what could have happened."

He looked truly shaken. Emily stared at him for a moment, then a broad smile crossed her face.

"Thomas! You do care about me, I knew it! Rosie said you did, but I didn't believe her!"

Thomas groaned, rolling his eyes heavenward. But the struggle within him was over almost immediately, and he swept Emily into his arms, burying his face in her hair. Pressing heated kisses along her throat, he growled softly, "You're damned right, I care about you, and I am not standing by any longer and letting this nonsense continue. I am moving you today, and that's final."

"But Thomas, I can't move! You know the mystery is tied up in this house! I can't leave it!" Emily protested. His eyes narrowed and she backed slowly away, dropping her hands from his shoulders. He stepped closer, and she felt an odd sense of threat as he faced her down.

"This is not up for discussion, Emily. I'll give you the morning to pack, then I'm going to the hotel and making your reservation. If you don't go there peacefully, I promise you that you won't like what happens."

And then he stormed out, slamming the door behind him. Tears of frustration stung her eyes as Emily felt a tumult of emotions inside her, and she longed to throw something breakable.

How could she leave now? The solution to this mystery could be at her very feet! Yet the danger was evident, even to her. Somehow she sensed that the answer to everything was under her nose—and someone else knew it, too. Someone desperate enough to break in to find it.

"Excuse me, Miss Potter." Lynette spoke from the threshold, then gasped at the sight inside. "My word! What happened?"

"I had a robbery last night." Emily sighed, explaining the morning's events.

Lynette shook her head in sympathy. "That's terrible, it truly is! I was worried about you this morning, when you didn't show up at the shop. I hope you don't mind, but it occurred to me that you're out here all alone, and that is never a good thing. Perhaps . . . no, it would be too bold of me to ask."

"What?"

"I was going to talk to you about this at the shop today. I just received notice that my room has to be vacated," Lynette explained. "My landlady is very kind, but says she has a brother coming to visit and needs the use of my room. I was going to register at the boardinghouse, but it occurred to me that perhaps . . . we could share lodgings."

"What a wonderful idea!" Emily's eyes brightened as she turned the thought over in her mind. Lynette's presence would soften Thomas's objections to her remaining in the house. It would also appear more respectable, for a woman alone was always subject to rumor.

"I thought it might help both of us," Lynette was saying. "I know the business isn't entirely profitable yet. You could reduce my wages a bit, since I wouldn't have to pay for the room, and I could help you here as well. If it didn't work out, I could always go to the boardinghouse."

Emily nodded. "I think it's a grand idea. Why don't you move your things in today? I'll mind the shop. I'd feel better having someone keep an eye on the place after what happened last night."

Lynette smiled. "Thank you so much, Miss Potter. You've been so kind to me. I feel you're almost like . . . a sister."

Emily smiled, taking Lynette's hand. It felt good to know someone else cared about her. And now she had a plan that would benefit everyone.

It had to work.

It was late in the day, and a lone customer was looking over the hats while Emily sorted through her notes. She added the details she had accumulated that morning to her casebook, then studied everything again, looking for some kind of pattern.

Why had her father hidden the will so meticulously? That was the thought that niggled constantly at Emily. The man had given a copy to Ewert, one that he was certain Emily would have. Why, then, did he go to all the trouble to wall up the original?

She'd come up with fourteen possible reasons, but none of them convinced her. John Potter was an intelligent man. If he did something so strange, he did it for a reason. Now Emily only had to figure it out. . . .

"Emily, I thought I told you I wanted you to move into the hotel." Thomas's voice shattered her reverie and she glanced up, quickly shutting the casebook. The single customer, hearing the tone in his voice, left quickly. Thomas looked forbidding as he put his hat down on top of the book and leaned slowly toward her.

"Thomas! What a nice surprise! I . . ."

Emily felt a knot form quickly in her throat. Swallowing hard, she backed up against the wall until her bustle prevented her from moving any farther.

"I can see that my words didn't carry much weight

with you this morning. Funny, I sort of thought we had an understanding." Thomas's voice was cold and she could sense the anger inside him. "I don't know if you saw the paper, but Bertie Evans is dead."

"What?" Emily was stunned.

"Yes. Shot to death, on the train while she was going to her sister's house. I came looking for you as soon as I heard. Imagine my surprise when I stopped by the hotel and was told at the desk that you hadn't checked in."

Emily looked up into steel blue eyes that promised retribution. "Thomas, I came up with another plan—"

"I'm not interested in any more of your plans," he said sharply. His fist struck the counter and Emily squeaked like a frightened mouse. She'd never seen him this angry! "I told you I wanted you at the hotel. Dammit, do you have a death wish or something? Where the hell is your common sense?"

Emily faced him bravely, squinting through her spectacles. "Thomas, you have no right to bully me like this! You are being totally irrational! I appreciate your concern, and have taken appropriate measures to ensure my safety—"

"Emily, I don't have the time or patience for this. I have no desire to find you dead. If you won't listen to common sense, then I'll walk out of here, and you won't see me again. I'll continue my own investigation, but I will refuse to act as your protector any longer. Now, what will it be?"

He'd spoken as calmly as if he had just asked about the price of eggs. Emily's eyes widened. Just as she started to protest, Lynette came in from the rear of the shop.

"Mr. Hall. How wonderful to see you again! I suppose Emily told you the good news about me moving in with her. I understand that you've been concerned about her situation. I'm sure you'll be gratified to know that she will no longer be alone in that house."

Thomas's gaze swept from one woman to the other. Emily nodded, her hands outstretched, as if she were still trying to explain, but Lynette had smoothly done the talking for her. But instead of seeming relieved, Thomas picked up his hat and stormed out.

The door slammed behind him, rattling the shop windows. Emily sighed, then turned to Lynette in apology. "I don't know what's gotten into him. He's not normally that rude."

"He's worried about you," Lynette said with a smile. She turned her face away from Emily. "And I also think he's very smitten with you. I wouldn't be concerned about him walking out like that. My guess is that he's just angry. Men don't like to realize they can't boss us around, you know."

Emily nodded slowly. When Thomas calmed down, he'd understand that this was the best possible solution for everyone.

He'd have to.

There wasn't enough whiskey in the world to get this woman off his mind.

Thomas stared into the amber depths of his

glass, cursing Emily Potter for the fiftieth time. He couldn't believe her audacity, standing there and openly defying him after everything they'd been to each other.

What he couldn't admit, even to her, was that he was afraid for her. Emily seemed drawn to danger the way most women were to perfume. It was as if she were galloping toward a brick wall and there was nothing he could do but watch.

Ordering another drink, he placed his hat and the book he was carrying on the bar. Glancing down in puzzlement, Thomas realized what he'd done. In his anger, he must have picked up Emily's casebook along with his hat and taken it with him. Ruefully he flipped a few of the pages, reading the notes in her odd, crabbed hand.

He smiled reluctantly. She was brilliant. As he scanned her journal, he was astounded by the logic that glimmered on every page, the courage, the attention to detail, and the amazing deductions. They were all there, from the women on the stage-coach to the shopkeeper in town to the postal clerk who'd helped her. Emily catalogued people the way others did postage stamps, and her insights were mesmerizing.

Her skeletal outline of the case fascinated him as well. Every detail they'd discovered, every implica-tion or suspicion, was neatly diagrammed. He could glance at the page and instantly see all of the tangled threads. Page after page attested to her genius, and he felt his outrage lessen with each notation.

She had a gift, a burning gift, that she was compelled to use. It was as simple as that. Thomas had to face facts. No lawman he'd ever met, no marshal or sheriff, possessed her uncanny ability to get to the heart of a matter. Although her talent put her in danger, she really couldn't avoid it. Criminals did not want to be discovered. And to prevent Emily from sleuthing, he saw, would be like asking Mozart to stay the hell away from the piano.

On the last page there was a notation about the gold. He read it absently, looking over her calculations concerning the secret room and her entry about her disappointment upon finding nothing of value there. But it was her final paragraph that stopped him cold.

> To my dismay, I discovered I was relieved that we had failed in our objective. I had to examine my own emotions, for they ran totally contrary to the purpose of the case. Logic, one must always deal in logic. Yet I found I couldn't.
>
> So I finally admitted the truth to myself—I am in love with Thomas Hall, and this gold hangs between us like a glittering barrier. I must forget what I feel and pursue the case, for his sake as well as my own. And if our success leads to my despair and I lose him in the process, then I will live out my days with a memory that shines brighter than any treasure, so wondrous is this thing we have together. Holmes may have had his Irene

Adler, but I have Thomas Hall, and perhaps,
he will also be my defeat.

Thomas closed the book, feeling a jolt in his belly
that he couldn't attribute to the liquor. Something
suspiciously moist stung his eyes. He could no longer
hide from the truth, either. Emily knew that to succeed would lead to the ultimate failure, yet she
doggedly pursued the case anyway.

Why?

Because she loved him. It was as simple and as
complicated as that.

Thomas sighed. Somehow, from the moment he'd
met her, he'd known it would come to this. Emily
had peered through her magnifying glass and seen
right into her heart. Using her unerring logic, she
had deduced her own feelings, but had forgotten to
take one thing into account: his own.

He rose, and picked up his hat and the casebook.
A pretty, red-haired saloon girl approached him, giving him a saucy smile. Thomas saw that her low-cut
dress exposed a generous white bosom, and that her
apricot-colored mouth looked extremely kissable.
She leaned closer, and the scent of her perfume en-
veloped him.

"Hi, honey. You look lonely. Want some company?"

He stared at her for a long moment, then asked,
"Do you know Sherlock Holmes?"

The girl looked honestly puzzled. "No, but if you
hum a few bars I'll get the piano player to fake it.
Why, does it mean something special to you?"

"Yes, it absolutely does." Thomas grinned, handed

her a bill, then walked out of the bar. Hard as it was to believe, he understood now that his taste ran quite differently. It ran, in fact, toward a slender, stubborn, sometimes bespectacled woman with an incredible figure and a brain to match.

A woman who would give him a lifetime of trouble.

25

China Blue

"Are you certain it was her?" Emily asked Darrel again. "You really saw Sung He?"

She was trembling with excitement. Lynette had gone to mind the shop, so Emily had had the whole morning to dream up this plot. Little did she know it would prove so fruitful so quickly. Emily shook Darrel so hard that the boy's teeth rattled. He didn't appear to mind, though. In fact, being one of Potter's Irregulars was a job he seemed to enjoy far more than carting wood.

"Yes, I saw her! I know it's her. She looked awful, though. Sick-like."

"And you say she was in a tent full of men?"

Darrel's head bobbed excitedly. "There were lots of 'em. Old men, young men. Cowboys. A few women, too. They was all smoking some stuff that made them sleepy. Some of them kept talking, rambling and such, but none of them 'peared to be listenin'."

"Was China Blue working there?"

"No. I think she was one of 'em. Like I said, she looked sick. She kept falling asleep, then would wake up fast, like this." Darrel demonstrated, his head weaving down toward his shoulder, then snapping back up as if startled.

"I see." Emily frowned thoughtfully. China Blue, an opium addict! This twist certainly explained a lot. Like why no one had seen her.

She patted Darrel's head proudly, then placed a large coin in the boy's hand. He beamed at her, and she reminded herself that once again she had Holmes to thank for this idea. Sending Darrel for information had turned out to be a stroke of sheer genius. No one suspected an adolescent boy of being an informant, and he was free to wander the Chinese encampment at his leisure.

Emily had decided to pursue this lead even more aggressively after Thomas stormed out on her. She didn't know if he'd meant what he said about being through with her, and she couldn't blame him if he did. The case grew darker by the moment, and the danger was drawing close. But why didn't he understand that it was only by solving the crime that they could find happiness?

Another disturbing thought came to Emily as she envisioned Darrel finding China Blue amid the scoundrels and addicts. "She didn't recognize you, did she? After all, she knew you from Shangri-La."

Darrel shook his head furiously. "Naw. For a

minute, she looked right at me, but her eyes were almost shut. She couldn't even stand."

"That's so sad. I wonder why she turned to drugs?"

"I think it's because of what happened here." The boy nodded thoughtfully, as if given to deductions himself.

"You mean the murders?"

"Yeah. I think she knows something and doesn't want to think about it. Why else would she be like that? She worked hard when she was here. Did all the sheets, the girl's dresses, pert' near everything. Ma said she had the roughest job at the place, and I swear she did."

"I see." Emily thought he could be right. Witnessing a murder and waiting for the killer to find you would wear down a soul all right. Maybe enough to turn to opium. China Blue wouldn't have been the first to hide in a pipe, and Emily was certain she wouldn't be the last.

"Thanks, Darrel." She patted him one last time and waited until he was gone before racing upstairs. Sitting at the dressing table, she applied dark kohl to make circles beneath her eyes. Next, she lightened her complexion with powder, changing her normally healthy color to pale white. She artfully tangled her hair and threw on some dirty clothes. A few more adjustments, then she turned to face the mirror.

Rosie gasped, slowly coming into view. "Why, honey, if I didn't know it was you, I'd never know it was you! Good Lord, woman, you look horrible!"

Emily grinned, dragging her leg behind her as if

in a stupor. Her mouth hung open and her eyes seemed to fight to stay open. Her shoulders thrust upward like a wooden hanger that the rest of her body simply dangled from, and her gait was rolling and unsteady. She looked like a derelict, someone who had spent her life searching for the next drug lift.

"I'm posing as an opium addict," Emily explained. "Sir Arthur Conan Doyle describes one in a story of his. And I need to find China Blue. This seemed like the best way to do that."

"My goodness! It's not just the clothes, it's everything! You've actually assumed the manner of a real opium user!"

Emily bowed, blushing at the compliment, then turned toward the door. "I'll be back before dark. I'll have to go through the woods so no one sees me."

"Be careful, Emily," Rosie said seriously.

Emily's smile faded. "I'm always careful." She closed the door behind her, then slipped quietly along the trail at the back of the house into the dense foliage. She didn't see the horse that followed, nor did she see the rider, who grinned at this stroke of luck.

The only thing on Emily's mind was China Blue. She had to solve this mystery—for Thomas.

Thomas knew what he had to do. Slipping on his coat, he reached for his gun belt, heedless of the fact that he was about to destroy his false identity. The chambers of both pistols were loaded, and he spun them carelessly before snapping the barrels shut and thrusting the guns into his belt.

He had to find China Blue. A good night's sleep

had brought him to several conclusions. One: Emily Potter would never stop investigating, not while she had breath in her body. Two: In spite of what he'd said to her, he couldn't let her get herself killed, and he couldn't stand by and watch this web close around her. She simply meant too much to him. Three: The best way to thwart her would be to solve the case himself. Then, once they had Emmet behind bars, he'd lay down the law. Until then, he knew it was futile.

At least he'd have some help this time. He'd finally talked the sheriff into making one last effort to bring China Blue in for questioning. The lawman had reluctantly agreed, for poor Bertie's death had convinced him that the time for waiting had passed.

Thomas grinned, tossing his collar aside for the first time since he'd come to town. It was a relief to show himself for what he really was, not a traveling preacher but a man determined to get the truth.

The sheriff awaited him downstairs, and the two men mounted their horses in silence. They rode past the townspeople, who gaped at him, through the mining district to the very outskirts of town.

The encampment was quiet, just as it was the last time Thomas had been there. As they approached, he saw a few figures scrambling frantically among the tents. By the time they actually dismounted, it seemed that everyone already knew they were there.

The sheriff headed straight for the trading tent, his gun drawn for all to see. Thomas followed, aware of the silent eyes that watched him. The tradesman behind the crates, the same man who'd previously told him nothing, turned expectantly toward the sheriff.

"Yes, sir?"

"I want to know where that girl is. Sung He, the one they call China Blue."

The tradesman lifted his shoulders in a puzzled shrug. "No English!"

Thomas cocked his own gun and raised it to eye level. The Chinaman paled, but kept shaking his head, his gaze riveted to the weapon.

"No English! So sorry!"

"Well, then we'll have to tear this place apart until we find her. I suggest you tell your friends to lend a hand—for her sake as well as your own."

The sheriff spoke firmly, but if the words had any effect on the tradesman, it wasn't obvious. He walked outside with Thomas and spat on the ground in disgust.

"Damn! He knows exactly where she is. Now we're going to have to waste half the morning looking through these tents."

"I guess we'd better get started," Thomas said, looking out over the green canvas town before them.

They split up, Thomas taking the east, the lawman focusing on the west. Thomas went to the first tent in the row and flipped open the cloth door.

Inside a family huddled in wordless confusion, their eyes staring. Fishing into his pocket, he found the composite drawing of Sung He that the sheriff had given him, a crudely etched likeness that the few witnesses had provided. There was no China Blue, just a woman, two children, and an elderly man gazing sightlessly at the open flap. The next tent again yielded no suspects, and the following tent was empty. Frustration ate at Thomas as he realized the near impossibility of their task. If someone had warned the girl, she could be heading off into the mountains even now, laughing at their efforts.

That thought nearly made him crazy. Thomas paused at the tenth tent, wiping the sweat from his brow, when he saw a young girl looking at him.

She was beautiful, but even more startling, looked like Sung He. Thomas stared at the girl, noting her ragged dress and broken shoes. He looked at the drawing again, then his gaze went back to the little girl.

They could have been twins. Except for the difference in years, the same lovely almond eyes peered out at him, the same perfectly curved mouth, and the same look of determination and secretiveness. She was only about six years old, but already, Thomas could see the woman she would become.

Guided by instinct, he lowered himself to his knees and smiled softly at the child.

"Hello. My name is Thomas. I wonder if you can help me. I'm looking for someone." He showed her the picture.

"Mama!" the little girl said immediately, pointing to the likeness.

Thomas tried to keep the excitement from his voice. "That's right. Do you know where she is?" His blood pounded as the child stared at the drawing.

"Ming!"

An elderly man with a long white beard appeared suddenly and clapped his hands together in a harsh manner. He said something in Chinese to the girl, and she looked as scared as a rabbit. Thomas rose and stared at the man. Dressed in a beautiful but faded costume of blue silk embroidered with white thread, he was obviously someone of importance.

The child scampered into the tent, disappearing in an instant and taking his last hope with her. Frustrated beyond measure, Thomas turned to the elderly man and forced his words through his gritted teeth.

"You speak English. I need your help. I'm trying to find this woman." Once again, he held out the drawing.

But the old man stared back at Thomas, ignoring the picture, and his eyes gleamed with hatred. "No help. You did this to her, you and your kind. You killed her."

Thomas felt his throat tighten. He thrust the paper into his pocket. "She's dead? Sung He is dead?"

The man's eyes narrowed, then he raised his head with dignity. "She might as well be dead. She is in the black dream. You and your kind took her to that big house. She did work there, honorable work. Washed. Cleaned. Then they came and killed."

The man lowered his eyes, as if reliving some awful memory. When he lifted his head once more, Thomas searched his face and found what he was looking for. The resemblance was there, harder to find because of the years, but it was there.

"You're her grandfather," Thomas said softly. The elderly man didn't respond, but Thomas pushed on. "I'm so sorry about what happened. But I want to save her life. Too many people have died already. Men are after her. Bad men. If you don't help me, I can't keep them from killing her, and maybe other people here, too."

The man stared at the shirt he wore and gestured to the collar. "I thought you a holy man."

Thomas bowed his head. "I wore a clerical collar as a disguise, so I could find out what had happened here. But now these men are closing in. I've got to get to Sung He before they do."

"Why?"

Thomas stared at the man in confusion. "What do you mean, why?"

"Why does she matter to you? You don't know my granddaughter."

"No. But she has a beautiful daughter who needs her mother." Thomas sighed. "And because . . . because I'm in love with Miss Emily Potter and I'm trying to help her as well."

The man seemed to measure this, and his eyes seemed to sear Thomas's very soul. Thomas himself was surprised at how easily those words had come.

And the Chinaman must have felt their truth as strongly as Thomas suddenly did, for he nodded, as if Thomas had passed some crucial test. The eyes buried in layers of paperlike flesh squinted, and he gestured with one gnarled finger toward the road.

"You follow me. I take you to her."

Relief broke over Thomas and he eagerly followed the Chinaman down the winding paths. He was amazed when they came closer to town, nearer to the mining area. He would have thought Sung He hidden in the farthest tent, but that didn't seem to be the case. The man never stopped until he reached one of the tents near the mines. He stood to one side, his head held high.

"She there. You go. See what they've done to Sung He."

Apprehension crawled up Thomas's spine. Stepping past the old man, he opened the tent flap and was immediately hit by the smoky fumes of opium.

It was a den all right, the worst Thomas had ever seen. The acrid smoke stung his eyes and made the back of his throat dry. Dizziness began to overcome him just from inhaling the air, and Thomas whipped out his handkerchief, tying the thin cloth over his face. Clutching his weapon, he proceeded into the tent, amazed at the sight that greeted him.

Dozens of men and a few women sat on the floor of the tent, smoking from odd-looking pipes or dozing against the walls. A single Chinaman scurried back and forth, refilling the pipes, sometimes arranging one of the dozing bodies to make room for another. An air of languor and dreamlike unreality filled the place and the faces that stared at Thomas were devoid of expression. They all seemed to look inward, lost to the allure of a drug-induced dream, blithely unaware of their physical appearance or surroundings.

The cloying smoke began to make him feel nauseous. Thomas ignored the unintelligible murmurings around him, the tugs at his clothes, the outstretched hands, and began to look for the girl. Roughly he pulled up one head after another, searching their faces, a task made even more difficult by the smoke. Coughing, Thomas stumbled toward a knot of several women at the back of the tent then pulled one of them to her feet.

"Please, do you know this girl . . ."

The words died even as he spoke them. Appalled, he recognized the eyes that gazed back at him, though he saw little else that was familiar. Emily stared back at him in equal horror, even as she struggled to remain in disguise.

"Emily." Thomas gripped her arm, blind fury flooding through him. Nothing except the eyes gave her away. Her hair, clothes, even her demeanor all bespoke one of the wretches inhabiting this terrible place. He couldn't believe what he was seeing. Before he could begin to shout at her, she reached up and whispered in his ear.

"Thomas, please don't identify me. It's too dangerous. People are looking. I've found Sung He. She's there."

His gaze swiveled and he saw the young Chinese woman lying on the floor, staring at him sightlessly her mind fixated within.

Thomas looked from Sung He to Emily, as if uncertain of which one to rescue first.

Emily shook her head at him, gesturing to a mark on the ground. It was so faint that if he hadn't known where to look, Thomas would never have seen it. Still battling his anger, he managed to control himself long enough to squat down and examine the writing.

It was an *L*. Thomas traced the delicate lines, and his eyes met Emily's. She nodded.

"That's our only clue, Thomas. I asked her who she saw that night. We have to help her, or they'll come and kill her."

Thomas clenched his jaw. "I'll deal with you later. Let's get her out of here. I have a horse at the edge of the camp. The sheriff is with me."

Emily's eyes widened, but Thomas forced her to walk ahead of him. The two of them emerged into the blinding sunlight. Thomas gulped a mouthful of fresh air, snatching the cloth from his face, feeling the wretched burn of the opium smoke in his lungs. As soon as his head cleared, he took hold of Emily again, intending to head for the sheriff. Instead, he found himself looking down the barrel of Emmet's gun.

"Well, howdy there, Preacher. Fancy meeting you here. It's a mighty nice day for dying, isn't it?"

26

———❦———

Showdown

Thomas faced the desperado down, pushing Emily behind him. She tried to peek through Thomas's legs, but could only observe the outlaw's boots. Rising on her tiptoes, she could just see Emmet's cruel face above Thomas's left shoulder.

Emmet chewed on a plug of tobacco, spitting, now and then, on the ground. The air was strangely still. Emily felt as if every detail of this scene were being seared into her brain. Emmet had on a dark blue shirt and vest, his trousers slit to accommodate his wooden leg. The black Stetson he wore slanted down over his face, but couldn't hide the menace in his eyes, nor the purposeful way he held his gun. His sneer deepened as his gaze shifted to Emily. Fingering his weapon, he grinned at Thomas once more.

"Taken up opium smoking, too, preacher man? You are the oddest minister I've ever seen. Drinking, cursing, smoking, and wearing a gun. One might think you're not what you appear."

Emily felt Thomas stiffen. "What the hell do you want, Emmet?"

"I reckon same thing you do," Emmet answered coldly. "Just give me that China girl."

"No!" Emily gasped, determined to throw herself at this rotten, two-bit outlaw and scratch his eyes out, if that were the only weapon she had. But Thomas held her firmly behind him.

"The girl is of no use to anyone, Emmet," Thomas said firmly. "She's an addict. There's nothing she can tell anyone, even if she wanted to. Now why don't you head on out of here before the law arrives."

Emmet's grin grew broader and he glanced back over his shoulder. It was then that Emily saw Jake, covering his partner with his own gun. The glint of the rifle showed clearly between the green canvas tents. Emmet turned back to Thomas, his voice rough.

"I don't give a damn what that China girl is or isn't, and I don't care if ten lawmen show up. Git outta my way, preacher man. Or you and your little lady will have to die, too."

Panic suffused Emily as she felt Thomas reach for his gun. Two simultaneous explosions filled the air, and Emily tumbled to the dirt under Thomas's weight.

Slowly, Emily lifted her head. Her heart pounded with relief. Emmet was sprawled in the dirt like a broken doll. His peg leg lay beside him, fractured in the fall, and he stared up at the heavens, directly into the sunlight.

Her gaze swung quickly to Thomas. His face was turned away from her, but his body was motionless. Panic choked her as he lay perfectly still, almost as if . . .

"Thomas!" Emily cried out. *Oh, God, please don't let him die.* . . . The words pounded in her brain like a refrain. She tried to move, tried to force her body into action, but her limbs seemed frozen with shock. She had succeeded in getting to her knees when Thomas rolled suddenly to his feet.

"Stay the hell down! There's one more!" he shouted hoarsely.

Gunfire filled the air. Emily shrieked in terror. The sounds died as quickly as they'd come. Silence followed. Then she saw the sheriff walk slowly out into the open. He held his weapon aloft. "It's all right. He's dead."

Emily looked past him and saw Jake's body slumped against the tent. Thomas stood, moving cautiously toward Emmet's body, lying less than ten feet away. The sheriff kept his gun trained on the outlaw as Thomas kicked Emmet's gun out of reach. He sank down next to the bloody form. But he didn't have to touch the man to know his condition: Emmet Colter was finally dead.

"Well, you saved the townsfolk the trouble of hanging him," the sheriff said grimly. "Been after these two for quite a spell. The good citizens of this town will sleep better tonight."

Thomas rose and turned to look for Emily. On her knees, Emily shakily accepted his hand. Her eyes fell on the soft red stain slowly oozing through his shirt. "Thomas, you're hurt! Why didn't you say something? We have to get you to a doctor right away!"

He stared down at her, his harsh expression softening. "It's just a flesh wound," Thomas replied, though he stopped to wrap his arm with his handkerchief. His gaze drifted toward the tent. "We have to get China Blue to safety. Jake wasn't the only member of Emmet's gang. They may disperse now that Emmet's dead, but we can't take that chance."

"I'll take care of it," the sheriff said. "Your woman's right. Get yourself to a doctor. We don't need gangrene setting in."

Thomas nodded, then put his good arm around Emily. Together they walked back toward the entrance of the camp. Putting Emily onto his horse, Thomas swung up behind her.

Neither of them spoke for a long time. Emily relaxed into his arms, feeling drained. The depth of her feelings for Thomas nearly overwhelmed her, especially now that she'd been confronted with the thought of losing him. She finally understood his fears for her safety. If he was half as scared for her as she was for him, it must be unbearable. Somehow, in the midst of all this, they had found something more priceless than gold.

Wordlessly, Thomas pulled her closer to him. The sun set lower, splashing the sky with crimson, scarlet, and amber. A lone hawk circled above, and the cottonwoods sighed in the wind. Emily felt warm and secure. Emmet was dead. And the man who held her had risked his life to save her.

Altogether too soon, the horse stopped at the hitching post in town. Reluctantly Emily slipped from the mount, shivering after the warmth of Thomas's body. But instead of following her, he remained stiffly on the horse.

"Thomas? Are you all right?"

She waited for him to answer. He turned to her slowly. His face was pasty white and his eyes were glassy. Sweat beaded his brow. Her eyes fell to his sleeve and she gasped as she saw the vivid red blood.

"No," Thomas said, then slid from the horse into the dirt.

Pain. That was all he felt when he awoke.

Thomas grimaced, feeling the torturous needles pricking at his arm, racking his brain, making him feel like crawling back inside the darkness. Recollection came slowly to him. There had been a gunfight. Emmet. Had to get Emily home safely. Then . . . the darkness.

His arm throbbed hotly and he frantically reached out to touch his hand, sighing with relief when he felt the limb still attached.

"You almost did lose it, my friend, but we managed to save your gun hand. Good thing your lady friend got you straight here. A hell of an infection set in. Never seen anything like it."

Thomas opened his eyes finally and saw the doctor grinning down at him. Beside him were the sheriff and Emily. Emily looked incredibly scared. Her eyes were tired, as if she'd been sleepless a long time, reminding him all at once of her dangerous masquerade as an opium addict. That thought brought back his ire and he glared at her, but for once she didn't seem interested in defending herself. Instead she smiled, as if welcoming his wrath.

"How long have I been here?" He sat up, looking around at the unfamiliar room.

"Three days," the doctor told him. "You had a high fever. Your lady friend there tended you all day and night. That's a good woman you've got there."

"I'm aware of that." Thomas's eyes met Emily's. To his delight, he saw her blush profusely. Knowing that she'd nursed him back to health made him decide to let her off the hook. For now. She was trouble, all right, a whole package of it. But she also had character and depth, loyalty, and love. What more could a man ask for?

Emily leaned over and felt his forehead. "He feels much better," she pronounced. Her hand moved down to hold Thomas's good one tightly. "Thank you, Doctor."

"You and he did all the work." The man beamed. "I have to say I wouldn't want to be on the opposite end of your gun. You hit the notorious Emmet Colter almost before he drew."

"That was mighty fine shooting," the sheriff agreed. "In fact, if you ever want to consider a deputy position, it's yours. I could use a man with aim like yours."

"Then it's all over." Thomas collapsed back onto his pillow.

"Yes. Might as well tell both of you now, we found their hideout this morning. It was just up Ridge Mountain. As soon as they heard about Emmet, the rest of the boys all ran scared. We found someone there, though."

Emily and Thomas stared at the sheriff in confusion. "Miss Lizzie," the sheriff answered their unspoken question. "She was tied up in the outlaw's den. Claims to have been kidnapped, but that's not the way we see it. Apparently she's been involved with Jake all along."

"Lizzie?" Emily repeated, stunned. She turned swiftly to Thomas. "Do you think that's what China Blue was trying to tell us? She drew an L in the sand, remember?"

"Makes sense." Thomas shrugged. "You never think a woman could do something as brutal as this, but some women don't care about anything except their man."

Emily shook her head, far from satisfied. "So has Lizzie confessed to the killings?"

"She hasn't said much yet, but we'll get it out of her. I have to say, I agree with Thomas. Lizzie certainly had motivation. She was in love with one of these outlaws, she knew about the money, and had easy access to Rosie and your pa. I remember the night of the murders, being clearly struck that your pa expected someone, someone he must have known. She probably set him up, then either by herself or with the help of these outlaws, killed them both."

"What about Sung He?" Emily asked. "How is she doing?"

The doctor smiled. "That story, at least, has a happy ending. She's in another physician's care, and shows every sign of recovering from her addiction. She needs help, but she has her grandfather, and the deepest motivation to get well. And she has you both to thank for her life, for it's apparent Emmet meant to kill her if the opium didn't do it first. By the way"—he turned to Emily—"how did you get in that opium den?"

"I think that conversation is better saved for another time," Emily said quickly, avoiding Thomas's eyes.

The sheriff chuckled, watching the exchange. "Yes, I'd like to hear about it as well, but we can discuss it when Thomas is better. I think we can say the case is pretty much wrapped up. Except for the gold."

Emily shook her head. "I wish I were convinced of that. Still, I do feel safer knowing that Lizzie's behind bars and Jake and Emmet are dead."

"And I feel better knowing your case is closed," Thomas said firmly. He tightened his grip on her hand. "After all, I plan to make an honest woman of you. I understand that detecting is part of your soul. If you want to consult, and I mean consult, that's fine. What I don't plan to do is spend the rest of my days worried about you traipsing into opium dens, chasing down outlaws, or investigating murders. Is that clear?"

The sheriff and the doctor exchanged a look, and the two men bowed out of the room, leaving Emily and Thomas alone.

"Thomas!" Emily cried. "Do you mean you really want to marry me?"

"I don't see anyone else here I'd like to marry," Thomas said with a grin, then his face turned serious. "Emily, I love you. I think I've loved you from the first day we met. I never realized how much until I was facing down Emmet, and knew I could lose you forever. I don't have much to offer at this point, but I can start over, make a new life. Maybe I'll accept the sheriff's offer. I don't care about the gold anymore, or Wells Fargo. I see now that nothing matters as much as what we have between us. If you feel the same way, then yes, I want to marry you."

Emily's answer was a squeak of delight. Thomas chuckled, gently disengaging himself so that he could see her face. "Does that mean yes?"

"Oh, yes, Thomas." She sighed, plastering kisses all over his face. "Yes."

27

The Game Is Afoot

Emily was exhausted when she returned to Shangri-La. Thomas had insisted that she go home, seeing the effects the last three days had had on her. When Emily tried to protest, he had become obstinate, advising her that she still hadn't accounted for her presence in the opium den, and that she shouldn't push her luck. Emily had smiled, given him a quick kiss, and promised to return in the morning.

The door to her house opened easily, and she reminded herself for the thousandth time that she had to be more careful about locking up. Yet now that Emmet was dead, she had nothing really to fear. The peace of mind the man's demise brought made her feel a little guilty, but grateful all the same.

Leaving her shoes at the door, she started up the steps in her stockinged feet. Even though she was exhausted, she couldn't stop the bubble of joy that welled up inside of her.

Thomas wanted to marry her. The idea made her feel like singing. If she had a whit's strength left, she would have done just that. Giddy, she couldn't wait to share her news with Rosie. Perhaps the two of them could celebrate after she'd gotten some rest. Rosie, she was certain, would have some grand ideas about the wedding, and even grander ideas about the honeymoon. Emily could just imagine her bridal advice, which was certain to be much different from the normal mother-daughter talk. Suppressing a giggle, Emily dashed into her room.

And found Lynette standing at her bureau, rifling through her clothes. She froze when Emily burst in, then glanced down at the hand that was still in the drawer.

"Lynette, what are you doing in my room? And why are you going through my things?" The question wasn't accusatory, but firmly worded just the same.

Lynette stammered for a moment, then she lifted her head high and stared Emily down. "I was missing an earring, and I thought maybe you picked it up by mistake."

Her voice rang clear, but Emily knew a lie when she heard one. It didn't take a lot of detecting to figure out that something was wrong here.

"I see," Emily said. "Well, I suggest you pack your things, because I won't be needing a boarder any longer. Especially one I can't trust. I would like your room vacated within the hour."

Lynette didn't speak for a moment, and Emily was startled by the hard glint of hatred in her eyes. It was gone quickly, replaced by the subservient expression the seamstress normally wore.

"Yes, if that's what you wish." She started past Emily, then paused in the doorway. Her face was contrite. "Miss Potter, I'm very sorry about this misunderstanding. I thought we worked well together. I didn't mean to cause any trouble. I just didn't know when you'd be home."

"I'm sorry, too, but my mind is made up. Please leave."

Lynette walked out of the room, and Emily softly closed the door behind her. All was quiet for a short time and Emily assumed she was packing her things, then her footsteps sounded in the hallway. Finally Emily heard the porch door swing shut, and she knew the woman was gone.

Rosie swam into view, but this time, her reflection was fainter than ever. "Rosie?" Emily cried in dismay. "Why are you so blurry?" Rosie tried to smile, but her features seemed to blend together. Her black plume was like a soft brush stroke, and her dress a wash of scarlet. She looked like a beautiful but runny watercolor painting.

"Hello, sweetie. I wanted so badly to warn you. That woman's been looking through everything while you were gone. I wanted to scare her, but it would have used up the last of my energy. I'm fading more and more. I almost couldn't come back this time, but I forced myself. I wanted to see you again."

"I'm so glad you did." Emily couldn't stop the tears that choked her. "Oh, Rosie, I wish you weren't going! Especially now! Thomas—he asked me to marry him! I wanted to share it all with you, every last minute. . . ."

"I'll be there, sweetie," Rosie said, though Emily could tell she was crying, too. "Do you think I'd miss your wedding? Like I told you before, I'll always be with you, even if you don't see me. It's getting so hard to focus now. I feel something pulling me toward this light. I don't want to go there, because I think if I do, I won't ever return. . . ."

"Rosie!" Emily cried, pressing her hands against the mirror. "Please don't go! I don't want you to leave me!"

Rosie's hand lifted to the glass. Emily, still sobbing, touched her fingertips to the ones in the reflection. For one brief second, Emily felt heat, as if the ghost's life force joined hers. A glimpse of gold light, green grass, and roses filled her mind, and her body tingled. The feeling was wonderful, warm and comforting, and Emily knew she would never fear dying again.

"Oh, Rosie! What will I do without you?"

"I'm getting real tired, sweetie. I love you, remember that. I'm so glad for you and Thomas. You deserve it, honey. Love him, Emily. And let him love you back. Only in love is there no time and no death."

"Rosie!" Emily cried.

But the spirit was gone.

The house was intensely quiet when Emily awoke
the next morning. She braced herself, waiting for the
anguish she expected to engulf her at the loss of her
friend, but thankfully, a peaceful, happy sensation
came over her, and a sense of things being as they
should. Rosie must be happy wherever she was,
Emily concluded. As she wished her well, she felt a
flush of comforting warmth, as if the phantom had
kept her promise to always be with her.

Rising from bed, she recalled what had happened
between herself and Thomas yesterday, and utter joy
washed all over her once more. His words had meant
so much to her, especially his reassurance that the
gold no longer mattered. He was right. What they
had was already worth a fortune.

The top drawer of her dresser remained open,
and when Emily attempted to push it shut, she saw
the papers stuffed inside. Lynette. The woman must
have been rifling through her personal effects. Taking the documents from the drawer, she held them
up to the morning sunlight, puzzled. They were the
original copy of her father's will, and the duplicate
that Ewert had brought.

That's odd, Emily mused, laying them side by
side. The thought that the will her father had hidden
was somehow a factor in the case had never left her.
Now Lynette's interest in the papers aroused her
sleuthish instincts. Whipping out her glass, she examined the two documents closely.

The wording was precisely the same, as Emily had

already surmised. There was a notation by Ewert Smith that a letter had been sent to Emily, advising her of her father's death. Following that was another stating that Emily had refused to sell the house. Other than those notations, the two documents seemed identical.

It has to be here, Emily thought. *But what is it?* Holding the duplicate wills toward the lamp, she turned the gaslight up as high as it would go, eliminating every possible shadow. Lowering the glass to the papers once more, her heart skipped a beat. There was something odd. . . .

It was a pinprick. Emily squinted as she turned the paper to fully examine the tiny dot. Directly beneath a letter *T*, it showed up clearly on the original will, but not on the attorney's copy.

A thrill raced up Emily's spine, and she slowly read the next sentence. There was another dot. Then another. Two sentences down, a fourth.

She snatched up a paper and a pencil, copying the letters above each dot in order. Good Lord, what a fool I've been! she berated herself. Her father had left her a clue all right, but she'd been too thick-headed to find it.

Forcing herself to remain calm, she focused on what she had written on the page: T-H-E-G-O-L-D-I-S-I-N-T-H-E-M-I-R-R-O-R-G-U-A-R-D-A-G-A-I-N-S-T-L-Y-N-E-T-T-E.

Emily tested the verbiage out loud: " 'The gold is in the mirror. Guard against Lynette.' "

Emily reached out to touch Rosie's mirror.

Where? Her hand fell on the gilt that encased the glass, and her pulse began to pound. What if it wasn't gilt? What if . . .

A reflection swam before her in the glass. This time, it wasn't Rosie who stared back at her. This time, it was—

"Lynette!"

"Back away from that mirror. That's right. Pretty clever of your father, to hide the gold that way. It's been right here all this time, molded around the mirror beneath the gilt paint, and none of us thought to look twice at it. You saved me quite a bit of time and effort. Too bad you won't be around to enjoy it."

Emily's gaze fell helplessly on the pearl-handled pistol in the woman's grip.

Thomas walked toward the former bordello, absently rubbing his aching arm. Although the doctor had advised more bed rest, he had to see Emily. The thought of her brought a smile to his lips, one that died instantly when he approached the house. Shangri-La was eerily dark, except for one light upstairs. Stranger still, the door was not only unlocked, but ajar. While he knew Emily was oddly absent-minded when it came to such details, he didn't think her so foolish as to leave the door wide open. On alert now, a sixth sense made him remove his boots before padding cautiously up the stairs.

Something was wrong. He could feel it in his bones. Thomas tried to fight the sense of doom that swept over him, but it was useless. Feeling for his gun, Thomas recalled that the sheriff had taken possession of it, and invited him to pick it up at his convenience. With Emmet dead and Jake behind bars, Thomas wouldn't have thought he'd need it so quickly, but at this moment, he heartily wished for the reassurance of the heavy Colt at his side.

Emily's bedroom door stood open. As Thomas drew nearer, he saw her standing beside the mirror, her face ashen, yet her voice—it was Emily, after all—coldly logical. Her gaze was not directed at him. Someone else occupied the bedroom, someone whose gun was reflected in the glass, as well.

"Lynette," Emily said simply. "Of course."

"I had you fooled. I had everyone fooled."

Thomas froze. Lynette's ladylike voice sounded hard. A chill passed through him as he thought of China Blue, weakly etching the letter *L* in the dirt. It was this woman she had been trying to warn them against, and not Lizzie Wakefield after all. Good God, what a fool he'd been!

Lynette gave a harsh laugh. "You thought you were so smart and so clever, a real detective! Chasing after Emmet and Jake, when all along *I* was pulling the strings."

"You were my father's partner," Emily said softly.

"You could say that." Lynette laughed again. "He was transporting the payroll, along with another employee, when your pa stole it out from under the other fella, then let him take the blame. Funny thing was, I'd planned to steal the gold from your pa and kill him myself. But he must have sensed something amiss, for he knocked me out and disappeared, only to turn up at this whorehouse. He was right about one thing, though. It's the last place I would have looked, if it hadn't been for Emmet."

"The outlaw told you where he was?" Emily asked, putting the pieces together.

Good Girl, Thomas thought, *keep her talking.* Without his gun, his only chance to save Emily was to get close enough to tackle Lynette, and he needed the element of surprise on his side. Otherwise they, too, would become victims of Shangri-La. He inched his way toward the two women. With every second, he got closer. . . .

Lynette was talking again. "Of course. Emmet was my pawn, too, just like your pa. But before I kill you, I want to know something. What made you suspect me? And why did you let me live in your house if you did?"

Emily waved her hand as if it were simplicity itself. "I knew a woman had broken into Shangri-La that night. I never saw a man yet who would avoid a flower bed when breaking in to a house. And then the coroner's report, feeble as it was, indicated that the bullet wounds in Rosie and my father were from a pistol. Men out here in the West aren't much for small guns, so I deduced a woman."

"Clever."

"Elementary. So you see, you were always on my list of suspects. In fact, there is some information due to arrive any moment that I am now certain will totally incriminate you. Unfortunately for you, you told me a piece of your history that was true. Mrs. Bates did remember you, but said you had worked in Philadelphia under another name. I am positive the local police departments will produce records of Lynette Armstrong. Until I had such proof, however, it made perfect sense to keep you under scrutiny."

"Well, then. More's the pity. The world will lose a real talent when I get rid of you. Too bad you're going to meet such a sudden end at such a youthful age. But it's sort of fittin', don't you think? You and your pa dying in the same house, by the same gun? I couldn't think of a more poetic justice myself."

She pointed the gun at Emily. Thomas could see its deadly reflection in the glass. He was within ten feet of her—not close enough, but there was no more time. Lunging into the room, he tried to reach Lynette before she could fire, but it was too late. Her cruel smile was illuminated in the silver glass as she pulled the trigger.

"No!" Thomas cried.

As if in slow motion, he saw Lynette's arm jerk back with the force of the gunshot, and Emily's eyes widen in horror. Just at that moment, to his disbelief, a woman's arm thrust through the mirror and yanked Emily out of the way. Thomas gaped in surprise even as he grabbed Lynette. The gun flew out of her hand, smashing into the mirror, breaking it into a dozen glittering shards.

"Did you see her, Thomas? Did you?" Emily cried, staring at the broken glass in shock.

Wrestling Lynette to the floor, Thomas bound her with one of Emily's scarves. When he stood up he took Emily into his arms and they both turned to the shattered looking glass. To Thomas's astonishment, their fractured reflection vanished, replaced by the vision of a dozen Rosies, laughing merrily and fanning themselves with black plumes. Thomas's mouth went dry. Every brain cell he possessed told him this couldn't be true, and yet he knew it was. He was seeing a ghost. A bunch of ghosts!

"Rosie!" Emily cried, delighted. "It is you! You saved me! But how—"

The spirit laughed naughtily, then gestured to the woman on the floor. "I acted a bit sicker than I was, sweetie. I was saving up my energy. I thought you might need my help. I knew the night that spider came into this house that something was wrong. It was a feeling. Know what I mean?"

Emily nodded, wiping away tears. "Yes, I know."

"I couldn't let her kill you, too, honey. I didn't know if I could do it, but I was watching her in the mirror the whole time. I thought maybe, if I just concentrated enough, I could pull you away. I did good, didn't I?"

"You sure did," Emily said. "Real good."

"Then you're really a . . ." Thomas's voice trailed off in wonder, and Rosie giggled uproariously.

"Yes, I'm a real 'live' ghost. Miss Emily's gotten rather used to me, but I guess it's sort of a shock to you."

"Rosie, I can't . . ." Thomas shook his head in wonder. "I can't thank you enough. You don't know what this woman means to me."

"Oh, I think I have an idea." Rosie winked flirtatiously. "Now, you be good to her, preacher man. She deserves someone nice. And honey, don't let your father's wrongs keep you from being happy. You'll never know his side of the story, so don't judge him too harshly. I just know he loved you, and that's all that counts."

"I know," Emily said tearfully. "Oh, Rosie, I'm so glad to see you again! Will you be able to stay?"

The ghost shook her head sadly. "No, it's time for me to go. It's over; I'm sure of it now. Remember when I told you about the light? I can feel it shimmering all around me. Good-bye, honey. Remember what I told you."

"Rosie!" Emily cried, but the vision had already faded.

"Remember," she called. "Remember love."

A long moment passed. Emily sobbed quietly as the mirror became just so much broken glass again. Lynette had stopped swearing and stared in disbelief at the vision that faded before their eyes. "Good God, it's a ghost!"

"Yes, the ghost of the woman you killed," Thomas said. He trained the pistol on her, his face an icy mask.

"Emily, go get the sheriff. Tell him this time we can deliver the real murderer right into his hands."

As Emily dashed from the house, she saw a shooting star.

Rosie, she thought. *She's going home.*

28

The Denouement

"That was an uncommon fine job of detecting, Miss Emily. Ain't seen nothing better."

Emily blushed at the sheriff's praise, then quickly turned to the business at hand. "I should have put Lynette together with Emmet long ago! I'm still kicking myself over that one."

Another man, who'd been sitting quietly behind the desk, rose from his position and came over to shake hands with Emily. Dressed in a wool tweed suit and a derby, he looked like a successful businessman, but when he handed her a card with a single eye in the center, Emily's mouth dropped.

"I'd like to introduce myself. I'm Charlie Hopkins of the Pinkerton Agency. We've been investigating this case for some time, but I have to admit, none of my men ever got as far as you did. Tell me, please, where were you trained?"

Emily opened her mouth to reply when Thomas stepped forward. "She is self-trained, but out of the business."

The detective looked from the lean, dangerous-looking man beside her, back to Emily. His smile dimmed somewhat. "I see. I was just hoping to understand your methods. I must say, our agency was most impressed."

"Maybe you could clear a few things up for the lady," the sheriff said smoothly. "Like how Lynette plays into all this."

"Well, we've been trailing Lynette Armstrong for years," the detective said slowly. "She has a long record of this sort of thing, but always stays well in the background, so we've never been able to pin anything on her. People never suspect a woman, so it's easier for her to stay hidden. She always gets someone else to do her dirty work, whether it was your father, whom I suspected she blackmailed, or Emmet. She doesn't soil her pretty hands."

"I knew it was a woman who had broken into Shangri-La," Emily confirmed. "By that time, I assume Lynette was growing frustrated with Emmet and had decided to take matters into her own hands."

"Right. But still, no one could find that gold. It wasn't until you deciphered the message in the will that the thieves really closed in."

Thomas nodded thoughtfully. "But how did Lynette know that? She must have crept in right at the moment that Emily figured out where the gold was."

"She did. I think her plan was to continue to

follow Emily until the gold turned up. As her assistant, it was a perfect setup, for anything you did, she would instantly know about. Once you caught her sneaking through your things, she knew the jig was up. She got desperate."

"I still can't figure out what she had on my father." Emily sighed. "Or why he would agree to steal the gold, only to hide it so well all this time."

"That part I think we'll never know, for it certainly isn't in Lynette's best interest to inform on herself. We do know that she found out about the payroll shipment through an informant at Wells Fargo, and then ingratiated herself with your father. By the time he realized what he was dealing with, it was too late. Either way, I think she would have killed him. Potter bought himself a year by running away."

"I guess that's it, then," Emily said briskly. "The rest is obvious. Emmet's participation was easy to deduce, especially once I'd heard about my father's fear of a wooden-legged man. The night of the killings, Lynette must have shown up alone. He probably thought it was a peace offering."

"No doubt. He invited her in, gave her a drink, and she shot him. She probably thought it would be a simple matter to find the gold. But there your father fooled her again. And poor Rosie was murdered simply for being in the wrong place at the wrong time. May she rest in peace."

"I don't think that's a problem," Thomas said, choking back what might have been laughter. Emily sent him a wicked smile, then turned back to the sheriff.

"You've been most kind, and I trust you'll take care of Lynette," Emily said to the sheriff. "If you need any more help from me, you know where to find me."

"You're staying here, then?" the sheriff asked hopefully.

In answer, Emily slid her arm through Thomas's. "If he'll still have me."

Amid the uproarious congratulations, the sheriff turned to Thomas, a sly twinkle in his eyes. "I meant what I said to you about needing a deputy. I don't know what your plans are, or if you want to go back to Wells Fargo, but if not, you're certainly welcome here."

Emily looked at Thomas, who grinned broadly. "I might just take you up on that. I'm glad my name has been cleared, and with delivery of the gold back to the company, I'm sure they'd reinstate me. Still, I think I've had it with transporting other men's wealth. A position here sounds a lot more palatable."

"Good." The sheriff turned to Emily, the twinkle in his eye increasing. "Perhaps then, if we come across a case that is too difficult for us, you would lend a hand? Maybe look over the facts?"

The Pinkerton man frowned, then spoke quickly, as if determined not to be outdone by this rustic sheriff. "Miss Emily, our firm thinks you have a bright future, should you ever turn to detecting. In fact, my boss, Mr. Pinkerton himself, would like an interview."

But it was Thomas who spoke first.

"Miss Emily, soon to be Mrs. Brant, is retired. She

can help by consultation only. Am I making myself clear?" He directed the question not to the men, but to Emily.

"Certainly," Emily said in all innocence, though a smile glimmered around her mouth. "I wouldn't dream otherwise."

The detective looked crestfallen, but the sheriff hid a speculative grin as Emily and Thomas walked out of the sheriff's office, arm in arm. A strange peace seemed to settle over Emily, now that all the loose ends were tied up. Thomas turned her to face him when they reached the porch of the former bordello, and he gazed into her eyes.

"Emily, I'm sorry about your father. I know you never wanted to believe him capable of stealing that gold."

Emily nodded. "I do think he meant for me to find it and perhaps return it to Wells Fargo. Maybe he knew he hadn't the strength of character to do so himself. Truthfully, it doesn't matter anymore."

"Are you sure?"

Emily examined the part of herself that had refused to accept the truth for so long. She nodded. "Yes. I feel better now that the gold is being returned to Wells Fargo. It never brought anyone pleasure—only death or jail. And I finally feel like the cloud that's been hanging over us is gone, that we can make a fresh start and truly find happiness. Do you feel that way, too?"

Thomas lowered his head and kissed her thoroughly. Emily sighed, wrapping her arms around

him, feeling the heady sensations flood through her.
When he withdrew from her embrace, he smiled
down at her.

"Does that answer your question?"

Emily nodded. It certainly did.

Epilogue

"I'm so sorry, Miss, I mean Madam, to disturb you on your wedding day, but there is an urgent telegram for you."

The new postal clerk thrust the missive at her as the couple stood together outside the church. Emily glanced at Thomas, who looked concerned, then she tore open the envelope. It read:

Murder at Graystone Lodge. Damien's Curse missing. Perhaps you can shed some light on what is so dark. Please help. Your cousin, Mary Lou Finch.

The postmark was Boston. Emily turned to her husband. "Thomas! My cousin is in trouble. I can help—"

"Oh no." Thomas said firmly, leading her back toward the carriage. "You aren't getting involved in any more murders. I won't have you recklessly endangering your life again. You mean too much to me."

His lips claimed hers in a ravishing kiss. The townspeople applauded as he hoisted her into the carriage, then gave the driver instructions as to their destination.

Emily nodded, settling into the carriage. "You are right, Thomas. I will correspond with her immediately. By the way," she turned to him with an expression of complete innocence. "Just how far is Boston from Niagara Falls?"

"Driver, move on." Thomas's face was set firmly, but Emily was undaunted. Folding the telegram into a tiny square, she put it in her bridal bag. It would simply be a stop to visit family.

Nothing more.

About the Author

KATIE ROSE is thrilled to be a part of Bantam's Fanfare program. Her first book, *A Hint of Mischief,* won *RomCom's* Reviewer's Choice Award and achieved a five-star rating on Amazon.com. A lifetime resident of South Jersey, Katie lives with her daughter in Marlton and spends much of her free time horseback riding, exploring old houses, and researching American history. She is fascinated with the Victorian period, and sees a distinct parallel in the industrial revolution and the technology revolution today. Katie has a degree in journalism, and has also written for magazines and newspapers.